The Garrison Dynas
unforesee

The Garrisons: Cassie, Adam & Brooke

Three passionate novels from favourite
authors Brenda Jackson, Emilie Rose
and Catherine Mann

The Garrisons:
Cassie, Adam
& Brooke

BRENDA JACKSON

EMILIE ROSE

CATHERINE MANN

First published in Great Britain 2012
by Mills & Boon, an imprint of Harlequin (UK) Limited,
Eton House, 18-24 Paradise Road, Richmond, Surrey TW9 1SR

THE GARRISONS: CASSIE, ADAM & BROOKE
© by Harlequin Enterprises II B.V./S.à.r.l 2012

Special thanks and acknowledgement are given to Brenda Jackson, Emilie Rose and Catherine Mann for their contribution to THE GARRISONS series.

Stranded with the Tempting Stranger, Secrets of the Tycoon's Bride and *The Executive's Surprise Baby* were published in Great Britain by Harlequin (UK) Limited.

Stranded with the Tempting Stranger © Harlequin Books S.A. 2007
Secrets of the Tycoon's Bride © Harlequin Books S.A. 2007
The Executive's Surprise Baby © Harlequin Books S.A. 2007

ISBN: 978 0 263 89708 1
ebook ISBN: 978 1 408 97076 8

05-1112

Printed and bound in Spain
by Blackprint CPI, Barcelona

STRANDED WITH THE TEMPTING STRANGER

BY
BRENDA JACKSON

Dear Reader,

I hope you are enjoying the stories in the THE
GARRISONS series. I enjoyed working closely with
the other five authors to bring you a scintillating tale
of a family's hidden secrets, skyrocketing passion and
endless love.

In my story, Brandon Washington was a man with a
plan…or so he thought. Until he meets the heroine,
Cassie Sinclair-Garrison. Then he finds out the hard
way that no matter what your intentions are, when
emotions get in the way even the best-laid plans can
get kicked to the curb.

I love writing romance stories in which the hero and
heroine are pitted against each other, but in the end,
true love prevails.

I hope you enjoy Brandon and Cassie's story and their
journey to finding everlasting love.

Best,

Brenda Jackson

Brenda Jackson is a die 'heart' romantic who married her childhood sweetheart and still proudly wears the going steady ring he gave her when she was fifteen. Because she's always believed in the power of love, Brenda's stories always have happy endings. In her real-life love story, Brenda and her husband live in Jacksonville, Florida, and have two sons.

A bestselling author, Brenda divides her time between family, writing and working in management at a major insurance company. You may write Brenda at PO Box 28267, Jacksonville, FL 32226, USA, by e-mail at WriterBJackson@aol.com or visit her website at www. brendajackson.net.

To Gerald Jackson, Sr.

Thank you for thirty-five years of love and romance.
To my Heavenly Father for giving me the gift to write.

My beloved *is* mine, and I *am* his:
he feedeth among the lilies.
—*Song of Solomon* 2:16 II

One

October

Cassie Sinclair-Garrison released an uneven breath when she rounded the corner in the lobby of her hotel. She stopped, totally mesmerized by the man standing at the counter to check in to the Garrison Grand-Bahamas. It had been a long time since any man had captured her attention like this one. He was simply gorgeous.

He stood tall at a height of not less than six-three with an athletic build that indicated he was a sportsman or someone who made it his business to stay in great physical shape. He was an American, she knew at once, studying his coffee-brown skin, his dark brown eyes and closely shaved head. And he wasn't here on business, she thought, noting the way he was immaculately dressed in a pair of dark brown trousers and a tan shirt that brought out the beautiful coloring of his skin.

She didn't know what, but there was something about him that demanded attention and from the way other women in the lobby were also staring, it was attention he was definitely getting.

Deciding she had more to do with her time than to practically drool over a man, Cassie pushed the button to the elevator that would take her to her office on the executive floor. It was an office that once belonged to her father.

Five years ago, when she was twenty-two, her father had made her manager and there hadn't been a time when he hadn't been pleased with the way she had handled things. That's why she wasn't surprised that upon his death he had left full ownership of the hotel to her. In doing so he had only confirmed what some of her employees had probably suspected all along— that she was John Garrison's illegitimate child.

A flutter of pain touched her heart as she thought of her parents. She stepped inside the elevator, glad it was vacant because whenever she encountered these types of moments, she preferred being alone. Although she had tried putting on a good front over the past five months, it had been hard to first lose her mother in an auto accident and, little over a month later, lose her father when he'd died of a heart attack...although it was probably more of a broken heart.

She had wondered how he would be able to go on after her mother's death. The last time she had seen her father—just days before he passed when he had come to visit her—Cassie had seen the depths of pain in his eyes and she had wondered how he would get over the loss. He had said more than once that losing his Ava was like losing a part of him.

Even though he was a married man that hadn't stopped him from falling in love with her mother, the beautiful and vivacious Ava Sinclair. And she had been John Garrison's true love for more than twenty-eight years.

According to her mother, she had met the wealthy and very handsome American in the States when he had been a judge and she a contestant in the Miss Universe beauty pageant as Miss Bahamas. Their paths had crossed a few years later, when he had visited the Bahamas to purchase land for this grand hotel he intended to build.

Although he had a family in Florida consisting of five kids, he was an unhappy man, a man who was no longer in love with his wife, but too dedicated to his children to walk away from his marriage.

Cassie hadn't understood their relationship until she was older, but it was beyond clear her parents had shared something special, something unique and something few people had. It was a love of a lifetime. Ava never made any demands on John, yet he had freely lavished her with anything and everything, and provided her and the child they had created with complete financial support.

Cassie knew that others who'd seen her parents together over the years had formed opinions on what the relationship was about. He was a married American and Ava was his Bahamian mistress. But Cassie knew their relationship was so much more than that. In her heart she believed they had been soul mates in the truest form. She had loved her parents deeply and they had loved her, a product of their love, and there hadn't been a day they hadn't let her feel or know it.

She had resented those times when her father would leave them to return to his family in Miami, a family she'd only found out about when she became a teenager. The truth had hurt, but then her mother and father had smoothed away the pain with the intensity of their love and had let her know that no matter what the situation was, the one thing that would never change or diminish was their love for her, as well as their love for each other. From that day forward, whether others did or not, Cassie understood and accepted her parents' unorthodox love affair.

She stepped off the elevator and walked into her office, stopping to smile at her secretary while picking up her messages off the woman's desk. "Good morning, Trudy."

"Good morning, Ms. Garrison."

Cassie liked the sound of that. She had begun using her father's last name within a week of his death. With both of her parents deceased, there were no secrets to protect and she had no reason to continue to deny herself the use of his name.

"Any additional messages?" she asked the older woman whom she had hired a few months ago.

"Yes. Mr. Parker Garrison just called and would like you to return his call."

Cassie forced the smile to stay on her face while thinking that no matter what Parker liked, he wouldn't be getting things his way since she wouldn't be returning his call. She could not forget the phone conversation they had shared nearly four months ago. He'd called within a week of the reading of John Garrison's will and he'd kept calling. Eventually, she had taken his call.

At the time she had been very aware that he, his siblings and mother had been shocked to discover at the reading of the will that John Garrison had an outside child. Of the five Garrison offspring, Parker had been the most livid because the terms of their father's will gave her and Parker equal controlling interest in Garrison Inc., an umbrella corporation that oversaw the stocks and financial growth of all the Garrison-owned properties. He wasn't happy about it.

Their telephone conversation hadn't gone well. He had been arrogant, condescending and had even tried being intimidating. When he'd seen Cassie would not accept his offer to buy her out, he had done the unthinkable by saying she had to prove she was a Garrison, and had threatened her with a DNA test as well as the possibility of him contesting the will. Parker's threats had ticked her off and she was still angry.

"Ms. Garrison?"

Her secretary's voice recaptured her attention. The forced smile widened. "Thank you for delivering the message."

Cassie entered her office. She would think Parker would have more to do with his time these days. It didn't take long for news to travel over the hotel grapevine that the handsome and elusive playboy had gotten married. And not that she cared, but she'd also heard that another Garrison bachelor, Stephen, had gotten hitched, as well.

She had no intention of ever meeting any of her "siblings." She didn't know them and they didn't know her and she preferred things stayed that way. They had never been a part of her life and she had never been a part of theirs. She had a life here in the Bahamas and saw no need to change that.

As she sat behind her desk her thoughts shifted back to the guy she'd seen in the lobby. She couldn't help but wonder if he was married or single, straight or gay. She shrugged her shoulders knowing that it really didn't matter. The last thing she needed was to become interested in a man. Her man was the beautiful thirty-story building that was erected along the pristine shoreline of the Caribbean. And "her man" was a beautiful sight that took her breath away each time she entered his lobby. And she would take care of him, continue to make him prosper the way her father would want her to do. Now that her parents were gone, this hotel was the only thing she could depend on for happiness.

Brandon Washington glanced around the room he had been given, truly impressed. He had spent plenty of time at the Garrison Grand but there was something about this particular franchise that left him astonished. It was definitely a tropical paradise.

The first thing he'd noticed when he had pulled into the parking lot was that the structure was different from the sister hotel in South Miami Beach, mainly because it was designed to take advantage of the tropical island beach it sat on. And it was nested intimately among a haven of palm trees and a multitude of magnificent gardens that were stocked with flowering plants.

The second was the warmth of the staff that had greeted him the moment he had walked into the beautiful atrium. They had immediately made him feel welcome and important.

And then it was his hotel room, a beautiful suite with a French balcony that looked out at the ocean. It had to be the most stunning waterscape view he'd ever seen.

Brandon was more than pleased with his accommodations. And since he planned to stay for a while, his comfort was of the utmost importance. He had to remind himself that this was not a vacation, but he'd come here with a job to do. He needed to uncover any secrets Cassie Sinclair-Garrison might have that could be used to persuade her to give up her controlling interest in Garrison, Inc., his most influential client. Not to mention that members of the family were close friends of his.

His father had been John Garrison's college friend and later his personal attorney for over forty years and Brandon had been a partner in his father's law firm. When his father was killed in a car accident three years ago, instead of transferring the Garrison business to a more experienced and older attorney, John had retained Brandon's firm, showing his loyalty to the Washington family and his faith in Brandon's abilities.

Brandon had known John Garrison all of his thirty-two years and he was a man Brandon had respected. And he considered Adam Garrison, one of John's sons, his very best friend. Now Brandon was here at the request of Parker and Stephen Garrison. It seemed

John's illegitimate daughter refused to deal with the corporation in any way and had refused to discuss any type of a buyout offer with Parker.

Before resorting to a full-blown court battle, the two eldest brothers had suggested that Brandon travel to the Bahamas, assume a false identity to see if he could get close to Ms. Garrison and dig up any information on her present or her past, which would give them ammunition to later force her hand if she continued to refuse to sell her shares of Garrison, Inc. Another smart thing John had done was retain exclusive control of this particular hotel, the one Cassie had managed and now owned. No doubt it had been a brainy strategic move to keep his secrets well-hidden.

Brandon pulled his cell phone from his coat jacket when it rang. "Yes?"

A smile touched his lips. "Yes, Parker, I just checked in and just so you'll know, I'm registered under the name of Brandon Jarrett."

He chuckled. "That's right. I'm using my first and middle name since I want to keep my real identity hidden." A few moments later he ended his phone call with Parker.

Brandon began unpacking. He had brought an assortment of casual clothes since it was his intent to pose as a businessman who'd come to the island for a short but very needed vacation. That shouldn't be hard to do, because since John Garrison's death and his secrets had been revealed, Brandon had been working long hours with the Garrison family to resolve all the unwanted issues.

Contesting the will had been out of the question. No

one wanted to air the family's dirty laundry. Doing so would definitely send John's widow, Bonita, over the edge. There were a number of people who would not sympathize with the woman, saying it was her drinking problem that had sent John into the arms of another woman in the first place and that he had stayed married to her longer than most men would have.

Then there would be others who would think that John's extramarital affair is what had driven the woman to drink. As far as Brandon was concerned, there was no way Bonita hadn't known about John's affair, given the amount of time he spent away from home. But from the look on her face during the reading of the will, she had not known a child had been involved. Now she knew, and according to Adam, his mother was hitting the bottle more than ever.

Brandon rubbed his chin, feeling the need of a shave. As he continued to unpack he knew that sometime within the next couple of days he would eventually cross paths with Cassie Sinclair-Garrison. He would make sure of it.

Cassie stood on one of the many terraces on the east side of the hotel, which faced Tahita Bay. It was late afternoon yet the sky was still a dazzling blue and seemed to match the waters beneath it. There were a number of yachts in the bay and several human bodies were sunbathing on the beach.

She smiled and waved her hand when a couple she'd met yesterday when they'd checked in recognized her and gave her a greeting as they glided by on a sailboat. At least she had met the woman yesterday; the man she already knew from the numerous times when his family's corporation—Elliott Publishing Holdings; one of the largest magazine conglomerates in the world—had utilized the hotel to host their annual business conference. Their main office was located in New York and the Garrison Grand-Bahamas was the ideal place to hold a seminar during the winter months.

Teagan Elliott was here vacationing with his wife of eight months, a beautiful African-American by the name of Renee. An interracial couple, the two looked very good together and reminded Cassie of what she thought every time she would see her parents together. And just like her parents, it was easy to see their love was genuine.

Thinking of her parents sent a feeling of forlornness through her. Now that the business of the day had been handled, she decided to stay at the hotel for the night instead of taking the thirty-minute drive to her home, which was located on the other side of the island. Maybe later she'd take a leisurely stroll along the shoreline in an area that wasn't so crowded.

She thought of the Diamond Keys, an exclusive section of the hotel that had beachfront suites with parlors and French doors that opened directly to the water, providing a commanding view of endless beach and ocean. The rooms, which were extremely expensive but definitely worth it, were nestled in the hotel's most intimate settings.

Cassie headed back inside, making her way to her bedroom to change out of her business suit and slip into a pair of silk lounging pants and matching camisole with a print design. It had been a long time since she'd carved out some time for herself. Over the past months she had spent the majority of her time wallowing in work and mourning the loss of her parents, as she tried to move on through life, one day at a time.

She had been at her mother's funeral, standing beside her father, who'd remained in shock over their unexpected loss. What hurt so much even now was that she hadn't attended her father's funeral. By the time she had received word of his death, the funeral had already taken place. All she had was the memory of the last time they had spent together, a few days before his death.

He had shown up on the island unexpectedly, not at the hotel but at her condo, waiting for her when she had arrived home from work that day. The handsome and charismatic man she'd always known and loved had held sadness in his eyes and pain in his features.

That night he had taken her out to dinner and before he had returned to Miami, he had placed in her hand the deed to the beautiful ten-acre estate in the exclusive Lyford Cay community that he had purchased for her mother fifteen years ago. It was the home she now occupied and called her own.

Cassie took a glance around as she stepped out onto the sandy shores. Daylight had faded and dusk had set in. But that didn't bother her. In fact she much preferred it. She always thought the beach at night was breathtakingly beautiful. In the background she heard the band from the lounge as it mixed with the sound of the waves crashing against the shore. She leaned down and took off her sandals, wanting to feel the sand beneath her feet. Being on the beach always made her feel better. It helped her momentarily forget her pain, and made her feel carefree, energized and invigorated.

She bit back a smile and glanced around again, just to make sure she was alone, before pretending to play hopscotch on the sand. She laughed out loud when she almost slipped as she continued to hop around on one foot from one pretend square block to another. What a wonderful way to work off the day's stress, she thought, and today had definitely been a busy one. The hotel's capacity was at an all-time high, with requests for extended stays becoming the norm. They even had a waiting list for weeks not considered as prime time. The man she had chosen to succeed her as a manager, Simon Tillman, was doing an excellent job, and now she was able to concentrate on doing other things, such as expanding her business in various ways.

She had received a call from her accountant that profits for the hotel were surging. Once it had become official that she was the owner of the Garrison Grand-Bahamas, she had begun implementing the changes she had submitted to her father in a proposal just a month before his death. Over the last dinner they had shared together, he had given his blessing to move ahead with her plans. Today after meeting with her staff, she had a lot to be happy about, for the first time in months.

"May I play?"

Cassie lowered her leg as she swung around at the sound of the deep, masculine voice, angry at the intrusion. She narrowed her eyes, at first not seeing anyone, but then she watched as a man seemed to materialize out of the darkness.

She recognized him immediately. He was the man

she had seen earlier today when he had checked into the hotel. He was the man every woman in the hotel had been watching, and a man who even now was taking her breath away.

Two

Brandon stared at the woman standing a few feet from him. He had been watching her, barely seeing her features in the shadows, and now with her standing so close, he thought she had to be the most beautiful woman he had ever seen. He immediately wanted to know everything about her.

He glanced at her left hand, didn't see a ring and inwardly let out a relieved breath. But that didn't necessarily mean she didn't have a significant other, even perhaps a boyfriend. What were the chances of her spending time at this hotel, one known for rest, relaxation and romance, alone?

But still, that didn't stop his hormones from going into overdrive when he stared into her face, seeing the cocoa color of her complexion, the dark curly brown hair that fell to her shoulders, the darkness of her brown eyes and the shape of her curves in the outfit she was wearing.

Disgusted, he was reminded of why he was there, which was not to concentrate on a woman whose looks were so striking they could almost blind him, but to get close to a woman who was causing problems to his biggest client—a woman he had yet to meet, although he'd hung around the hotel the majority of the day hoping that he would. When he had discreetly asked about her, he'd been told that Cassie Sinclair-Garrison had been in meetings all day and chances were she had already left for her home, which was on the other side of the island.

In that case, since it wasn't likely he would be running into Ms. Garrison anytime tonight, why not spend time with this beauty…if she was free and available.

He watched how she tilted up her chin and narrowed her eyes at him. "You intrude on my privacy."

Her Bahamian accent was rich, just as rich as the curly brown hair that flowed around her shoulders, he thought. With the lifting of her chin he zeroed in on more of her features. In addition to her creamy brown skin, she had high cheekbones, a cute dimple in her chin, a straight nose and lips so full and generous they were downright sexy. There was something so feminine about her it actually made him ache.

"And I apologize," he said quietly, accepting what she felt was her need to take him to task. "I was out for a walk and couldn't help but notice the game you were playing. "

"You could have said something to let me know you were there," she said directly, eyeing him.

"And you're right, but again, I got so caught up in watching you that I didn't want to interrupt, at least not for a while. If I upset you, I'm sorry."

Cassie realized she really shouldn't make such a big deal out of it. After all it wasn't just her section of private beach, but belonged to anyone who was staying at Diamond Keys, and evidently he was. "Since there hasn't been any harm done," she said in a muffled voice, "I will accept your apology."

He smiled. "Thank you. And I hope you will let me make it up to you."

"And how do you pose to do that?"

"By asking you to be my guest at dinner tonight," he said lightly, watching the look of surprise skim her features at his request.

She shook her head. "That's not necessary."

"I think it is. I offended you and want to make it up to you."

"You didn't offend me. You just caught me off guard."

"Still, I'd like to make it up to you."

Cassie bent her head, trying to hide the smile that suddenly touched her lips. If nothing else, he was persistent. Shouldn't she be as persistent, as well, in turning down his offer?

She lifted her head and met his gaze and for a period of time she was rendered speechless. He had moved into into her line of vision and she thought he was so incredibly handsome, she could actually feel a rush of blood flow through her veins. She doubted that very few women turned down anything coming from him.

"Maybe we should introduce ourselves," he said,

taking a step forward and smiling. He extended his hand out to her. "I'm Brandon Jarrett."

"And I'm Cassie Sinclair-Garrison."

It took everything Brandon had to keep the shock that rocked his body from showing in his face. This was Cassie Garrison? The woman who was causing Garrison, Inc., all kinds of trouble? The woman who had been giving Parker heartburn for the past four months? The woman who was a sibling to the Miami Garrisons whether she wanted to acknowledge them or not? The woman who was the main reason he was here on the island?

"Hello, Cassie Sinclair-Garrison," he said, forcing the words out of his mouth and hesitantly releasing her hand. It had felt good in his, as if it had actually belonged there. He had looked forward to meeting Cassie, but without this element of surprise. He didn't like surprises and this one was a biggie.

"Hello, Brandon Jarrett," she said, smiling. "I hope you're enjoying your stay here."

"I am. Are you?" he asked, not wanting to give anything away that he recognized her name or knew who she was, although she carried the same last name as the hotel.

"Yes, I'm enjoying myself."

No doubt at my expense, he thought, when he saw she had no intention of mentioning that she was the hotel's owner. "I think you might enjoy it even more if you have dinner with me."

A feeling of uneasiness crept over Cassie. The moment her fingers had slid into the warmth of his when they had shaken hands, she had felt a surge of sensations that settled in the middle of stomach. This guy was smooth and the problem was that she wasn't used to smooth guys. She dated, but not frequently, and definitely not someone like Brandon Jarrett. It was quite obvious he knew how to work *it* and it was also quite obvious that he thought he had a chance of working her. That realization didn't repulse her like it should have. Instead it had her curious. He wouldn't be the first man who'd tried hitting on her, but he was the first who had remotely triggered her interest in over a year or so.

"We're back to that, are we?" she asked, chuckling, feeling a little more relaxed than she had earlier.

"Yes, I'm afraid we're back to that, and I hope you don't disappoint me. We can dine here at the hotel or go someplace else that's close by. It will be your choice."

She knew if would be crazy to suggest to a perfect stranger to take her someplace other than here, but the last thing she wanted was to become the topic of conversation of her employees. Some of them hadn't yet gotten over the shock that John Garrison was her biological father and that he had left the hotel to her. Making a decision she hoped that she didn't later regret she said, "I prefer going someplace else that's close by."

She could tell her response pleased him. "Is there any place you want to recommend or do you prefer leaving the choice to me?" he asked.

Again putting more trust in him than she really should, she said, "I'll leave things to you."

"All right. Do you want us to meet in the lobby in about an hour?"

She knew that wouldn't work. "No, we can meet

back here, at least over there on that terrace near the flower garden."

"Okay."

If he found her request strange he didn't let on. "Then I'll see you back here in an hour, Cassie Sinclair-Garrison," he said, smiling again.

Her heart missed a beat with his smile and, holding his gaze a bit longer than she should have, she said goodbye and then turned and quickly began walking back across the sand to her suite.

As Brandon headed back toward his room, he felt more than the October breeze off the ocean. A rush of adrenaline was pumping fast and furious through his veins. What were the chances of the one woman he had been attracted to since his breakup with Jamie Frigate a year ago to be the woman he had purposely come here to get to know?

Jamie.

Even now he had to steel himself against the rising anger he always felt when he thought about his fiancée's betrayal. How any woman could have been so shallow and full of herself he would never know. But more than that, she had been greedy as hell. She hadn't been satisfied with just having the things he could give her. While engaged to him she'd had an affair with a California businessman. He had found out about her duplicity when he had returned to Miami un-expectedly from a work-related trip to find her in bed with the man.

He entered his suite, not wanting to think about Jamie any longer, and instead his thoughts shifted back to Cassie. Any information he shared about himself to her would basically be false. But under the circumstances, that couldn't be helped. Tonight things had fallen into place too nicely for him and for some reason he was bothered by it. The woman he had seen playing a game of hopscotch had had an innocent air about her, definitely not what he had expected. And he had detected some sort of vulnerability, as well.

And he couldn't dismiss just how incredibly beautiful she was. With her striking good looks he would think she would have a date every night of the week. So the question that was presently popping in his mind was why didn't she?

In just the brief time he had spent with Cassie he had a feeling she was extremely bright. Maybe it had been the way she had studied him before making the decision to join him for dinner tonight that had given him that perspective.

A chuckle welled up inside of Brandon. He would find out just how bright she was at dinner when he really got into the game of wining and dining her. Whatever it took, he needed her to feel comfortable enough with him to share things about herself; things that could possibly damage her reputation if they became public knowledge.

He was suddenly unnerved by what he had to do and if he dwelled on it too long he would probably find the entire thing disgusting. But he could not let personal feelings or emotions intervene. He had a job to do and he intended to do it well.

Cassie glanced at herself in the mirror once more. She had taken another shower and changed outfits.

This one was a dress her mother had bought her earlier in the year that she had never worn until tonight.

It was a slinky thin-strapped mini-dress, fuchsia in color, and what made it elegant was the silver-clasp tie neck. She nervously smoothed the dress down her body, wondering if perhaps in trying to make a good impression she was making some sort of a statement, as well.

She ran her fingers though the long, dark brown curls on her head, fluffing them around her face. A face she thought had a remarkable resemblance to both of her parents, but mainly her father. She had her mother's eyes but her father's mouth, nose and cheekbones. And then there was that cleft in her chin that definitely came from him.

Her skin coloring was a mixture of the both of them, but her smile was that of John Garrison. She chewed her bottom lip nervously, thinking her smile was something she hadn't shown much of lately. But tonight she had smiled more than once already, although she had lowered her head so Brandon wouldn't see it the first time she'd done so.

She inhaled deeply, thinking for the umpteenth time that Brandon Jarrett was so drop-dead gorgeous it was a shame. No man should be walking around looking like he did and with a well-toned muscled body in whatever clothes he wore, made him downright lethal. He had to be the most beautiful man she'd ever met. On the beach he had been wearing a pair of jeans and a white shirt. And like her, he had removed his shoes. The outfit would have been casual on any other man but not on him.

Evidently he was single. At least he hadn't had a

ring on his finger, but that meant nothing since her father had rarely worn his wedding ring, either. She wondered if Brandon had someone special living in the States. A businessman traveling alone often forgot certain details like that. As owner of the hotel she was observant and perceptive and knew such affairs were going on under her roof, but as long as they were of mutual consent it was no business of hers.

Cassie reached for the matching shawl to her dress and placed it around her shoulders. The air tonight was rather breezy. Forecasters had reported a tropical storm was stirring up in the Atlantic. Hopefully, it wouldn't become a hurricane, and if it did she hoped that it would not set its course toward the islands.

She glanced at her watch. It was time to meet the very handsome Brandon Jarrett.

Brandon stood near the flower garden, his body shadowed by numerous plants and an abundance of palm trees. He watched Cassie as she left her suite and strolled along the private brick walkway. Like earlier, she hadn't detected his presence and this gave him a chance to study her once again.

The dress she was wearing seemed to have been designed just for her body and was definitely working for her, and for him as well. Just watching her made his pulse rate increase. The lantern lights reflecting off the building highlighted her features. Her hair flowed around her shoulders, tossing around her face with every step she took.

Sensations he hadn't felt in a long time gripped him and they were of a degree he'd never experienced before. John Garrison's youngest daughter was definitely a looker and was having an impact on his senses as well as his body. He inhaled deeply. He had to regain control. He had to remember his plan.

Deciding it wouldn't be in his best interest to catch her off guard for a second time, he deliberately cleared his throat. When she glanced his way their gazes met. He almost forgot everything, except the way she was looking at him. He had never been swept away by a woman, but he felt that he was now standing in sinking sand and quickly decided, just for that moment, he would forget the real reason he was on the island. The woman was too stunningly beautiful for him to do anything else.

"I hope you haven't been waiting long," she said, coming to stand directly in front of him, giving him a close view of her outfit.

"Not at all, but any time I've spent waiting has been worth it," he said, taking her hand in his and feeling the way her hand trembled beneath his fingers. In response, he felt his insides quiver and primitive emotions began stirring in his gut. He was discovering just how strong his sexual attraction to her was.

"Have you decided where we're going?"

Her question invaded his thoughts and he wished he could respond by telling her they were going to find the nearest bed. "Yes, the Viscaya Restaurant. Have you ever heard of it?"

"Yes, I've heard of it," Cassie answered, drawing in a deep breath. "It has an astounding reputation."

"I heard that, as well," he said, holding firm to her hand as he led her through the gardens and toward the parking lot where his rental car was parked. It was a beautiful October night and the breeze off the ocean made it somewhat cool.

"You look nice," Brandon said, opening the door to the Lexus.

She glanced up at him and smiled as she slid onto the car seat. "Thanks. You look nice yourself."

He smiled back at her. "Now it's my time to thank you."

"And you are welcome."

Cassie watched as Brandon crossed in front of the car to get into the driver's side. He did look nice in his dark trousers and crisp white shirt and looked the epitome of sexy. Everything about him appealed to her female senses. His walk was smooth and self-assured.

Before starting the engine he glanced over at her. "The lady at the front desk said the restaurant is only a five-minute drive from here."

Cassie nodded. "All right."

He pulled out of the parking lot and she leaned back into her seat, her body relaxed. She was looking forward to this evening; especially his company. There was a lot she wanted to know about him and decided that now was the time to ask. "So where are you from?"

"I'm from Orlando, Florida," he answered.

"Disney World."

He chuckled. "Yes, Disney World. Have you ever been there?"

"Yes, when I was about ten my mom took me there. We were there for a whole week."

"What about your father?"

A small smile touched her lips. "Dad traveled a lot

and joined us later, but for only a few days." And then, as if she wanted to know more about him, she asked, "And what sort of work you do?"

"I'm an investment broker. My motto is 'If you have any monies to invest then entrust them with me and I'll do the rest.'"

"Umm, that's clever. I like it."

"Thanks. And where are you from, Cassie, and what do you do?" he asked.

Brandon had come to a traffic light and he glanced over at her and saw her nervously rubbing her palms against the side of her dress. Her actions caused him to look at her thighs, the portion her minidress wasn't covering. It took everything within him to force his eyes back on the road when the light changed.

"I was born here on the island and I'm in the hotel business," he heard her say.

Deciding not to put her on the spot by asking her to expound more regarding her occupation he said, "The Bahamas is a beautiful island."

He could tell she had relaxed by the sound of her breathing. "Yes, it is. I take it that this is not your first visit here."

He smiled, liking the sound of her sexy accent. "No, I've been to the island several times, but this is the first time I've stayed at the Garrison Grand-Bahamas."

He didn't think it would be appropriate to mention that he had flown here last year with Jamie in his private plane. It had been then that he had asked her to marry him. She had accepted and they had spent the rest of the week on a yacht belonging to one of his clients, who was also a good friend.

He was grateful when they pulled into the parking lot of the Viscaya Restaurant. For a little while he was getting a reprieve from having to weave more lies.

Less than an hour later Cassie had determined a number of things about Brandon. In addition to being breathtakingly handsome, he was also incredibly charming and outrageously smooth. She'd discovered during dinner that he was also someone who was easy to talk to; someone who had the ability to make her feel comfortable around him. And she noticed he had a tendency to treat all people—from the restaurant's manager to the waiter to the busboy who'd come to clear off their table—with respect. He had made each individual feel important and appreciated.

"That was kind and thoughtful of you," she said when they were walking out of the restaurant.

He glanced over at her. "What?"

"The way you treated everyone back there. You didn't hesitate to let them know how much you appreciated their services. You would be surprised at how many people don't do that," she said, thinking how rudely her hotel workers were often treated by people who thought they were better than them.

He shrugged. "It's something I got from my father. He believed it wouldn't take much for a person to let others know when they've done something right, especially when we are quick to let them know when they've done something wrong."

"It sounds like your father is a very smart man."

"He *was* a smart man. Dad passed away a few years ago," he said.

She glanced over at him and a look of sorrow touched her features. "I'm sorry. Were you close to your father?"

"Yes, we were extremely close. In fact we were partners at our firm," he said truthfully. "My mother died of cancer before I reached my teens so it had been just my dad and I for a long time."

She nodded and then said, "My father passed away a little over four months ago and my mom a month before that."

Brandon heard the pain of her words in her voice and from the light from the electrical torches that lit the parking lot, he actually saw tears in her eyes. He stopped walking just a few feet from where their car was parked and instinctively pulled her into his arms. She offered no resistance when he gathered the warmth of her body against his. He briefly closed his eyes, regretting this cruel game he was playing with her.

"I'm sorry," he whispered in her ear, in a way for both her loss as well as his lies. Her loss was sincere and he actually felt her pain. She had loved both her parents immensely. For the first time since John's death, Cassie Sinclair-Garrison had become a real person and just not a name on a document on a file in his office. And not just the person with whom Parker had a beef.

"I didn't mean to come apart like that," Cassie said, moments later, stepping back out of Brandon's arms, looking somewhat embarrassed.

"It's okay. I can understand the depth of your pain. I've lost both of my parents, but when my mom died at least I had my dad to keep things going, providing a sense of stability in my life. But your parents died fairly close to each other. I can't imagine how you endured such a thing. Do you have other siblings?" he asked, wondering if she would acknowledge the Miami Garrisons.

She gave him a distracted look, as if thinking deeply on his question. Then she said, "My father had other children but I've never met them."

"Not even at the funeral?" he asked, already knowing the answer.

She shrugged. "No, not even then." Then she quickly said, "I'd rather not talk about it anymore, Brandon. It's rather private."

He nodded. "I understand. Sorry for prying."

She reached out and took his hand. "You weren't prying. Everything's sort of complicated right now."

"Again I understand, but if you ever need to talk or need—"

"A shoulder to cry on again," she said, trying to sound cheerful.

He chuckled. "Yes, a shoulder to cry on. I am available."

"Thank you. How long will you be staying at the hotel?"

He paused to open the car door for her. "A week. What about you?"

She waited until she was inside and glanced up at him and said. "Indefinitely. I work at the hotel and depending on how my days are, I sometimes spend the night there instead of driving all the way home. I have a private suite. My home is on the other side of the island."

"I see," Brandon said before closing the door. He

had given her another opportunity but she had yet to tell him she owned the hotel.

After walking around the car and getting inside he turned to her before starting the ignition. "I'm glad you came to dinner with me tonight. What are your plans for tomorrow?"

She smiled. "I have a meeting in the morning and then I'll be leaving for my home. I won't be returning to the hotel until Thursday morning."

Brandon leaned forward and smiled. "Is there anyway I can weasel another dinner date out of you?"

Cassie laughed. "Another dinner date?"

"Yes, I'll even be happy if you wanted to treat me to some of your good cooking."

"And what makes you think I can cook?"

"A hunch. Am I wrong?"

She shook her head. "No, you're right. Not to sound too boastful or conceited, although I don't spend a whole lot of time in the kitchen since I usually eat at the hotel, I can cook. That was one of my mom's biggest rules. And because of it, I was probably one of the few girls in my dorm at college who could fend for herself."

He chuckled. "And where did you attend college?"

"I went to a school in London and got a degree in business administration."

Brandon was still smiling when he finally decided to dig deeper by asking, "And just what is your position at the hotel? You never did say."

From her expression he could tell she was somewhat startled by his question. He was forcing her to make a decision as to whether or not she trusted him enough to tell him that much about herself.

"Evidently," she finally said, "you didn't make the connection when I gave my name earlier tonight."

He lifted a dark brow. "And what connection is that?"

Cassie held on to his gaze. "Garrison. I own the Garrison Grand-Bahamas."

Three

"You own the hotel?" Brandon asked, seemingly surprised by what she'd said and trying not to place much emphasis on what she'd just revealed and raise her suspicions about his motives for being there.

"Yes, my father left it to me when he died."

Brandon brought the car to a stop at a traffic light and used that opportunity to look directly at her. "Then you must feel proud that he had such faith and confidence in your abilities to do such a thing."

The smile she gave him extended straight from her eyes and he suddenly felt his gut clench from the effect those dark eyes had on him. "Thanks. And he did know of my capabilities because I'd managed the hotel for the past five years."

He nodded when the car began moving again. "That

might be true but I'm sure managing a hotel is a lot different than owning it. It's a big responsibility to place on anyone's shoulders and evidently he felt, and I'm sure justly so, that you could handle the job."

"Thank you for saying that," she said softly. "That was very kind of you."

"I'm just telling you the way I see it," he said, bringing the car to a stop in the parking lot of the hotel. "Now getting back to the subject of seeing you again tomorrow…" he said smoothly.

She shook her head, grinning. "You don't give up, do you?"

"Not without a fight," he said sincerely. "And if you don't feel like having me try out your cooking skills, I'd love to take you to another restaurant tomorrow evening. I understand several in this area come highly recommended."

Trying to ignore the urge to laugh from the intensity of his plea, she smiled. Since she'd taken ownership of her mother's home a few memths ago, no man had crossed its threshold and she hadn't planned for one to cross over it anytime soon. But for some reason the thought of Brandon visiting her home didn't bother her, which could only mean one thing. She really liked him.

Pushing her hair away from her face she said, "I would love having dinner again with you tomorrow and I insist it be my treat. At my home. And I will proudly show you just what a good cook I am."

Brandon grinned. "I'll look forward to it."

He got out of the car and walked around it to open the door for her. What he'd said was true. He was looking forward to it but not for the reason that he should be. A part of him wished like hell that her last name wasn't Garrison.

"Thank you, Brandon," she said when he offered her his hand. "I'll leave a sealed envelope with directions to my home for you at the front desk tomorrow," she added when they stood at her door. "It's in Lyford Cay."

"And is there a particular time you prefer that I show up?"

She tilted her head back to look up at him. "Anytime after four will be fine. I won't be serving dinner until around six but I think you might enjoy taking a walk through the aquarium."

He lifted a brow. "The aquarium?"

She smiled. "Yes, my mother loved sea life and ten years ago for her fortieth birthday my father had a beautiful indoor aquarium built for her."

"You live in your mother's home?" he asked when she had lowered her head to get the door key out of her purse.

She glanced back up at him. "It used to be Mom's, but Dad signed it over to me when she died. I really had thought he was going to sell it, but I think the thought of parting with it bothered him since the place held so many special memories."

Brandon didn't know what to say to that. He did know there was no mention of John Garrison owning a home in the Bahamas in any of the legal papers he had. It was a moot point now since, according to Cassie, John had signed it over to her.

"I enjoyed your company tonight," she said, unlocking her door.

Cassie's words drew back his attention. "And I, yours. I'm looking forward to tomorrow."

"So am I. Good night, Brandon."

Although they had just met tonight, he had no intentions of letting her escape inside her suite without them sharing a kiss. All night he had focused on her lips, wondering how they would taste and how they would feel beneath his. He could feel the sizzling tension between them and took a step closer to her, deciding to draw it out and pull it in. He was powerless to do anything less.

He reached out, cupped her chin gently in his hand and studied the dimple she had there. "Nice place for a dimple," he said in a husky voice.

She smiled up at him. "My dad said it's a cleft. He had one, too."

So do his other five children, Brandon thought. "I'm going to have to disagree with your father on that. I have it on good authority that on a man it's a cleft but on a woman it's a dimple."

"Nothing wrong with disagreeing," Cassie said.

His hand felt warm and when he moved it from her chin and took the backside of his hand and caressed the side of her face, she felt her entire body tingle from sensations that not only flooded her mind but also her senses. Without any self-control she released a deep sigh and closed her eyes, thinking his touch felt so soothing. And before she could reopen her eyes she detected the warmth of his lips close to hers, and then she felt it when he placed them softly against her own.

She released another sigh and her lips parted, giving his tongue the opportunity to slip inside and capture hers. She had thought of tasting him all night and she was getting more than she had bargained for. His taste was manly, sexy, delicious—everything she had imagined it would be and more. She couldn't stop the quiver that passed through her body or the moan she heard from low in her throat. He was a master at his game, definitely an expert at what he was doing and how he was making her feel.

Her fingers gripped the sleeve of his shirt when she felt weak in the knees, and in response his arms wrapped themselves around her waist, pulling her closer to him. And she could actually feel his heat, his strength, everything about him that was masculine. Moments later when he broke off the kiss, she opened her eyes.

"Thank you for that," he whispered hoarsely, just inches from her lips. And before she could draw her next breath, he was kissing her again and the pleasure of it was seeping deep into her bones. Instinctively she responded, feeling slightly dizzy while doing so, and she could hear the *purr* that came from deep within her throat.

Moments later he ended the kiss and she regretted the loss, the feel of his mouth on hers. Her gaze latched onto his lips and she felt a warm sensation flow between her legs. Without much effort, he had aroused impulses within her that she had never encountered before. It was like her feminine liberation was threatening to erupt.

"I'm looking forward to seeing you tomorrow, Cassie," he said, taking a step even closer.

The light that shone in her doorway cast the solid planes of his face into sharp focus. She watched as his gaze moved slowly over her features before returning to her eyes. And while his eyes held hers, she studied the deep look of desire in them. For some reason the look didn't startle her, nor did it bother her. What it did do was fill her with anticipation of seeing him again.

"And I'm looking forward to seeing you, as well." When she realized she was still clutching his sleeve she quickly released it, turned and, without wasting time, opened the door and went inside.

A few moments later Brandon entered his own suite as he took a mental note of what had transpired that night. Frankly, he wasn't sure what to make of it. Cassie Garrison was definitely not what he had anticipated. He had expected a woman who was selfish, spoiled, inconsiderate and self-centered. Definitely temperamental at best. However, the woman he had spent time with tonight, in addition to her physical perfection, had possessed charm, style and grace, warmth and sensuality, even while not knowing she was eluding the latter. Then there was her keen sense of intelligence, which was definitely obvious. She was not a woman who acted irrational or who didn't think through any decision she made. Even when she had ordered dinner she had expounded on the advantages of eating healthy. And when she had spoken of her parents he could feel the pain that she'd endured in losing them, pain she was still mending from.

He shook his head, remembering how comfortable she had gotten with him. Surprisingly, they had discovered over the course of their conversation that they had a lot in common. They enjoyed reading the same types of books, shared a dislike of broccoli and had the same taste in music. And when she had opened up to him and revealed she had owned the hotel, he had seen the trusting look in her eyes.

A part of him wished the circumstances were different, that she hadn't lost her parents; that the two of them had met before John's death. And more than anything a part of him wished that he wasn't here betraying her.

In truth, he didn't want to think about that part— he really didn't want to think about Cassie Garrison at all. If only he could let it sink into his mind, as well as his body, that his only reason for being here was purely business and not personal. He of all people knew how it felt to be betrayed. How it felt to have your trust in someone destroyed. And that was not a comforting thought.

He walked out on the balcony and took a moment to stare out at the ocean, hoping he could stop Cassie from whirling through his thoughts. It was a beautiful night, but instead of appreciating the moon and the stars, his mind was getting clouded again with thoughts of a pair of long, gorgeous legs, a mass of curly brown hair cascading around a strikingly beautiful face and the taste of a mouth that wouldn't go away. Kissing her, devouring her lips, had been better than any dessert he'd ever eaten.

Closing his eyes, he breathed in the scent of the ocean, trying to get his mind back in check. That wasn't easy when instead of the ocean's scent filtering through his nostrils it was the scent of Cassie's perfume that wouldn't leave him.

A feeling of uneasiness crept over Brandon. He definitely didn't need this. He was not a man known to get wimpy and all emotional over a woman. Okay, so he had enjoyed her company, but under no circumstances could he forget just who she was and why he was here.

With that thought embedded into his mind and back where it belonged and where he intended for it to stay, he turned and went into his suite.

Craning her neck, Cassie stood at the floor-to-ceiling window in her living room and looked out, watching Brandon's car as it came through the wrought-iron gates that protected her estate.

As the vehicle made its way down the long winding driveway she forced back the shivers that tried over-taking her body when she remembered the night before—every single thing about it. For the first time in a long time she had spent an evening very much aware of a man. No only had she been aware of him, she had actually lusted after him in a way she had never done with a male before. But somehow she had managed to maintain her sensibility and control—at least she had until he had kissed her. And it had been some kiss. Even now those same shivers she tried forcing away earlier were back.

A part of her mind relayed a message to move away from the window when Brandon's car got closer, or else he would see her and assume she was anxiously waiting for him. She lifted her chin in defiance when another part of her sent a different message. Let him think what he wants since she *was* anxiously waiting.

He brought his car to a stop in front of her house and from where she stood she had a very good view of him; one he wouldn't have of her until he got out of the car and halfway up her walkway. She studied his features through the car window and in the light of day he was even more handsome. And when he got out of the car he was dressed as immaculately as he had been the night before.

Today he was wearing a pair of khaki trousers and a chocolate-brown polo shirt. The man was built. He exuded so much sensuality she could actually feel it through the window pane.

She watched him walk away from his car toward her door and suddenly, as if he somehow sensed her, he looked toward the window. His eyes held hers for a moment and then he lifted his hand in a wave, acknowledging her presence.

The heat she had felt earlier in her body intensified and the shivers she couldn't fight slithered through her once more. She lifted her hand to wave back, wondering what it was about him that affected her so. What was there about this man that had her inviting him to her home, her private sanctuary, her personal domain, the place where she felt the presence of her parents the most? Why was she sharing all of that with him?

She discovered she didn't have time to ponder those questions when he disconnected his eyes from hers and headed toward her door. She sighed deeply, her nerves stretched tight. The air she took into her lungs was sharp, and the quickening she felt in her veins was absolute.

Not waiting for a knock at her door, she moved away from the window and headed in that direction, very much aware of the magnetism, the attraction and the lure of the man who was now standing on her doorstep.

* * *

"Welcome to my home, Brandon."

Brandon gazed at Cassie, telling himself that just like last night, his reaction to her was strictly sexual, which accounted for the ache he suddenly felt below the belt. The effect did not surprise him. He accepted it although he didn't like it.

He immediately picked up her scent, the same one that had tortured him through most of the night as if it had been deeply drenched into his nostrils. Reaching out, he took her hand in his, leaned closer and placed a light kiss on the dimple in her chin and finally said, "Thank you for inviting me, Cassie."

He released her hand and she smiled before taking a step back, letting him inside her home. The moment he crossed the threshold he beheld the stunning splendor of the décor. It wasn't just the style and colors, there were also the shapes and designs that combined traditional flare with that of contemporary, colonial and Queen Anne. The mixture in any other place would look crammed, definitely busy. But in this monstrosity of a house it demonstrated a sense of wealth combined with warmth. It also displayed diversity in taste with an unmistakable look of sophistication.

"You have a beautiful home."

Her smile widened. "Thank you. Come let me give you a tour. I haven't changed much since Mom died because she and I had similar taste."

She led and he followed. "Do you take care of this place by yourself?" he asked, although he couldn't imagine one person doing so.

She shook her head. "No, I have a housekeeping

staff, the same one Mom had when she and Dad were alive. My staff is loyal and dedicated and," she said grinning, "a little overprotective where I'm concerned since they've been around since I was twelve."

They came to a spacious room and stopped. He glanced around, appreciating how the entire width of the living room had floor-to-ceiling windows to take advantage of the view of the ocean. He also liked the Persian rugs on the floor.

Beyond the living room was the dining room and kitchen, set at an angle that also took advantage of the ocean's view. The first thing he thought when they walked into the kitchen was that that she had been busy. Several mouthwatering aromas surged through his nostrils and he successfully fought back the grumbling that threatened his stomach.

Both the dining room and kitchen opened to a beautiful courtyard with a stunning swimming pool and a flower garden whose design spread from one area of the yard to the other. Then there was the huge water fountain that sprouted water to a height that seemed to reach the roof.

"Did you live here with your mother?" he asked, moving his gaze over her, taking in the outfit she had chosen to wear today, tropical print tea-length skirt and matching peasant blouse that was as distinctly feminine as she was. The way the skirt flowed over her curves only heightened his sexual desire and made him aware, and very much so, just how much he wanted her.

"Until I left for college," she said, leading him up the stairs. "When I returned from London I got an apartment, but a year later for my birthday Dad bought me a condo. When he gave me the deed to this place, I moved back."

Moments later after giving him a tour of the upstairs, she said with excitement in her voice, "Now I must show you the aquarium."

Once they returned downstairs and rounded corners he saw other rooms—huge rooms for entertaining, a library, a study and room that appeared lined with priceless artwork. He suddenly stopped when he came to a huge portrait hanging on the wall. The man in the painting he recognized immediately, but the woman…

"Your parents?" he asked, staring at the portrait.

"Yes, those are my parents," he heard Cassie say proudly.

Brandon's gaze remained on the woman in the portrait. "She's beautiful," he said. He was so taken by the woman's exquisiteness that he took a step closer to the painting. Cassie followed and glanced over at his fixed look and smiled.

"Yes, Mom was beautiful."

When Cassie began walking away, he strolled beside her, noticing several other photographs of her parents together and some included her. In every one of them John was smiling in a way Brandon had never seen before. To say the man had found true happiness with Ava would be an understatement. The image portrayed on each picture was of a couple who was very much in love, and the ones that included Cassie indicated just how much they loved their daughter, as well.

When they approached another room she stood back to let him enter. His breath literally caught in his throat. On both sides of the narrow but lengthy room were high mahogany cabinets that encased floor-to-ceiling aquariums, each one designed to hide the aquarium frames and waterlines, they were filled with an abundance of tropical and coldwater sea life, seemingly behind a glass wall.

"So what do you think?"

The sound of her voice seemed subdued, but it had a sexy tone just the same. He turned to her. "I think your mother was a very lucky woman to have your father care so deeply to do this for her."

Cassie chuckled. "Oh, Dad knew what would make Mom happy. She had a degree in marine biology and for years worked as a marine biologist at the largest mineral management company on the island."

"Your mother worked?" he asked before he could stop himself.

Cassie didn't seem surprised by his question. "Yes, Mom worked although Dad tried convincing her not to. She enjoyed what she did and she refused to be a kept woman."

At his raised brow, she explained. "My parents never married. He was already married when they met. However they stayed together for over twenty-eight years."

Surprised she had shared that, he asked, "And he never got a divorce from his wife?"

"No. I think at one time he intended to do so when their children got older, but by then things were too complicated."

"Your mother never pushed for a divorce?"

Cassie shook her head. "No. She was comfortable with her place in my father's life as well as his love for her. She didn't need a wedding band or a marriage certificate."

He nodded slowly and deliberately met her gaze when he asked. "What about you? Will you need a wedding band or marriage certificate from a man?"

She grinned. "No, nor do I want one, either. I'm married to the hotel."

"And what about companionship?" he murmured softly, his head tilting to one side as he gazed intently at her. "And what about the idea and thought of a man being here for you? A person who will be there for you to snuggle up to at night. Someone with whom you can get intimate with?"

If the intent of his latter questions were meant to arouse her, it was definitely working, Cassie thought, when a vivid picture flashed through her mind of the two of them sharing a bed, snuggling, making love. Shivers slid down her body and the passion she saw in his eyes was incredibly seductive, too tempting for her well-being.

Trying to maintain her composure with as much effort as she could, she said, "Those happen to be ideas or thoughts that don't cross my mind."

He lifted a dark brow. "They don't?"

"No."

"Umm, what a shame."

"I don't think so. Now please excuse me a moment. I need to check on dinner."

She turned and swiftly left the aquarium.

The moment Cassie rounded the corner to her kitchen she paused and leaned against a counter and inhaled deeply. She had quickly left Brandon because her self-confidence would have gotten badly shaken had she stayed.

He had asked questions she'd only recently thought about herself, but only since meeting him. Last night she had gotten her first experience of a real kiss. She had been filled with the intensity of desire and had never felt such passion. And for the first time in her life she had longed for male companionship, someone to snuggle up close to at night. Someone with whom she could make love. The very thought sent heated shivers down her spine.

Grabbing the apron off a nearby rack and tying it around her waist, Cassie moved away from the counter and went to the sink to wash her hands. She then walked over to the stove where she had a pot simmering…the same way she was simmering inside. It was a low heat that if she wasn't careful, could escalate into a full-fledged flame. And truthfully, she wasn't ready for that.

Four

Following the smell of a delicious aroma, Brandon tracked his way to the kitchen and suddenly paused. He had seen a lot of feminine beauty in his day, but Cassie Garrison took the cake. Even wearing an apron while standing at a stove stirring a pot, she looked stunning.

She was wearing her hair up but a few errant curls had escaped bondage and were hanging about her ears. Because of her peasant blouse, the top portion of her shoulders was bare and a part of him wanted to cross the room and kiss her, then take his lips and move downward toward her throat and place butterfly kisses along her shoulder blades.

"Something smells good," he said, deciding to finally speak up to remove such lusty thoughts from his mind.

She turned and smiled and not for the first time he

thought she had a pretty pair of lips, ones that had felt well-defined beneath his.

"I hope you're hungry."

He chuckled. "I am. I missed lunch today."

She lifted a brow. "And how did that happen when our brunch buffet is to die for?"

It wouldn't do to tell her that he had missed lunch because he had gotten a call from one of the Miami Garrisons, namely her brother Stephen. "I can believe that. In the two days I've been here I've found your hotel staff to be very efficient at everything they do. The reason I missed out on what I'm sure was such a very delicious meal was I got a call from the office on a few things I needed to finalize."

"Don't they know you're on vacation? My father's rule was to tell the office to hold the calls when you're taking a much-needed break from work, unless it was an extreme emergency."

"Sounds like your father was a smart man."

"He was," Cassie said proudly as her lips formed into another smile. "You would have liked him."

I did, Brandon quickly thought. He leaned against one of the many counters in the kitchen and asked. "So what are you cooking?"

"A number of dishes for you to enjoy. Right now I'm stirring the conch chowder. I've also prepared crab and rice, baked macaroni and cheese and potato salad. For dessert I decided to give you a taste of my grand-mother's famous recipe of guava duff."

Brandon felt his lips curve, thinking he wouldn't mind having a taste of her, too. That thought instantly sent his pulse thumping wildly. "Anything I can do to help?" he asked, thinking the best thing to do to keep his mind from wandering was to get busy.

"Let me see…" She said glancing around the room. "I've already washed everything if you want to put the salad together in a bowl."

Relief swept through him, glad she had found him something to do. If he were to continue to stand there and look at her while having all kinds of sexual thoughts, he couldn't be held responsible for his actions.

"Considering my skills in the kitchen, doing what you asked should be reasonably safe," he said, moving toward the sink to wash his hands.

Moments later he was standing at the counter putting the lettuce, tomatoes, cucumbers and onions in a huge bowl for their tossed salad. Knowing he needed to use all the time he had to get to know her, or to find out everything he could about her, he asked, "So, why are you still single, Cassie?"

"Why are you?"

Brandon could tell by her tone that he had once again put her on the defensive. To counter the effect he decided to be honest with her. "Up to a year ago I was engaged to get married."

She stopped stirring the pot and slanted him an arch glance. "If you don't mind me asking, what happened?"

He did mind her asking, but since he initiated the discussion, he would provide her an answer. "My fiancée decided a few months before the wedding that I wasn't everything she needed. I discovered she was unfaithful."

He watched her expression. First surprise and then regret shone in her eyes. "I'm sorry."

"Yes, so was I at the time, but I'm glad I found out before the wedding instead of afterward." Not wanting to discuss Jamie any further, he said, "Salad's done."

She turned back to the stove. "So is everything else. Now we can eat."

Brandon leaned back in his chair after glancing at his plate. It was clean. Cassie hadn't joked when she'd said she knew her way around a kitchen. Everything, even the yeast rolls that had been so fluffy they almost melted in his mouth, had been totally delicious.

He glanced across the table at her. She was finishing the last of the dessert, something that had also been delectable. "The food was simply amazing, Cassie. Thanks for inviting me to dinner."

"You're welcome and I'm glad you enjoyed everything."

"You never did answer the question I asked earlier, about why you're still single. Was I out of line in asking?" he asked, studying the contents of his glass before glancing back at her.

She met his gaze. "No, but there's not a lot to explain. After high school I left home for London to attend college there. I spent my time studying, more so than dating. I didn't see going to college as a way to escape from my parents and start proclaiming my freedom by exerting all kind of outlandish behavior."

"You mean you didn't go to any naked parties? Didn't try any drugs?" He meant the comment as a joke and he could tell she had taken it that way by the smile he saw in her eyes.

"No, there were no naked parties, no drugs and no

eating of fried worms just to fit in with any group." She grinned and added, "I mostly hung alone and I lived off campus in an apartment. Dad insisted. And the only reason he agreed that I have a roommate was for safety reasons."

"So you never dated during college?"

"I didn't say that," she said, taking a sip of her wine. "I dated some but I was very selective when I did so. Most of the guys at college enjoyed a very active sex life and didn't mind spreading that fact or the names of the girls who helped them to reach that status. I didn't intend to be one of them. I had more respect for myself than that."

Brandon stared down at his wine, considering all she had said. He then looked back up at her. "Are you saying you've never been seriously involved with anyone?"

She smiled warmly. "No, that's not what I'm saying." She paused for a moment before adding softly, "There was someone, a guy I met after college. Jason and I dated and thought things were working out but later discovered they weren't."

"What went wrong?"

The memory of that time filled Cassie's mind and for some reason she didn't have a problem sharing it with him. "He began changing in a way that wasn't acceptable to me. He would break our dates and make dumb excuses for doing so. And then out of the clear blue sky one day he broke off with me, and it was then that he told me the reason why. He had taken up with an older woman, a wealthy woman who wanted him as a boy toy, and he felt that was worth kicking aside what I thought we had."

Brandon stared at her. "How long ago was that?"

"Almost four years ago."

"Have you seen him at all since that time?" he asked.

She took another sip of her wine and suddenly felt quite warm. "Of course we haven't dated since then, but yes, I've seen him. He was thoughtful enough to attend my mother's funeral."

And then Cassie said, "And when I saw him I knew that our breakup was the best thing and I owed him thanks. That was a comforting thought and I no longer could hate him."

Brandon stared down into his wine, absently twirling the glass between his fingers, wondering if she ever discovered the truth about him—who he was and why he was there—would she end up hating him, too.

"You've gotten quiet on me," she said.

He glanced back up at her, held her gaze and then reached across the table and took her hand in his. "Have I? If so, it's because I can't imagine any man letting you go," he said softly, tightening his hold on her hand.

A shiver ran down Cassie's spine. She felt the sincerity in Brandon's words and they touched her. She stared at him, totally aware of his physical presence, and with his hand holding hers she felt his strength. Warmth flooded her from the heat she saw in his eyes and for a tiny moment a wealth of meaning shone in them.

"And while you were telling me about your ex-fiancée," she said, her eyes holding steady on his face, "I couldn't help thinking the same thing. I can't imagine any woman letting you go, either."

It seemed the room suddenly got quiet. The only sounds were that of their breathing in a seemingly strained and forced tone. And he was still holding her hands and she felt his fingers move as they brushed across her hand in soft, featherlike strokes. The beating of her heart increased and his gaze continued to hold hers. The expression on his face was unreadable but the look in his eyes was not.

He slowly stood and pulled her out of her seat. Wordlessly, he brought her closer to him. Heat was thrumming through her and she drew in a slow breath. She slid her gaze from his eyes and lowered them to his lips. He leaned in closer, inching his mouth closer to hers.

Cassie felt the heat within her intensify just seconds before he brushed his lips across hers, causing a colossal sensation that she felt all the way to her toes, before spreading to areas known and unknown. And when a sigh of pleasure escaped her lips, easing them apart, with a ravenous yet gentle entry he began devouring her mouth.

Brandon felt the rush of blood that started in his head, and when it got to his chest it joined the rapid pounding of his heart. This was what energized passion was all about. And as he deepened the kiss all kind of feelings reverberated through him, searing awareness in his central nervous system. When he took hold of her tongue, he was filled with intense yearning and a craving that for him was unnatural.

He slightly shifted his stance and brought her closer to the fit of him, and to a body that was getting aroused by the minute. By the moans he heard coming from her he could tell she was enjoying the invasion of his tongue. That realization had him sinking deeper and deeper into the taste and texture of her mouth.

Her body pressed against his hard erection, making him want to sweep her into his arms and carry her to the nearest bedroom. He knew it would be sheer madness. And it would also be wrong. She deserved more than a man making love to her for all the wrong reasons, a man who had walked into her life without good intensions. A man who was even now betraying her.

That thought had him ending the kiss but he couldn't let her go just yet, so he pulled her closer into his arms. How had he allowed himself to get into this situation? How had he let Cassie get to him so quickly and so deeply?

She pulled slightly back, glanced out the window and then back at him and smiled. "Do you want to take a stroll on the beach before it gets too dark?"

"I'd love to," he said, releasing her.

"It will only take a minute for me to get my shawl. You can wait for me on the terrace if you'd like."

"All right."

She shifted to move past him and he suddenly reached out and gently locked his hand on her arm. Then he raised his hands to her hair and brushed back the strands that had fallen in her face. He felt the shiver that touched her body the moment he leaned down and brushed a kiss against her lips. "I'll be waiting," he whispered.

A few moments later Cassie quietly slipped out on the terrace to find Brandon standing with his back to her, staring out at the ocean with both hands in the pockets of his trousers.

His stance radiated so much sex appeal it should

have been illegal. He seemed to be in deep thought and she couldn't help wondering what he was thinking about. Had talking about his ex-fiancée opened up old wounds? Having someone you loved betray you wasn't easy to take. She had discovered that with Jason.

"I'm ready."

He turned at the sound of her voice and across the brick pavers she met his gaze. He then looked at her from head to toe, zeroing in on her bare feet for a few seconds.

She laughed. "Hey, don't look surprised. You never walk on the beach with shoes on. That's an islander rule, so please remove yours."

He chuckled as he dropped into a wicker chair to take off his shoes and socks. She thought the feet he exposed were as sexy as the rest of him. Placing his socks and shoes aside, he stood and smiled at her. "Happy now?"

"Yes, extremely. Now we can make footprints in the sand." She held her hand out to him. "Let's go."

Brandon took the hand she offered and together they walked down the steps toward the private beach.

"So, tell me about your life in Orlando."

Her question reminded him of the lies he had planted, as well as those he had to continue to tell. He glanced over at her and asked, "What do you want to know?"

Smiling curiously, she asked, "Is there someone special in your life waiting for your return?"

"No," he responded with no hesitation. "I date occasionally but there's no one special."

Seconds ticked by and when she didn't say anything he decided to add, "And it isn't because I mistrust all women because of what my ex-fiancée did. I got over it and moved on. I buried myself in my work because while with her I spent a lot of time away from it. That's what she wanted and what I thought she needed."

"But you found it wasn't?"

"Yes, I found it wasn't, especially when it wasn't for the right reason. Jamie had an insecurity complex and I fed into it. But that wasn't enough. She had to feel doubly safe by having someone else in her life, besides me."

"Did she not care how that would play out once you discovered the truth?"

He shrugged. "I guess she figured she would never get caught. She even went so far to admit that she would not have given up her lover after we married."

"Sounds like she was pretty brazen."

His jaw tightened. "Yes, she was."

When they reached the end of the shore they stopped and looked out at the ocean. Standing beside her Brandon could feel Cassie's heat, and even with the scent of the sea he inhaled her fragrance. He allowed the rest of his senses to appreciate her presence, being with her at this time and place.

She turned and flashed him a brilliant smile. "The sunset is beautiful, isn't it?"

"Yes, and so are you."

She lowered her head as if to consider his words. She then looked back at him. "Are you always this complimentary with women?"

"No, not always."

"Then I should feel special."

"Only because you are."

She turned and pressed her lithe body against his aroused one, and he was tempted to lower his head and connect to the lips she was so eagerly offering him. Instead he stepped back and said, "I think it's time for me to leave and go back to the hotel now."

He saw the questions in her eyes and really wasn't surprised when she asked, "Why, Brandon?"

He understood her reason for asking. But there was no way he could be completely honest with her. "I don't think we're ready for that step yet," he murmured softly, moving forward to pull her in his arms.

She leaned back and looked at him as her lips curved into a smile. "Are you talking for yourself or for me?"

He ignored the underlying challenge in her words. "I'm trying to be a gentleman and speak for the both of us."

"I'm a grown woman, Brandon. I can speak and think for myself."

He looked down at her, studied her eyes and saw the deep rooted stubbornness glaring in them. "I know that, but I want you to trust me to know what's best for the both of us right now."

She paused then said, "All right, but only on one condition."

He raised a dark brow. "And what condition is that?"

"That we have dinner again tomorrow night."

It was on the tip of Brandon's tongue to tell her that he was thinking seriously about returning to Miami tomorrow. Parker and Stephen would know soon enough that his mission hadn't been accomplished. The thought of spending time with Cassie one more night over dinner was something he couldn't pass up. But then, he would give her an out by suggesting a place she probably wouldn't go along with.

"Dinner will be fine as long as we can dine at the hotel," he said.

He was surprised when she nodded and said, "All right."

Brandon nodded. "Come on, let's go back."

When they reached the terrace he stopped and turned to her. "And I might have to go back to the States on Thursday. Something has come up that needs my attention."

He could see the disappointment in her face and it almost weakened his resolve.

"I understand. I'm a businesswoman, so I know how things can come up when you least expect them to…or want them to."

He eased down in the wicker chair to put back on his shoes and socks. He waited and then said, "I'm looking forward to having dinner with you tomorrow."

"So am I."

He glanced up at her, intrigued by the eagerness in the tone of her voice, and wondered if perhaps she was plotting his downfall. He wanted her with a fierce passion and it wouldn't take much to push him over the edge.

Brandon stood, knowing it was best for him to leave now. Hanging around could result in more damage than good. "Will you walk me to the door?"

He reached for her hand and she didn't resist in giving it to him. When they reached her front door he gazed at her, thinking he wouldn't be forgetting her for a long time. "Thanks again for a beautiful evening and a very delicious dinner."

The smile that appeared on her face was genuine. "You are welcome." And then she leaned up on tiptoes and brushed a kiss across his lips. "I'll see you at dinner tomorrow, Brandon. Please leave a note at the front desk regarding where you want us to meet and when."

Brandon held her gaze for a moment, and then nodded before turning to walk down the walkway to his car.

Five

Brandon glanced at the table that sat in the middle of the floor. Room service had done an outstanding job of making sure his orders were followed. He wanted Cassie to see the brilliantly set table the moment she arrived.

He had tried contacting Parker earlier today to let him know his trip hadn't revealed anything about Cassie that they didn't already know. He shook his head, thinking that he stood corrected on that. There was a lot about her that he knew now that he hadn't known before, but as far as he was concerned it was all good, definitely nothing that could be used against her.

Parker's secretary had told him that his friend had taken a couple of days off to take his wife Anna to New York for shopping and a Broadway show, and wouldn't be returning until the beginning of next week. Brandon couldn't help but smile every time he thought about how the former Anna Cross had captured the heart of the man who had been one of Miami's most eligible bachelors and most prominent businessman.

He turned at the sound of the knock on the door and quickly crossed the room. As he'd expected, she was on time. He opened the door to find Cassie standing there, and smiled easily. As usual she looked good. Tonight her hair was hanging around her shoulders. He studied her face and could tell she was wearing very little makeup, which was all that was needed since she had such natural beauty.

His gaze slid down her body. She was no longer wearing the business suit he had seen her in earlier that day when he had caught a glimpse of her before she had stepped into an elevator. Instead she had changed into a flowing, slinky animal-print dress that hugged at the hips before streaming down her figure. A matching jacket was thrown over her arm. A pair of black leather boots were on her feet, but how far up her legs they went he couldn't tell due to the tea-length of her dress. He knew she was wearing the boots more for a fashion statement than for the weather.

"May I come in?"

He pulled his gaze back to her face and returned her smile. "Yes, by all means."

Her fragrance filled his nostrils when she strolled by him and after closing the door he stood there and stared at her with his hands shoved in the pockets of his trousers. He had placed them there so he wouldn't be tempted to reach out and pull her into his arms. That temptation was becoming a habit.

"You look nice," he couldn't help but say because she did look nice, so nice that he felt the fingers inside his pockets beginning to tingle.

"Thank you. And you look nice yourself."

When he lifted a skeptical brow he saw her smile widen, and then she said, "You do look nice. I thought that the first time I saw you."

"That night on the beach?"

"No, that day you checked in to the hotel. I happened to notice you and immediately knew by the way you were dressed that you were an American businessman."

He nodded, not wanting to get in to all the other things that he was, especially when his conscience was getting pinched. He decided to change the subject. "I hope you're hungry."

"I am." She glanced around and saw the table. "They've delivered already?"

Freeing his hands from his pockets, he moved away from the door to cross the room to where she stood. "No, they've just set up everything. I didn't want to take the chance of ordering something you didn't like."

He reached for the menu he had placed on the table. "You want to take a look?"

She shook her head. "No, I have every entrée on it memorized."

He chuckled. "I'm impressed."

She grinned. "Just one of my many skills. And if I may…"

"And you can."

"Then I would recommend the Salvador. It's a special dish that's a combination of lobster, fish, crawfish and various other seafood that's stewed and then served over rice."

"Sounds delicious."

"It is, but I have to warn you that it's kind of spicy."

A smile curved his lips. "I can handle a little bit of spicy. And please make yourself comfortable while I phone room service."

Cassie placed her jacket across the back of the sofa and sat, crossing her legs. She hadn't missed the look of male appreciation in Brandon's eyes when he had opened the door. His already dark gaze had gotten darker and his seductive look had sent heat flowing through her body.

Deciding she needed to cool down, she glanced around. The layout of this suite was similar to one she used whenever she stayed overnight at the hotel. However since hers was an executive suite, it was slightly larger and also had a kitchen, although she never used it.

"Our dinner will be delivered in about thirty to forty-five minutes," he said, sitting on the sofa beside her and shifting his position to face her. "So, how was your day?"

She rolled her eyes and shook her head. "Crazy. Hurricane Melissa can't seem to make up her mind which way she wants to go, so we're taking every pre-caution. Just yesterday she was headed north, but now she's in a stall position as if trying to decide if she really wants to go north after all. We had a number of people who decided not to take any chances and have checked out of the hotel already."

Brandon nodded. He'd been keeping up with the

weather reports as well and understood her concern. Being a native of Miami, he had experienced several hurricanes in his lifetime, some more severe than others. Earlier that day he had spoken with his secretary, Rachel Suarez. A Cuban-American, Rachel had been working for his firm for over thirty years, and had started out with his father. When it came to handling things at the office she could hold her own—including the possibility of an oncoming hurricane.

"And if the hurricane comes this way I'm sure your staff knows what to do," he said, tempted to ease over toward her and run his hands up her legs to see how far up her boots went.

"Trust me, they know the drill. Every employee has to take a hurricane awareness course each year. It prepares them for what to do if it ever comes to that. Dad mandated the training after we went through Hurricane Andrew."

Brandon remembered Hurricane Andrew, doubted he would ever be able to forget it. It had left most of Miami, especially the area where he had lived, in shambles. "Well, hopefully Lady Melissa will endure a peaceful death before hitting land," he said mildly.

He then asked, "Would you like anything to drink while we wait? How about a glass of wine?"

"That would be nice. Thanks."

He stood and Cassie watched as he did so. She watched him walk across the room, thinking he was so sinfully handsome it was a shame. His gray trousers and white shirt were immaculate, tailored to fit his body to perfection. Last night he had done the gentlemanly thing and had stopped anything from escalating further between them, and after he had left her home she had felt grateful. Now she felt a sense of impending loss. He would be leaving tomorrow and chances where they would never see each other again.

For the past two days she had felt alive and in high spirits, something she hadn't felt in the last five months—and all because of him. He hadn't pushed for an affair with her. In fact when he'd had a good opportunity to go for a hit, he had walked away. Had he exerted the least bit of pressure, she would have gladly taken him into her bed. There had never been a man who'd had her entertaining the idea of a casual fling before. But Brandon Jarrett had.

"Here you are."

She looked up. Their gazes connected and she reached out to take the wineglass he offered, struggling to keep her fingers from trembling. "Thanks." She immediately took a sip, an unladylike gulp was more like it. She needed it. The heat within her was intensifying.

"You okay?"

She favored him with a pleasing smile. "Yes, I'm fine." She held on to the look in his eyes and then asked, "And are you okay?"

He returned her smile. "Yes."

She lowered her head to take another sip of her drink, trying to ignore the towering figure standing in front of her. She sensed his movement away from her, but refused to lift her head just yet to see where he had gone. Moments later when she did so, she drew in a quick breath. He was standing across the room with a wineglass in his hand, leaning against the desk and staring at her. Not just staring, but he seemed to be stirring up the heat already engulfing her. Then there were pleasure points that seemed to be touching various parts of her body. She was a sensible woman but at the moment she felt insensible, deliriously brazen. She knew what she wanted but inwardly debated being gutsy enough to get it. But then, as awareness flowed between them, she was compelled to do so.

With his eyes still holding hers, she stood and slowly began crossing the room to him. His strength, as well as his heat, was filtering across to her, touching her everywhere, and putting her in a frame of mind to do things she'd never done before. He watched her every step, just as she watched how the darkness of his eyes did nothing to cloak the desire in his gaze. It was desire that she felt in every angle of her body, in every curve and especially in the juncture of her legs. Especially there.

When she reached him she stood directly in front of him, still feeling his strength and heat, and still radiating in desire. With great effort she held on to the wineglass in her hand, needing another sip to calm her nerves, to quench her heat.

She lifted the glass to her lips and after taking a quick sip, Brandon reached out and took the glass from her, leaned in and placed his lips where the glass had been.

Brandon's heart was pounding furiously in his chest and every muscle in his body ached. Fire was spreading through his loins and a quivering sensation was moving through him at a rapid pace. Her mouth had opened beneath his and he tasted her with a ravenous hunger that was gripping him, conquering with a need he could no longer contain.

Pulling back, he placed both of their glasses on the table, and with his hands now free he took her into his arms and quickly went back to kissing her with a passion that was searing through him. With very little effort his mouth coaxed her to participate. Once he took hold of her tongue, he strived to reach his goal of ultimate satisfaction for the both of them.

What they were exchanging was a sensual byplay of tongues that was meant to excite and arouse. Their bodies were pressed so close that he could feel the tips of her breasts rub against his chest. He could feel the front of her cradle his erection in a way that had his heartbeat quickening and his body getting harder. A need to make her his was seeping through every pore. He lowered his hand and pulled her even closer to his aroused frame, as he was in serious danger of becoming completely unraveled.

She pulled back and breathed in deeply, her arms wrapped tightly around his neck. It only took a look into her eyes to see the fire burning in their depths. That look made him feel light-headed. The room seemed to be revolving, making him dizzy with smoldering desire. The experience was both powerful and dangerous. His lungs released a shuttering breath and a part of him knew he should do what he'd done last night and walk away. But his wants and needs had him glued to the spot.

And then she rose on tiptoe and whispered. "Make love to me, Brandon."

Her words, spoken in a sexy breath, broke whatever control he had left, every single thread of it. With a surge of desire that had settled in his bones, he swept her off her feet and into his arms and headed straight for the bedroom.

Cassie's heart began thumping in her chest when Brandon placed her on the king-size four-poster bed. And when he stood back and gave her that look, like she was a morsel he was ready to devour, she automatically squeezed her legs together to contain the heat flowing between them. There was an intensity, a desperation bursting within her, but not for any man. Just this one.

Since meeting him she hadn't been able to put him out of her mind. Even as crazy as today had been, periodically he had found a way to creep into her thoughts. And she had felt herself getting flushed when she thought about the kisses they had shared. The memories had been unsettling on one hand and then soothing on the other. His kisses had easily aroused her and had made every nerve in her body quiver…like they were doing now.

She watched as he slowly began unbuttoning his shirt before shrugging broad shoulders to remove it. Her gaze zeroed in on his naked chest and suddenly her mind began indulging in fantasies of placing kisses all over it. She held her breath watching, waiting for him to start taking off his pants. However, instead of doing so, he walked back over to the bed.

"Do you know what I want to know? What I have to know?" he asked, staring at her from top to bottom.

Her mind went blank. She didn't have a clue. "What," she murmured, feeling the sexual tension that had overtaken the room.

"I have to know how far up your legs those boots go."

That definitely was not what she had expected him

to say and couldn't help but smile. "Why don't you find out," she challenged silkily.

Brandon took a couple of steps toward the bed, reached out and slowly raised her dress. He sucked in a deep breath as he lifted it higher and higher. The top of the boots ended just below her knee, giving him a tantalizing view of her thighs.

"Satisfied?"

He shifted his gaze from her legs and thighs back to her face. "Partially. But I will be completely satisfied in a moment."

Cassie swallowed when Brandon unzipped her boots and began removing them, taking the time to massage her legs and ankles and the bottom of her feet. "Do you want to know something else?" he asked her.

"What?"

"I stayed awake most of the night just imagining all the things I'd like doing to you if ever given the chance," he said in a husky tone.

"Now you have the chance."

He smiled. "I know." He took a step back. "Scoot over here for a second."

She eased across the bed to him on her knees and he tugged her dress over her head, leaving her clad in a black satin bra and a pair of matching panties. He tossed the dress aside with an expression on his face denoting he was very pleased with what he had done.

Cassie was very pleased with what he had done, too. "Not fair," she said sulkily. "You have on more clothes than I do."

He chuckled. "Not for long." His hands went to the snap on his pants.

Reasonably satisfied with his answer, as well as more than satisfied with what she was seeing, Cassie watched as Brandon begin easing down his zipper, her gaze following every movement of his hand. This wasn't her first time with a man, but it had been a while. And this was the first time one had gotten her so keyed up. What she was seeing was sending shivers rippling down her spine.

She nearly groaned when he stepped out of his pants. The only thing covering his body was a pair of very sexy black briefs—briefs that could barely support his huge erection, but were trying like hell to do so. She stared when he removed them. Then she blinked and stared some more. And in a move that was as daring as anything she had ever done, she scooted to the edge of the bed, reached out and stroked over his stomach with her hand before moving it lower to cup him.

She glanced up when she heard his sharp intake of breath. "Am I hurting you?" she asked softly, as she continued to fondle him in a way she had never done with a man before. Even with Jason she hadn't been this bold.

"No, you're not hurting me but you are torturing me," she heard Brandon say through clenched teeth. "There's a difference."

"Is there?"

"Yes, let me show you." He reached his hands behind her back and undid her bra clasp. He eased off her bra and tossed it aside and his hands immediately went to her naked breasts. And then he began stroking her as precisely and methodically as she was stroking him. A startled gasp erupted from her throat when he took things just a little further and leaned over and caught a nipple between his lips.

Suddenly, she understood the difference between pain and torture. She understood it and she felt it. This was torture of the most exhilarating kind. It was the type that filled you with an all-consuming need, an intense sexual craving. When he switched his mouth to the other breast she released a deep moan, thinking his tongue was wonderfully wicked.

"I can't take much more," she muttered in an abated breath.

"That makes two of us," he said, lifting his head. "But I'm not through with you yet."

He moved to grab his pants off the floor, pulled a condom packet from his wallet and put it on. He then eased her back on the bed and gently grabbed a hold of her hips to remove her panties. She heard the deep-throated growl when she became completely bare to his view. She saw the look in his eyes; felt the intensity of his gaze, and immediately knew where his thoughts were going. He glanced at her, gave her one hungry, predatory smile and before she could draw in her next breath he lifted her hips to his mouth.

Cassie screamed out his name the moment his tongue invaded her and she grabbed on to the bed-spread, knowing she had to take a hold of something. He was taking her sensuality to a whole new dimension and shattering her into a million pieces, bringing on the most intense orgasm ever. She continued writhing under the impact of his mouth while sensations tore through her. And while her body was still throbbing, he pulled back and shifted his body in position over hers. Their gazes locked, held, while he eased into her, joining their bodies as one.

Brandon sucked in sharply as he continued to sink deeper and deeper into Cassie's body, fulfilling every fantasy he'd had about her. Securing his hips over hers he then used both hands to lock in her hair as he lowered his head to capture her mouth. He began rocking against her, thrusting into her as she gave herself to him, holding nothing back. He felt her inner muscles clench him, while a whirlwind of emotions washed over the both of them.

"Brandon!"

When he felt her come apart under him, he followed suit and exploded inside of her. He felt heaven. He felt overwhelmed. He felt a degree of sensuality that he knew at that moment could only be shared with her.

Moments later he gathered her closer into his arms, their breathing hard, soft, then hard again. He slowly moved his hand to caress her thigh and stomach, still needing to touch her in some way.

Deep down Brandon knew he should not have made love to her without first telling her the truth of who he was and why he was there. He didn't want to think about how she would react to the news and hopefully, she would hear him out and give him time to explain. More than anything, she deserved his honesty. "Cassie?"

It took her a long time to catch her breath to answer. "Yes?" She lifted slightly and looked at him for a moment before saying, "Please don't tell me that you regret what we shared, Brandon."

He shook his head. Boy, was she way off. "I have no regrets but there's something I need to tell you."

She lifted a brow. "What?"

He opened his mouth to speak at the exact moment there was a knock on the door. A part of him felt temporary relief. "Dinner has arrived. We can talk later."

Like Cassie had said it would be, dinner was delicious. But it would be hard for any man to concentrate on anything when he had a beautiful woman sitting across from him wearing nothing but a bathrobe. And the knowledge that she was stark naked underneath was not helping matters.

He had assumed, when he had slipped back into his shirt and trousers to open the door for room service, that she would put back on her clothes, as well. He had been mildly surprised, but definitely not disappointed, when she had appeared after the food was delivered wearing one of the hotel's complimentary bath robes.

Deciding to take his mind off his dinner guest and just what he would love to do to her…again, he glanced out the French doors and onto the terrace. In the moonlight he could tell that the ocean waves were choppy and by the way the palm trees were swaying back and forth, he knew there was a brisk breeze in the air. Even if Hurricane Melissa decided not to come this way, she was still stirring up fuss.

"Brandon?"

He glanced over at Cassie. She had said his name with a sensual undercurrent, making him get aroused again, especially when he saw the top of her robe was slightly opened, something she'd evidently taken the time to do while he had been looking out the French doors. A smile tugged at his lips. She was trying to tempt him and he had no complaints. In fact, he more than welcomed her efforts. When it came to her he was definitely easy. "Yes?"

"Right before dinner you said you needed to talk to me about something."

He nodded. He had dismissed the thought of discussing anything over dinner. The last thing he'd wanted was the entire meal flung at his head. And in a way he didn't want to talk about anything now since he knew how the evening would end once he did so. But he couldn't overlook the fact that he owed her the truth.

She was giving him a probing look, waiting on his response. He was about to come clean and tell her everything when a cell phone went off. From the sound of the ringer he knew it wasn't his and she jumped up and walked quickly to grab her purse off the sofa and pulled her cell phone out.

"Yes?" After a few moments she said, "All right, Simon. Let me know if anything changes." Cassie held the phone in her hand for a moment before putting it back in her purse.

"Bad news?"

She glanced up and met Brandon's gaze. "Nothing that surprises me. Forecasters predict Hurricane Melissa will escalate to a category three whenever she makes it to shore."

Brandon nodded. "So she's moving again?"

"No, she's still out in the Atlantic gaining strength. Wherever she decides to land is in for a rough time."

And more than anyone Cassie knew what that meant. Because of the uncertainty, more people would be checking out of the hotel. She really didn't blame them and didn't begrudge anyone who put their safety first. But that also meant chances were Brandon would be leaving tomorrow, as well, possibly earlier in the day than he had planned. If Hurricane Melissa turned its sights toward the Bahamas, the airports would be closing, which wouldn't be good news to a lot of people.

Today things at the hotel had been crazy, but she had a feeling tomorrow things would get even crazier. She would probably be too busy to spend any time with Brandon before he left, which meant tonight was all they had. The thought of never seeing him again pricked her heart more than she imagined it would. And she knew what she wanted. She wanted memories that would sustain her after he left. They would be all she would have in the wee hours of the morning when she would want someone to snuggle close to, someone to make love to her the way he had done earlier. Those nights when she would ache from wanting the hard feel of him inside of her, she would have her memories.

He had said that he had something to tell her and a part of her had an idea just what that something was. A disclaimer that stated spending time with her, sharing a bed with her, had been an enjoyable experience, but he had to move on and he wouldn't keep in touch. She couldn't resent him for it because he hadn't made any promises, nor had he offered a commitment. What they were sharing was an island fling and nothing else and chances were he wanted to make sure she understood that.

She did.

And she wouldn't have any regrets when he left. Knowing all of that, she knew what she wanted. More than anything, tonight she wanted to spend the rest of her time making love and not talking.

Deciding not to be denied what she wanted, and knowing his eyes were on her, she untied the sash at her waist to remove her robe and dropped it where she stood. She brazenly moved to cross the room to him stark naked. He stood and began removing his clothes, as well. For the second time that night she felt daring and the look in his eyes while he pulled a condom out of his pocket and put it on over his huge erection, once again made her feel desirable.

They stood in front of each other completely naked and their mouths within inches of each other, emanated intense heat. He leaned down and captured her mouth. Unlike earlier that night, there was nothing gentle about this kiss. It conveyed a hunger that she felt as he plunged deeply and thoroughly in her mouth, at the same time he wrapped her arms tightly around her. His taste was spicy and reminded her of the food they'd eaten for dinner. The flavor of him exploded against her palate when her tongue began tangling with his.

Her body began quivering, all the way to her bones, and she felt heat collect in the area between her legs. Only Brandon could bring her to this state, escalating her need for passion of the most intense kind. She felt the powerful beating of his heart in his chest, sending vibrations through her breasts, tantalizing her nipples and making them throb, the same way she was throbbing in the middle.

She pulled back, hauled in a gasping breath, and before she could recover, he began walking her backward toward the sofa. She was glad when they finally made it there since her knees felt like they would give out at any moment. She sank back against the sofa cushions, and then he was there, his mouth and hands everywhere, and it took all she had not to give into the earth-shaking pleasure and scream.

And then he did the unexpected, he pulled her up with him turning her so her back pressed against his chest. He leaned over and began placing kisses along her throat and neck while his hand moved up and down her stomach before capturing her breasts in his hand. He cupped them, gently squeezed them, teased her sensitive nipples to harden beneath his fingertips.

"Open your legs for me." He murmured the request hotly against her ear while his hands moved from her breasts and traveled lower to the area between her legs. He stroked her while breathing heavily in her ear. Electric currents, something similar to bolts of lightning, slammed through her with his touch. Moments later another orgasm exploded within her but she had a feeling he wasn't through with her yet.

"Lean forward and hold on to the back of the sofa," he said with a raw, intense sexuality in his breath.

As soon as she stretched her arms out and grabbed hold of the sofa, she felt him grind the lower part of his body against her. He took his hands and tilted her hips before easing his shaft into her. He went deep, and she felt him all the way to her womb.

"Brandon!"

He began thrusting back and forth inside of her, sending sensations rippling all through her. Establishing a rhythm that was splintering her apart both inside and out, he grabbed hold of her breasts again and used his fingertips and thumb to drive her over the edge.

She cried out his name when her body exploded and when he plunged deeper inside of her she could feel the exact moment an explosion hit him, as well. She groaned when a searing assault was made on her senses, and when he pulled her head back and took control of her mouth she felt his possession.

Before she could get a handle on that feeling, she felt him scoop her into his arms and carry her into the bedroom.

The ringing phone woke Cassie and, instinctively, she reached over and picked it up. When she heard Brandon's voice engaged in a conversation with someone, she quickly recalled where she was and realized that he had gotten out of the bed earlier to take a shower and had picked up the bathroom's phone.

She was about to hang up when she recognized the voice of the man he was talking to. She immediately sat up straight in bed, knowing she was right when she head Brandon call the man by name. Why would Brandon be talking to Parker Garrison? How did they even know each other? Just what was going on?

Hanging up the phone, she angrily slipped out of bed. Ignoring the soreness in the lower part of her body, she glanced around, looking for her clothes, and hurriedly began putting them on. Her mind was spinning with a thousand questions as she tried getting her anger under control. She had just tugged her dress over her head when she heard Brandon enter the room.

"Good morning, sweetheart."

She swung around after pulling her dress down her body. Trembling with rage, she tried remaining calm as she crossed the room to face Brandon. A part of her didn't want to believe that this man, who had tenderly made love to her last night, who had taken her to the most sensuous heights possible in his arms, could be anything other than what she saw. Utterly beautiful. The epitome of a perfect gentleman, who was thoughtful and kind.

Something in her eyes must have given her away, and when he reached for her hand, she took a step back. "What's wrong, Cassie?" he asked in a voice filled with concern.

Instead of answering his question she had one of her own. Swallowing the lump she felt in her throat and with a back that was ramrod straight, she asked, "How do you know Parker Garrison, Brandon?"

Six

There was a long silence as Brandon and Cassie stood there, staring at each other. Tension in the room was thick, almost suffocating. Brandon inhaled deeply, wishing like hell that he'd told her the truth last night as he had intended and not have her find out on her own. Apparently, she had listened to his phone conversation long enough to know the caller had been Parker.

"I asked you a question, Brandon. How do you know Parker?"

Her sharp tone cut into his thoughts and he could tell from her expression that she was beginning to form her own opinions about things. He didn't want that. He took another deep breath before saying, "He's a client."

She turned her face from him with the speed of someone who had been slapped and the motion made his heart turn over in his chest. He had hurt her. He could actually feel it. The thought that he had done that to her appalled him and at that moment he felt lower than low. "Cassie, I—"

"No," she snapped, turning back to him.

She reached up as if to smooth a strand of hair back from her face, but he actually saw her quickly swipe back a tear. Brandon winced.

"And just what do you do for Parker, Brandon? Are you his hit man? Since I'm not being cooperative did he decide to do away with me all together?"

"I'm his attorney, Cassie," he asserted, his brows drawing together in a deep frown, not liking what she'd said.

"His attorney?" she whispered, her eyes widening in disbelief.

His stomach tightened when he saw the color drain from her face. "Yes," he said softly. "I represent Garrison, Inc."

She didn't say anything for a few moments but the shocked eyes staring at him appeared as jagged glass. Then they appeared to turn into fire. "Is Brandon Jarrett even your real name?" she blurted.

He exhaled a long breath before answering. "Yes, but not my full name. It's Brandon Jarrett Washington."

Cassie frowned. She recalled seeing the name of Washington and Associates law firm on a letterhead sent to her on Parker's behalf a few months ago when she had refused to acknowledge any more of his phone calls. "I should have known," she said with anger in her voice. "Anything that's too good to be true usually isn't true. So what sort of bonus did Parker offer you to make me change my mind about the buyout? He evidently told you to succeed by using any means necessary. You wasted your time in law school since you would make a pretty good gigolo."

"Don't say that, Cassie."

"Don't say it?" she repeated as intense anger radiated from every part of her. "How dare you tell me not to. You came here pretending to be someone you are not, to get next to me, to sleep with me to change my mind because Parker paid you to do it?"

"That's not the way it was."

"Oh? Then what way was it, Brandon? Are you saying you didn't come here with me as your target, and our meeting had nothing to do with Parker wanting me to give up my controlling share of the company?"

Brandon felt the floor beneath him start to cave in, but he refused to lie. "Yes, but that changed once I got to know you."

That wasn't good enough for Cassie. She shook her head and began backing away from him. She felt both hurt and anger when she thought of all the time they had spent together, all the things they had done. And all of it had been nothing more than calculated moves on his part.

That realization filled her with humiliation. "You bastard! How dare you use me that way! I want you out of here. Out of my hotel," she all but screamed. "And you can go back and tell Parker that your mission wasn't accomplished. Hell will freeze two times over before I give him anything!"

It only took her a minute to snatch her boots off the floor and then she stormed past him and went to the sofa to grab her jacket and purse. Brandon was right on her heels.

"Listen, Cassie, please let me explain. I told Parker just now that I was going to tell you the truth."

She whirled on him. "You're lying!"

"No, I'm not lying, Cassie. I tried telling you the truth last night."

"It doesn't matter. You lied to me, Brandon, and I won't forget it. And I meant what I said. I want you out of my hotel or I will order that my staff put you out."

With that said and without taking the time to put on her boots, a barefoot Cassie opened the door and raced out of the suite.

Brandon studied the roadway as he drove toward Cassie's home, barely able to see due to the intense rain pouring down. By the time he had made it out of the suite after Cassie, she had gotten into her car and driven off. He had gone back inside and done as she'd demanded by packing, and within the hour he had checked out.

He had called his pilot to cancel his flight off the island. He refused to leave the Bahamas until he had a chance to talk to her again, to clear himself. Nothing mattered other than getting her to believe that although his intentions might not have been honorable when he'd arrived on the island, after getting to know her, he had known he could not go through with it. And he had tried telling her the truth last night.

But deep down he knew that none of that excused his behavior in her eyes. He also knew that she had a right to be angry and upset. He owed her an apology,

which he intended to give her, and nothing would stop
him from doing so. Not even the threat that Hurricane
Melissa now posed since she had decided to head in
this direction.

The hotel had been in chaos with people rushing to
check out. No one wanted to remain on an island that was
in the hurricane's path. But even with all the commotion,
Cassie's staff had everything under control and was doing
an outstanding job of keeping everyone calm and getting
them checked out in a timely manner. For Cassie to be
at home and not at the hotel was a strong indication of
how upset she was and just how badly he had hurt her.

He inhaled a deep sigh of relief when he pulled into
Cassie's driveway and saw her car was there. He hoped
she had no intentions of going back out in this weather.
From the report he'd heard on the car's radio, the authorities were saying it wasn't safe to travel and were
asking people to stay off the roads since there had
been a number of major auto accidents.

He glanced at her house when he brought the car to
a stop. Judging the distance from where he was to her
front door, chances were he would be soaked to the
skin by the time he made it, but that was the least of
his concerns. He needed to clear things up between
them and he refused to entertain the thought that she
wouldn't agree to listen to what he had to say.

He opened the car door and made a quick dash for
the door. The forecasters still weren't certain if Hurricane Melissa would actually hit the island or just come
close to crossing over it. Regardless of whether it was
a hit or a miss, this island was definitely experiencing
some of the effects of her fury. He was totally drenched

by the time he knocked on Cassie's door. He had changed into a pair of jeans and the wet denim material seemed to cling to his body, almost squeezing him.

The door was snatched open and he could tell from Cassie's expression that she was both shocked and angry to see him. "I can't believe you have the nerve to come here."

"I'm here because you and I need to talk."

"Wrong, I have nothing to say to you and I would advise you to leave," she said, crossing her arms over her chest.

"We have a lot to say and I can't leave."

She glared at him. "And why not?"

"The weather. The police asked drivers to get off the road. If I go back out in that I risk the chance of having an accident."

Her glare hardened. "And you think I care?"

"Yes, because if there's one thing I've discovered about you over the past few days, it's that you are a caring person, Cassie, and no matter what kind of asshole you undoubtedly think I am, you would not send me to my death."

She leaned closer and got right in his face. "Want to bet?"

From the look in her eyes, the answer was no. At that particular moment he didn't want to bet, but he would take a chance. "Yes."

She glared at him some more. "I suggest that you go sit in your car until the weather improves for you to leave. You're not welcome in my home."

"If I do that then I run the risk of catching pneumonia in these wet clothes."

Evidently fed up with what she considered non-sense, she was about to slam the door in his face when he blocked it with his hand. "Look, Cassie, I'm not leaving until you hear me out, nor will I leave the island until you do. If you refuse to do so here today then whenever you go back to the hotel I'll make a nuisance of myself until you do agree to see me."

"Try it and I'll call the police," she snapped.

"Yes, you could do that, but imagine the bad publicity it will give the hotel. I'd think the last thing you'll want for the Garrison Grand-Bahamas is that." He knew what he'd said had hit a nerve. That would be the last thing she would want.

Except for the force of the rain falling, there was long silence as she stonily stared at him before angrily stepping aside. "Say what you have to say and leave."

When he walked across the threshold he glanced around and saw what she'd been doing before she'd come to answer the door. She had been rolling the hurricane shutters down to cover the windows. "Where's your staff?"

She glared at him. "Not that it's any of your business but I sent them home before the weather broke. I didn't want them caught out in it."

"But you have no qualms sending me back out in it," he said, meeting her gaze.

"No, I don't, so what does that tell you?" she stormed.

He crossed his arms across his chest and gave her a glare of his own. "It tells me that we really do need to talk. But first I'll help you get the shutters in place."

Cassie blinked. Was he crazy? She had no intention of him helping her do anything. "Excuse me. I don't recall asking for your help," she said sharply.

"No, but I intend to help anyway," he said, heading toward the window in the living room.

She raced after him. "I only let you in to talk, Brandon."

"I know," he agreed smoothly, over his shoulder. "But we can talk later. A hurricane might be headed this way and John would roll over in his grave if he thought I'd leave his daughter defenseless," he said, taking hold of the lever to work the shutter into place.

A puzzled frown crossed Cassie's brow and she stopped in her tracks. "You knew my father?"

He glanced over at her, knowing he would be completely honest with her from here on out and would tell her anything she wanted to know, provided it wasn't privileged information between attorney and client. "Yes, I knew John. I've known him all my life. He and my father, Stan Washington, were close friends, and had been since college."

He saw the surprised look in her eyes seconds before she asked, "Stan Washington was your father?"

"Yes. You'd met him?" he asked, moving to another window.

"I've known him all my life, as well," she said. "But I never knew anything personal about him other than he and Dad were close friends. He was the person Mom knew to contact if an emergency ever came up and she needed to reach Dad."

Brandon nodded. He figured his father had been. As close a friendship as the two men shared, Brandon had been certain his father had known about John's affair with Ava. Besides that, Stan had been the one who'd drawn up John's will and who had handled any legal matters dealing with the Garrison Grand-Bahamas exclusively. Once Cassie had taken ownership of the hotel she had retained her own attorneys.

"What about all the other windows?" he asked, after securing the shutters in place.

"I had my housekeeping staff help me with them before they left."

"Good," he murmured as he glanced over at her. She was still barefoot but had changed into a pair of capri pants and a blouse. And like everything else he'd ever seen on her body, she looked good. But then she looked rather good naked, too.

"Now you can have your say and leave."

His eyes moved from her body to her face. He had been caught staring and she wasn't happy about it, probably because she had an idea what thoughts had passed through his mind.

"I'd think my help just now has earned me a chance to get out of these clothes."

Her back became ramrod straight. "You can think again!"

He suddenly realized how that might have sounded. "Calm down, Cassie," he said, running his hand down his face. "That's not what I meant. I was suggesting it would be nice to get out of these wet things so you can dry them for me. Otherwise, I might catch pneumonia."

Cassie bit down on her lip to keep from telling him that when and if he caught pneumonia she hoped he died a slow, agonizing death, but then dished the thought from her mind. She wasn't a heartless or cruel person, although he was the last human being on earth who deserved even a drop of her kindness.

"Fine," she snapped. "The laundry room is this way," she said, walking out of the room knowing he had to walk briskly to keep up with her. "And I suggest you stay in that room until your clothes are dry."

"Why? Don't you have a towel I could use while they're drying?"

She shot a look at him that said he was skating on thin ice and it was getting thinner every minute. "I have plenty of towels but I prefer not seeing you parade around in one."

"Okay."

She abruptly stopped walking and turned to face him. "Look, Brandon. Apparently everything you've done in the last three days was nothing but a joke to you but I hope you don't see me laughing. You don't even see me smiling."

The humor that had been in Brandon's eyes immediately faded. When he spoke again his voice was barely audible. "No, I don't think the last three days were a joke, Cassie. In fact I think they were the most precious I've ever spent in my entire life. The only thing I regret is coming to this island thinking you were someone you are not and because of it, I screwed up something awful. The only thing I can do is be honest with you now."

She refused to let his words affect her in any way. There was no way she could trust him again. "It really doesn't matter what you say when we talk, Brandon. I won't be able to get beyond the fact that you deliberately deceived me."

"Not all of it was based on deceit, Cassie. When I made love to you it was based on complete sincerity. Please don't ever think that it wasn't."

"You used me," she flung out with intense anger in her voice.

He reached out and gently touched the cleft in her chin and said in a low voice, "No, I made love to you, Cassie. I gave you more of myself than I've ever given another woman, freely, unselfishly and completely. "

Knowing if she didn't take a step back from him she would weaken, she said, "The laundry room is straight ahead and on your right. And since you're so terrified of catching pneumonia, there's a linen closet with towels in that room. But I'm warning you to stay put until your clothes dry. I have enough to do with my time than worry about a half-naked man parading through my house. I need to fill all the bathtubs with water in case I lose electricity."

"And if you do lose electricity, the thought of being here in the dark won't bother you?"

"For your information, I won't be here. As soon as your clothes dry and you have your say, I'm going to the hotel to help out there."

"You're going out in that weather?" he asked in a disbelieving tone.

"I believe that's what I said," she said smartly.

"Weren't you listening when I said the authorities are asking people to stay off the streets?" he asked in-credulously, refusing to believe anyone could be so pigheaded and stubborn.

She lifted her chin. "Yes, I was listening with as much concentration as you were when I was telling you to leave." She narrowed her eyes and then said, "Now if you will excuse me, I have things to do. When your clothes are dry and you're fully dressed again, you should be able to find me in the living room."

Narrowing his eyes, Brandon watched as she turned and walked away.

Cassie kept walking on shaky legs, refusing to give in to temptation and glance over her shoulder to look at Brandon once again. The man was unsettling in the worst possible way and the last thing she needed was having him here under her roof, especially when the two of them were completely alone.

She shook her head. At least he was taking off those wet jeans. She hadn't missed seeing how they had fit his body like a second layer of skin. She was glad he hadn't caught her staring at him when he had been putting the shutters up to the windows. Every time he had moved his body her eyes had moved with it. Not only had his wet jeans hugged his muscular thighs but they had shown what a nice tush he had, as well as a flat, firm stomach.

She sighed deeply, disgusted with herself. How could she still find the man desirable after what he had done? And she'd had no intention of accepting his help with the shutters but he hadn't given her a choice in the matter. He did just whatever he wanted. Even now his behavior and actions were totally unacceptable to her.

After filling up all the bathtubs and making sure there were candles in appropriate places and extra batteries had been placed beside her radio, she called the hotel. Simon had assured her that he had everything under control and for her to stay put and not try to come out in the weather. The majority of the people who had wanted to leave had checked out of the hotel without a hitch. The ones that had remained would ride the weather out at the Garrison Grand-Bahamas. If the authorities called for a complete evacuation of the hotel, then they would use the hotel's vans to provide transportation to the closest shelters that had been set up. Simon had insisted that she promise that if needed, she would leave her home and go to the nearest shelter, as well.

Satisfied her staff had everything under control, she walked into the living room, over to the French doors and glanced out. The ocean appeared fierce and angry, and the most recent forecast she'd heard—at least the most positive one—said that Melissa would weaken before passing over the Bahamas. But Cassie had lived on the island long enough to know there was also a chance the hurricane would intensify once it reached land as well.

She glanced up at the sky. Although it was mid-afternoon the sky had darkened to a velvet black and the clouds were thickening. Huge droplets of rain were drenching the earth and strong, gusty winds had trees swaying back and forth. She rubbed her arms, feeling a slight chill in the air. Even if Melissa did become a category four, Cassie wasn't afraid of losing her home. Her father had built this house to withstand just about anything.

Except pain.

It seemed those words filtered through her mind on a whisper. And she hung her head as more pain engulfed her, disturbed by the emotions that were scurrying through her. She drew in a deep breath, thinking she hadn't shed a single tear for what Jason had done to her, yet earlier today she had cried for the pain Brandon had caused her. Inwardly her heart was still crying.

Cassie lifted her head. She smelled Brandon's scent even before she actually heard him. She knew he was there and had known the exact moment he had entered the room. However, she wasn't ready to turn around yet, at least not until she had her full coat of armor in place. For a reason she was yet to understand, Brandon Jarrett Washington had gotten under her skin and even with all the anger she felt toward him, he was still embedded there.

"Cassie?"

She stiffened when the sound of his voice reached her. She tried ignoring the huskiness of his tone and the goose bumps that pricked her skin. Saying a silent prayer for strength, as well as the retention of her common sense, she slowly turned around. Because all the windows were protected by shutters, the room appeared slightly dark, yet she was able to make him out clearly. He stood rigid in the doorway and thankfully, fully dressed. He took a step into the room and heat coursed through her, and to her way of thinking she might have been thankful way too soon.

Although she didn't want to admit it, even in dry jeans and a shirt, Brandon looked the picture of a well-developed man. And she was reacting to his presence in a way she didn't want to and that realization was very disconcerting. The silence shrouding them within the room was a stark contradiction to the fury of the storm that was raging outside.

She tightened her hands into fists at her side when he slowly crossed the room to her. His gaze continued to touch hers when he reached out his hand to her and said in a soft voice, "Come, Cassie, let's sit on the sofa and talk."

Seven

Cassie glanced down at the hand Brandon was offering her. That hand had touched her all over last night, as well as participated in their no-holds-barred lovemaking. Finding out about his betrayal had hurt and she wasn't ready to accept anything he offered her. She would listen to what he had to say and that would be it.

Refusing to accept his hand, she returned her gaze to his face and said, "You can sit on the sofa. I'll take the chair." Her lips tightened when she moved across the room to take her seat.

Brandon was still considering Cassie's actions just now when he headed toward the sofa. It was apparent she didn't intend to make things easy for him and he could accept that. He had wronged her and it would be hard as hell to make things right. He wasn't even sure it was something that could be done, but he would try. Nervous anxiety was trying to set in but he refused to let it. Somehow he had to get her to understand.

Once he was settled on the sofa he glanced over at her, but she was looking everywhere but at him. That gave him a chance to remember how she had looked that first night he'd seen her on the beach. Even before knowing who she was, he had been attracted to her, had wanted to get to know her, get close to her and make love to her.

He shifted in his seat. Intense desire was settling in his loins, blazing them beyond control. Now was not a good time for such magnetism and he figured if she were to notice, she wouldn't appreciate it. Not needing any more trouble on his plate than was already there, he shifted on the sofa again and found a position that made that part of his body less conspicuous, although his desire for her didn't decrease any.

"Before you get started would you like something to drink?"

He glanced up and met her gaze, surprised she would offer him anything. "Yes, please."

She left the room and that gave him a few moments to think. In a way it was a strange twist of fate that had brought him and Cassie together. Their fathers' friendship had extended from college to death and unless he cleared up this issue between them, he and Cassie could very well become bitter enemies. He didn't want that and was unwilling to accept it as an option.

She returned moments later with two glasses of wine, one for him and the other for herself. Instead of handing him his wineglass directly, she placed it on the table beside him. Evidently, she had no intention of them touching in any way. He picked up his glass and took a sip, regretting he was responsible for bringing their relationship to such a sorrowful state.

"You wanted to talk."

Her words reminded him of why she was there, not to mention the distinct chill in the air. He took another sip of his wine and then he began speaking. "As you know, the Garrisons didn't know about your existence until the reading of John's will. I'm not going to say that no one might have suspected he was involved in an affair with someone, but I think I can truthfully say that no one was aware that a child had resulted from that affair. You were quite a surprise to everyone."

When she didn't make any comment or show any expression on her face, he continued. "But what came as an even bigger surprise was the fact that John left you controlling interest to share with Parker. That was definitely a shocker to everyone, especially Parker, who is the oldest and probably the most ambitious of John's sons. It was assumed, as well as understood, that if anything ever happened to John, Parker would get the majority share of controlling interest. Such a move was only right since John had turned the running of Garrison over to Parker on his thirty-first birthday. And Parker has done an outstanding job since then. Therefore, I hope you can understand why he was not only hurt and confused, but also extremely upset."

He could tell by the look on Cassie's face that she didn't understand anything, or that stubborn mind of hers was refusing to let her. "As I told you earlier," he continued, "my father is the one who drew up John's will, so I didn't know anything about you until I read over the document a few days before I was to present the will to the family. Once I discovered the truth, I knew the reading of it wouldn't be pretty."

He took a deep breath and proceeded on. "Pursuing normal legal action in this case, we took moves to contest the will but found it airtight. And—"

"I guess Parker smartened up and thought twice about pushing for a DNA test, as well," she interrupted in a curt tone.

Brandon nodded. "Yes, I advised him that nothing would be gained from it. John claimed you as his child and that was that. Besides, there was no reason to really believe that you weren't. You and Parker made contact and he offered to buy out your share of the controlling interest. You turned him down."

"And that should have been the end of it," she snapped.

Brandon couldn't help the smile that touched the corners of his lips. "Yes, possibly. But that's where you and Parker are alike in some respect."

At the lifting of her dark, arched brow, he explained. "You're both extremely stubborn."

She narrowed her eyes at him. "That's your opinion."

He decided not to waste time arguing with her by telling her that was what he knew, especially after spending time with her. Although she and Parker had never officially met, the prime reason they didn't get along was because they were similar in a lot of ways. Besides being stubborn, both were ambitious and driven to succeed. Apparently John had recognized that quality in the both of them and felt together they would do a good job by continuing the empire he'd created.

"I'm waiting, Brandon."

He glanced over at Cassie and saw her frowning in irritation. "I want to apologize for assuming a lot of incorrect things about you, Cassie, and I hope you will find it in your heart to forgive me."

Cassie wasn't ready to say whether she would or would not forgive him. At the moment she was close to doing the latter. However, she was curious about something. "And just what did you assume about me?"

Brandon inhaled before speaking. "Before answering that, I need to say that when you decided to be a force to reckon with by not responding to my firm's letters or returning any more of Parker's phone calls, it was decided that I should come and meet with you and make you the offer in person. It was also decided that I should first come and see if I could dig up any interesting information on you and your past, to use as ammunition to later force your hand if you continued your refusal to sell."

By the daggered look she was giving him, he knew she was surprised he had been so blatantly honest. He could also tell she hadn't liked what he'd said. "You might be stubborn, Cassie, but I'm a man who likes winning. I'm an attorney who will fight for my clients, anyway that I can…as long as it's legal. Garrison Incorporated is my top client and I had no intention of Parker not getting what he wanted. My allegiance was to him and not to you."

Cassie straightened in the chair and leaned forward. Her eyes were shooting fire. "Forget about what's legal, Brandon. Did you consider what you planned to do unethical?" she snapped.

He leaned forward, as well. "At the time, considering what I assumed about you, no, I didn't think anything I had planned to do as being unethical. By your refusal to even discuss the issue of the controlling shares in a professional manner with Parker, I saw your actions as that of an inconsiderate, spoiled, willful, selfish and self-centered young woman. And to answer your earlier question, that's what I assumed about you."

That did it. Cassie angrily crossed the room to stand in front of him. With her hands on her hips, she glared at him. "You didn't even know me. How dare you make such judgments about me!"

He stood to face off with her. "And that's just it, Cassie. No one knew you and it was apparent you wanted to keep things that way, close yourself off from a family that really wants to get to know you. And if my initial opinion—sight unseen—of you sounds a bit harsh then all I have to say in my defense is that's the picture you painted of yourself to everyone."

Cassie turned her head away from him, knowing part of what he said was true. She'd still been grieving her mother's death when she'd gotten word of her father's passing. He had been buried without her being there to say her last goodbye and a part of her resented that, and had resented them for letting it happen. But then the truth of the matter was that they hadn't known about her, although she had known about them. They would not have known to contact her to tell her anything.

"Imagine my surprise," she heard Brandon say,

"when I arrived here and met you. You were nothing like any of us figured you to be. It didn't take long for me to discover that you didn't have an inconsiderate, spoiled, willful, selfish or self-centered bone in your body. The woman I met, the woman I became extremely attracted to even before I knew her true identity that night on the beach, was a caring, giving, humane and unselfish person."

He took a step closer to her when Cassie turned her head and looked at him. "She was also strikingly beautiful, vivacious, sexy, desirable and passionate," he said, lowering his voice to a deep, husky tone. "She was a woman who could cause my entire body to get heated just from looking at her, a woman who made feelings I'd never encountered before rush along my nerve endings every time I got close to her."

He leaned in closer. "And she's the woman whose lips I longed to lock with mine whenever they came within inches of each other. Like they are now."

An involuntary moan of desire escaped as a sigh from Cassie's lips. Brandon's words had lit a hot torch inside of her and as she gazed into his eyes, she saw the heated look she had become familiar with. And she couldn't help but take note that they were standing close, so close that the front of his body was pressed intimately against hers, and the warm hiss of his breath could be felt on her lips. Another thing she was aware of was the hardness of his erection that had settled firmly in the lower center of her body.

She shuddered from the heat his body was emitting. Luscious heat she was actually feeling, almost drowning in. And then there was the manly scent of him that was sending a primal need escalating through her. It was a need she hadn't known existed until she had met him and discovered that he had the ability to take her to a passionate level she hadn't been elevated to before.

She knew he was about to kiss her. She also knew he was stalling, giving her the opportunity to back up and deny what the two of them wanted. But that wasn't what she wanted. Although they still had a lot more talking to do, a lot more things to get straight, she felt at that particular moment that they needed time out to take a much needed break from their stress.

And indulge in a deliriously, mind-boggling kiss.

When to her way of thinking he didn't act quickly enough, she stuck out her tongue, and with a sultry caress, she traced the lining of his lips from corner to corner. She saw the surprise on his face and the darkening of his pupils just seconds before a deep guttural groan spilled forth from his throat. He reached out and wrapped his arms around her waist, and like a bird of prey, he swooped down and captured her lips with his.

He had a way of devouring her mouth with the finesse of a gazelle and the hunger of a wolf, sending shivers all the way through her. And when he began mating with her tongue with a mastery that nearly brought her to her knees, she released a moan deep in her throat.

He tasted of the wine he had drunk and had the scent of man and rain. And he was consuming her with such effectiveness that she could only stand there and purr. His kiss was turning her into one massive ball of desire and she felt a dampness form between her legs.

He pulled his mouth free. His breathing was heavy

when he said huskily, "If you don't want what I'm about to give you, stop me now, Cassie. If you don't, I doubt I'll be able to stop myself later."

She had no desire to stop him. In fact she intended to help. To prove her point, she pulled his shirt from where it was tucked inside his jeans, before freeing the snap and easing down his zipper. And with a boldness she'd only discovered she had last night, she slipped her hand inside his jeans and felt her fingers grip the rigid hardness of him. She cupped him, fondled him and felt him actually grow larger in her hand.

"I want to be inside of you, Cassie," he whispered hotly in her ear. "I want to feel your heat clamp me tight, squeeze me and pull everything I have to give out of me. I want to make love to you until neither of us has any energy left. And then, when we regain our strength I want to do it all over again. I want to bury myself inside you so deep, neither of us will know at what point our bodies are connected."

His erotic words sent fire flaming through her body. The dampness between her legs threatened to drench her thighs. "Then do it, Brandon. Do me. Now."

As far as Brandon was concerned, her wish was his command and he eased her down on the Persian rug with him and quickly began removing their clothes. The logical part of his brain told him to slow down, she wasn't going anywhere, but another part, that part that was throbbing for relief said he wasn't going fast enough.

When he had her completely naked he turned his attention to removing his own clothes. And she was there helping him by pulling his shirt over his head and tugging his jeans down his legs after she had removed his shoes and socks.

He made a low growl in his throat when she straddled him and began using her tongue to explore him all over, starting with the column of his neck. She worked her way downward, tasting the tight buds on his chest before easing lower and giving greedy licks around his navel. She left a wet trail from his belly button to where his erection lay in a bed of tight, dark curls.

Cassie paused only long enough to raise her head to look at Brandon before gripping the object of her desire in her hands again. Lowering her head, she blew a warm breath against his shaft before clamping her mouth over him. Then she simply took her time, determined to give him the same kind of pleasure he had given her last night.

His body arched upward, nearly off the floor, and he released a deep groan before reaching down and grabbing hold of her hair. She thought he was going to jerk her away from him. Instead he entwined his fingers in her hair and continued to groan profusely. And then he started uttering her name over and over from deep within his throat. The sound had her senses reeling and made the center part of her wetter than before.

"No more," he said, using his hands to pull her upward toward him to capture her lips. And then he was kissing her with a need she felt invading her body. And suddenly she found herself on her back, her legs raised over his shoulders, nearly around his neck. He then lifted her hips and before she could catch her breath, he swiftly entered her, going deep, embedding himself within her to the hilt.

And then he began those thrusts she remembered so well, she tried grabbing hold on his buns, but they were moving too fast, pumping inside of her too rapidly. So she went after the strong arms that were solid on both sides of her and held on to them.

Their eyes met. Their gazes locked. The only thing that wasn't still was the lower part of their bodies as he kept moving in and out of her, filling her in a way that had sweat pouring off his forehead and trickling down onto her breasts. And then she felt her body shudder into one mind-blowing orgasm, the kind that made her go wild beneath him while screaming out his name and digging her fingernails into his arms.

And then he threw his head back and screamed out her name, as well. She felt him explode inside of her and she clenched her muscles, pulling more from him and knowing what had just happened could have very well left her pregnant with his child if she weren't on the pill. But the thought of that didn't bother her like it should have because she knew at that moment, without a doubt, that she had fallen in love with him.

"The power's out."

Cassie's head snapped up when she felt a movement beside her. She quickly remembered where she was. On the floor in the living room in her home, naked. She had dozed off after making love to Brandon, several times and then some.

She squinted her eyes in the darkness, missing the warmth of his body next to hers. "I put the candles out. I just need to get up and light them."

"Can you see your way around in the dark?"

"With this I can," she said, reaching for a large flashlight nearby. She smiled. "I figured we might lose power so I was ready."

She turned the light toward him and, seeing his naked body, she deliberately aimed it on a certain part of him. She chuckled. "Does that thing ever go down?"

He grinned. "Not while you're around." He walked over toward her. "Where's your radio?"

"On that table over there."

"Let me borrow this for a second. I don't know my way around in your house in the dark as well as you do." He took the flashlight and slowly moved around the room. When he located the radio he turned it on. It was blasting a current weather report that turned out to be good news. The island had been spared the full impact of Melissa but another tropical island hadn't been quite as lucky. The worst of the storm was over and everyone without power should have it restored by morning.

Cassie crossed the room. "I want to call to make sure everything is okay at the hotel."

"All right. I'm going to get dressed and check to see how things are outside."

By the time Brandon returned he found Cassie in the kitchen. She had put back on her clothes and was standing over a stove…with heat. Seeing his raised brow she said, "Mom preferred gas when it came to cooking, so if nothing else, we won't starve."

He nodded as he leaned in the doorway. "How are things at the hotel?"

"Fine. The power went out but the generator kicked

in," she replied. "A few fallen trees but otherwise nothing major. How are things outside?"

"The same. A few fallen trees but otherwise nothing major. And it's still raining cats and dogs." He crossed the room to look into the pot she was stirring. "What are you cooking?"

She smiled up at him. "The conch chowder from the other night. I grabbed it out of the freezer. You said you liked it."

"I do. It's good to know you plan on feeding me."

She chuckled. "That's not all I plan to do to you, so I have to keep your strength up."

He came around and grabbed her from behind and pressed her against him. "For you I will always keep my strength up. What can I help you do?"

"Put the bowls and eating utensils on the table and pour some tea into the glasses."

Moments later they sat to eat and Brandon decided to use that time to finish the talk he had started earlier. "So now you know why I did what I did, Cassie. I'm not saying it was right." At her narrowed eyes he changed his strategy and said, "Okay, it was wrong but you weren't making things easy for anyone."

She leaned back in her chair. "Tell me, Brandon. What part of 'no' didn't Parker understand? No means no. He asked to buy me out and I said no, I wasn't interested. What was the purpose of him calling when my answer wasn't going to change?"

"The reason he refused to let up is because he's a staunch businessman, Cassie. Parker is a man who is used to going after what he wants, especially if it's something he felt was rightfully his in the first place. Besides, you never took the time to hear what he was offering."

"It would not have mattered. What Dad left me was a gift and there's no way I'd sell my shares, no matter how much Parker offered me. And if he keeps it up, you'll be representing him on harassment charges."

Brandon stared at her for a moment, knowing she was dead serious. He chuckled. She lifted a brow. "What's so funny?"

"You, Parker and all the other Garrison siblings, but specifically you and Parker. At first I wondered what the hell John was thinking when he put that will into place. Now I think I know, although I didn't before coming here and meeting you."

"Well, would you like to enlighten me?"

"Sure. Like I said earlier, you and Parker are a lot alike and I think John recognized that fact. Besides the fact that both of you are stubborn, the two of you have an innate drive to succeed. Apparently John recognized that quality in both of you and felt together you and Parker would do a good job by continuing the empire he'd started."

She shook her head. "That can't be it. Dad knew how much I loved it here. He of all people knew how I missed the islands while attending college in London. To do what you're insinuating would mean moving to Miami and he knew I wouldn't do that. I told him after returning from college that I would never leave the island again. It's my home and where I want to stay."

"Then why do you think he gave you and Parker sharing control?"

Cassie inhaled deeply. "I wished I knew the answer."

Brandon's face took on a serious expression before

he said, "Then hear me out on my theory. John loved all of his children, there's no doubt in my mind about that. I also believed that he recognized all of their strengths…as well as their weaknesses. Not taking anything away from the others, I think he saw you and Parker as the strongest link because of your business sense. Parker is an excellent businessman, a chip off the old block. He's done a wonderful job of running things while John was alive, so John knew of his capabilities. And I understand that you did a fantastic job managing the hotel, so he was aware of what you could do, as well. Personally, I don't think it was ever John's intent for you and Parker to share the running of Garrison, Inc. Both of your personalities are too strong for that and he knew it. I think he put you in place to serve as a check and balance for Parker whenever there's a need."

She gazed at him thoughtfully before saying, "If what you're saying is true then it would serve no purpose if I were to sell my share of control to Parker. I wouldn't be accomplishing what Dad wanted."

"No, you wouldn't."

She studied him for a moment. "You haven't forgotten that you're Parker's attorney, have you?"

He smiled as he shook his head. "No, and I wasn't speaking as Parker's attorney just now. I was speaking as your friend…and lover." After a brief moment, he said, "I'd like to make a suggestion."

"What?"

"Take a few days off and come to Miami with me. Meet Parker, as well as your other sisters and brothers. I know for a fact that they would love to meet you."

"I'm not ready to meet them, Brandon."

"I think that you are, Cassie. And I believe John would have wanted it that way. Otherwise, he would have given you ownership of the hotel and nothing else, but he didn't do that. He arranged it where sooner or later you would have to meet them. And why wouldn't you want to meet them? They're your siblings. Your family. The six of you share the same blood."

He laughed. "Hell, all of you certainly look alike."

She raised a surprised brow. "We do?"

"Yes. All of you have this same darn dimple right here," he said, leaning over and reaching out to touch the spot.

She tilted her chin, trying to keep the sensations his touch was causing from overtaking her. "It's a cleft, Brandon."

He chuckled, pulling his hand back, but not before brushing a kiss across her lips. "Whatever you want to call it, sweetheart."

His term of endearment caused a flutter in her chest and the love she felt for him sent a warm feeling flowing through her. A few moments passed and then she said in a soft voice, "Tell me about them."

Knowing her interest was a major step, Brandon bit back a smile. "All right. I think I've told you everything there is about Parker. He's thirty-six. No matter how arrogant he might have come across that time when you did speak to him, he's really a nice guy. He used to be a workaholic but things have changed since he's gotten married. His wife Anna is just what he needs. She was his assistant before they married."

He took a sip of his tea and then said, "Stephen is

thirty-five. Like Parker, he's strong-willed and dependable. He's also compassionate. He's married and his wife is Megan. They have a three-year-old daughter named Jade."

Cassie lifted her brow. "Correct me if I'm wrong but it's my understanding that he got married a few months ago."

Brandon smiled. "You are right."

"And he has a daughter that's three?"

Brandon chuckled. "Yes. He and Megan had an affair a few years ago and she got pregnant. He didn't find out he was a father until rather recently. Now they're back together and very happy."

A huge smile touched Brandon's lips when he said, "And then there's Adam. He and I share a very close friendship and I consider him my best friend. As a result, I spend more time with him than the rest. He's thirty and operates a popular nightclub, Estate. And last but not least are the twins, Brooke and Brittany. They're both twenty-eight. Brittany operates a restaurant called Brittany Beach, and Brooke operates the Sands, a luxury condominium building."

Cassie took a sip of her own tea before asking, "What about my father's wife?"

Brandon glanced at her over the rim of his glass. "What about her?"

"I'm sure she wasn't happy finding out about my mom," Cassie said.

Brandon put his glass down and met her gaze. "No, she wasn't. But finding out about you was an even bigger shock. A part of me wants to believe she had an idea that John was having an affair with someone, but I think finding out he had another child was a kicker. Needless to say, she didn't take the news very well."

Brandon decided not to provide Cassie with any details about Bonita, especially her drinking problem. He would, however, tell her this one thing. "If you decide to come to Miami with me, I want to be up front with you and let you know that Bonita Garrison won't like the fact that you there. Trust me when I say that it wouldn't bother her one bit if you decided to drop off the face of the earth."

Cassie almost choked on her tea. Once again Brandon had surprised her. Now that he had decided to tell her the truth about everything, he was being brutally honest. "If she feels that way then I'm sure the others—"

"Don't feel that way," he interrupted, knowing her assumptions. "Their mother doesn't influence how they treat people in any way. Come to Miami with me, Cassie, and meet them."

She ran her hands through her hair as she leaned back in her chair. "I don't think you know what you're asking of me, Brandon."

"And I think I do. It's the right thing to do. I know it and I believe you know it, as well. This bitter battle between you and Parker can't go on forever. Do you think that's what John would have wanted?"

She shook her head. "No."

"Neither do I." He paused, then he asked, "Will you promise that you will at least think about it?" He reached across the table and took her hand in his.

"Yes, I promise."

"And will you accept my apology for deceiving

you, Cassie? I was wrong, but I've told you the reason I did it."

She thought about his words. He had tried telling her the truth last night, and if sex was all he'd wanted from her, he'd had a good opportunity to get it the night she had invited him to her home for dinner. But he had resisted her advances. And even last night, she had been the one to make the first move.

She stared into his face knowing the issue of forgiveness had to be resolved between them. She could tell he was fully aware that he had hurt her and was deeply bothered by it. "Yes, now that you've explained everything, I accept your apology." She saw the relieved look that came into his eyes.

He hesitated a moment. "And another thing. I didn't use any protection when we made love, so if you're—"

"I'm not. I've been on the pill for a few years now, and I'm healthy otherwise."

Brandon nodded. "So am I. I just don't want you to think I'm usually so careless."

"I don't." She smiled, thinking of the way he handled their lovemaking, always making sure she got her pleasure before he got his. "In fact, I think you are one of the most precise men that I know."

Later that night Cassie lay snuggled close to Brandon in her own bed. She was on her side and he was behind her in spoon position, holding her close to the heat of him. The power had come back on a few hours ago and they had taken a shower together before going to bed and making love again.

He was sleeping soundly beside her, probably tired

to the bone. He had taken her hard and fast, and she had enjoyed every earth-shattering moment of it. Her body trembled when she remembered the mind-splitting orgasm they had shared. Brandon was undoubtedly the perfect lover.

And she appreciated him sharing bits and pieces about her siblings, satisfying a curiosity she hadn't wanted to acknowledge that she'd had. And then he had been completely honest with her about how her father's wife would probably feel toward her if she decided to do what Brandon had suggested and go to Miami with him.

She inhaled deeply. A part of her wanted to go and resolve this issue between her and Parker once and for all, and then another part didn't want to go. What if Brandon was wrong and they really didn't want to meet her like he thought?

Deciding she didn't want to bog her mind with thoughts of them anymore tonight she let her thoughts drift to the issue of her and Brandon. She knew that true love was more than a sexual attraction between two people. It was more than being good together in bed. It was about feelings and emotions. It was about wanting to commit your life to that person for the rest of your life.

It was about the things she and Brandon didn't have.

She loved him. That was a gimme. But she knew he didn't love her. He was attracted to her and he enjoyed making love to her. For him it had nothing to do with feelings and emotions. Her heart turned in her chest at the realization, but she couldn't blame him for lacking those things. He hadn't made her any promises. He hadn't offered her a commitment. She was okay with that. She had no choice.

Moments later when she discovered she couldn't get to sleep, she knew the reason why. She quietly eased out of bed, put on a robe to cover her naked body and slipped down the stairs. She entered the room where her parents' huge portrait hung on the wall and turned on the light. Whenever she had problems and issues weighing her down, she would come in here where she would feel their presence and remember happier times.

A few moments later she went to the aquarium, sat on a love seat and observed the many species of marine life in the tanks all around her. The sight and sound created a relaxing atmosphere and she sat there with her legs tucked beneath her and enjoyed the peaceful moments.

She left the aquarium a short while later and when she eased back in the bed, Brandon tightened his arm around her, pulled her closer to his warmth and whispered in her ear, "Where were you? I missed you."

She cuddled closer to him. "Umm, I went downstairs to think about some things."

"About what?"

"Whether I should go to Miami with you to meet my sisters and brothers and resolve the issue between me and Parker." She cupped Brandon's face in her hand. "I've decided to go, Brandon."

And then she leaned up and kissed him, believing in her heart that she had made the right decision.

Eight

Cassie glanced over at Brandon, who was sitting across from her in his private plane. They had boarded just seconds ago and already his pilot was announcing they were ready for take off from the Nassau International Airport.

The last week had been spent preparing for this trip, both mentally and physically. As strange as it seemed, she was a twenty-seven-year-old woman who would be meeting her siblings, all five of them, for the first time. And surprisingly enough, once Brandon had told them of her decision to visit, she had heard from each of them…except for Parker. However, his wife Anna had contacted her and had seemed genuinely sincere when she'd said that she was looking forward to meeting her.

After remnants of Melissa's presence had left the island and the sun had reappeared, it was business as usual. Cassie had gone to the hotel that first day to check on things, and her other days she had spent with Brandon.

They had gotten the trees taken care of that had fallen on her property and then the rest of the time had been used taking care of each other. She'd given him a tour of the island and had introduced him to some of her mother's family. They had shopped together in the marketplace, had gone out to dinner together several times and had taken her parents' boat out for a cruise on the ocean. But her favorite had been the times she had spent in his arms, whether she was making love with him or just plain snuggling up close.

She would be spending two weeks in Miami as a guest in his home. After that, she would return to the Bahamas and resume her life as it had been before he'd entered it. She tried not to think about the day they would part, when he would go his way and she would go hers. In reality, they lived different lives. He had his life in America and she had hers in the islands.

And even now, she still wasn't sure of Brandon's feelings for her, but she was very certain of her feelings for him. She loved him and would carry that love to the grave with her. Like her mother, she was destined to love just one man for the rest of her life.

She continued to stare at Brandon, and as if he felt her eyes on him, he glanced up from the document he was reading and met her gaze. "You okay?" he asked, with concern in his voice, as he put the papers aside.

"Yes. I'm fine." And she truly was, because no matter how things ended between them, he had given her some of the best days of her life and she would always appreciate him for it.

"How about coming over here and sit with me."

She took a perusal of his seat. It couldn't fit two people. "It won't work."

He crooked his finger at her. "Come here. We'll make it work."

The raspy sound of his voice got to her and she unsnapped her seat belt and eased toward him. He unsnapped his own and pulled her down into his lap. "Don't be concerned with Gil," he said of his pilot. "His job is to get us to our destination and not be concerned with what's going on in here."

She snuggled into his lap, thinking this was what she would miss the most when he left—the closeness, the chance to be held tight in a man's arms, to be able to feel every muscle in his body, especially the weight of that body on hers. Not to mention the feel of him inside of her. Then there was his scent…it was one she would never forget. It was a manly aroma that reminded her of rain, sunshine and lots of sex.

"I spoke with Parker before we left."

She'd heard what he said but didn't respond. She was still thinking of lots of sex.

He tightened his arms around her as he glanced down. "Cassie?"

She tilted her head and looked up at him. "I heard you."

He didn't say anything for a moment, just reached out and softly caressed the cleft in her chin. She swallowed with his every slow, sensuous stroke. He was trying to get next to her. And it was working.

"What did he want?" she asked, forcing the words out from her constricted throat. His hand had moved from her chin and was now stroking the side of her face, the area right below her ear.

He pretended not to hear as he continued to trace a path from her ear to her neck. "Brandon?" she said, to get his attention.

"I heard you," he answered, meeting her gaze and grinning.

She grinned back. "What did Parker want?"

"He has summoned you to the compound for Sunday dinner."

She raised up and glanced at him with a perturbed look on her face. "He did what!"

He laughed. "I was joking. I knew you wouldn't like the word *summoned*. I like getting a rise out of you."

She eased her hands between his legs to his crotch. "I like getting a rise out of you, too. Now stop teasing and tell me what Parker wanted."

He pulled her hand back and drew her closer into his arms. "He wants to *invite* you to Sunday dinner at the Garrison Estate. It's a weekly affair for the Garrison family."

She nodded as she thought about what he'd said. "And what about Bonita Garrison? The woman who wouldn't care if I dropped off the face of the earth."

Brandon inhaled deeply. "I wondered about that myself, but knowing Parker he'll have everything under control."

Cassie glanced up at him. "You don't sound too convincing."

He lowered his head. "Maybe this will help," he

breathed against her lips while his hand lifted her skirt to stroke her thigh. He then stroked his tongue across her lips the same way his hand was massaging her thigh, gently, pleasurably and methodically. And if that wasn't enough, he inserted his tongue into her mouth and the impact shattered her nerve endings. Her lips parted on a sigh, which gave him deeper penetration, something he was good at taking advantage of. And he was doing so in a way that had her moaning from the sensations escalating through her. His exquisite tongue was doing wild and wonderful things to hers. Devouring her mouth. Deepening her desire.

"Buckle up for landing."

He lifted his head when his pilot's command came across the speaker. And then as if he couldn't resist, he lowered his head and kissed her again. This time it was Cassie who pulled back and whispered against his moist lips. "I think I need to go back to my own seat."

"Yes, you do," he agreed, tracing his tongue around her mouth before finally releasing her from his lap.

She eased back to her seat and quickly buckled in. She lifted her head. Their gazes met. She smiled. So did he.

The thought that suddenly ran though her mind was that they hadn't missed making love one single time since that first experience and they hadn't gone a day without sharing a kiss, either. Those would be memories that would have to sustain her. Memories she would forever cherish.

"Cassie?"

She glanced over at him. "Yes?"

"Welcome to Miami."

* * *

"Do you mind if I make a quick stop by my office to check on things?" Brandon asked Cassie as he drove his car down Ocean Drive. Her attention was on the happenings outside the car's window. During this time of the day, it wasn't unusual to spot models, vintage cars, Harleys and people on Rollerblades mixing in with the many tourists that visited South Beach.

She turned to him, smiling. The sun coming through the window seemed to place golden highlights in her hair. "No, not at all. I'm sure you want to check to make sure nothing was damaged during the storm, although from the looks of things, all this city got was plenty of rain."

"Which seem to have grown more people," Brandon said, chuckling. "This area gets more popular every day. Daytime is bad enough but wait until darkness falls and all the nightclubs open. South Beach becomes one big party land."

"Umm, sounds like fun."

He chuckled. "It is, and Adam's nightclub is right there in the thick of things. It's doing very well. Before you return to the Bahamas, I plan to make sure I take you out on the town one night, and Adam's club is just one of the many places we'll visit."

Cassie slanted a smile over at him. "Don't tell me you're one of those party animals."

He laughed. "Not anymore, but I used to be. Adam and I have a history of spending many a nights out partying and having a good time. We were intent on experiencing as much of the wilder side of life as we could. But after Dad's death I had to buckle down and get serious when everything fell on my shoulders. I will always appreciate your father for having faith in my abilities and retaining our firm after Dad died. John didn't have to do that, but by doing so, he gave me a chance to prove my worth."

Cassie nodded as her smile deepened. "So you settled down, but is Adam still the party animal?"

"Not to the degree he used to be," he said. "He's become a very serious businessman. You're going to like him."

"You would say that because he's your best friend," she said.

"Yes, but I think you're going to like all the Garrison siblings."

She gave him a doubtful look. "Even Parker?"

"Yes, even Parker. Once you get to know him you'll see he's really a nice guy, and like I told you before, his marriage to Anna has changed him in a lot of ways. He loves her very much. I would be the first to admit that I never thought I'd see the day he would settle down. After all, he was one of the city's most eligible bachelors, a status he liked having."

Cassie considered his words and wondered if there would ever be a woman in Brandon's life that he would fall in love with and want to marry and spend the rest of his life with.

"We're almost there, just another block. And you'll be able to see the Garrison Grand once I turn the corner. It's on one corner of Bricknell and my office is on the other."

No sooner had he said the words than she saw what had been her father's first hotel. A sense of pride flowed through Cassie. It was a beautiful high-rise, a stately structure.

"It's beautiful," she said, getting to study it in more detail when they came to a stop at a traffic light right in front of the grand-looking building. The Garrison Grand was a perfect name for it.

"Stephen's in charge of running it now and he's doing an excellent job. He has exemplary business skills, but he's going to have his hands full when the Hotel Victoria open its doors."

Cassie glanced at Brandon. "The Hotel Victoria?"

"Yes, it's a hotel that's presently under construction and is being built by Jordan Jefferies. It will be a competing hotel that will be slightly smaller in size but will rival the Garrison Grand in luxury and prestige and attract the same type of clientele. Jeffries is a shrewd businessman who can be rather ruthless at times. He's a person who's determined to succeed by any means necessary."

"Sounds a lot like Parker."

Brandon chuckled. "Yes, which is probably why the two can't get along. There's a sort of family rivalry going on between the Garrisons and the Jeffrieses and has been for a while. However, a couple of months ago, Brittany defied the feud and recently became engaged to Emilio, Jordan's brother."

"I can imagine Parker not being too happy about that," Cassie said.

"No, and neither is Jordan. But Brittany and Emilio seem very much in love and intend to live their lives the way they want without family interference."

"Good for them."

Brandon glanced over at her as he pulled the car to a stop in a spot in a parking garage. A name plate indicated the spot was designated for his vehicle only. "You sound like a rebel."

She unsnapped her seat belt, stretched over and placed a kiss on his lips. "I am. My mom told me how her family was against her dating my dad since he was a married man. She defied them and dated him anyway."

"What about you? Would you date a married man?"

She shook her head. "No, I'm more possessive than my mom ever was. I couldn't stand the thought of sharing. That's why I feel somewhat sympathetic to Bonita Garrison. I can only imagine how she must have felt finding out her husband had had a long-term affair with another woman. But then another part of me, the part that knew my father so well and knew what a loving and loyal man he was, feels there was a reason he sought love and happiness elsewhere."

Brandon shrugged. "Perhaps."

Cassie really didn't expect him to say any more than that. Even if he knew anything about her father and his wife's relationship, he wouldn't say. No matter what she and Brandon had shared, he was very loyal when it came to the Garrison family.

A few moments later they entered the lobby of the Washington Building. "My father purchased the land for this building over forty years ago from your father. At the time a young John Garrison, who was in his early twenties, was on his way to becoming a multimillionaire. He was single and one of the most eligible bachelors in Miami. My father was his attorney even then."

Cassie nodded as she glanced around before they stepped on the elevator. "Nice building."

"Thanks. My firm's office is on the twentieth floor," he said, pressing a button after the elevator door closed shut. "I lease out the extra office space to other businesses."

When the elevator came to a stop on the twentieth floor they began walking down a carpeted hall. Brandon's law firm's glass doors had his named written in bold gold script. The receptionist area was both massive and impressive, and a young lady who sat at the front desk smiled and greeted them when they entered.

Passing that area they rounded a corner that contained several spacious offices, where she noticed people working at their desks. Some looked up when she and Brandon passed their doors and others, who were busy working or talking on the phone, did not. Cassie figured since it was Friday, most were probably trying to bring their work week to an end at a reasonable time so their weekend could begin.

She admired the layout of the offices. She knew that every office was made up of three fundamental elements—architecture, furniture and technology— and it appeared that Brandon's firm emphasized all three. The interior provided a comfortable work environment where anyone would want to spend their working hours. The painted walls, carpeted floors in some areas and marble tile floors in others, modern furniture and state-of-the-art equipment all provided an upscale image of what she'd thought Brandon's place of business would be like and she hadn't been wrong.

"I should have warned you about my secretary,

Rachel Suarez," he said in a low voice. "She's been here for ages, started out as my dad's first secretary, and she thinks she owns the place. But I have to admit she does a fantastic job of running things. I have ten associates working for me and she keeps everyone in line, including my other thirty or so employees."

Cassie glanced over at him, not realizing his firm was so massive. "You have a rather large company."

"Yes, and they are good people and hard workers, every one of them."

"The layout is nice and no one is cramped for space," she openly observed.

Brandon's secretary's desk appeared to be in the center of things. The sixty-something-year-old woman's face broke into a bright smile when she saw her boss. "Brandon, I wasn't expecting you back until sometime next week."

He smiled. "I'm still officially on vacation. I just dropped by to see how everything faired during the storm."

The woman waved off his words with her hands. "It wasn't so bad. I'm just glad it didn't get worse. I understand the islands got more rain that we did."

She then glanced over at Cassie and gave her a huge smile. "Hello."

Cassie smiled back. "Hello to you."

Brandon began introductions. "Rachel, this is—"

"I know who she is," the woman said, offering Cassie her hand. "You look a lot like your daddy."

Cassie raised a surprised brow as she took the hand being offered. Her surprise had nothing to do with being told that she looked like her father since she knew that was true. Her surprise was that the woman knew who she was.

At Cassie's bemused expression Rachel explained. "I was Stan Washington's secretary when you were born."

Cassie nodded. In other words the woman had known about her parents' affair and, like Brandon's father, had been sworn to secrecy.

"I'm going to give Cassie a tour of my office, Rachel. And like I said, I'm still on vacation so I won't be accepting any calls if they come in."

Rachel grinned. "Yes, sir."

Brandon ushered Cassie down the carpeted hall to his office. When they entered he locked the door behind him. She only had time for a quick glance around before he pulled her into his arms. "Now to finish what we started on the plane," he said, before lowering his head for a kiss.

Their mouths had barely touched when Brandon's cell phone rang. Muttering a curse, he straightened and pulled it out of his pocket. He rolled his eyes upon seeing whose telephone number had appeared. "Yes, Adam?" he said, a split second from letting his best friend know he had caught him at a bad time.

"Yes, Cassie is here and yes, she's with me now." A few moments later he said. "No, she's not staying at the Garrison Grand. She'll be a guest in my home." He winked his eye at Cassie before she moved to sit on the sofa across the room, crossing her legs in a very sexy way.

"And, no," he continued, trying to concentrate on what Adam was saying and not on Cassie's legs, "you won't be able to meet her until dinner on Sunday. You might be my best friend but I can't let you use that fact to your advantage since Parker has requested that the family all meet her at the same time. Besides, I'm taking her to dinner tonight and tomorrow I plan to give her a tour of the town."

Brandon laughed at something Adam said and replied, "Okay, Adam. I'll let Cassie know." He then clicked off the phone and placed it back in his pocket.

"Let me know what?" she asked, returning to where he stood.

Brandon smiled. "If you want to go ahead and make him your favorite brother, he's fine with it."

A smile touched Cassie's lips. She had a feeing she was really going to like him. "He seems nice."

"He is. Like I told you, all of them are, including Parker. The two of you just rubbed each other the wrong way in the beginning."

"And what if he doesn't agree with the counteroffer I intend to make him? I want you to know that I won't back down. He can either take it or leave it."

Brandon grinned. Sunday dinner at the Garrisons would be interesting, as usual. "I wouldn't worry about it if I were you. Like I said, Parker is a sharp business-man and I believe he wants to end the animosity between the two of you and come up with a workable solution as much as you do."

He reached out and caressed the cleft in her chin. "Every time I touch this I get turned on."

Cassie smiled, shaking her head. "I think you get turned on even when you're not touching it."

He laughed. "That's true." And to prove his point he lowered his mouth and joined it with hers. Their lips locked. Their tongues mated. Desire was seeping into both of their bones. Brandon thought he would never get enough of this woman no matter how much he tried.

Moments later he lifted his head and drew back from the kiss, his gaze on her moist lips. "I better get you out of here. It's not safe to be in here alone with you. I've never made love to a woman in my office, but I might be driven to do that very thing with you."

On tiptoe she stretched up and brushed a kiss across his lips. In a way she wanted him to take her here. That way when they did go their separate ways, her presence would always be in here, a place where he spent the majority of his time working.

"Maybe not today, but promise you'll do it before I leave to return home."

He lifted a brow. "Do what?"

"Make love to me in here," she said, stepping closer and sliding her fingers to his nape to caress him there.

He released a shuddering sigh at her touch before asking, "Why would you want me to make love to you in here?"

"So you could always remember me, especially in here."

He was taken aback by her words, and then murmured softly, in a husky tone, "Do you honestly think I could forget you, Cassie? Do you think I'd be able to forget everything we've shared together?"

Before she could answer he bent his head and claimed her lips, kissing her with so much passion it made her stomach somersault. It made the lower part of her body feel highly sensitive to his very presence.

Reluctantly, he pulled his mouth away and gazed at her in a way that sent sensations rushing all through her. He took her hand in his. "Come on and let's get out of here before I do just what you ask and not care that I have an office full of people working today."

A smile touched his lips when he added, "They're a smart group of people who will get more than suspicious about all the noise we'll make."

"Umm, you think we'll make a lot of noise?" she asked when he unlocked the door.

"He glanced over at her before opening it and chuckled. "Sweetheart, we always do."

Later that night Cassie could feel the soft pounding of Brandon's heart against her back. His arms were wrapped around her as he slept. The warm afterglow of their lovemaking had lulled her to sleep, as well, but now she was awake.

And thinking.

He had a beautiful home, and after showing her around, she had felt the love he had for it while he'd given his tour. She had watched him carefully when he had shown her with pride the things that were his. They were possessions he had worked hard to get and he was still working hard to retain. He'd told her that a number of his father's clients had dropped his firm after his father's death, citing Brandon's youth and lack of experience. John Garrison had been one of the few who'd kept him on, and had gone even further by recommending him to others. With hard work Brandon had rebuilt the legacy his father had started.

When Brandon stirred in his sleep, she glanced over her shoulder and her gaze touched his sleeping face. She wanted him. She wanted to marry him. She wanted to have his babies. But most of all, she loved him. However, this would be one of those situations where she couldn't have any of the things she wanted.

Because he didn't love her in return.

And she could never spend her life with a man who didn't love her. She had grown up in an environment that was filled with too much love to want something less for herself.

She closed her eyes to blot out the advice her mind was giving her. *Get out while you can do so without getting your heart shattered. Take your memories and go.*

Cassie opened her eyes, knowing she would take the advice her mind was giving her. This was Brandon's world and hers was in the Bahamas. Instead of staying the two weeks she'd originally planned, she would let him know after dinner on Sunday that she would be leaving in a week. It was important that she and Parker resolved the issues between them, and she was looking forward to meeting her other siblings. After that it was time to move on. The more time she spent with Brandon, the more she yearned for things she could not have. Already her love for him was weakening her resolve and undermining her defenses.

It was time for her to make serious plans about returning home. There was no other way.

Brandon walked off the patio and back into his home to answer the ringing telephone. He stood in a spot where he could still see Cassie as she swam around in his pool.

The two-piece bathing suit she was wearing was sexual temptation at its finest, and he was quite content to just stand there and stare at her. But when his phone rang again, he knew that wasn't possible. He reached on the table to pick it up. "Yes?"

"Brandon, this is Parker."

He wondered when Parker would get around to calling him back. They had been playing phone tag for the better part of the day. He understood Parker had been in meetings most of yesterday, and Brandon and Cassie had left the house early this morning when he had taken her to breakfast and later on a tour of South Beach.

When she had mentioned that she had a taste for Chinese food, they had dined for lunch at one of his favorite restaurants, an upscale and trendy establishment called the China Grille. After lunch, instead of taking in more sights, he had done as she requested and had taken her to the cemetery where her father was buried. He had stood by her side when she'd finally got a chance to say goodbye and then he had held her in his arms while she cried when her grief had gotten too much for her.

Afterward, they had returned to his place to take a swim in the pool and relax a while before getting dressed for dinner and the South Beach night life.

"Yes, Parker, I'm glad we finally connected."

"I am, too. How's Cassie?"

Brandon turned and glanced out the bank of French doors to stare right at her. She was no longer in the water but was standing by the edge of the pool, getting ready to dive back in. It was his opinion—with the way she looked with the sunlight made the wet strands of her hair gleam, and her body made his breath catch every time he saw it, naked or in clothes—Cassie was every man's fantasy. That was definitely not something her oldest brother would appreciate hearing from him.

"Cassie's fine and is out by the pool. She wanted to take a swim before we go out to dinner."

"Everyone is looking forward to meeting her tomorrow," Parker said.

"Glad to hear it. I had a hard time convincing her of that, but I did, which is the main reason she's here in Miami."

"Just so you know, I haven't mentioned it to Mom."

Something in Parker's voice forced Brandon to ask, "But you will, right?"

"I don't think that will be a wise thing to do at this point."

Brandon didn't like the sound of that. Chances were Bonita would be home since she rarely left the house on Sundays. And, for that matter she was rarely sober after lunchtime, as well. "And why not, Parker? I've been totally up front with Cassie since she discovered our association and I'm not going to have her start doubting my word or intentions about anything. If Bonita will be at dinner tomorrow, before I agree to bring Cassie, I need a good reason why you won't be telling Bonita she's coming. That wouldn't be fair to either of them." He knew Cassie could hold her own against anyone, but in this particular situation, he felt she shouldn't be placed in a position where she had to.

For the next ten minutes Parker explained to Brandon why he'd made the decision he had, and after discussing it with his siblings, they felt Bonita being caught unaware would be the right approach to use. "That might be the right approach for Bonita, but what about Cassie? I can see an ugly scene exploding, one I don't like and wouldn't want to place her in."

Brandon rubbed his hand down his face. "I'm going to tell her, Parker, and explain things to her the way you have explained them to me. It's going to be her decision as to whether or not she still wants to come."

"And I agree she should know, which is the reason I wanted to talk to you. So when will you tell her?"

Brandon sighed deeply. "I'd rather wait until in the morning. I don't want anything to ruin the plans I have for dinner," he said, fighting for control of his voice. He still wasn't sure not telling Bonita was the right thing, although he understood Parker's reason for it.

"Please inform me of Cassie's decision one way or the other," Parker said. "If she doesn't want to join us for dinner at the Garrison Estate tomorrow evening, then we can all get together and take her out somewhere else. Mom will wonder why we're not eating Sunday dinner at her place though, so either way, she's going to find out Cassie's in town and that we've made contact with her. I just think it's best if we all stand together and face Mom as a united front."

"I understand, Parker, but like I said, it will be Cassie's decision."

Nine

Frowning, Cassie stared over at Brandon. "What do you mean Bonita Garrison doesn't know I was invited to dinner?"

Brandon sighed. He had known she would not like the news Parker had delivered yesterday. "Considering everything, the Garrison siblings felt it would be best if she didn't know," he explained.

From where he was standing, with his shoulder propped against the bookshelves in his library, he could tell that Cassie, who was sitting on a sofa, was confused by that statement.

"But it's her house, right?" she asked, as if for clarification.

"Yes, it's her house."

"Then am I to assume she's out of town or something and won't be there?"

"No, you aren't to assume that." He saw the defiant look in her eyes, a strong indication as to what direction this conversation was going.

"Then I think you need to tell me what's going on, Brandon."

He sighed again, more deeply this time. What he needed was a drink, but that would have to come later. He really did owe her an explanation. Straightening, he crossed the room to sit beside her on the sofa. His gaze locked on her face when he said, "Bonita Garrison is an alcoholic and has been for years. She's always had a drinking problem and John's will only escalated the condition. Like I told you before, considering the state of their marriage, I think she had an idea he was having an affair, but she didn't know anything about you. That was one well-kept secret."

Cassie's frown deepened. "Have any of her children suggested that she seek professional help?"

"Yes, countless times. I understand John even did so, but for the longest she wouldn't acknowledge she had a problem. She still hasn't."

Cassie nodded. "But what does that have to do with me? Wouldn't seeing me in her home uninvited, the person who is living proof of her husband's unfaithfulness, push her even more over the edge?"

He reached for her hand. "Parker and the others are hoping it doesn't. Their relationship with her is strained and has been for some time. I'm talking years, Cassie. They'd decided, and unanimously I might add, that they want to meet you, build relationships with you, include you in the family mix, and they refused to sneak behind their mother's back to do so. They believe it's time to mend the fences and move on, and want Bonita to see that as a united group they plan to do just that, with or without her blessings."

He chuckled. "I've known those Garrisons most of my life and this is the first time they've ever been in complete agreement about anything."

Brandon got quiet for a moment and then said in a serious tone, "John would be proud of them. And knowing the type of man he was, a man who loved his children unconditionally, I want to believe that had he lived, he would have eventually gotten all of you together. He was a man who would have made it happen."

His words had Cassie staring at him thoughtfully. What he'd said was true. She believed that, as well. She had learned about her siblings' existence from her father, and she had known he had loved them as much as he had loved her. He had said so a number of times.

"But…" she said, frowning still. "What if things get ugly?"

"And there's a possibility that they might," he said honestly, needing to make her aware of that fact. "But Parker wants you to know that no matter what, they intend to finally bring things to a head, a forced-feeding intervention, so to speak."

Cassie inhaled a deep breath. She just hoped Parker and the others were right. The last thing she wanted was to be responsible for Bonita Garrison getting pushed over the edge. But then her children knew her better than anyone and Cassie was sure that no matter how strained their relationship, that they loved their mother. And if they felt what they had planned for this afternoon was the right approach to use then she would trust their judgment.

She met Brandon's gaze. "Okay, thanks for telling me."

"Are you still going?"

"Yes. I'm going." After a moment, she asked, "You will be there, too, right?"

A smile touched the corners of his lips. "Yes, I was invited, as well, and I will be there," he said. Tugging on the hand he still held he pulled her closer to him and whispered, "But even if I weren't invited I would still be there, Cassie. You would not be alone."

Cassie glanced around when Brandon brought the car to a stop in front of the massive and impressive Spanish-style villa that was the Garrison Estate. Everywhere she looked she saw a beauty that was spellbinding. From the brick driveway to the wide stucco stairs that led to the entrance, she thought there weren't many words that could be used to describe the house that could sufficiently do it justice.

She inhaled a reverent breath in knowing this is where her father had lived, the place he considered home when he wasn't in the Bahamas with her and her mom. And even now a part of her could feel his presence. What Brandon had said earlier that day was true. Her father would want his offspring to meet.

"You've gotten quiet on me. Are you okay?"

She glanced over at Brandon, hearing the concern in his voice. From the moment his plane had landed in Miami, he had been attentive, considerate of her well-being and so forthcoming with his affection. More than once she'd had to stop and remind herself that his affection had nothing to do with love, but was a result of his kindness. There was a natural degree of warmth and caring about him. Those were just two of the things that had drawn her to him from the first.

"Yes, I'm okay. I was just thinking about Dad and how much I loved him and how much I miss him, and how today I can feel his presence more so than ever."

"And you never resented him for having another family besides you and your mom?"

"I never resented Dad, but when I was a lot younger, after having found out he was a married man with another family, for a long time I resented them. In my mind, whenever he would leave me and Mom it would be to return here to them. I never gave thought to the fact that whenever he was in the Bahamas with me and Mom, he wasn't with them, either. I was too possessive of him in my life to even care."

"But now?"

"But now I want to believe that somehow he was able to give all six of us equal time, special time, as special as he was," she said softly.

"I think he did," Brandon said in a quiet tone. "I believe he knew what each of his kids needed and gave it to them. He was an ingrained part of each of their lives and they loved him just as much as you did."

Her eyebrows lifted. "Do you think that even now? After finding out he'd had a long-term affair while married to their mother? You don't think that love was tarnished because of it?"

Brandon shook his head. "No. Adam is the only one

I've spoken to in depth about it, basically to garner his personal feelings. He said they all knew their parents' marriage was on the rocks for years. Bonita's abuse of alcohol led to a friction that couldn't be mended."

Cassie nodded, then dragged in a deep breath and said, "It's time we go inside, isn't it?"

"Yes. Nervous?"

"I would be lying if I were to say no. But I can handle it."

Brandon chuckled as he unbuckled his seat belt. "Cassie Sinclair-Garrison, I think you can handle just about anything."

He exited the car and came around to open her door for her, admiring what she was wearing. Although it was the middle of fall, the weather was warm and the sky was clear and she was casually dressed in a pair of black slacks and a velvet plum blouse. The outfit not only brought out the natural beauty of her skin coloring, but added a touch of exuberance to her brown eyes, as well. She smiled at him.

He offered his hand and she took it. The sensation that immediately flowed through him was desire that was as intoxicating as the strongest liquor.

After closing the door, he placed her hand on his arm and walked her up the wide stucco stairs that led to the front door. Before he could raise his hand to knock, the door opened and Lisette Wilson stood there smiling at them. The woman had been the Garrison's housekeeper for as long as Brandon could remember and, according to Adam, Lisette was a force to reckon with when he'd been going through his mischievous teen years. Now she seemed older, and although a smile was bright on her face, she looked tired. She was probably worn out from having her hands full these days with Bonita's excessive drinking. With none of the Garrison siblings living at home, they depended on Lisette to keep things running as smoothly as possible on the home front.

"Mr. Brandon, good seeing you again, and I want to welcome the both of you to the Garrison Estate."

Brandon returned the woman's smile. "Thanks, Lisette. Have Parker and the others arrived yet?"

"Yes, they're on the veranda," she said, stepping aside for them to enter. "I'll take you to them."

Lisette led the way. Brandon could feel the tenseness of Cassie's hand on his arm. He smiled over at her as they passed a wide stone column that marked the entrance to the living room. After passing through several beautifully decorated rooms, they walked through a bank of French doors to the veranda. The Garrison siblings were there. All five of them. Along with three of their significant others.

"Your dinner guests have arrived," Lisette announced.

The group immediately ended whatever conversation they were engaged in and turned, seemingly all at once. Eight pairs of eyes stared at them, mainly at Cassie. They appeared stunned. The look on their faces confirmed that they were thinking what Brandon already knew. She was definitely a Garrison.

It was Parker who made the first move, crossing the veranda with an air that was cool and confident. He came to a stop in front of them. He continued to stare at Cassie, studying her features, probably with the same intensity that she was studying his.

For her it was like seeing what she figured was a younger version of their father. He looked so much like John Garrison it was uncanny. All three Garrison men did. That was the first thought that had crossed her mind when they had looked at her. But Parker, the first-born, had acquired nearly every physical feature their father had possessed, including his height, build and mannerisms—especially how his dark brow creased in a deep, thoughtful frown when he analyzed anything.

Not feeling at all intimidated, Cassie tilted her head back as she met his intense stare. Then she watched his eyes soften speculatively when he said, "Umm, the famous Garrison cleft. Was there ever a time you thought it was a curse rather than a blessing?"

Refusing to let her guard down, not even for a second, Cassie said, "No, that never occurred to me. Anything I inherited from my father I considered a blessing."

A semblance of a smile touched his arrogant lips and he said, "So did I." Extending his hand out to her, he said, "I'm Parker, by the way."

She accepted it. "And I'm Cassie."

He nodded before glancing over at Brandon. "Good seeing you again, Brandon."

"Likewise, Parker."

Parker's eyes then returned to Cassie. "There's a group of people who're anxious to meet you. Please come and let me introduce them."

"All right," she said, giving Parker the same semblance of a smile that he'd given her as she held his gaze steadily. Their opposing wills seemed to be squaring off, but in a sociable way. "I'd love to meet everyone," she said.

Cassie glanced over at Brandon and he smiled at her, and immediately his strength touched her, gave her the added confidence she needed. She fell in love with him even more.

She inhaled deeply as the two men escorted her across the veranda to meet the others. As much as she didn't want them to be, butterflies were flying around in her stomach at the round of introductions she was about to engage in.

She forced herself to relax and smiled when they came to a stop before a woman she quickly assumed to be Parker's wife, from the way he was looking at her. He might have been a happy bachelor at one time, but from the way he gently placed an arm around the beautiful woman with shoulder-length dark hair and green eyes, it was quite easy to tell he was a man very much in love.

He smiled affectionately at his wife before returning his gaze to Cassie. "Cassie, I'd like you to meet my wife, Anna."

Instead of shaking her hand, Anna gave her an affectionate hug. "It's nice meeting you, Cassie, and welcome to the family."

"Thank you."

Without taking more than a step, Cassie came to stand in front of two men she immediately knew were her other two brothers, since their clefts were dead giveaways. The woman standing between them had green eyes and wavy red hair. And just like Parker's wife, she was gorgeous.

"Cassie, welcome to Miami and I'm Stephen," the man standing to her left said, making his own introductions while slanting a smile at her and taking the hand she offered. "And this is my wife, Megan."

Like Anna, Megan automatically reached out and hugged her. "It's nice to finally get to meet you," Megan said, smiling at her with sincerity in her eyes. "And you have a three-year-old niece name Jade who I'm hoping you'll get to meet before you return to the Bahamas."

"I would love that and can't imagine leaving Miami before I do."

She then glanced at the other man, who was tall, dark and handsome—common traits, it seemed, with Garrison men. "And you must be Adam," she said.

A broad grin flitted across his face and suddenly two words came to her mind regarding him—loyal and dedicated. He reached out and gave her a hug and a kiss on the cheek. "Yes, I'm Adam, and remember, I'm to be the favorite brother."

She met his gaze and had a feeling that he would be. "I'll remember that."

She then turned and saw two women and a very handsome man of Cuban descent. She knew immediately that the two women were her identical twin sisters.

"Cassie, I'd like you to meet Brooke, the oldest of the twins by a few minutes," Parker said of the tall, attractive, model-thin woman with long dark brown hair and brown eyes. "And this is Brittany and her fiancé, Emilio Jeffries."

Cassie faintly raised a brow at the derision she'd heard in Parker's voice when he had introduced Emilio. She then remembered what Brandon had shared with her about there being bad blood between the Garrisons and the Jefferieses, and how Brittany had basically fallen in love with one of her brother's enemies. But still, she couldn't help but admire

Brittany for her bravery, as well as her good common sense. No woman in her right mind would let a hunk like Emilio slip through her fingers, regardless of how her family felt about it.

"It's nice meeting all of you," Cassie said, glancing around at everyone and very much aware of the moment Brandon came to stand next to her side.

"It's good to know I'm no longer the baby in the family," Brittany said, grinning.

The next few minutes Cassie mingled with everyone while answering numerous questions about her life in the Bahamas, without any of the inquiries getting specific about the relationship between their father and her mother. Stephen asked about the activities at the Garrison Grand-Bahamas and complimented her on the great job she was doing.

For the most part Parker didn't say anything, and knowing the astute businessman that he was, she figured he was hanging low and listening for any details regarding her business affairs that might interest him.

"Dinner is ready to be served."

Everyone glanced over in Lisette's direction before the woman disappeared back inside.

"Would you give me the honor of escorting you in to dinner?" Adam asked as he appeared at her side. "I'm sure Brandon won't mind," he added, winking an eye at the man he considered his best friend.

Cassie smiled serenely, wondering how much her siblings knew…or thought they knew of her and Brandon's relationship. Did they assume they were friends, lovers or what? Did she care? She knew the terms of their relationship, the boundaries as well as the life span of it.

She smiled over at Brandon before returning her gaze to Adam. Before she could open her mouth to say anything, she felt Brandon's hand at her back when he said in a low tone, "I think we will both do the honor, Adam. I've appointed myself her escort for the evening."

She saw the two men exchange meaningful looks. She was aware, as much as they were, that Bonita Garrison had not yet made an appearance. "I think having two escorts is a splendid idea," she said.

When they reached the dining room she noted Parker had taken the chair at the head of the table. Brandon took the chair on one side of her and Adam took a chair on the other side. Emilio was sitting across from her and they shared a smile. She suspected that he felt as much an outsider as she did. There was the easy and familiar camaraderie the others shared, including Brandon. He'd evidently shared Sunday dinner with the group before because he seemed to be right at home.

"So when can I come visit you in the Bahamas?" Brooke asked, smiling over at Cassie.

Before she could respond, Adam said, "Trying to get the hell out of Dodge for some reason, sis?"

She rolled her eyes at him. "Not particularly," she said, not meeting his gaze as she suddenly began concentrating on the plate Lisette set in front of her.

"You're welcome to visit me any time," Cassie said and meant it. When Brooke glanced up, Cassie could have sworn she'd seen a look of profound thanks in her eyes. That made Cassie wonder if perhaps what Adam had jokingly said was true and Brooke was trying to escape Miami for a reason.

Conversation was amiable with Adam, Brooke and Brittany telling her about the establishments they owned and ran under the Garrison umbrella. Stephen discussed the Miami Garrison Grand and even asked her advice on a couple of things that he'd heard she had implemented at her hotel.

When Brooke excused herself for the second time to go to the bathroom, Cassie overheard Brittany whisper to Emilio that she thought her twin was pregnant. Cassie was grateful everyone else had been too busy listening to Megan share one of her disastrous interior decorating experiences to hear Brittany's comment.

Suddenly, the dining room got deathly quiet and Cassie knew why when Brandon reached for her hand and held it tight in his. She followed everyone's gaze and glanced at the woman who was standing in the entrance of the dining room. Regardless of what curiosity she had always harbored about her father's wife, she never in a million years thought such disappointment would assail her body like it was doing now.

It was easy to see that at one time Bonita Garrison had been a beautiful woman, definitely stunning enough to catch a young John Garrison's eye. But the woman who appeared almost too drunk to stand up straight while holding a half-filled glass of liquor in her hand looked tired and beaten.

"Mother, we weren't sure you would be joining us," Parker said, standing along with all the other men at the table.

"Would it have mattered?" Bonita snapped, almost

staggering with each step she took. She made it to the chair on the other side of Parker and sat.

Resuming his seat, Parker glanced at Lisette, who had entered, and said, "Please bring my mother a plate as well as a cup of coffee."

The woman glared at her oldest son. "I don't need anything to drink, Parker. I have everything I need right here," she said in a slurred voice, saluting her glass at him.

"I would say you've had too much, Mom."

The comment came from Stephen and whereas Bonita Garrison had glared at Parker just moments earlier, she actually smiled at Stephen. She didn't say anything to Stephen directly, but instead announced, "Maybe I'll have a cup of coffee after all."

Cassie knew it was then that Bonita noticed her presence. She saw Brandon sitting beside her and holding her hand, and said, "Brandon, how nice, you've brought a date."

Brandon didn't say anything but merely nodded, while Bonita continued to stare. Cassie figured that it wouldn't take long before her identity became obvious with her sitting so close to Brittany. Other than the color of their skin, the two women favored. In her drunken state such a thing could go over Bonita's head.

But it didn't.

Cassie found herself the object of the woman's intense attention and then suddenly Bonita rose on drunken legs and, not speaking to anyone in particular, she asked, "Who is she?"

It was Parker who spoke. "Cassie. Cassie Sinclair-Garrison."

The woman snatched her gaze from Cassie and glared at Parker. "That woman's child? You invited that *woman's* child to our home?"

"No, I invited our *father's* child to our home, Mother. Cassie is our sister and we thought it was time we met her," Parker answered with the same mastery in his voice that Cassie was certain he used in the boardroom.

Bonita's features took on a stony countenance. "Meet her? Why would you want to meet her after what your father and her mother did to me?"

"Whatever happened between you and Dad was between you and Dad," Adam said firmly, his jaw set.

"And no matter what happened, Mother, or the participants involved, nothing changes the fact that Cassie *is* our sister and we want to get to know her," Stephen added.

Bonita slowly glanced around the table and saw a look of conformity on the faces of Brooke and Brittany as well. Angrily, she slammed her glass down. "Don't expect me to be happy about it." She then stormed out the room.

"Maybe we should consider cancelling her sixtieth birthday party," Brittany said softly.

No one agreed or disagreed. Instead, Parker met Cassie's gaze and said, "I want to apologize for my mother's behavior."

Cassie shook her head. "You don't have to apologize. I just regret upsetting your mother."

"Don't sweat it," Adam said, smiling as he took a sip of his wine. "Everything upsets Mother. We're used to it and have been for a long time. Over the years we've learned to deal with it. Some better than others."

Dinner resumed and the tension eventually passed. Cassie, like everyone else, indulged in the shared discussions, murmurs, chuckles and laughter around the table. Feeling more comfortable, she began to relax and more than once she glanced over at Brandon to find him staring at her.

When dinner was over everyone retired to the family room. Moments later, Brandon asked to speak with Parker privately. She knew he would be telling them of her wish not to discuss any business today, and that she preferred meeting with Parker tomorrow.

Moments later, she found herself alone with Brittany, Brooke and Emilio. Anna and Megan, who were close friends, took a walk outside to admire one of the many flower gardens surrounding the estate, and Stephen and Adam had excused themselves to speak with Lisette.

"I see your brother still doesn't care for me," Emilio said, chuckling to Brittany.

She leaned up and kissed his cheek. "Doesn't matter, since I like you."

Fascinated, Cassie decided to ask, "Do you think he'll ever soften up?"

Brooke lifted an arched brow. "Who, Parker? No. That would be too easy," she said, with more than a trace of annoyance in her voice.

"And he's really upset now that he knows that Jordan has acquired a piece of land he had his sights on," Emilio said. Then since he thought Cassie didn't know, he added, "Jordan is my brother."

"Excuse me, please. I think I'll join Anna and Megan in getting some fresh air," Brooke said rather tersely before turning and walking out the French doors.

Brittany watched her twin leave. "I wonder what that was about?" she said thoughtfully. "Something's up with her."

"Pure speculation on Brittany's part," Emilio added. "She thinks Brooke's been acting strange lately."

"It's not what I think, sweetheart. It's what I know. She's my twin, so I can't help but notice certain things."

Before Brittany could speculate any further, Brandon, Parker, Stephen and Adam returned. Brandon came up to her and slipped his hand around her waist. "Ready to leave?"

Cassie smiled up at him. "Yes, if you are."

She promised Brittany she would drop by her restaurant this week and gave Brooke her word she would visit the condominiums that Brooke owned.

Before leaving she made more promises. Adam wanted her presence at his club at least once and Stephen asked her to come by the Garrison Grand so he could give her a tour. Parker hadn't asked her to promise him anything since he was meeting with her first thing in the morning at his office. The most important thing to him was for them to come together and find a resolution to what was keeping them at arm's length.

When she and Brandon walked to the car she smiled over at him. "Dinner wasn't so bad."

He grinned. "No, I guess not. What did you think about Bonita?"

"I hope that she'll get professional help, and soon."

"What about your siblings?"

She tilted her head and said, "To be quite honest, I like them."

He opened the car door for her. "I told you that you would. Even Parker softened up some."

When he came around and got inside the driver's side he glanced at his watch. "I know just the place I want to take you now."

She glanced over at him upon hearing the sensual huskiness of his tone. "Oh, really? Where?"

"My office."

Ten

After walking down the carpeted hallway holding hands, they reached Brandon's office. There was no guesswork as to why they were in an empty office on a Sunday night.

Cassie could unashamedly remember her request to him a couple of days ago, and there was no doubt in her mind that he was going to give her just what she'd asked for.

She chewed her bottom lip, not in nervousness but in anticipation. Goose bumps had begun forming on her arms, desire was making her panties wet and her tongue ached to mingle with Brandon's in a hot-and-heavy kiss. From the time he had announced just where he would be taking her and they had pulled out of the brick driveway of the Garrison Estate, sensations, thick and rampant, had flowed through her, making her shift positions in her seat a few times.

Cassie's thoughts shifted back to the here and now when Brandon released his hold on her hand and she immediately felt the loss of his touch. Opening the office door, his touch was back when he guided her inside before closing the door behind them. He tugged on her hand and brought her closer to him.

She felt weak in the knees, and to retain her balance, she placed her hands on his chest and gazed up at him, remembering the last time they had made love. It had been early that morning when they had awakened. And his lovemaking last night had given her a good night's sleep and been the very thing that had lulled her awake that morning as well. She'd wanted more of what he had the ability to give her. He had been more than happy to oblige her in the most fervent and passionate way.

She knew she should tell him of her decision to return to the Bahamas sooner than she'd originally planned, but at the moment she couldn't. The only thing she could do while standing in his embrace was get turned on even more by the gorgeous brown eyes looking down at her. Being the sole focus of his attention was causing all sorts of emotions to run through her; feelings that were intimate and private, feelings that could only be shared with him.

"Do you know what I think about whenever I look at you?" Brandon asked in a low husky voice, taking his forefinger and tracing the dimple in her chin.

She shook her head. She only knew what she thought about whenever she looked at him. "No. Tell me. What do you think when you look at me, Brandon?"

He took a step back and his gaze flicked over her from head to toe, and then he met her eyes. "I think about stripping you naked and then kissing you all over. But I want to do more than just kiss you. I want to taste you, to savor your flavor, get entrenched in your heated aroma, and to get totally enmeshed in the very essence of you."

Cassie was caught between wanting to breathe and not wanting to breathe. His words had started her heart to race in her chest and was making heat shimmer through all parts of her. Whenever they made love he had the ability to let go and give full measure, holding nothing back and making her the recipient of something so earth-shattering and profound.

With a heated sigh, she recovered the distance he had placed between them and reached out and wrapped her arms around his neck. She stared into his face, studied it with the intensity that only a woman in love could do, taking in every detail of his features—the dark brown eyes, sensual lips and firm jaw. Despite her determination to return to the island and live her life alone, she knew there was no way she would ever forget him and how he made her feel while doing all those wonderful things to her.

"On Friday you said you wanted me to make love to you in here because you didn't want me to forget you. Why do you think I'd forget you, Cassie?"

Chewing her bottom lip, she met his gaze knowing his inquiry demanded an answer, one she wasn't ready to share with him. If she did, she would come across as a needy person, a woman wanting the love of a man who wasn't ready to give it. A man she figured had no intention of ever getting married after what his fiancée had done to him. But then, hadn't she figured that same thing about her own life after Jason?

"Cassie?"

Giving him an answer that was not the complete truth she said, "Because I know this is just a moment we are sharing, Brandon, and nothing more. I know it and you know it, as well. But I want you to remember me like I will always remember you. And since this is where you spend a lot of your time, I want you to remember me here."

He smiled with a touch to his lips that made more heat flow through her. "Especially in here?" he asked in a deep, throaty voice.

"Yes, especially in here," she replied silkily. "I want to get into your mind, Brandon." What she wouldn't say is that she wanted to get in his heart, as well, but she knew that was wishful thinking.

With all amusement leaving his face, he said in a serious tone and with a solemn expression, "You *are* in my mind, Cassie."

She swallowed. She had all intention of making some kind of sassy comeback, but didn't. She so desperately wanted to believe him, and in a way she did believe him. He might not be in love with her, but over the past couple of weeks they had bonded in a way that went beyond the bedroom. He had come to the island seeking her out with a less than an honorable purpose, but in the end he had come clean and had been completely truthful with her, telling her more than she'd counted on.

And he had brought her here tonight to make the

memories she wanted him to have, even when she would be across the span of an ocean from him, he would remember her in here. The happiness she felt at that moment made her feel light-headed and she automatically breathed air into her lungs, picking up his manly scent in the process. "Then let's make memories, Brandon. Let's make them together."

Brandon stared at Cassie. He wanted her with a desperation he almost found frightening. The intensity of his desire was almost mind-boggling. It had been that way each and every time they made physical contact. She was an itch he couldn't scratch enough, a meal he could never get tired of consuming.

With the way she was standing so close to him, he could feel the hard tips of her breasts pressing against his chest, and the heated juncture of her legs aroused his erection even more. And if those things weren't mind-wrenching enough, he pulled her closer to the fit of him, needing the intimacy of their bodies joined first in clothes and then without.

The thought of making love to her in his office suddenly sent a sexual urgency as strong as anything he'd ever encountered to fill him to capacity. And with a sharp hunger that could only be appeased one way, he lowered his head and greedily consumed her mouth, devouring its taste and texture. He felt her lips tremble beneath his, he knew the exact moment her tongue engaged in their sensuous play, something so powerfully erotic it made him growl deep in his throat. He knew the air conditioning was on and was working perfectly, yet he felt hot and the only way to cool off was to remove his clothes. Their clothes.

He broke off the kiss and quickly began unbuttoning his shirt, driven by graphic images flowing through his mind of just what he wanted to do to her. The thought made his lips curl into a smile.

"What are you smiling about?" she asked when he began removing his shoes and socks.

He glanced at her and chuckled. "Trust me, you don't want to know so I'd rather not tell you."

"But you will show me?" she asked when he began removing his pants.

He nodded. "Oh, yes, I will definitely show you."

Totally naked, he stood in front of her. He wanted to take her hard and fast, then slow and easy. He wanted to brand her. He wanted to …

Sensing he was suddenly about to lose it, he took a condom out of his wallet and quickly put it on before stepping closer to her to begin removing her clothes, appreciating the fact that she was helping. Otherwise he would have ripped them off her in his haste, his greed, his obsession.

When she stood before him completely nude, he knew that this was one immaculate woman, a woman who could turn him on like nobody's business. She was elegant and sexy, all rolled into one. He reached for her hand, took it in his and began walking backward toward his desk. He'd been fantasizing about taking her on it since the last time he'd brought her here. He could imagine her legs spread wide, with him standing between them and making love to her in a way that had his body hardening even more just thinking about it.

And they would be making memories. There would never be a time that he wouldn't enter his office without thinking about her, remembering what they had done in here, and remembering her being a part of him for this short while.

When they reached his desk he picked her up and sat her on it. A hot surge of desire rammed through him and he wanted his hands all over her, he wanted his body inside of her. He wanted it all. He reached out and let his fingers trace a path all over her, and pretended to write his name on her chest, stomach, thigh, everywhere.

And then he captured her mouth, sank into it with a hunger that was more intimate than any kiss he'd ever shared with a woman. She was consuming all of him, whether she intended to or not. Deliberate or accidental, he didn't care, she was doing it, taking him to a level that was physically exciting and emotionally draining all at the same time.

And when he gently leaned her back on the desk he spread her thighs and took his place between them— a place at the moment that was rightfully his. She looked beautiful with her hair a tousled mass on her head, flowing over her shoulders and falling in her face. He pushed the soft, curly strands back, not wanting anything to obliterate her vision. He wanted her to see every single thing he would do to her.

Her warm scent assailed him and he leaned forward and took her lips with an urgency, his tongue invading her mouth the way his erection was about to invade her body. Not wanting to wait any longer, knowing he couldn't even if he did, he pressed his engorged flesh against her and then when he felt her ultrawet heat, he eased it into her, clenching his teeth the deeper it went.

The sound of her moan pushed him into moving, stroking her body with his, thrusting in and out of her while holding her hips immobile. He made love to her with a primitive hunger that had him feeling every single sensation right down to his toes. Every stroke seemed keyed to perfect precision and his heart was pounding with each and every thrust.

He felt her shudder and his reaction to it was instantaneous. He was overtaken with pleasure so intense his body exploded in a million tiny rapturous pieces. Releasing the hold on her hips, he reached up and tangled his fingers in her hair as his entire body became one huge passionate mass. He pressed into her deeper still, when he felt the essence of him shooting into her womb as her flesh still continued to throb while his senses raged out of control. It was as if this part of her knew exactly what he needed and was giving it in full measure.

When she went limp, he somehow found strength to gather her into his arms to hold her, not wanting to let her go, wondering how he would do so when she left in two weeks. Not wanting to think about their parting, he picked her up and moved to sit behind the desk with her nestled protectively in his lap.

He glanced down at her. Her face wore the glow of a woman who'd just been made love to, a woman who had enjoyed the shared intimacy of a man. Not being able to stop himself from doing so, he reached out and began touching the swollen tips of her breasts. And when he noticed her breathing change, he leaned forward and took a tip into his mouth.

He wanted her again.

He lifted his head and met her gaze and his hand

began trailing down her body, seeking out certain parts of her. He heard her sharp intake of breath when his fingers touched the area between her legs.

"Had enough yet, baby?" he asked huskily in a low voice.

She clutched at his shoulders and whispered the one single word he wanted to hear. "No."

"Good."

He stood with her in his arms and headed toward the sofa. Tonight was their night. In the coming days the Garrisons would want to spend time with her before she returned home. But tonight was theirs and they would make memories to last.

Parker's secretary glanced up and gave Cassie a thoroughly curious look as she stood from her seat. "Mr. Garrison is expecting you and asked that I escort you to his office the moment you arrived, Ms. Garrison."

"Thank you."

Cassie followed the woman, knowing she had made the right decision in deciding to meet with Parker this morning alone. Regardless of her and Brandon's relationship, Parker was still his client.

She had talked to her own attorney and taken in all the advice he had given her. He had indicated he wanted to be included—whether in person or via conference call—in any business meetings that she and Parker conducted that included Brandon, as a way of making sure she was well-represented and not being compromised in any way. She came to the conclusion that things would be less complicated and more productive if she and Parker discussed things and tried to reach an agreement without any attorney involvement for now.

The secretary gave a courtesy knock on Parker's door before opening it and walking in. He turned from the window, which overlooked Biscayne Bay, and gazed at her. With his intense eyes on her she was struck again with just how much he looked like their father.

"You're staring."

She could feel herself blush with his comment. She noticed his secretary had left and closed the door behind her, and she was grateful for that. "Sorry, I can't get over just how much you look like Dad."

He chuckled slightly. "That's funny. I thought the same thing about you on Sunday. And I hadn't expected you to look so much like him."

The guard she put up was instinctive and immediate. Tilting her head back, she asked, "Who did you expect me to look like?"

He shrugged. "I don't know, probably more like your mother, a stranger, someone I really didn't have to relate to. But seeing you in the flesh forced me to admit something I've tried not to since the reading of Dad's will."

"Which is?"

"Admit that I do have another sister—one my father evidently cared for deeply to have done what he did," he said, while motioning to a chair for her to have a seat.

"But I'm a sister you'd rather do without," she said, accepting the seat.

He moved to take the chair behind his desk and grinned sheepishly. "Yes, but don't take it personal. I've felt the same way about Brittany and Brooke one time or another when they became too annoying. It was hard as hell being an oldest brother." And then he added thoughtfully, "As well as an oldest son."

A part of Cassie refused to believe her father had been so ruthlessly demanding of his firstborn. "Did Dad make things hard for you since you were the first?" she couldn't help but ask.

He seemed surprised by her question. "No, I made things hard on myself. I admired everything about him and wanted to be just like him. He was a high achiever in everything he did—sports, business, financial success. He was a man who was well-liked and admired by many. I never knew if I'd be able to grow up and fit his shoes, but God knows I always wanted to."

He paused then said, "But one thing about Dad was that he was fair, with all of us. At an early age we were encouraged to enter the family business and that's something none of us have regretted doing."

Cassie nodded. He had encouraged her to join the family business, as well. At sixteen she had worked part-time for the hotel and when she had graduated from college he had given her the responsibility of managing it. It had been a huge responsibility for a twenty-two-year-old, but he had told her time and time again how much faith he had in her abilities.

And she hadn't wanted to let him down…just like Parker had probably grown up not wanting to let him down as well. Did he assume that since their father hadn't left him the bigger share of the pie that somehow he had?

"Dad was proud of you, Parker," she decided to say.

She saw the glint of surprise that shone in his eyes. "He discussed us with you?" he asked.

"Of course, considering the circumstances, he wasn't able to tell all of you about me, but I've always known about the five of you. He used to talk about what a wonderful job you were doing and that he had no qualms about turning the running of the entire company over to you one day."

Parker leaned back in his chair and Cassie felt him study her intently while building a steeple with his fingers. "If what you're saying is true then why are you and I sharing controlling interest?"

Cassie smiled. His arrogance was returning. "Because I'm good at what I do just like you're good at what you do. He knew both of our strengths, as well as our weaknesses, and although you can't quite grasp it now, I think he figured that over the long run, the two of us would work together for the betterment of the company. You even admitted that Dad was a fair man."

"Yes, but—"

"But nothing, Parker," she said, leaning forward in her seat. "He was a good and fair man, point blank. And I'm sure Brandon has told you by now that I won't sell my portion of the controlling shares."

"Yes, he did say that," Parker said, and Cassie smiled at the tightening of his lips. There was no doubt in her mind that Parker Garrison was used to having his way, something she hoped his wife Anna was working diligently to break him out of.

"I'm here to make you another offer, one we can both live with," she said.

The look in his eyes said he doubted it. "And what offer is that?"

"Like I've told you, the Garrison Grand-Bahamas

is my main concern, but I won't give away a gift Dad gave to me. However, I will agree to sign my voting proxy over to you with the understanding that you inform me of all business decisions, not for my approval but just to keep me in the loop on things, since I'll be in the Bahamas."

Cassie saw the protective shield that lined the covering of his gaze when he asked, "Are you saying you won't sell the controlling shares but you'll give them to me by way of proxy?"

"Yes, that is exactly what I am saying. Since I'm signing them over to you it will basically mean the same thing, except I retain ownership. Yet it removes me from having to provide my feedback and vote on every single business decision you make."

The room got quiet and she saw the protective shield become a suspicious one when he asked, "Why? Why would you do that?"

A quiet smile touched the corners of her lips. "Because I believed Dad all those times when he said you were one of the most astute business-minded persons that he knew, and because I also believe that you will do what you think is best for the company and keep Dad's legacy alive for the future generation of Garrisons."

She could tell for a moment that Parker didn't know what to say. And then finally he said, "Thank you."

She nodded as she stood. "No need to thank me, Parker. Have Brandon draw up the papers for me to sign before I leave."

He stood, as well. "You'll be here another week, right?" he asked.

"That had been my original plan but I've decided to leave at the end of the week. I haven't told Brandon of my change in plans. I will tell him tonight."

Parker came from around the desk to stand in front of her. "Cassie, Brandon is a good man. In addition to being my attorney, he's also someone that I consider a good friend. The reason he did what he did when he came to the Bahamas—"

She waved off his words. "I know, he explained it all to me. Although I was furious at the time I'm okay now." *I'm also very much in love,* she couldn't add.

"Anna and I would like to have you over for dinner before you leave. Will you be free Wednesday night?"

Cassie smiled, feeling good that she and Parker had formed a truce. She thought about all the other dinner engagements she had scheduled that week with Stephen, Adam, Brittany and Brooke, and said, "Yes, I'd like that and Wednesday night will be fine. Thanks, Parker."

Brandon sat looking at Cassie on the dance floor with Stephen, who had dropped by to see her before she left for the Bahamas. Tonight was her last night in Miami and he had brought her to Estate, Adam's night-club. It was Thursday night, which Adam had long ago designated as ladies' night.

Brandon had been surprised and disappointed when Cassie had told him a few nights ago that she would be leaving Miami a week earlier than she had originally planned. He had come close to asking her not to go, to stay with him, and not just for another week but for always. But then he remembered what she had said about the Bahamas being her home and not ever wanting to live anywhere else. Little did she know that when she left she would be taking a piece of his heart right along with her.

"Brandon, got a minute?"

He glanced up at Adam. "Sure, what's up?"

Adam straddled the chair across from him and glanced around as if to make sure no one was in close listening range. He then met Brandon's curious gaze. "I've decided to run for president of the Miami Business Council."

Brandon smiled. "That's great, Adam. Congratulations."

Adam grinned. "Thanks, but don't congratulate me yet. Already there's a problem."

Brandon raised a curious brow. "What kind of a problem?" Both he and Adam had been members of Miami's elite Business Council for years, and evidently Adam felt it was time to step up and take control. Brandon saw no problem with him doing that. Like his brothers, Adam was an astute businessman and the success of Estate could attest to that.

"Some of the older members, those with clout, aren't taking me seriously. They see me as a single man who is a notorious playboy, and since I work in the entertainment field, they also see me as someone not suited to lead the business council."

Brandon stared over at Adam. Unfortunately, he could imagine the older, more conservative members saying such a thing to Adam. "So what are you going to do?"

"One of the things that someone suggested that I do is easy."

"Which is?"

Adam smiled. "Work on expanding the club's clientele beyond the young, rich and famous. But the other suggestion won't be so easy."

"And what was that suggestion?" Brandon asked, hearing a hint of despair in his best friend's voice.

"To clean up my playboy image it was suggested that I find a wife."

Brandon blinked. "A wife?"

Adam nodded. "Yes, a wife. So what do you think?"

Brandon frowned. "I think you should tell whoever told you that to go to hell."

"Be serious, Brandon."

Brandon's frown deepened. "I am serious." He then sighed as he leaned back in his chair. "Okay, what if you did consider doing something like that? What woman will marry you just to help you advance your career that way?"

Then before Adam could respond, Brandon said, "Don't bother answering that. For a split second I forgot your last name is Garrison. You'll have all kind of greedy-minded, money-hungry women lining up at your door in droves. Is that the type of woman you'd want to be strapped to for the rest of your life?"

"It won't be for the rest of my life. I'm only looking at one year, possibly two. I want a woman who'll agree to my terms. We can get a divorce at the end of that time."

Brandon took a sip of his wine and asked, "And where do you intend to find such a woman?"

Adam shrugged. "I don't know. Do you have any ideas?"

Brandon chuckled and said the first name that came to his mind. "What about Paula Franklin?"

Adam glared at him. "Don't even think it."

Paula had first made a play for Parker a few years ago and when Parker hadn't shown her any interest, she had moved on to Stephen. Stephen had avoided her worse than Parker had, and she'd finally turned her sights on Adam, determined to hook up with a Garrison.

Adam had been forewarned about Paula from Parker and Stephen and hadn't been surprised when she had shown up at the club one night, ready to make a play for him and willing to do just about anything to succeed. When he had refused her advances, she had all but stalked him for a few weeks until he had threatened her with possible harassment charges.

Brandon gazed at him thoughtfully for a minute and then smiled and said, "Okay then, what about Lauryn Lowes?"

Adam gave Brandon a look that said he'd lost his mind. "Straight-laced Lauryn Lowes?"

Brandon ignored the look and said, "Yes, that's the one. You have to admit she's a picture of propriety, something those older, conservative members would want in a wife for you, so consider it a plus. And she's not bad-looking, either."

Brandon's words got Adam to thinking. "Lauryn Lowes."

Brandon stood and clapped Adam on the shoulder. "Yes, Lauryn Lowes. And while you're giving that some thought, I'm going to steal my girl from Stephen for a dance."

"Umm, that's interesting," Adam said, looking at him.

Brandon paused. "What is?"

"That you consider Cassie *your girl*. If she's your

girl then why is she leaving town tomorrow to return to the Bahamas?"

Brandon frowned. "She said she needed to go. What was I supposed to do? Hold her hostage? The Bahamas is her home, Adam, and she doesn't want to live anywhere else. She told me that a few days after we met."

"Have you given her a reason to change her mind?" Adam asked. "Maybe it's all been for show and you really don't care about her as much as I assumed you did. But if I cared for a woman, I mean really cared for one—although mind you, I don't—I would do whatever it took to make sure we were together, and nothing, not even the Atlantic Ocean, would be able to keep us apart." Before Brandon could say anything, Adam got out the chair and walked away.

Brandon took that same chair and sat, thinking about what Adam had said and his mind began racing. Although Cassie never said she loved him, a part of him had always felt that she did whenever they made love. She would always give herself to him, totally and completely.

And although he had never told her how he felt, he knew in his heart that he loved her, as well. He loved her and he wanted her, but he didn't want her to be with him in Miami if she wasn't going to be happy. Besides, her hotel was in the islands. It wasn't like she could fly over there every day for work.

He suddenly rolled his eyes when a thought flickered through his mind and he wondered why he hadn't thought of it before. He took a few moments to consider the idea, evaluate the possibility and then decided he would make it work. He laughed out loud, pretty pleased with himself.

"What's wrong with you?"

Brandon looked into Stephen's concerned face. Instead of answering he glanced around and asked, "Where's Cassie?"

"She's still out there dancing," Stephen responded, sitting down at the table. "Another song came on and this guy asked her to dance."

"And you let her?" Brandon asked, actually feeling a muscle tick in his jaw.

The sharp tone of his voice actually surprised Stephen. "Was I supposed to stop her or something?" When Brandon didn't respond, Stephen asked, "What's going on, Brandon?"

Brandon searched the dance crowd for a glimpse of Cassie. He saw her dancing to a slow song in another man's arms.

"Brandon?"

He glanced across the table at Stephen. "What?"

"I asked what's wrong with you?"

Brandon stood again. "Nothing's wrong with me. In fact at this moment everything is right with me. I think I'll go dance with Cassie."

Stephen shook his head, hiding his grin. "She's already dancing with someone."

"Too bad."

Like a man on a mission, Brandon crossed the room and tapped the man dancing with Cassie on the shoulder. The man turned and glared at Brandon, but instead of saying anything, he graciously moved away.

As soon as he did so, Brandon took hold of Cassie's hand and pulled her into his arms.

She glanced up at him and smiled. "The song is almost over so you didn't have to cut in, Brandon."

"Yes, I did."

"Why?"

"Because I didn't like the thought of another man touching you."

This was the first time she'd ever witnessed Brandon in a possessive mood and she made a half-hearted attempt at a chuckle. "And why would that bother you?"

"Because it does."

"Why?"

The song had ended and when others began returning to their tables, he took a firm hold of Cassie's hand and said, "Come on, let's take a walk."

They went outside and moments later they walked down a group of steps that led to the beach. Cassie paused long enough to remove her sandals. Her heart was beating fast and furious within her chest. Why had Brandon gotten all possessive and jealous all of a sudden? Could it mean that he cared for her more than she'd thought? A degree of hope stirred within her chest.

She decided to break the silence surrounding them. The only sound was the waves hitting the shoreline. "Estate is a very nice club."

Brandon stopped walking and she did likewise. She looked up at him and the bright lights from all the businesses on the beach lit his features. He was staring at her, his dark gaze intense. "I didn't bring you out here to talk about Adam's club," he said.

She looked away for a moment, across the span of the Atlantic Ocean, trying to maintain her composure. When she turned back to him, glancing up at him through her lashes, she asked, "Then what did you bring me out here to talk about, Brandon?"

For a brief moment Brandon couldn't speak. All he could do was stare at Cassie while his throat was constricted. Slowly expelling a deep breath, he said, "Our feelings for each other."

She met his gaze. "Our feelings for each other?" she repeated.

"Yes. I want to know where do you see our relationship going after you leave here tomorrow?"

As far as Cassie was concerned, the question he asked wasn't a difficult one to answer. "Nowhere."

Brandon tried to ignore the sharp pain that touched his chest. "And why do you think that?"

"Why would I not think that?" she responded in an irritated tone. "You've never said anything about continuing a relationship with me."

She was right. He hadn't. "I was afraid to," he said honestly.

She met his gaze. "Afraid? Why?"

"I knew what you told me weeks ago about how much you loved your homeland and not ever wanting to leave the island again to live anywhere else. I knew I could never take you away from that so I couldn't see a future for us. I was giving in to our demise too easily. But now I know what my heart is saying."

She studied his intense features before asking in a soft voice. "And what is your heart saying, Brandon?"

He took hold of her hand and brought her closer to

him and then placed that same hand on his chest and over his heart. "Listen."

She felt the gentle, timely thump beneath her hand and then heard him when he said, "It's a continuous beat that's saying over and over again, I, Brandon Jarrett Washington, love Cassie Sinclair-Garrison, with all my heart, soul and mind. Don't you hear it, sweetheart?"

Cassie fought back the tears that threatened to fall. "Yes, I can hear it now."

He smiled. "And do you also hear the beats that are saying that I want to marry you, make you my wife and give you my babies."

She chuckled. "No, I don't hear those ones."

"Well the beats are there, drumming it out loud and clear. What do you think? And before you answer I want you to know that I have no intention of asking you to leave the island to move here to accomplish any of those things."

She lifted a brow. "You're anticipating a long-distance marriage?"

He heard the disappointment in her voice. She was probably remembering the sort of absences her parents had endured. "Not hardly. I plan for us to live together in the Bahamas as man and wife and I will use my private plane to commute to Miami each day. It's less than a thirty-minute flight. Some people spend more time than that on the highways to get to work."

Her heart was filled with even more love when she said, "You would do that for me?"

He smiled and took his thumb to touch the dimple in her chin. "I would do that for us. I love you and I am determined to make things work." He then leaned down and captured her mouth with his and she shuddered under the mastery of his kiss. Moments later, when he pulled back, she was left quivering.

"Are you with me, sweetheart?"

She reached up and placed a palm to his cheek and smiled. "All the way."

He tightened his hold on her hand and tugged her in another direction. "Where are you taking me?" she asked, almost out of breath."

"Home. And I think we need to cancel your flight in the morning. My heart is beating out plenty of other words that you need to listen to, so I think you need to stick around."

Cassie smiled, totally satisfied that her heart belonged only to this man, and that it would always be that way. "Yes, I think I will stick around for another week after all, especially since my heart has a few special beats of its own, as well, Mr. Washington. And they are beating just for you."

* * * * *

SECRETS OF THE TYCOON'S BRIDE

BY
EMILIE ROSE

Dear Reader,

This book was extra special for me because it gave hubby and me the perfect excuse to take our first real adults-only vacation in years. Research! We left our four sons and the dog behind—the boys didn't miss us but the dog did :)—and travelled to South Beach. We even took a short cruise—our first—to the Bahamas.

South Beach was nothing like the laid-back North Carolina beaches I usually visit, but I did my best to give you a slice of the atmosphere. So when you get to the part about South Beach coffee shops selling condoms, they do!

I hope you can kick back, imagine the sand beneath your toes and palm fronds stirring above your head in a brisk ocean breeze and enjoy Lauryn and Adam's story.

Best,

Emilie

Emilie Rose lives in North Carolina with her college sweetheart husband and four sons. Writing is Emilie's third (and hopefully her last) career. She's managed a medical office and run a home day care, neither of which offers half as much satisfaction as plotting happy endings. Her hobbies include quilting, gardening and cooking (especially cheesecake). Her favourite TV shows include *ER, CSI* and Discovery Channel's medical programs. Emilie's a country music fan, because she can find an entire book in almost any song.

Letters can be mailed to:
Emilie Rose
PO Box 20145
Raleigh, NC 27619
USA
E-mail: EmilieRoseC@aol.com

To my husband for never saying no. Heaven knows I've given you plenty of reasons and opportunities to do so. You spoil me rotten. Don't think I haven't noticed.

One

Lauryn Lowes would make him a perfect wife because he didn't love her and wasn't attracted to her.

Hell, Adam Garrison realized, he barely knew her.

Their bi-weekly meetings since she'd started working for him seven months ago had never allowed time for get-to-know-you chatter. She worked days when the club was closed, and he worked nights when Estate was open. He knew little about her except what he'd read on her job application.

A tap on his open door revealed the woman in question. "You wanted to see me?"

"Come in, Lauryn. Close the door. Have a seat."

She did as he instructed and perched on the edge of the visitor chair in front of his desk.

According to his lawyer, who happened to be Adam's best friend and someone whose judgment Adam trusted, Lauryn was the perfect wife candidate.

Adam's leather chair creaked as he leaned back to make his own assessment. Lauryn wasn't bad-looking. Bland. No make-up. Pale-blond hair which she always kept pinned up. An intelligent and independent worker. Otherwise he never would have hired her to handle his nightclub's multimillion-dollar books.

"Is something wrong? This isn't our usual meeting day." Lauryn pushed the narrow rectangles of her tortoiseshell glasses up her straight nose, and then with slender, ringless fingers adjusted the longish skirt of her boring navy suit.

He'd never noticed her hands before. But then he'd never considered those hands touching him. Intimately. Her short, unpainted nails were a far cry from the lacquered claws the majority of women in his life preferred.

Besides a manicure, she'd need new clothing to carry off this charade. Maybe contacts. Better shoot for a complete makeover. Otherwise no one would believe he'd chosen her out of all the fashion models and celebrities who frequented Estate and/or his bed.

He had his pick of women. Just not the type he needed for this assignment. The council already considered him a playboy. His female equivalent would not help his cause. Lauryn was far from a party girl. If she'd dated at all in the past months no one on the staff knew it. He'd asked. Discreetly, of course.

She shifted in her chair, reminding him he hadn't answered her question. That was something else he'd always admired about her. She knew how to be quiet instead of chattering endlessly.

"Nothing's wrong, Lauryn. In fact, I'd like to offer you a raise and a…promotion of sorts." He punctuated that with what he hoped would be a reassuring smile. Whether for her or for himself, he couldn't say.

God knows he had reservations about this plan. He was

only thirty and he *liked* being single. Between witnessing his parents' far-from-perfect union and his front-row seat to the nightly dating safaris at the club, he'd never planned to marry for any reason, but he couldn't see any other way to achieve his goals.

He wanted a bigger stake in the family business and there was only one way short of murdering his two older brothers to get it. He had to gain their respect. His father had died unexpectedly in June, and here it was the first of November, and Parker and Stephen still hadn't given Adam more responsibility in Garrison, Inc., because they didn't take him seriously. Frustration burned Adam's stomach.

Lauryn's smooth brow furrowed. "I'm confused. I'm Estate's only accountant. How can I get a promotion? Are you planning to hire an assistant for me? Because I assure you, Mr. Garrison, I can handle the workload. I don't need help."

"Adam," he corrected not for the first time. She never relaxed around him. In fact, she always seemed on edge, and he didn't know why. People—women in particular—liked him. More than one reviewer had attributed Estate's popularity to Adam's charm. He knew how to work a crowd, how to make guests feel welcome and want to return.

Of course, he'd never tried to charm Lauryn Lowes. She was an employee and that was a line he'd never crossed. But he would today.

"The president of the Miami Business Council is retiring next year. As you may have heard, it's a pretty conservative group."

She nodded.

"I've been an active member for years, but the council's not willing to entertain the idea of a single guy—especially one who runs a scandalous South Beach nightclub—being in charge no matter how qualified he might be."

"You mean *you* want to run for president?"

The surprise in her voice stung like salt in a fresh wound. "Yes. And the only way for me to have a chance at that nomination is to become the stable, settled guy they require. I won't give up Estate. That means I need to acquire a wife."

Her look of confusion grew. "What does that have to do with me?"

"You're the perfect candidate."

She blinked once, twice, a third time. "To be your *wife?*"

"Yes."

She sat back in the chair, her posture stiffer than usual. After a few moments an uncertain smile wobbled on her lips. "I—I— You're joking. Right?"

Nice lips, he noted. Pale pink. No lipstick. Not collagen enhanced.

Natural. That's it. Lauryn's a natural.

Too bad that would have to change.

"No." He leaned forward and pulled the file pertaining to this merger from the stack on the side of his desk. "Brandon Washington—you've met my attorney—has drawn up the necessary paperwork. I'll pay you five hundred thousand per year for two years plus reasonable living expenses. After that we'll quietly divorce. We'll have a contract and a pre-nuptial agreement. What's yours stays yours including any gifts I buy you. What's mine stays mine."

Extracting the relevant documents, he pushed the pages across the polished wood surface toward her. She didn't take them. "You're welcome to have your attorney look over the agreement."

Tightening her grip on the arms of the chair, she eyed the papers like she would a hungry gator. "You actually expect me to agree to this…proposition?"

"You'll be paid a million dollars to do nothing for two years. Why wouldn't you accept?"

"Because I don't love you?"

A little surprised by her reluctance, he shrugged. He could think of several dozen women who'd jump at this chance, but they weren't the type he needed.

"I don't love you, either, but it's an advantageous match for each of us and a sound business decision. You'll move into my loft and I'll buy you a new car. Maybe a Mercedes or a Volvo wagon. We need to give the impression we'd like to start a family soon."

Eyes wide with shock, she made a choking sound. "A family?"

"We won't of course, but we need to play the part."

"Part?" she echoed.

Lauryn's quick grasp of details was one of the things he'd liked about her at that first interview and in subsequent meetings. But she wasn't picking up quickly now. He stifled his impatience. "The picture of domestic bliss. Stable. Settled. Rooted in the community."

She shook her head as if bewildered. "I'm sorry. I just can't wrap my brain around this. You're seriously asking me to marry you?"

"Yes."

"Mr. Garrison—*Adam*—" Her lips stretched in a fleeting and clearly forced smile. "I'm not the woman for this…position."

"I think you are. You're poised, articulate and conservative. You're exactly what—who—I need, Lauryn."

Although she flushed at his compliments, the words didn't ease the starch from her spine. Biting her bottom lip between straight white teeth, she rose. Her fingers knotted so tightly at her waist that her knuckles gleamed white in the overhead fluorescent light.

"I am extremely flattered by your, um…proposal, but I'm afraid I'll have to decline."

"Lauryn—"

She gasped and worry pleated her brow. "My refusal isn't going to cost me my job, is it?"

"Of course not. What kind of jerk do you think I am? But if you marry me you'll be too busy doing whatever it is South Beach socialites do to put in a forty-hour workweek here."

He came around the desk and stopped just inches from her. For the first time he noticed her scent. She smelled like the night-blooming vines growing on his condo neighbor's patio with an additional kick of something spicy and alluring mixed in. "Consider it a two-year paid vacation. Pampering, shopping—"

"But I enjoy my job. And I like working. I'm sorry, but no thank you. I'm sure you can find someone else who—"

"I don't want anyone else. I want you."

She snapped to attention at his adamant tone and lifted a trembling hand to push her glasses up the bridge of her nose. Adam intercepted, curling his fingers around hers. A spark ignited on contact. He blamed it on the knowledge he was crossing the employee/employer line by touching her and invading her space. Always a risky proposition in this litigious age.

He removed her glasses with his other hand. She had extraordinary eyes. Brighter than olives. Darker than grass. The exact shade of the waters off Miami's coast.

His pulse quickened and his mouth moistened.

Because of what's at stake, he told himself.

He sure as hell wasn't attracted to his mousy bookkeeper. But not being repelled by her was good. Considering…

"I'd be a good husband." His voice came out huskier than

intended. He cleared his throat and continued. "I guarantee you'll be satisfied."

A beat later her eyes widened. "You're saying we'd sleep together?"

"Maybe not sleep. I like my space. I have a study we can convert into a bedroom for you. You'll have privacy when you need it. But for appearances' sake this must appear to be a normal marriage in every way."

"But you'd expect sex. With me." She didn't sound as if she relished the idea and that pricked his pride. He was good in bed, dammit. He'd been perfecting his technique since he was sixteen. And he never left a woman unsatisfied.

"Definitely. We'll be together for two years. That's a long time to be celibate. Infidelity would negate the purpose of the union by showing I couldn't be trusted."

She gaped for a full ten seconds and then yanked her hand free, plucked her glasses from his grasp and backed toward the door. "No. I can't. I won't."

She was turning him down? When had a woman ever turned him down? Hell, when had he ever even had to voice an invitation? Usually he cocked an eyebrow and his choice for the night rushed forward to do whatever he asked. *Whatever* he wanted.

He had to change Lauryn's mind. She was the right woman for the job—an outsider who wouldn't spill all his secrets to the very community of people he was trying to fool. She was smart enough to pull this off, and the timing was too tight for him to search for another candidate. The final slate of business council nominees would be proposed in six months. That meant he needed to prove his stability *now*.

"Name your price, Lauryn."

"I don't have a price. And I think I'd better go."

"I'll call you tomorrow."

"*Don't,* Mr. Garrison. Don't call. Not about…this."

This wasn't going well. "Besides the money, think of the advantages—"

"Of selling my body?"

"—of being my wife. Of being one of the Garrisons of Miami. Doors will open for you."

She gurgled a disgusted sound. "I don't care about getting into A-list nightclubs. I'm not even awake when they're open."

She tilted her head and appraised him through narrowed eyes. The angle revealed the pulse fluttering rapidly at the base of her slender neck. Her ivory skin looked smooth not sun-baked or covered with sprayed-on tan. Was she as pale all over?

"I suppose it's because of your family's wealth and power that you believe you can buy anyone or anything. Like a wife. Or the presidency of the business council."

Damn. "Lauryn—"

She held up a hand. "You should stop now. Before this becomes harassment. Surely your attorney warned you about that?"

Oh yeah. Brandon had warned him in the same breath he'd insisted Lauryn was The One. That warning was the only reason Adam hadn't planted a hot kiss on Lauryn's lips to prove to her that he could please her in bed. But he would never convince her that the marriage could work when she was in this frame of mind. Time for a strategic withdrawal.

"Let me remind you of the confidentiality agreement you signed as part of your employment contract. Anything related to my business, and that includes my strategy to win the Business Council nomination, does not leave this room."

"No one would believe me if I told them Adam Garrison tried to buy a wife. But don't worry. I won't blab unless you make that necessary." She hustled out, closing the door behind her.

Adam shoved a hand through his hair, expelled a frustrated breath and dropped back into his desk chair. He was used to women chasing him—not running from him as if he'd suddenly announced he had the avian flu.

As one of the heirs to the Garrison hospitality and entertainment empire he was a great catch. All the society columns and his tax returns said so. Not only did his family have deep pockets, but Adam's personal investments had exponentially increased his net worth. Add in his recently inherited fifteen percent of Garrison, Inc. and saying he was financially comfortable would be a gross understatement.

And he'd seen a mirror. He wasn't ugly.

So why wasn't Lauryn biting?

There must be something she wanted. Something he could use for leverage.

All he had to do was find it.

The man had to be crazy.

Lauryn placed her purse, car keys and glasses on the kitchen counter of her minuscule apartment and then headed for the bedroom, tugging the pins from her hair as she went.

A marriage of convenience.

What was this? A romance novel? She read them. But she didn't *live* them.

Admittedly, she'd moved to Florida specifically to befriend Adam Garrison.

But she didn't want to *marry* him.

He was a known womanizer who dangled a different celebrity or socialite from his arm almost every night. And with his longish inky dark hair, lady-slayer smile and devastating blue eyes, he invariably chose women equally as gorgeous as himself.

But good looks, she'd learned the hard way, were superficial and sometimes covered an ugly personality. They definitely attracted the wrong kinds of attention, which was why she'd quit flaunting her curves and started dressing to fade into the background.

She removed her suit, returned it to the hanger, toed off her pumps and placed them on the shoe rack.

"Huh. He says he likes his space, but I'll bet he never goes to bed alone," she muttered to herself as she pulled on a pair of faded sweats and an old T-shirt of her father's. "He probably serves his women's orgasms with a cab fare chaser."

As an accountant she couldn't help but consider all she could accomplish with a million dollars, starting with replenishing the bank account she'd depleted to move cross country and take a job with Adam's club—a job she'd specifically targeted when her research revealed he was the new deedholder to her family's estate.

But marriage? No way. She'd had one disastrous marriage that began for all the wrong reasons. It wasn't an experience she ever intended repeating.

Not even as a business deal.

A very lucrative business deal.

Forget it.

She padded barefoot to the kitchen, withdrew last night's Chinese takeout leftovers and popped them in the microwave. The scent of Hunan shrimp mingled with citrus in the air as she peeled an orange to go with her dinner.

If you lived with him you'd get to know him well.

Well enough to convince him let her pry up a few closet floorboards in the fifteen-million-dollar estate he'd bought eighteen months ago?

Why had he spent a fortune on a house if he wasn't going to live there? She'd thought maybe he intended to remodel first, but a check at the courthouse revealed no building permits had been issued prior to her arrival, and as far as she could tell with her frequent drive-bys nothing beyond routine mainte-nance had been done to the house since her move to Florida.

A lawn-care company groomed the lush yard, and she'd seen a pool-service company's van in the circular driveway. She thought she'd spotted tennis courts on the other side of the stone and wrought iron fence but the bougainvillea hedge was too thick to be certain, and the exclusive Sunset Island wasn't exactly the kind of neighborhood where you could climb fences to peer over the top without getting arrested.

The estate wasn't within walking distance of the club like Adam's condo, but even in heavy traffic and with all the South Beach road construction the commute would take less than twenty minutes.

While the food heated she set the table. Her mother—her heart hitched—her *adoptive* mother, she corrected, had always made a big production of setting the table. It was one of the many things she and Lauryn had done together. All that had changed eleven months ago when Lauryn's father died and her "mother" had shared the letters.

Letters that had been locked in a safety-deposit box for decades.

Letters from her father's former lover.

Letters that had upended Lauryn's life and sent her on a three-thousand-mile quest to find the woman who'd loved her enough to have her but not enough to keep her.

Adrianna Laurence.

Her birthmother.

How could her father have lied? Lauryn asked herself for the billionth time. And how could her mother have let him?

The timer beeped. On autopilot Lauryn retrieved the carton, scraped the contents onto a plate and pulled a Diet Coke with lime from the fridge.

Hadn't her father realized what a shock it would be for Lauryn to suddenly discover she wasn't who she'd thought she was for the past twenty-six years?

Hadn't he known finding out she was the by-product of her father's affair with a Miami Beach socialite would make Lauryn doubt everything she'd once held as truth?

Why hadn't he guessed that finding out he'd married his deceased buddy's pregnant wife only to provide a mother for his infant daughter would make Lauryn question the very fabric of her parents' marriage? Or that discovering the child growing in her "mother's" rounded tummy in all those pictures wasn't Lauryn at all, but a baby boy who had died before taking his first breath?

Why couldn't her father have told her about her birthmother earlier? Before Adrianna had died. If he'd done so Lauryn would have had a chance to meet the woman who'd given her life and ask questions. She could have heard her mother's voice, seen her face and learned about her parents' relationship. What attracted them? What separated them? What had driven Adrianna to give her baby away and why had she died so young?

Even Lauryn's name was part of the mystery. *Laur*ence. *Laur*yn. According to Lauryn's adoptive mother, Adrianna Laurence had insisted on the name. Was it because she wanted Lauryn to find her one day? Or because she couldn't bear not being a part of her daughter's life in some small way?

Lauryn might never discover the reason, but it wouldn't be from lack of trying on her part.

If her father had told the truth then Lauryn wouldn't be forced to use subterfuge to find her answers.

Answers that, according to the letters, might be found in a diary hidden in a secret compartment beneath the closet floorboards of the estate Adam Garrison now owned.

Were the diaries still there? Or had someone besides her mother known about them and removed them from their hiding place long ago? From Lauryn's research she knew that her grandmother, the last surviving member of the Laurence clan, had died shortly before Adam bought the property.

Doors will open for you, Adam had said.

The only doors Lauryn wanted to open were the ones to that house. Her birthmother's house. But she couldn't just blurt out her odd request. If she did and Adam turned her down, then she'd have nowhere else to turn, and she'd never have her questions answered.

And so the deceit began. She'd moved from California to Florida planning to befriend her new boss and gain his trust. She'd believed that once she did that, once she'd proven she wasn't some flake with outlandish ideas, he'd be more likely to grant her bizarre request to pry up a few floorboards.

Only it hadn't worked out the way she'd hoped. She and Adam only saw each other in a business setting at biweekly meetings. There was nothing remotely personal in discussing the club's bottom line and there were always other employees in the vicinity.

And now…

She stared at her steaming dinner with absolutely no appetite.

Now, Adam's crazy plan and her refusal to participate in it had probably ruined any chance of friendship or trust ever developing. She'd be lucky if she escaped this situation with her job.

She'd have to find a way—short of marriage—to make amends or kiss her quest for answers goodbye.

Two

Getting out of the building for an hour on Friday appealed to Lauryn about as much as winning the lottery.

With the club operating from 11:00 p.m. to 5:00 a.m., Adam didn't usually make appearances in the Estate offices until late afternoon. While he slept, a hive of office staff, custodians and food and beverage restockers did their jobs to prepare for the night ahead. Nevertheless, Lauryn had jumped at every sound this morning and looked forward to taking the bus to her favorite Dolphin Mall deli and spending a relaxing hour not worrying about Adam Garrison's bizarre proposition.

The clock ticked noon. *Time to escape.* Tension drained from her knotted shoulders. She pulled her purse from her desk and took her usual circuit through the club. With the lights turned low, the antebellum structure that had begun life as a French-owned casino looked as if it, too, were sleeping.

Later this afternoon the building would awaken as the technicians tested every speaker and bulb and set up whatever stage requirements tonight's entertainers demanded.

The club was designed around a "night out at home" theme, and each room in the vast building had been set up with trendy leather sofas and chairs arranged in conversational nooks. There were multiple bars and dance floors on both levels, each having its own color scheme. State-of-the-art lighting and sound systems and top-notch live entertainment kept the place packed to its twenty-five-hundred-person capacity with an A-list crowd every night. Or so she'd heard. She hadn't been a customer yet and probably never would be since she'd given up late-night partying years ago and she didn't fit the guest profile.

She paused to caress the carved newel post of the grand staircase sweeping up to the second floor. This was her favorite part of Estate. She'd always thought it resembled a stage from a Hollywood movie set.

Thinking of Hollywood reminded her of California and home.

Home. And the mother she'd inadvertently hurt when Susan Lowes had revealed Lauryn's true parentage.

Way to go, Lauryn. Shoot the messenger.

Lauryn hadn't meant to imply Susan had been anything less than a perfect mother. But Lauryn had questions about her heritage. Questions Susan couldn't answer. And then there was the anger. Anger toward her father and Susan for withholding the truth. Anger toward Lauryn's birthmother for rejecting her without even giving her a chance to fit into her world.

Shaking off her unproductive emotions, Lauryn circled back toward the employee exit, shoved open the side door and stepped into the Miami sunshine and balmy November day.

The first thing she saw once her eyes adjusted to the brightness was Adam Garrison leaning against a silver BMW convertible parked by the curb.

Her stomach dropped like a cruise ship anchor and her nerves knotted like a snarled line. So much for avoiding him after yesterday's fiasco. She hoped he wasn't waiting for her.

Reluctantly, she made her way down the sidewalk. She had to walk past him to get to the bus stop a block away. Lauryn had quickly learned that driving in South Beach was a disaster, not due to the traffic but because of the parking. Specifically, the lack thereof. So she relied on the bus system to get to and from work most of the time.

"Good afternoon, Lauryn." Adam straightened as she neared.

At several inches over six feet, he looked lean and athletic in sharply creased chocolate slacks that accentuated his height and a cream silk T-shirt that emphasized the breadth of his shoulders. A breeze ruffled his dark hair, which always looked in need of a trim. She'd bet he paid a fortune for that casually unkempt look. Thankfully, his designer sunglasses covered his gorgeous make-Jell-O-of-her-kneecaps blue eyes.

She was ashamed to admit that in the beginning she'd had a bit of a crush on her boss, but then stories of his swinging bachelor lifestyle and short attention span with women had eroded those feelings. She'd been there, done that and didn't ever want to live that kind of superficial, self-absorbed life again.

Adam was gorgeous, but good-looking men were a dime a dozen in South Beach. Not that she was shopping for one. You couldn't walk down the sidewalk without passing a bare-chested guy showing off his tan and pecs—either of which may or may not be real here in a city where artificial beauty was as common as a cold.

But most of those guys didn't make her pulse blip unevenly.

And none of them had proposed.

"Good afternoon, Mr.—Adam. Did you need me for something?"

Please say no.

"Lunch."

Not the answer she wanted. "I...have plans."

He frowned. "A date?"

She hesitated and debated lying. But she couldn't. Her presence in Miami was already complicated by too many half-truths. "No. I was going to the mall."

"I have a better idea. Get in." He opened the passenger-side door.

Would he fire her if she refused? Not something she wanted to find out. She eased into the leather seat and fastened her safety belt. Adam slid into the driver's seat, started the engine and merged into the Washington Avenue traffic.

"I only have an hour," she reminded him.

"Not a problem. Besides, you're with the boss. Who's going to report you?" He drove north for a couple of miles and then cut through to North Bay and turned back south. Seconds later he pulled up to the curb in front of an exclusive restaurant overlooking Biscayne Bay—one she'd never been to because A, she couldn't afford it, and B, she couldn't get a reservation even if she wanted one.

He climbed from the car and tossed the keys to the valet. Another uniformed employee opened Lauryn's door, handed her out and escorted her to Adam waiting on the sidewalk as if she were a prized possession. Or a ditz who couldn't be trusted next to the busy street.

"Good afternoon, Mr. Garrison," the hostess greeted him

the second they stepped through the doors. Her cool gaze assessed and dismissed Lauryn in two seconds flat. "Your table is ready."

Adam motioned for Lauryn to precede him, but then followed so closely she could feel his heat and his gaze on her back. She hoped her pin-striped navy skirt didn't make her butt look big. And then she mentally kicked herself.

His opinion of your butt is irrelevant.

Conscious of the curious stares and her department-store clothing so different from the rest of the clientele's designer wear, Lauryn followed the hostess to a waterfront table on the outside deck, took a seat beneath the umbrella and accepted a menu. A breeze teased strands of her hair from the knot at her nape to tickle her cheeks.

She looked up and directly into Adam's blue eyes. He'd removed his sunglasses. As always, the intensity and intelligence in his gaze made her breath hitch.

Tension invaded her limbs as she waited for him to bring up the proposal because there was no doubt that's why he'd brought her here. She hadn't changed her mind about marrying him, although the idea had monopolized her thoughts and cost her a decent night's sleep. Lunch at an exclusive restaurant wouldn't sway her.

What kind of man coolly plotted to buy a wife, sleep with her for two years even though he didn't love her and then discard her and walk away? But then Adam probably hadn't loved any of the women who'd creased his sheets.

Having been burned by love, Lauryn could see the advantages of avoiding the unpredictable emotion, but call her a romantic sap; she actually wanted to find her soul mate one day.

She ducked her head and fussed with her napkin. She'd thought her parents had been soul mates, but discovering the letters and the lies had made her question every tender gesture she'd witnessed over the years. What had been real? What had been staged? Had they fallen for each other after the convoluted coverup of Lauryn's adoption and the premature death of Susan's baby like Susan claimed? Or was that also a lie?

After the waiter took their orders Adam gave Lauryn his full attention. His gaze roamed her features as if cataloging each one. "You moved here from California. Which part?"

Small talk. She could do small talk. Although it had been so long since she'd been on a date she was probably rusty. Was this a date? She hoped not. "Northern."

"Why Florida?"

She'd had enough doors slammed in her face to know she certainly couldn't blurt out the whole truth. Adam belonged to the same upper class who'd closed ranks and shut her out when she'd come here ten months ago to ask questions about one of their own. No one would confirm that Adrianna had given birth to an illegitimate child, and no one would tell Lauryn how her birthmother died. In fact, conversations ended pretty quickly as soon as she mentioned Adrianna Laurence's name.

Adrianna's obituary hadn't listed a cause of death or even an organization to which one could donate in lieu of flowers as a clue. She'd only been thirty-six, ten years older than Lauryn was now. If there was a ticking time bomb in Lauryn's genes she would like to know.

"My father used to be stationed at Tyndall Air Force Base. I grew up hearing stories about Florida, the Everglades and the beaches. After he died I decided to check them out for myself."

"And yet you settled on the east coast rather than panhandle."

"Better job opportunities," she replied and hoped he'd drop the subject. He'd been the only job opportunity she'd pursued, and she considered it an amazing stroke of luck that his previous accountant had quit to stay at home with her new baby around the same time Lauryn had needed her job.

"California's loss is my gain." He accompanied the words with a smile she'd only seen in the South Florida Album section of the newspaper, but those grainy pictures in no way had the same lung-emptying impact as the real deal. No wonder flocks of women fell at his feet. She felt almost dizzy.

She transferred her gaze to the islands across the bay. The Sunset Islands were a tiny cluster of outrageously priced real estate. Could you see Adam's other home—her birth-mother's family estate—from here? She counted until she found the correct channel to mark the way to the waterfront property. Lauryn had considered renting a boat and trying to get a better view of the house from the bay side, but the only thing she knew about boats was that they made her seasick.

The man in front of her held the answers. "Didn't I hear someone say you own a house on one of those islands?"

Adam nodded. "Ricco?"

What did the club's booking agent have to do with the estate? But he wasn't her source. She'd discovered that tidbit during a search of the county records, but if she told Adam that she'd come across as a stalker. Which she was…sort of. And she didn't want to get Ricco in trouble. "I don't remember."

"I bought the house at auction the same way I bought the building now housing Estate and a few other properties. Bargain prices. Good investments."

"And yet you don't live on the island."

"I use the Sunset estate to house certain VIPs who are performing at the club. The ones who prefer privacy to hotels."

That explained the maintenance crews. "I didn't know that."

He reached across the table and covered her hand with his. A zing shot up her arm—the same kind of tempting tingle she'd experienced yesterday when he'd held her hand. Lauryn was no stranger to sexual attraction, but she'd learned the hard way to ignore it because sex inevitably led to complications. Complications she didn't need.

She tried to pull away, but Adam's grip tightened around her wrist. He turned her hand over, used his other hand to pry open her clenched fist and then drew on her palm with his fingertip. The impact hit her libido like a car bomb. Shockwaves plowed through her and shattered defenses she'd thought unbreachable. She gulped and squeezed her knees against the warmth gathering between her thighs.

"I apologize for springing my proposal on you so abruptly yesterday. I realize it's a pretty radical idea."

"No kidding," she croaked and tugged her hand to no avail.

"You don't know me well enough to know I always give one hundred ten percent to any endeavor. I can and will be a great husband." He stroked up and down between each of her fingers. Her pulse bounded like popcorn in a popper. No doubt he felt it beneath the thumb he feathered over the inside of her wrist. "We'll get to know each other better. Date a few times."

"I—I don't think that's a good idea. And it won't change my answer."

"You can't deny there's chemistry between us."

His deep, velvety tone immediately made her think of

dark nights, tangled sheets, a lack of clothing and his hands on her skin.

Heat flushed her from the inside out. How long had it been since she'd had really good sex? Or sex, period, for that matter.

Did he really feel the attraction, too, or was he just saying what he needed to say to close this deal? God knows she'd fallen victim to plenty of smooth-talking guys who'd made her feel like the most important person on the planet until they had what they wanted. But then she'd been known to use guys, too, to get a rise out of her father.

She scanned Adam's face, noting the dusky color on his cheekbones and the way he breathed through slightly parted lips.

Adam Garrison attracted to *her?* Impossible. She'd seen his usual bimbos and she didn't even come close to the models and starlets he dated, especially the way she dressed these days.

"You're my boss. Office relationships always turn out badly—usually for the employee."

"They don't have to. Besides, you won't be working for me after the wedding," he enunciated very clearly and a tad too loud. Before she could figure out why he'd spoken that way a woman jerked to a halt behind him.

"Adam?" The lady could have been anywhere from fifty to a well-preserved seventy, but it was impossible to gauge by her tightly stretched skin.

Adam looked up and hesitated just the right amount of time before releasing Lauryn's hand and standing. "Good afternoon, Mrs. Ainsley. This is Lauryn Lowes. Lauryn, Helene Ainsley. She's on the board of practically every charitable foundation in Miami."

Helene Ainsley. The same woman who'd refused to come

to the door when Lauryn had knocked and asked the maid who answered for a moment of her mistress's time. The Ainsley estate was four doors down from the Laurence property, and even though Mrs. Ainsley was older, she or her children had probably known Adrianna Laurence.

"It's nice to meet you, Mrs. Ainsley." It would have been nicer ten months ago.

The woman looked from Adam to Lauryn through her nipped and tucked eyes. "Do we have news?"

Lauryn tensed and held her breath.

Adam sent a lingering look her way and then smiled tenderly before replying without breaking eye contact, "No news."

Good grief, the man should be an actor. His tone, expression and body language spoke the opposite more eloquently than words.

"I could have sworn I heard you say 'wedding.'"

Adam returned his attention to Mrs. Ainsley. "You could have. There have been a few weddings in the Garrison family lately. And of course, my sister Brittany is engaged."

But Mrs. Ainsley didn't believe him. Lauryn could see the curiosity in the woman's overstretched face. How smart of Adam to plant the seed—just in case he convinced Lauryn to say yes. Not that he would.

The woman's searching gaze focused on Lauryn. "Have we met, dear? You look familiar."

Lauryn's heart skipped a beat. Did she take after her mother? The only photos she'd found of Adrianna had been blurry black-and-white newspaper shots that made identifying specific features difficult, but Lauryn had inherited her father's coloring. Her mother had been a brunette. "No, ma'am."

"Are you quite sure? I never forget a face."

She yearned to blurt out the truth, but the consequences of handling this badly were too great. "I'm sure. I haven't met many people because I haven't lived in the area very long."

"Then we should remedy that. We're having a few friends over on Saturday. Perhaps you and Adam will join us for couples' tennis?"

The invitation stole Lauryn's breath.

Doors will open, Adam had said. Lauryn hadn't considered that those open doors would offer an opportunity to join her birthmother's social circle.

If she married Adam Garrison she'd be one of the Miami elite and closer to getting her answers than ever before. The idea tempted her more than it should.

"Lauryn?" he asked.

"I, um…I'm sorry. I don't play tennis." She'd been too busy being a rebellious teen to learn. Just one more reason to regret her misspent youth.

Helene turned back to Adam. "Then perhaps you'll bring Lauryn to cocktails on Monday evening. The club is closed then, isn't it?"

"We'd like that," Adam accepted without consulting Lauryn. But she didn't care about his high-handedness. He was going to get her into a house her mother had probably visited and introduce her to people her mother had probably known. While they were on the island maybe she could convince him to show her his place and she could walk her mother's path.

"Lovely. See you at eight." Mrs. Ainsley glided off with the grace of the queen.

Adam sat quickly, followed by the arrival of their meal. After the waiter departed Lauryn looked at her companion. "You're very sneaky."

A mischievous smile slanted his lips, making him look like

a bad boy inviting her to come out and play. The dormant rebel in Lauryn raised its head, but she quickly reined in her naughty urges. She'd given up her penchant for bad boys.

"I know what I want and I'm not ashamed to go after it. Helene is one of the biggest gossips in the Greater Miami area. By the time we announce our engagement it will be old news."

She gaped at him. "Need I remind you that I turned you down?"

"You'll change your mind." He lifted his wineglass in a silent toast. His eyes held a challenge. "Or I'll change it for you. We'll be good together, Lauryn. In bed and out."

Tendrils of desire wound through her. And that, Lauryn realized, was the crux of her dilemma. The answers she wanted were right at her fingertips, but only if she broke the promise she'd made to her father and herself before the ink on her annulment had dried.

Next time, she'd vowed, she'd marry for all the right reasons.

And the business alliance Adam proposed didn't even come close.

He almost had her.

Adam didn't know why the idea of drinks with the Ainsleys' stuffy crowd excited Lauryn, but he'd seen the flash of interest in her eyes and the heightened color on her cheeks earlier at lunch.

He rinsed the last of the shaving cream from his face, patted dry and then padded naked into his bedroom to dress for a Friday night at the club. He fed off the pulse of the music, the flash of the lights and the energy of Estate's guests. Knowing he provided a good time for hundreds of people each night and was financially rewarded for doing so filled him with satisfaction.

Work. He lived for it. Why couldn't his family—specifically his brothers—see that? But they viewed his life as one big party and treated him like a perpetual frat boy.

He made it halfway across the room before the mental image of Lauryn in his bed stalled his steps. Hell, he couldn't be attracted to her, could he? Before Brandon's suggestion, Adam had never had a sexual thought about his accountant. Or any employee, for that matter.

Lauryn had done nothing to light his fire. She was cool and withdrawn. She didn't flirt. Even though he'd spent an hour with her today, he didn't know any more about her than he had before lunch except that the smiles he used to make other women melt didn't affect Lauryn Lowes.

But he had to admit something happened when he touched her to quicken his pulse and heat his blood. Was his interest piqued solely because she'd said no?

Shaking his head to clear the image of her pale skin spread across his black sheets, he headed for his closet. Any anticipation he might feel for seeing her again could be attributed to moving closer toward his goal. The marriage would be strictly business. Not pleasure. Although he was beginning to suspect Lauryn had a good body beneath her shapeless clothing and that he could derive a great deal of pleasure from exploring it.

All right, so he wanted to see her naked, but that was only because he was curious to know what she was hiding and why.

And if she wanted to dip her toes in Miami Beach society, he'd lead her to the water even though he usually avoided such events like he'd avoid swimming through a school of jellyfish. You never knew when you might get stung.

Drinks at the Ainsleys' could include anywhere from a half-dozen to a hundred guests. Adam hoped like hell his mother wouldn't be there drinking herself into oblivion. Lauryn would get a dose of Bonita Garrison soon enough.

After the wedding he and Lauryn would have to attend some of the Sunday family dinners, but until then he didn't dare risk letting his mother's increasingly bitter barbs scare off Lauryn because he didn't have the time or inclination to search out another wife candidate. The nominating committee had already begun their search.

Guilt nagged at Adam as he dragged on a silk shirt. Finding out her husband of thirty-eight years had a twenty-seven-year-old illegitimate daughter from a long-term and on-going affair couldn't have been easy for his mother. But that was no excuse for pickling her liver by living in a bottle of booze. His mother's drinking had been a problem for as long as Adam could remember, and with it came the lies and excuses to cover the things she'd done or forgotten to do. But the situation had worsened since the reading of the will and the open acknowledgment of Cassie, his father's illegitimate daughter by his Bahamian lover.

Adam made a note to hire a full-time driver for his mother. He couldn't risk letting her get behind the wheel of a car. And he needed to talk to his siblings about drying her out before she killed herself.

He stepped into his trousers and pulled them over his bare butt. He hadn't known about his halfsister, Cassie, but he had known about his father's affair for years. Should he have told his mother? Or had she already known? Was that why she drank?

Five years ago during a trip to the Bahamas, Adam had stumbled upon his father and Cassie's mother in an intimate clench. He'd tried to force his father to end the affair and failed. The confrontation had been ugly. Later that same year his father had turned over the running of Garrison, Inc. to

Parker and the hotel operations to Stephen. Adam had received nothing. Nada.

And now it was too late to make things right with his father.

He tamped down the loss and frustration tightening his chest and finished dressing, then grabbed his keys and cell phone and jogged down the stairs. He couldn't go backward. He could only move forward.

For his plan to work he needed absolute secrecy. Only Brandon knew the whole truth behind Adam's proposal. And even though his best friend was crazy in love with Adam's newly discovered half sister, Adam knew he could count on Brandon to keep his lips zipped. Not just because of client confidentiality, but because Brandon was that kind of guy— as honest and loyal as a summer day is long.

In the meantime, Adam would keep Lauryn away from his family until the contracts were signed and the wedding knot was tightly tied—and he had no doubt it would be tied. If Lauryn slipped up and revealed his strategy to his siblings he wouldn't have a chance in hell of gaining more involvement in Garrison, Inc.

But first he had to get through Monday evening. A night at the Ainsleys' wouldn't be pleasant, but neither would it be a total waste of time. With Lauryn on his arm he'd schmooze with the movers and shakers of the community who could aid in his quest for the council nomination.

A win-win situation.

He'd score points with Lauryn and for himself.

And he'd do what he did best.

He'd turn on the charm and land himself a bride.

Three

Yet another dead end.

Lauryn tried to keep her steps from dragging as she followed Adam into the moist evening air and across the brick courtyard toward his car. She'd pinned her hopes on walking in her birthmother's footsteps tonight. But Adrianna Laurence had never set foot in the Ainsleys' house. At least, not this one.

Lauryn's disappointment was almost enough to distract her from the feel of Adam's hand wrapped around hers. Hot. Firm. Electric.

He'd been attentive all evening with a casual touch at her waist here, a brush of his hand against hers there. It hadn't taken her long to realize his every move had been designed to convince the other guests they were a couple. And yet he hadn't said one dishonest word or made a single inappropriate gesture to which she could object.

Much as she disliked the situation, she had to face facts. Being a pawn in Adam's scheme had its benefits. She'd been the only outsider at the gathering tonight, but because she was Adam's date she'd been welcomed into her birthmother's stratum by the same people who'd refused to speak to her a few months ago. People who had very likely known her birthmother.

With a little Garrison grease to oil the hinges she'd made more progress tonight in two hours of chitchat than she had in weeks of knocking on doors and researching microfiche newspaper articles and county documents. She didn't have her answers yet because it was too soon to ask without risking rejection, but as long as she was beside Adam she could build the tentative connections to find out what she wanted so desperately to know.

Adam opened the car door, but Lauryn didn't climb in. She pivoted in her flat sandals and studied the ostentatious home. Lights streamed from every window, painting stripes across the dark grounds. "You're telling me the Ainsleys demolished a perfectly good house and built a new one in the same spot?"

"Five years ago."

"But why?" She turned back to Adam and realized he'd moved close enough to loom above her—far too close for her peace of mind. The tang of his cologne, a crisp lime scent, teased her senses, and she could see the fine lines at the corners of his eyes. Her body still hummed from his unexpected touches throughout the evening and his proximity overwhelmed her.

One small step and they'd be breast-to-chest, hip-to-hip. Her gaze drifted to his lips. With all the practice he'd had, she'd bet he was a great kisser. If he bent his head—

No kisses. Back up.

But she couldn't. Trapped as she was between the car and

Adam's lean frame, there was nowhere to run. She forced her eyes away from his mouth and dragged a lungful of the heavily scented night air into her chest, but she couldn't identify the flowers she smelled.

Had her mother known the names? Had Adrianna been a plant lover? A swimmer? A shopaholic? A night owl or morning person? Tall, short, introvert or extrovert? Had she been a rule follower or a rule breaker? Knowing nothing frustrated Lauryn and left her feeling empty. Adrift.

Adam shrugged. "With the shortage of land and surplus of cash in South Florida it's a common practice to tear down and start fresh. Sometimes massive reconstruction is due to hurricane damage, but in this case Helene wanted renovations that exceeded the value of the house."

Alarm streaked through her. "Your house hasn't been razed has it?"

His eyes narrowed as if he could hear the panic she couldn't quite keep out of her voice. "No. It's the original structure. Why?"

Get a grip, Lauryn. She forced a smile. "I…um, love history. I hate to see it erased. We're close to your place, aren't we? Would you show it to me?"

He hesitated so long she thought he'd refuse. "Sure. There's no one staying there this week."

She slid into the car with so much anticipation and excitement bubbling through her veins that she could barely sit still.

Adam drove off the Ainsley property, down the palm-shadowed street and then pulled into a short driveway blocked by another set of elaborately coiled iron gates and stopped the car. He tapped a security code onto a recessed keypad and the wide gates silently glided open.

Emotion clogged Lauryn's throat as the car rolled into a circular brick courtyard and around the center fountain.

Sensor lights flicked on, flooding the area with light. Scrambling to absorb it all at once, she ticked off details in her mind. Mediterranean style. Four-car garage to the left. Arched windows. Carved columns. Deep, shadowed porches.

Her birthmother's home. Lauryn's heart thumped as hard and fast as a helicopter's blades as she climbed from the car on trembling legs. She wished she could see the house in daylight instead of washed by a weak crescent moon. She wanted to examine every minute detail of the elaborately carved cornices above the windows and doors and under the gables and eaves.

"It's beautiful," she whispered.

"Like I said, it's a good investment. By the time I unload it, the property will have doubled in value."

Panic burst in her veins. He couldn't sell. Not yet. "You're going to sell it?"

"When the market and price are right."

She wiped her dampening palms on her simple black sheath and followed Adam onto the front porch, tangling and untangling her fingers while he unlocked the door.

How many times had her birthmother crossed this threshold?

He entered, hit a light switch and then punched a sequence on an alarm system concealed by a small mirror. He gestured for her to join him, but she couldn't move. A weird form of near-paralysis locked her muscles. She was so close to uncovering the truth. So close to the diaries and answers.

If they were here.

But what if she didn't like what she learned? What if her mother wasn't a nice person? What if her mother had died of some hideously debilitating and hereditary disease? And what if Lauryn possessed some flaw that made her unlovable?

Her father and Susan had loved her hadn't they? Maybe. Her parents had lied about so much that Lauryn didn't trust herself to recognize the truth anymore.

"Lauryn?" Adam's expression asked why she delayed.

She scrambled for a response. "This luxury is about as far as you can get from the military housing I grew up in."

"Didn't seem to bother you at the Ainsleys'."

"I guess I was too nervous about meeting all those people to be overwhelmed by the house. I, um…don't get out much." Not anymore.

She forced her feet forward and found herself in a soaring circular two-story domed foyer. She slowly turned around in the center of the Mariner's Compass pattern inlaid into the marble floor like a glossy stone quilt, and then crossed to the wide staircase sweeping up and around the foyer to the second floor.

Had her mother crept up and down these stairs, avoiding the squeaky treads in the middle of the night? If marble treads creaked, that is.

Had the wild streak that had landed Lauryn in so much trouble as a teen come from Adrianna Laurence? Lauryn certainly hadn't inherited it from her father, a regimented career military man, or learned it from her adoptive mother, a serene saint of a woman who never raised her voice or her hand no matter how obnoxious Lauryn had been.

"Want the ten-dollar tour?" Adam's voice intruded.

She blinked. "I thought that was a ten-cent tour."

"Inflation," Adam replied straight-faced. "If you don't have cash, I'll accept a more creative payment."

His gaze dropped to Lauryn's lips and her mouth dried. She cleared her throat and looked away. "I'd love a tour."

She had to get into this house without him dogging her footsteps. Maybe she could convince him to give her a key to drop stuff off for the VIPs and steal a few minutes to explore. "How many bedrooms?"

"Six bedrooms, seven and a half baths, plus servants' apartments over the garage."

Six! It would take hours or days to search each closet for loose floorboards and that was assuming the closets were empty and she wouldn't have to shift stuff out of the way first.

"This is definitely the kind of house to raise a family in." Her mother had grown up here, an only child, and according to what little Lauryn had uncovered, had moved back home after one semester at Vassar. Had Adrianna taken the diaries to college with her? Had she brought them home?

"Come on." He turned and headed through an archway.

Lauryn hustled after him. "Did you make many changes after you bought the estate?"

He strode past a stream of rooms, flipping light switches as he went. "Other than updating the electrical wiring, no. The previous owners kept the place well-maintained. I even bought some of the furniture in the estate sale."

Lauryn stumbled. She barely caught a glimpse of the book-lined library, home theater, massive kitchen, two-story living room and beamed-ceiling den as she hustled to keep up with Adam. The grandeur of the house blew her mind. She wanted to beg him to slow down, to let her soak up the details like a sponge, to ask which pieces of furniture had been the Laurences'.

Had her mother sat on that sofa or at that writing desk? But asking would require explanations. And explanations could lead to rejection. It was too soon to launch her appeal.

He didn't stop until he reached a circular sunroom jutting from the back of the house like a peninsula. Three of her tiny apartments would fit in this room alone.

To her right a wall of windows overlooked an expansive

pool and patio illuminated by subtle landscape lighting. The left side revealed tennis courts, and beyond the seawall at the back of the property stretched a private dock with a long, low and fast-looking boat floating in the channel.

With one sweep of his hand Adam extinguished the interior and exterior lights and the outside view vanished. Pale moonlight cast the sunroom in a mysterious combination of shadows and wavering silvery light.

"Ready to go?"

No! Not yet. "You're not going to show me the upstairs?"

He closed the distance between them in two lazy strides, lifted his hand and cupped her cheek. Surprise held her motionless. Shadows sharpened the angles of his face. His thumb brushed over her lips. Desire sparked instantly in her veins and judging by the sudden widening of Adam's pupils and the flare of his nostrils he felt something, too. The air suddenly turned hot, humid and heavy.

"If you want to get me into a bedroom, you're going to have to accept my proposal and sign the agreements first."

Her thoughts screeched to a halt. She could not let herself fall for Adam Garrison. She'd given up bad boys and shallow relationships a long time ago. And while Adam wore designer clothing instead of torn jeans, he was still a heartbreaker through and through.

Been there. Done that.

Tempting, but taboo.

But she had to have access to this house. She'd lost her father and her own identity eleven months ago and possibly shattered her relationship with her mother beyond repair. If she had any chance of getting her life back on an even keel then she had to figure out who she was—who she *really* was—not the fairy tale her parents had concocted.

There was only one way.

A chill raced through her. She spun away from Adam, wrapped her arms around herself and picked her way through the mottled shadows to stand by the window and stare out at the lights winking across the darkness from the houses on the island across the channel.

"I'll do it," she said in a rush with her gaze focused on the rocking boat instead of the man behind her.

Light filled the room once again. "Do what?"

She slowly turned and met Adam's direct gaze. "I'll marry you. But only if we live here."

"I have a condo within walking distance of the club."

"Have you ever considered you might appear more settled if you lived in a house instead of a bachelor pad?"

He dipped his head. "Good point."

"I won't give up my job."

"Lauryn, you won't need to work."

"But I want to." She took a slow breath and then blurted, "And I won't sleep with you."

"You'll have your own room."

"No, Adam, I mean no sex. You might be able to be intimate with someone you don't love, but I can't." Not anymore. She remembered all too well the self-loathing afterward. She'd wanted to hurt her father with her brazen behavior, but she'd only ended up hurting and hating herself.

"I'll get tested if that's what you're worried about."

"That has nothing to do with it. I mean, it is important given the legions you're rumored to have bedded, but—"

"Legions?"

"You're not known for your discriminatory tastes."

"There haven't been legions."

"How many then?"

"None of your business."

"It is when you're trying to talk me into bed."

He hesitated and then shrugged. "I don't know."

"You didn't count or you can't count that high?"

His chin jutted forward. "How many men have you slept with?"

Her shameful past crept over her. She'd wasted her youth looking for ways to flout her father's iron-fist authority, and she wasn't proud of that. She'd been a rebel, but she'd reformed. She'd practically become a nun. "Hey, if you don't have to answer then neither do I."

"What am I supposed to do for...relief?"

A slideshow flashed in her mind of ten different ways she could give him sexual relief, but she shut it down. The heat flushing her skin wasn't as easy to vanquish. "That depends on whether you're right- or left-handed."

"And you?"

Her cheeks ignited. "I can take care of myself."

His jaw muscles bunched as if he were gritting his teeth. He paced to the window, paused and then turned. "Fine. I accept your terms. Do you have a passport?"

For a moment she was too stunned to speak. "Yes. Why?"

"I'll have Brandon make the arrangements. He and Cassie can set up a quick, quiet Bahamas wedding. Does that suit you? Or do you need a circus?"

Cassie...it took a moment for Lauryn to place the name. Cassie Sinclair had been John Garrison's secret lovechild from an extramarital affair. Or so the papers reported. Even though Lauryn had never met the woman, she felt a kinship with her. Another outsider. But at least Cassie had known who her parents were. Cassie currently owned and managed the Garrison Grand-Bahamas and had recently hooked up with Brandon Washington, Adam's attorney—if the club's scuttlebutt was to be believed.

"I don't want a big wedding. But why the Bahamas?"

"If we get married in Miami my family would expect to be invited and there's a good chance there would be a media blitz."

Avoiding both the media and the Garrison family appealed. "Something quiet in the Bahamas is fine. I've never been there."

"We'll stay a few days and call it a honeymoon."

Honeymoon? "I won't change my mind about the sex."

"Lauryn, it's imperative we act like a couple who's fallen in love and eloped. If this marriage doesn't look real it'll do me no good. We'll have a honeymoon."

"The business council nomination is that important to you?"

Again he hesitated. "It's what the nomination represents that's important."

"And that is?"

"Personal." He glanced at his watch. "If we leave now we have time to swing by the club and pick up the agreements."

Personal.

Secrets weren't the best way to start a marriage—temporary or otherwise. But she'd let him get away with this one because she had a few of her own.

Some things were too shameful to share.

"You didn't have to drive me home," Lauryn said as Adam turned his BMW into her apartment complex.

"I told you I'm not letting you take the bus at this time of night."

"I always use the bus."

"Not anymore. My fiancée would never use public transportation."

Fiancée. She gulped down her rising panic. Her last marriage had been a horrific mistake. Would this one be better or worse since love wasn't involved?

"Your fiancée can't afford valet parking or dollar-an-hour parking meters."

"With the money you're about to receive that's going to change."

As bad luck would have it, one of the few visitors' parking spaces opened up as he turned into the lot. He pulled between the white lines, killed the engine and unlocked the doors.

She needed to get away from Adam, needed to rethink this crazy scheme and make sure there wasn't another way to accomplish her goal.

Admit it. There is no other way. You've pursued every other avenue. This is your best chance to uncover the truth.

Clutching her purse and the file containing the prenuptial agreement and marriage contract, she sprang from the car before he could circle to her side. "You don't need to walk me to the door. The area is well-lit and safe."

He grasped her elbow in a warm, firm grip. Even though he'd touched her dozens of times tonight her breath still caught on contact. "Which way to the elevators?"

He obviously planned to ignore what she'd said.

"There are no elevators. I'm on the third floor."

He swept his free hand toward the stairwell.

Reluctantly, Lauryn led the way, but even with her "leading" he was right beside her, matching his steps to hers. She didn't want him in her apartment. Not that there was anything wrong with the tiny, tidy space, but after seeing the luxury to which he was accustomed, her place felt dinky and inadequate. The Art Deco building had been renovated, but with white-collar instead of wealthy tenants in mind.

She hiked the stairs with him by her side, unlocked the door and entered. A quick glance revealed she hadn't left anything lying around that she didn't want him to see—like the thick folder she'd compiled on her mother. Or the thinner one on Adam and his business clearly marked with his name on the tab.

She faced him with the marriage file clutched to her chest. "I'm in. Safe and sound. Thanks for taking me to the Ainsleys' tonight and for showing me your house."

He stepped forward, forcing her to shuffle hastily out of the way. With his eyes sweeping her space, the tiny kitchenette to the left, the sitting room in front of him, the doors leading to the small bedroom and minuscule bathroom, he shrugged off his suit jacket and hung it over the back of a kitchen chair.

"What are you doing?"

"Making myself comfortable."

"You don't have to stay. I'll look these over and bring them to work with me in the morning." She remained by the open door, hoping he'd take the hint, get his coat and leave.

Instead, he unbuttoned his cuffs and rolled up one shirt-sleeve and then the other, revealing hair-dusted forearms. "I'll go over the documents with you."

"No need. If I have questions I'll write them down."

He prowled toward her, his blue gaze intent and unwavering, and palmed the door shut. "Trying to get rid of me, Lauryn?"

Her mouth dried and her pulse kicked erratically. "I have to get up early."

"It's only eleven and your boss will cut you some slack."

"I can't be late. I have to issue a check to the liquor supplier when he delivers first thing tomorrow."

"The truck comes at ten. You can sleep in. We have a few more details to work out." He parked his hands on his hips as if expecting an argument.

"Like what?"

"Like how you'll be paid. Brandon has spelled it out in

the marriage contract, but I'll recap. You'll receive just over forty-one grand every month. The first payment will be transferred into your account after the wedding ceremony."

"Why monthly?"

"So you won't skip out before the end of the second year."

"Once I give my word I don't break it." Not anymore. "But okay. Monthly is fine." She wasn't in this for the money anyway.

"I'll open bank and charge accounts for you. Because of the temporary nature of this marriage our money will be kept separate. If you blow your salary before the end of the month you're out of luck. I won't give you a dime more." When she didn't argue he continued, "And I'm going to hire an assistant for you."

"Wait a minute. You said I could keep my job, and I've told you, I don't need an assistant."

"I'll allow you to continue working, but only part-time. If we're inseparable newlyweds you'll be expected to make regular appearances by my side at the club. That means late nights. Your assistant will cover mornings."

His logic made sense. She reluctantly conceded by inclining her head. "What else?"

"A certain amount of PDAs will be required to make this marriage look real." He stood almost a yard away, but the distance and her apartment suddenly seemed to shrink.

"PDAs?"

"Public displays of affection. We'll need to touch. Like we did tonight."

She could handle that. "Okay."

"Kiss."

She gulped. "I don't think—"

"Newlyweds kiss and touch. Often. Making people believe we can't keep our hands off each other is part of the performance."

Her lips seemed to throb beneath his gaze. Tension stretched between them. Would he kiss her tonight? To seal the deal? To test her acting ability? Her heart pounded so hard she felt light-headed.

"Can you handle that?"

"I…um…yes. I can handle kissing you." She hoped.

Adam turned abruptly and strolled deeper into the living room. Her lungs emptied in a rush.

"You need different clothes, makeup, hair, a manicure—"

"You want me to get a makeover?" She didn't know whether to be insulted or pleased. She'd been downplaying her looks for so long it had become second nature. Apparently, she'd become good at looking drab.

He hitched his pants and sat on her sofa. Such a masculine man on flowered chintz just looked…wrong somehow. "To be believable as my wife you're going to need a little flash and a lot of style."

"To compete with your usual bimbos, you mean?"

"There will be no competition. I told you, Lauryn, I won't be unfaithful despite your ridiculous insistence on celibacy."

She marched across the room and stopped in front of him. "It's not ridiculous."

He stretched his arms along the back of the sofa and let his gaze coast from her face to her breasts, waist, legs and then back up again. Goose bumps sprouted in the wake of his examination.

"We'll see who can hold out the longest. And when you break, you come to me. No one else."

She wanted to smack that smug smile off his face. "I won't break."

"We'll see. I'll hire a personal shopper to help you choose appropriate clothing and make the beauty appointments."

"I'll choose my own clothes and make my own appointments."

"Lauryn—"

"And I won't dress like a tramp."

His eyes narrowed, "I don't date tramps."

"Didn't your last girlfriend recently make the news for flashing a pantiless crotch shot at the paparazzi?"

"She wasn't my girlfriend."

"The media says differently." She futilely tried to massage the headache squeezing the back of her skull beneath her knot of hair. "I can dress myself and do all the rest."

He sat forward, forearms braced on his knees. "Not from what I've seen. Keep your wardrobe conservative, but try to dress your age instead of matronly. Remember, people are supposed to believe I'm attracted to you."

Ouch. "You'll have to trust me."

"We can't afford mistakes. We have to get it right the first time."

"I'll get it right."

Tense, silent seconds ticked past. "You have a headache?"

"Yes. But it's nothing a good night's sleep won't cure. Please, Adam, go home. I'll read the documents and discuss them with you tomorrow."

He stared at her as if considering refusing, but then rose. "I'll pick you up at Estate at five tomorrow evening. We'll stop by Brandon's office for the notary to witness our signatures before going to dinner."

And then she'd be tied to Adam Garrison in a sham of a marriage for two years.

But what was two years when her entire life had been a lie?

Four

"Ready to roll?"

Lauryn nearly jumped out of her chair at the sound of Adam's voice behind her late Tuesday afternoon. She swiveled around and found him standing just inside her office.

Black suit, white shirt, conservative black-and-silver-patterned tie. Manly. Magnificent. He'd always been a sharp dresser, but she rarely saw him so formally attired.

"Almost. You're early. Let me print this last page." She caught the sheet before it could hit the tray. "I typed up an addendum."

"Addendum to what?" He crossed to her desk and took the papers she offered.

"Our agreement. These are the items we covered last night."

His gaze ricocheted from the pages to her face. He backtracked and closed her office door. "Our sex life is not going into a legal document."

"I want the terms spelled out."

"I won't have anything in writing that the press can use to discredit me. The prenup and marriage contract are risky enough. Delete that file," he ordered in an authoritative voice.

Her hackles rose in a conditioned response. Like a Pavlovian pooch. She'd never taken orders well. Her father had barked them as if she'd been a new recruit, and she…well, she'd rebelled. More often than not her response had landed her in hot water.

But that was then.

"Adam—"

"Do it now, Lauryn."

Grasping the arms of her chair, she sat back and counted to ten. "You're protecting your interests. Why shouldn't I protect mine?"

"I give you my word I will abide by your requests." He fed the pages into the shredder and then planted his palms on her desk and slowly leaned forward until he towered over her. He held her gaze without blinking. "Until you tell me otherwise."

The last phrase, delivered with a cocky half smile, oozed confidence and charisma. He thought she'd change her mind about the sex ban. He had no clue what kind of lockdown she'd put on her hormones since dissolving her hasty marriage or how good she'd become at ignoring the opposite sex. But he'd learn.

She deleted the file and even emptied her computer's recycle bin. "Done."

"Let's go."

"Wait. You need to approve the advertisement for my assistant."

"No need to advertise. Your predecessor is eager to come back to work. She's discovered she needs a break from full-time diaper duty."

Tension squeezed Lauryn's throat like an invisible strangler's hand. Silently, she collected her purse and the marriage agreement and followed Adam out of the building.

"Did your attorney look at the contract?" he asked.

"I don't have an attorney here and there wasn't time to find one."

Adam grasped her elbow and stopped her on the sidewalk. He met her gaze head-on. "I won't cheat you. The settlement is fair."

"I know. I read it." Five times. Pages of emotionless words promising twenty-four months of her life to a virtual stranger. A year to get Adam elected and then a year to keep him in office until he'd proven he could do the job.

Would she be able to remain as detached when she shared a home and a life with this man? Would she be able to walk away as if the marriage had never happened? Her reaction to Adam's stimulating touch said the time wouldn't pass without leaving its mark.

But she could control her body. Couldn't she?

She had to.

She turned, pulling free of his hand, and looked past him, but she didn't see his BMW by the curb. A dark blue Lexus sat in Adam's usual spot. It wasn't the first time someone had ignored the sign marking his reserved parking place. She scanned the street, but didn't see Adam's convertible in any of the other spaces, and the valet wouldn't arrive until later this evening. That meant a hike to the parking deck, which was one of the reasons—besides the prohibitive cost of parking—Lauryn always rode the bus. Thank goodness for her preference for flat-heeled shoes.

Adam reached into his pocket, withdrew a key ring and hit a button. The Lexus's lights flashed. He dangled the keys in front of her. "You wear a lot of blue. I hope that means you like it."

"What?" She gaped at the small SUV and then at him. "You're kidding, right?"

"No. You're driving." When she didn't reach for the keys he caught her hand, pressed them into her palm and closed her fingers around them.

She didn't know which startled her more. The pricey car or the contact with Adam. She'd have to work harder at reining in this taboo attraction. "I have a decent car."

"Now you have a better one. Keep the old one or sell it. I don't care."

"But…"

"Appearances, Lauryn. It's all about appearances." He checked traffic and then opened the driver's door for her. "Let's go. Brandon's staying after hours for us."

She slid into the buttery soft leather seat, filled her lungs with that new-car smell and checked out the tinted sunroof. Compared to her four-year-old economy sedan, this car's dashboard looked like something NASA built. GPS and satellite radio. Who knew what the other gizmos were? Her hand trembled as she slipped the key into the ignition and started the engine.

Adam climbed into the passenger seat. "You've delivered documents to Brandon for me before. Remember where his office is?"

"Yes." She wasn't looking forward to maneuvering a brand-new luxury vehicle through rush-hour traffic.

Adam gave her perhaps five minutes to get accustomed to the way the car handled before speaking again. "Bahamas law requires us to be in the country twenty-four hours before we can apply for a marriage license. We'll leave tomorrow morning, get married Thursday evening and then come home Monday morning and move our stuff into the house."

Thursday? She gulped. "So soon?"

"Waiting wastes time."

"You're willing to leave Estate that long?"

"The staff will survive without me, and Sandy will fill in for you."

He had it all figured out. "Sandy's my predecessor?"

"Yes."

"I won't have time for the makeover you requested by tomorrow."

She kept her eyes on traffic but caught his shrug out of the corner of her eye. "Do it on the island. Cassie's well put-together. She can tell you where to go."

All too soon they reached the high-rise housing Washington & Associates. Because so many of the building's workers were making the evening exodus, Lauryn easily found a spot near the entrance. She parked and climbed from the car. The knot between her shoulders from driving the unfamiliar vehicle sank to her stomach and expanded with each step she took beside Adam toward their destination.

He ushered her into the elevator and up to the law offices of Washington & Associates. A woman Lauryn guessed to be in her sixties waited for them by the reception desk with a big smile lined on her face. On past visits Lauryn had always left packages with the receptionist, who wasn't behind her desk.

"What is this I hear about an engagement? Both of your brothers, then Brandon and now you. Have the men in Miami suddenly become smarter?"

"Hello Rachel." Adam pulled the diminutive woman into a hug and then released her and extended his hand toward Lauryn. "This is Lauryn Lowes, my fiancée. Lauryn, this is Rachel Suarez."

Lauryn reluctantly put her left hand in Adam's and let him tug her forward. The shocking heat of his touch seeped up her arm and then oozed down deep inside her, but the woman thankfully broke the spell by enfolding Lauryn's right hand in both of hers.

"He'll be a good husband as long as you keep him on a short leash," she whispered.

Wide-eyed, Lauryn darted a quick glance at Adam to see if he'd heard, but his face remained impassive.

"Thanks for that tip," she replied and received a wink in return.

Movement down the hall drew Lauryn's attention. Brandon Washington strolled toward them. He was Adam's height, attractive and African-American. Lauryn had spoken with him on numerous occasions when he stopped by Estate.

The men shook hands and clapped shoulders before Brandon greeted her with a nod. Lauryn nodded back and tried to smile.

Adam indicated Mrs. Suarez. "Is she still running this place?"

"She likes to think so," Brandon replied. The warmth in his eyes belied his firm voice. "Let's step into my office." Brandon turned to Mrs. Suarez. "Give us five minutes and then join us, please."

Lauryn's mouth dried. The deal was all but done. Her feet felt weighted as she followed the men across the carpet. The point of no return lay directly ahead.

But if she walked away what would she have learned about her mother? Not enough. Not nearly enough. And she'd probably lose her job, too, for leading Adam on and then reneging.

The door closed behind them, sealing them into Brandon's office. He faced them across his desk and waited until they were seated before asking Adam, "Are you sure you want to do this?"

"I'm sure."

Dark brown eyes lasered in on Lauryn's. "Are you?"

"I—" She covered her flash of panic by clearing her throat and handing over the folder. "I am."

Brandon accepted it and withdrew the prenuptial agreement and marriage contract. "Did you have any questions, Lauryn? Is there anything that requires clarification?"

Is there another way? "No."

"She didn't have a lawyer read the agreements," Adam said.

Brandon stilled. "Would you like me to have one of my associates come in and go over the documents? I can assure you he'd be unbiased."

"No. I'm comfortable with the contracts."

Brandon nodded. "Once you get to the Bahamas you'll have to provide proof of arrival time in the country. The airport should be able to give you that. Then you'll swear before the U.S. Consul at the American Embassy that you're single American citizens who wish to get married. The next day you'll visit the Registrar General's office to get your license. No blood tests are required, but Adam says you're both going to be tested tomorrow morning anyway. Good decision."

That was news. Lauryn looked at Adam. He stared back. He must really believe he'd be able to charm her into bed.

Not going to happen, she told him silently with her eyes.

One corner of his mouth lifted, and she could practically hear his thoughts. *Wanna bet?*

"Lauryn, are you divorced or widowed?" Brandon asked as he laid the documents on the desk in front of them.

"Um…no." She'd been told annulments didn't count. Legally it was as if her marriage had never happened, which was only fitting since she couldn't remember the ceremony. Her skin burned with shame over that low point in her life. She'd just as soon nobody ever knew how stupid she'd been.

"Then that's all the paperwork you'll need. Cassie has arranged the rental of a cottage for you on a private beach. She's also hired the minister, photographer and caterers. The ceremony will take place Thursday evening on the beach at sunset. Cassie and I will be your witnesses. I'll issue a press release afterward. Any questions?"

Cold permeated Lauryn's hands and feet. She shook her head because she couldn't have spoken even if she'd tried.

A tap sounded on the door. It opened and Mrs. Suarez poked her salt-and-pepper head through the gap. "Ready for me?"

"Perfect timing as always," Brandon answered.

The petite woman bustled in carrying her notary stamp.

Brandon offered Lauryn a pen. "Lauryn, you sign first."

It took a second to find her nerve. She accepted the pen with an almost steady hand and scratched her name and the date where he indicated, first on the marriage contract and then on the prenuptial agreement. Adam did the same. And then Mrs. Suarez affixed her notary stamp, date and signature to each.

Done.

Heavy doubts rumbled through Lauryn like a California mud slide followed by a weird kind of numbness as Brandon matter-of-factly collected the documents and returned them to the file folder.

"I'll make sure you each have copies and I'll see you Thursday." Brandon stood and then extended his hand.

Thursday.

In forty-eight hours she'd be a married woman. Again.

And this time she couldn't call daddy to fix her mistake.

* * *

"Will you marry me, Lauryn?"

Stunned, Lauryn stared at Adam. The buzz in her ears drowned out the conversations around them in the elegant, exclusive restaurant. Or maybe a hush had fallen over the eavesdropping patrons awaiting her response.

She didn't know much about diamonds, but she'd bet the one pinched between Adam's finger and thumb cost a mint. The marquis stone had to be at least two carats. She forced her gaze from the mesmerizing sparkler to his eyes. Serious. Compelling. Intensely blue.

"I—I—"

Even though they hadn't rehearsed this, even though he'd surprised her with this very public proposal, she knew what she was supposed to say. She just couldn't get her mouth to work.

Flowers. Crystal. Candlelight. A strolling violinist. A prime table overlooking the bay. Adam had planned the perfect setting for a proposal.

And it was all fake. As fake as their marriage would be.

"Lauryn, baby, don't leave me hanging. You know we belong together."

She heard the warning in his deep voice and pressed a hand over her frantically beating heart. This wasn't right. And yet what choice did she have if she wanted to learn the truth?

Answer the man.

"Y-yes," she heard herself say. "Yes, Adam, I'll marry you."

A spattering of applause startled and embarrassed her. These days she hated being a spectacle as much as she'd once thrived on such attention. She briefly squeezed her eyes shut and then met Adam's gaze. He wore a wide smile—one that didn't reach his eyes—as he slipped the ring on her finger. And then he stood and pulled her into his arms.

His mouth covered hers so quickly she froze in shock. She hadn't expected such a public first kiss, nor had she expected his mouth to be soft. Or gentle. Or warm. Or persuasive. Or delicious. He sipped from her lips the way he had from his wineglass earlier.

Not that she'd been watching his mouth. Much.

He lifted his head a fraction of an inch, leaning his forehead against hers. "Put your arms around my neck."

His lips brushed hers with each whispered word and the eroticism nearly melted her. She lifted her arms as directed and his hands tightened on her waist, pulling her closer. The embrace mashed her breasts against the hard, hot wall of his chest and fused her hips to his. Desire swept through her like a California canyon fire, searing her deep inside. She planted her hands against his lapels, broke the kiss and looked away—right into the eyes of Helene Ainsley two tables away.

It's all about appearances, Adam had said.

And Lauryn had better not forget it. That's all this was. A charade. A setup. A chance for him to paint a convincing picture for the business council nominating committee. The heat in Lauryn's veins turned to ice.

Adam reclaimed her hand and carried it to his lips. He kissed her knuckle below the ring and reseated her. Leaning over her, he caressed her shoulders and then pressed another scorching kiss to the tender skin beneath her ear. Goose bumps rose on her skin.

Not good. She really, *really* didn't want to want him.

"Very convincing. Good job," he murmured low enough that only she could hear.

The waiter arrived immediately with a bottle of champagne and presented the label for inspection.

Oh yes, Adam had definitely planned this—right down to preordering his favorite vintage of the Salon Blanc champagne. Lauryn knew his preferences because the club kept the brand in stock. Rumor had it that when he requested a bottle he'd chosen his bedmate for the night.

Lauryn didn't want to be just another woman to share his sheets and his champagne. She'd better not forget the Adam Garrisons of this world bought what they wanted.

He might have bought her participation, but he couldn't buy her self-respect. And that meant she had to stay out of his bed no matter how easily he'd awoken the passionate hedonist she thought she'd buried years ago. Because when the hedonist came out to play, her common sense went away.

And she refused to be another man's puppet.

Lauryn stopped dead on the asphalt. "What is that?"

"A Columbia 400, turbo," Adam said with enough pride in his voice to clamp an iron band around Lauryn's chest. "My plane. Your ride," he added, confirming her worst fears.

He covered the last ten yards in quick, long strides and set their luggage down beside a tiny white airplane with a shiny propeller on its nose. His hand dipped into his pocket, reappearing with a set of keys.

She closed her eyes and gulped. This is so not good.

She should have known he wasn't just taking a different route to Miami International when he headed west of town.

Lauryn's shaking legs carried her forward at a much slower pace. "Why can't we fly commercial? You know, big jets with trained pilots, copilots and air hostesses who bring drinks?"

"Too slow." He shoved his aviator sunglasses into his hair and looked directly into her eyes as if he believed his calm assuredness would be contagious. "I am a trained pilot. I've had a license since I turned sixteen. You'll be safe with me."

Someone called out to him. Adam turned and walked to meet a guy in a khaki flight suit coming out of one of the hangars.

"I do not have a death wish," she muttered.

"Neither do I," he called over his shoulder.

She waited until he finished his conversation and returned. "I've never flown in a private plane."

"Good. I'll be your first, and I'll make it good for you." The gleam in his eyes as he opened a door on the side of the aircraft was purely sexual. Her body responded accordingly, warming, moistening. She shook off the unwanted response.

"My father died in a plane crash."

Compassion softened Adam's features. "I'm sorry. I didn't know. I take good care of my plane and I'll take care of you."

She wavered.

"Statistically, you're less likely to be in an accident in a plane than in a car. Climb in. Sit in the right front seat."

Her feet stayed planted. "Adam, I get seasick."

"Seasick and airsick are not the same. Trust me, Lauryn."

He grabbed her cold hands and carried them to the warmth of his cheeks, sandwiching her icy fingers between his smooth-shaven jaw and his warm palms. And then he leaned in and kissed her. One gentle, coaxing caress of his lips against hers followed another and another until the beginnings of arousal edged the fear from her stiff limbs. She was on the verge of responding, of threading her fingers through his hair and pulling him closer, when he lifted his head.

"Trust me," he repeated.

She was stuck. He was going to force her to ride in that dinky tin can. Grimacing, she pulled her hands free. "On three conditions. A, if I absolutely hate it you let me fly home on a regular plane. B, no fancy acrobatics. And C, I don't want to hear anything about the mile-high club. Not one word."

He grinned. "Deal. Now climb in."

He handed her into a compartment barely four feet high and wide. There were two leather bucket seats in the cabin and two more up front. She squeezed between the front seats and groaned as she sank into the one on the right. She was surrounded by glass, and she'd be able to see exactly how high they were off the ground. She buckled her seat belt. Tight.

She couldn't believe her father had flown for a living. Flying hadn't just been his job, it had been his passion.

Ten minutes later Adam eased his long frame in beside her. She gripped the armrests and watched him prepare for flight. Headset. Buttons. Dozens of them. And the she noticed the twin screens on the dash. One was GPS. She couldn't identify the other one. The propeller started, vibrating the plane.

He leaned over and pushed a headset over her hair. "Can you hear me now?"

He winked. Her stomach knotted. She closed her eyes.

Minutes passed while Adam communicated with the tower in the take-charge voice he used at work. She occupied herself with mental math. How much interest would a million dollars paid in twenty-four installments net over five years, ten, by retirement age?

The plane moved forward, bouncing gently down the runway before gathering speed and lifting off. She knew the exact second they left the ground. Squeezing her eyes closed, she tightened her grip on the armrests.

Moments later Adam's hand covered hers. "You can look now."

She eased open one eye and saw blue sky. She opened the other and risked looking down. Her stomach contents didn't rush to her throat. If anything, she wanted to see more and leaned closer to the window to do so. She could even identify some of the landmarks.

"The water's so green."

"Beautiful, isn't it? Same color as your eyes."

She snapped her head toward him and met his gaze. *Forget it. He's a natural-born charmer. Compliments come as easily to him as breathing.* But knowing the truth didn't lessen the impact of his words. "Thank you."

"Want to fly over the club and the estate before we head east?"

She considered it, realized she didn't feel the least bit sick and nodded. "Yes. I'd like that."

He didn't have to be nice. He had her where he wanted her, had her contracted to do exactly as he wished.

But it touched her that he made an effort.

Like a deer trapped in the headlights, Adam couldn't turn away from the view outside the window.

Mouthwatering curves. Amazing legs.

Cassie said something to Lauryn as the women walked toward the trunk of Cassie's car and Lauryn looked up at the cottage. Her gaze collided with his and the air dammed in his lungs.

She's beautiful. How had he missed that?

The raw material had to have been there because there was no way Lauryn could have worked major miracles in the five hours since Cassie had met their plane at the Nassau airport and whisked Lauryn away for an afternoon of shopping and…whatever. Adam had been more than happy to dodge that bullet by picking up the car Garrison, Inc. kept on the island and driving it and their luggage to the house.

Cassie hauled a number of shopping bags from the trunk and passed them to Lauryn. Adam snapped out of his trance and headed for the door. His legs felt rubbery as he jogged down the stairs. He blamed it on the blood drawn at his doctor's this morning and knew he lied.

He stopped beside the women. Adrenaline pulsed through his veins making him hyperaware of his bride-to-be. Sunlight gleamed off the hair streaming over Lauryn's shoulders. He'd never seen her hair down, and the urge to test the texture of the champagne-gold strands nearly overwhelmed him.

Thick lashes surrounded her sea-green eyes and a shell-pink gloss coated her lips. The breeze carried her incredible scent.

"Hello again, Adam."

He heard the smile in Cassie's voice and forced his stunned gaze from Lauryn to his grinning half sister. She seemed to be enjoying his stupefaction. "Thanks for helping, Cassie."

"My pleasure. So what do you think?"

His gaze devoured Lauryn from her satiny hair to her pink-painted toenails. He couldn't begin to put his thoughts into words. How had he ever believed her plain? Had he been so self-absorbed he'd missed the prize right in front of his face?

Apparently so.

"This cottage is one of my favorites," Cassie continued.

He jerked his attention back to his half sister. She meant the beach house? "It's very nice. Comfortable. Private."

"Excellent. I have to run. I have a hot date tonight with your best man. See you tomorrow."

"Bye, Cassie, and thanks again," Lauryn called out as Cassie climbed in her car.

"You're welcome. I had fun."

Adam watched the car pull away and then took another long look at Lauryn. He cursed the months of celibacy since his father's death. Despite what the tabloids said, Adam hadn't been in the mood to let anyone get close lately—not even physically. As peeved as he was with his father for refusing to acknowledge his accomplishments even after death, Adam still missed the old man.

Bags rattled as Lauryn shifted in her high-heeled sandals—sandals that made her legs look endless.

"Let me have those." He relieved her of her load, carried the loot inside to the room he'd chosen for her and dumped the bags on her bed. There were fewer bags than he'd expected. He'd expected her to try to bankrupt him.

Lauryn entered behind him. She scanned the space and then crossed the tile floor to peek into the luxurious bathroom. Her heels added a hypnotizing sway to her hips that he hadn't noticed before.

Her conservative clothing didn't scream "do me" like so many of Estate's patrons did. But there was a subtle sexiness in the way her new sundress skimmed her curves that yanked his awakened libido like an angler setting his hook.

Last night's kiss at the restaurant had rocked him with a tsunami of unexpected hunger. The one at the airport this morning had rocked him, too. And that was before he'd seen his soon-to-be wife looking like this.

He wanted her. Need pulsed in his gut. But he'd promised to abide by her no-sex rule until she said otherwise.

And dammit, he prided himself on being a man of his word.

That didn't mean he wouldn't try to change her mind. But

not until after the wedding. Judging by the wariness in her eyes if he tried to seduce her tonight he'd be missing a fiancée before the ceremony tomorrow.

"My bedroom's across the den." Desire roughened his voice.

"Okay." She looked and sounded relieved.

If he wanted to sleep better tonight than he had last night he needed to get out of this room, out of this house before he started picturing Lauryn wearing nothing but sleek, wet skin and a dusting of bubbles in that whirlpool tub. With him beside or beneath her.

Too late. He stifled a groan.

"Where are your glasses?" he asked in an attempt to sideline his illicit thoughts.

White teeth pinched her bottom lip and she wrinkled her nose. She looked so damned adorably guilty he almost whimpered. "I…um, don't really need them."

"Why in the hell did you hide behind shapeless clothing and ugly glasses?" It made no sense. The women he knew flaunted their assets. Hell, they paid good money to have bigger, better assets implanted.

"I learned not to draw attention to my looks a long time ago. Men assume if you're pretty, you're stupid and available."

"And you aren't available?" He knew she wasn't stupid.

"Not at the moment."

Her flip response stirred something unfamiliar in him. Possessiveness? No. *Determination* to make sure this plan worked. He couldn't afford slip-ups if he wanted the council and his brothers to believe he'd fallen for his straightlaced accountant and settled down. "And you won't be until after we're divorced."

"That won't be a problem."

The certainty in her tone raised red flags. Holy hell, was she gay? Did that explain why no one had seen her on a date? South Beach had a large gay population. Was that the real reason she'd moved to Florida? Because her story about her father had seemed a lame reason to move three thousand miles.

No, Lauryn couldn't be gay. He hadn't imagined the attraction between them or the hunger in her eyes. He'd felt the softening of her lips beneath his when he'd kissed her, and he'd heard her breath catch each time he'd touched her.

He wanted to kiss her now. To prove his theory.

But he wouldn't. Not yet.

Even though his neglected hormones had him in a tailspin.

Forget the candles, flowers and prepared meals he'd asked Cassie to arrange so he and Lauryn could play out the love-birds-needing-privacy farce. He couldn't handle a romantic dinner on the deck tonight. He needed crowds. Loud music. A noisy restaurant. Distractions. Anything but an intimate dinner for two.

"We're eating out tonight. Be ready in ten."

Lauryn's brow creased. "Cassie said she'd filled the refrigerator with local dishes for us."

Damn. He'd hoped his half sister had neglected to mention that detail. "She did."

Lauryn swept back her champagne locks with a newly manicured hand tipped in pearl-pink polish. The muscles of Adam's abdomen ripped as if she'd scraped those short nails across his flesh.

"Adam, I'd rather postpone the whole putting-on-a-show-for-the-locals thing, if you don't mind. I know we have to eventually, but it's our first night here and I'm kind of whipped. Cassie is a shopping machine. Surely if anyone is paying attention to our itinerary they'd expect us to want to be alone sometimes?"

Now that she mentioned it, he could see her fatigue in the faint shadows beneath her eyes and the slight downward turn of her mouth.

For sanity's sake he should be a bastard and insist on going out, but instead he ground his teeth on a frustrated curse.

It was going to be a long night.

"Pick whatever you want to eat and shove it in the microwave. I'm going for a run. I'll be back in an hour."

And then Adam did something he'd never done before.

He ran from a woman.

Five

Thursday. Her wedding day.

Lauryn had never been claustrophobic before, but she was getting there fast. The walls of the spacious oceanfront bedroom seemed to close in around her as the clock inched toward the time set for the ceremony. Her pulse raced and her mouth felt as dry and gritty as the sand dunes outside the cottage.

The silk chiffon of her strapless ivory tea-length dress fluttered against her shins as she paced from the window to the door and back, again and again, and the lace bolero jacket abraded her neck and shoulders. Since the ceremony would take place on the beach she'd decided against wearing shoes, and the floor tiles further chilled her already cold bare feet.

Cold feet. Appropriate.

She couldn't help comparing this wedding to her first. Her ex had had an agenda. So did Adam. Only Adam's wasn't illegal and no one would get hurt. Or arrested. Plus Lauryn knew what she was getting into this time. At least she hoped she did.

At eighteen and a day, she'd been incredibly young, naive and hardheaded when her father had forbidden her to see Tommy Saunders again. She'd foolishly believed herself old enough and wise enough to know better than her father. She and her dad had had another one of their legendary screaming matches, but this time Lauryn's mother hadn't played mediator the way she usually did when Lauryn's father went all dictatorial.

Afterward Lauryn had hidden in her room and called Tommy to vent. He'd insisted she was of age and her father couldn't tell her what to do anymore. On a wave of righteous indignation she'd agreed to go to Mexico with Tommy for spring break. Two days later she'd packed her bags, lied about spending the week at the beach with a girlfriend and left. Not one of her finest decisions.

In Tijuana Tommy had plied her with tequila and then asked her to marry him. She'd almost agreed, but even tipsy she'd known better than to cross her father that drastically.

The next morning she'd awoken hungover and with a cheap wedding ring on her finger that she couldn't remember putting there. When she'd freaked out Tommy had admitted he'd slipped something into her drink to loosen her inhibitions and help her make the decision he knew she really wanted to make.

His high-handedness had worried her but she'd loved him enough to make excuses for him. She hadn't panicked until he revealed his scheme over lunch to make them both rich and then she'd suddenly felt queasy and afraid.

Blaming her hangover, she'd excused herself to go to the bathroom, slipped out the backdoor of the cantina, found a phone and called her father.

That was the last time Lauryn had rebelled. After her father had rescued her from that disaster she'd become the perfect dutiful daughter, a straight-A student and as prim and proper as Emily Post.

Emily Post wouldn't be eloping in the Bahamas or neglecting to invite her mother to the ceremony.

Wincing, Lauryn paused by the glass doors leading to the deck. She hadn't called because she didn't want her mother to know about this marriage. Susan would be upset at how far Lauryn was willing to go to gain information about her birthmother, and she'd be hurt. She'd view this as another sign that she'd failed Lauryn as a parent. But other than not revealing the secret of Lauryn's birthmother sooner, that couldn't be further from the truth.

Lauryn studied the beach below her bedroom and tried to calm her agitated nerves. The flowered archway Cassie had ordered for the ceremony stood in the sand between the cottage and the lapping waves. The photographer hustled around checking shot angles or light or whatever it was photographers did.

The doorbell followed by muffled voices penetrated the closed bedroom door. Was that Cassie? The need to see a friendly face overwhelmed her. Lauryn yanked open the door.

Adam, Brandon and Cassie turned in unison.

"I take it you're not superstitious," Cassie said.

"I'm not." Lauryn's gaze slid to Adam as if dragged by a strong riptide. A black tuxedo complimented his ink-dark hair, made his shoulders look broader and his legs longer. His white shirt accentuated his tan and made his blue eyes and the flash of teeth in his slow smile seem brighter. He looked like every girl's fantasy groom. Handsome. Wealthy.

Sexy.

She tamped down that thought and dampened her dry lips.

No one will respect or value you if you don't respect and value yourself, her father's words came back to her.

So no sex and no more Mr. Right Nows. Not even the one she'd marry in a few minutes.

"If it's bad luck for the bride and groom to see each other before the ceremony then we're already cursed. Adam and I spent most of the day driving from one official's office to another's dealing with the legalities of this…marriage."

Adam crossed the room, looped his arms around her waist and pulled her close. Lauryn stiffened automatically. She couldn't let him keep getting to her like he'd done at the restaurant and airport. The heat of his body singed her at every contact point—breasts, waist, hips, thighs. He feathered his lips across hers and then lifted his head a fraction of an inch. Warning flashed in his eyes.

"You look beautiful, Lauryn."

Even knowing his compliment was part of the act didn't stifle the pleasure his words sent eddying through her.

"Thank you. So do you." Her cheeks warmed. She briefly ducked her head before daring to look into his eyes again. "I mean, you look good in a tux."

He dipped his head again. She forced herself to remain passive as he sipped from her lips once, twice more. Her heart raced and desire tugged like an undercurrent in her belly. She'd have to get used to being handled by him, kissed by him. But she had to shut down her response.

She heard Cassie's sigh. The woman believed this to be a true love match. Lauryn liked her new friend too much to lie to her, but Adam had ordered her to keep their secret.

Ordered. The back of Lauryn's neck prickled.

Only Brandon knew the truth behind this hasty marriage and Adam wanted to keep it that way.

On the pretext of examining the small wedding cake

sitting in the center of the dining room table Lauryn wiggled free. Adam let her go, but she could feel his gaze on her back. She fought the urge to lick her lips and lost. His taste lingered on her mouth and left her hungry for more.

Two bottles of champagne waited in sterling silver ice buckets on a sideboard and through the open kitchen door she spotted a pair of workers hustling around preparing food, presumably for the feast after the ceremony. Brandon, Cassie and the minister were staying for a wedding dinner. As much as Lauryn dreaded the lovey-dovey pretense, having company meant delaying the time alone with her groom, and that was good.

Last night… She exhaled slowly, trying to ease her overstretched nerves. Last night had been a nightmare. She couldn't remember ever being so aware of another person. Every shift of Adam's body on the sofa, each rustle of his clothing or chink of his glass on the coffee table had sounded as loud as a ship's horn. Finally, tension had driven Lauryn to her room for an early night of reading. *Attempted reading*. But a romance with steamy love scenes wasn't what she needed when she wanted to douse any potential flames for her groom. Even with the door closed she'd been aware of Adam's movements throughout the cottage.

Their marriage might be a business deal, but the whole wedding thing seemed so real. So…permanent. But it wasn't. And she didn't want it to be. One day she'd find the right man to build a future with—one who'd marry her because he loved her and not because he had a hidden agenda for marrying.

Like her father had had for marrying Susan. Like Tommy and Adam had for marrying Lauryn. Surely all men weren't that conniving? There had to be some good guys out there somewhere, and when this was over she'd find one.

She forced a smile and turned back to the trio in the den. "Cassie, this is incredible. I can't believe you pulled it all together so quickly."

"I've enjoyed it. Besides, it's good practice for when Brandon and I get married."

"And when is that going to be?" Adam asked.

"Soon," Brandon replied firmly with his dark eyes intent on Cassie.

Lauryn wanted a man who looked at her the way Brandon looked at Cassie—with his love shining like a lighthouse beacon from his eyes.

A brisk knock at the front door made Lauryn jump. Adam headed into the foyer and returned moments later with a dark-skinned, black-suited, white-collared minister by his side. Adam made the introductions.

Lauryn barely heard him through the alarms shrieking like hungry seagulls in her head. She wanted to run. All the way back to California. But she couldn't. Not until she found her answers.

She dug her toes into the rough sisal rug and the movement drew Adam's attention.

"Excuse me," he said and left the room. Moments later he returned without his shoes and socks. Lauryn's heart blipped irregularly. Adam had looked sexy before, but there was something dangerously appealing about a barefooted, tux-clad man that made her insides feel like a lava lamp.

His eyes met Lauryn's. "The sun is on the horizon. Ready?"

No. "Yes."

"Shall we?" He crooked his elbow in invitation.

Under a deluge of doubts Lauryn hesitated for precious seconds and then hooked her arm through Adam's. His muscles shifted beneath her fingers and her nerves and legs quivered.

He handed her a single long-stemmed red rose with an ivory ribbon twined around the thornless stem and then led her out the back door, down the porch stairs and across the warm sand to the archway.

An ocean breeze teased her hair, lifting the unbound strands and pulling at the wreath of flowers she wore instead of a veil. Adam caught a stray lock and smoothed it behind her ear. His fingertips glided down the hollow of her neck. She shivered. With awareness. With lust. Neither of which were welcome.

Cassie and Brandon flanked them and the beaming minister took his place and launched into the vows. At any other time Lauryn would have found the man's melodious accented voice beautiful, but the fragrant frame of the arch seemed to enclose her as securely as a locked jail cell.

A cold fog descended over her. She couldn't believe she was marrying a man she didn't love to find out more about a woman who'd discarded her.

But why hadn't Adrianna wanted her? That question kept Lauryn from running. She had to know. And she was counting on Adam's house holding the answers.

Adam's warm hands tightened around Lauryn's icy fingers. Did he sense her doubts? Her growing panic?

Too late to back out now.

As if he were willing her to finish what they'd started, his gaze never left hers as he stated his vows in a deep, steady baritone. If he had any doubts about the deception they were perpetrating he concealed them well. His hands were steady as he slid a platinum diamond eternity band onto her trembling finger next to the sparkling marquis.

And then it was Lauryn's turn. She numbly repeated the words the minister fed her and prayed this wasn't as big a mistake as her first wedding. She'd trusted Tommy and he'd betrayed her. Would Adam do the same?

She looked at the strong hand in her palm as she eased the wide platinum band they'd bought this morning over Adam's knuckle. Because he'd refused to put their amended agreement in writing, only his word would keep him from consummating their marriage tonight. Or any other night. Could she trust him?

A little late to worry about that now, isn't it?

A whirlpool of mixed emotions churned within her. This was so wrong. She was taking vows. Vows she had no intention of keeping. And yet what other choice did she have?

"I now pronounce you *mon*," the minister pronounced island-style, "and wife. Congratulations Mr. and Mrs. Garrison."

Mrs. Garrison.

Before she could digest those words Adam cupped her face in his palms and covered her mouth with his. This wasn't a tentative seal-the-deal peck. Adam kissed like a man assured of his welcome. His mouth branded hers, stamping her with ownership, and then his tongue separated her lips and swept the sensitive inside of her mouth as if he had every right to be there.

Tasting. Teasing. Tempting.

His kiss invited her to a party of sensual delights she had no doubt a man of his experience could provide. She hadn't had a lover since Tommy, and he'd been a twenty-three-year-old selfish jerk. The men before Tommy had been just as clumsy, just as selfish.

Adam's kiss promised satisfaction and she felt her control slipping. He overwhelmed her senses with his taste, his scent, his touch, and her hormones did a rain dance in hopes of ending the nine-year drought. The kiss felt so good, so right, that she lost herself in a hot rush of need, dug her toes in the shifting sand and pushed herself deeper into his embrace. Every inch of her body yearned to accept his invitation, to find out if lovemaking could actually be as good as it was in the romance novels she read.

She vaguely registered the birds screeching overhead, the waves crashing nearby, but it was Cassie's laughter that jarred Lauryn back to reality.

What are you doing?

She ripped her mouth free.

Adam breathed harshly. Hunger blazed in his eyes as he held her gaze, and she realized her mistake. She'd done a lot of less than honorable things in her time, things that made her cringe with shame. But she'd never been a tease.

That kiss, laden with years of pent-up passion, had promised something she had no intention of delivering.

"Sober enough to come to the phone?"

Lauryn nearly choked on her champagne when she heard Adam's question as she reentered the den after changing out of her wedding dress.

Okay, so maybe this was her second glass since Cassie and Brandon had left, and she'd had one two hours ago after dinner with her slice of wedding cake. Still, she should switch to coffee unless she wanted another wedding night like her first. One she couldn't remember. Drowning her nerves and her doubts wasn't working, anyway.

Adam's discarded tux jacket draped the back of a nearby chair. He stood facing the darkness outside the glass doors with both elbows bent beside his head and his white dress shirt stretched taut across his broad shoulders. The table lamp reflected off his wedding band drawing her attention to the cell phone pressed to his left ear.

"I'll wait while you get her, Lisette."

Lauryn realized he wasn't talking to her.

He turned. His gaze collided with hers and then slowly

drifted over her navy knit polo top, past her khaki knee-length shorts to her legs, bare feet and back up again. He'd unfastened his tie and the top three buttons of his shirt, but he looked tense instead of relaxed.

Welcome to the club.

He angled the phone away from his mouth. "I'm calling my mother to tell her about the wedding. Need to call anyone?"

Guilt sank its teeth into her like a great white shark. "No. Thanks."

"Do you have any family? I didn't ask or give you the option of having someone at the ceremony."

"There's only my…mother. But she's leaving in a few days for a fifteen-day South Pacific cruise. I didn't want to bother her."

Susan and Lauryn's father had booked the cruise before he died. Rather than cancel the trip Susan had decided to go in his memory and had asked Lauryn to accompany her. But Lauryn wasn't ready yet. Not ready to forgive the lie or to give up on her quest to learn about her birthmother.

"You're not concerned she'll hear about our marriage from another source? Brandon's sending out a press release tomorrow."

"She lives in Sacramento. I can't see the newspapers out there carrying the story. Can you?"

"Probably not."

"I'll tell her when she gets back." Or never. Lauryn had already disappointed Susan in a dozen different ways. Why do so again, especially now when their relationship was already strained?

His gaze raked her again. She bit her lip. Ever since that blasted wedding kiss he'd looked at her differently. Sexually. As if she'd slipped into something from Frederick's of Hollywood instead of Lands' End.

That wasn't good.

He stiffened and turned back to the window. "Hello, Mother… I'm in the Bahamas. I called to tell you I got married this afternoon…to Lauryn Lowes, Estate's accountant…. No, you've never met her.…"

Lauryn cringed. Rather than eavesdrop she retreated to the kitchen to give Adam privacy. She poured out the rest of her champagne, washed the flute and then put on the tea kettle more for something to do than for the need for caffeine. Her conscience probably wouldn't let her sleep tonight, anyway.

What would Adam's family think of this hasty wedding? Of her? She wasn't one of their affluent circle. At least, she hadn't been able to prove her connection yet. Would she ever? And would being Adrianna Laurence's illegitimate child be a detriment or an asset?

A sound made her turn. Adam stood on the threshold. "We need to make arrangements to move the stuff from your apartment into storage."

A mental door slammed shut. An escape route sealed. "My lease doesn't expire for months."

"You can sublet. For appearances' sake you need to vacate."

"I'll…I'll check into subletting." She knew wasting money on rent wasn't wise, but giving up her apartment seemed so…final.

She turned back to the mahogany variety box of Island Rose Tea, a Bahamian specialty, and dithered over her selection. Maybe the Cat Island Chamomile would calm her.

Fat chance.

Ever conscious of Adam watching and waiting only a few yards away, she found a mug in the cabinet and sugar on the counter and then pulled the creamer from the refrigerator.

When she could stall no longer she faced him. He'd propped a shoulder against the doorjamb. His hair looked a little more disheveled than usual, making her fingers itch to smooth it.

Ridiculous. No touching except when required by an audience.

"What did you tell your mother?" she asked. "About us, I mean. When Cassie asked today I didn't know what to say. We need to be to be on the same page."

"Agreed." His unwavering gaze made her fidgety. "What did you tell Cassie?"

She'd been caught off guard because she and Adam hadn't concocted a cover story. Reluctantly, Lauryn had admitted she'd developed a crush on Adam after meeting him at the initial interview. But she wasn't telling *him* that. "That we met at work and tried to keep our involvement quiet because fraternization is against Estate policy."

"That's good. I'll use that."

"But what did you tell your mother?"

"Just what you overheard. That I married Estate's accountant today. Mother wasn't sober enough to process more. You'll soon discover she has a drinking problem. If you want to have a coherent conversation with her then you have to do it before noon."

She heard suppressed anger—or was it frustration?—and maybe a hint of concern in his voice. "What about your brothers and sisters? Besides Cassie, you have two of each, right?"

"Right. My brothers, Parker and Stephen, are older, my sisters, Brooke and Brittany, the twins, are younger. I'll e-mail them."

"I don't have any siblings, but I can't imagine delivering such big news via an impersonal e-mail. Don't you want to call them?"

"We're not that close."

Sympathy welled within her—sympathy she couldn't afford to feel for him if she wanted to keep her distance. At least he had a family. Maybe it wasn't a perfect one, but he had them, and if he wasn't close to them that was his fault. "But—"

The tea kettle shrieked, making her nearly jump out of her skin.

Adam pushed off the jamb, turned off the stove and removed the kettle from the burner. "Lauryn, it would seem odd if I preferred to spend my wedding night talking on the phone with my family instead of alone with my bride."

The insinuation of what most newly married couples would be doing on their first night as husband and wife wound through her, tensing her muscles, shortening her breath, quickening her pulse.

She was attracted to Adam. Despite his alleged womanizing ways. Despite the fact that he was using her. Despite the temporary nature of this relationship. She'd believed it would be easy to ignore the chemistry for two years.

Wrong.

Forget the tea. She needed distance and solitude not a hot drink. And she needed to get her head together and her hormones under control. "Is it safe to walk on the beach here at night?"

"Probably not alone."

"Oh." Another escape route sealed and another bout of claustrophobia encroached. "Never mind then."

"Grab a jacket."

"But—"

"Lauryn. Grab a jacket. We'll walk." The words were an order, but also a warning. One she didn't dare ignore.

Not if she wanted to get through this night without doing something she'd regret.

Like consummating her marriage of convenience.

Six

Adam couldn't sleep.

No surprise.

He braced his forearms on the porch railing spanning the rear of the cottage and stared blindly into the night. The steady crash of the waves failed to soothe him, and the brisk sea breeze did nothing to cool his overheated skin. The woman sleeping on the other side of the closed glass doors behind him took a lot of the credit—or blame—for that.

Lauryn's kiss after the "I dos" had zapped him like an electric eel and then she'd turned off that sexual current like a circuit breaker.

How did she do it? Because he sure as hell hadn't been able to. His body still hummed.

Why now? Why her? Why did his hibernating libido have to jolt awake for a woman who wanted nothing to do with him?

It wasn't until after she had retired to her bedroom for the night that he'd realized he hadn't learned anything new about her during the long walk on the beach or the Scrabble game afterward except that she had a bigger vocabulary than he did and a competitive streak to rival his.

His wife played her cards close to her chest.

His *wife*.

Married. *Him*.

His mouth dried. He reached for his Kalik beer. The sparkle of moonlight on his wedding ring stopped him short of the bottle. He flexed his fingers, noting he didn't feel as trapped or freaked out as he'd expected.

Did he have it in him to be faithful to one woman even temporarily? God knows he'd never found a woman he wanted exclusively or one who'd seemed capable of fidelity to him. The women who came and went at Estate changed men as often as they changed clothes.

Two years with only Lauryn. One hundred four weeks. Seven hundred thirty days. And nights.

And no guarantee he'd get between her sheets.

Was infidelity encoded in DNA? If he ever fell in love, would he betray the woman the way his father had his mother? Nah, because he wasn't falling. He'd seen too many relationships turn acrimonious to ever want to go there. And knowing his father's secret and not being able to tell had been its own kind of hell.

He lifted the bottle and sipped. The Bahamas brew wasn't bad. Maybe he should check into ordering it for the club.

He couldn't check into the customs regulations tonight, but there was one decision he could make. Should he stay on the island until Monday as planned and risk driving himself nuts with need for his bride or return home early to the safety and separation a ten-thousand-square-foot house would allow?

An early return meant a command performance at the family's Sunday dinner—an event he'd prefer to postpone as long as possible. The Garrisons weren't a warm, fuzzy bunch. Scaring Lauryn off so soon in the game wouldn't be good.

They needed this honeymoon for a number of reasons.

One: appearances. A real newlywed couple would want solitude.

Two: he could hardly show up at dinner knowing nothing about the woman he'd married. If he did this charade would sink faster than lead.

Three: Lauryn jumped each time he touched her and, other than that wedding shocker, she still stiffened when he kissed her. That stung. Women didn't flinch from him. They melted, begged and wrapped themselves around him like a spider web.

But not Lauryn Lowes. Garrison. Lauryn *Garrison.*

Why not? What flipped her switches? And why didn't she desire him? Women wanted him. His bride shouldn't be an exception.

Changing her mind on the sex issue wasn't just about getting laid anymore. It was a matter of keeping the pretense. And pride. Staying in the Bahamas would give him time to diagnose and rectify the problem. He could hardly seduce her with work and family interrupting.

He needed a strategy.

The door opened behind him. Adam turned and almost choked on his beer. Lauryn stood framed in the doorway, a bedside lamp outlining her boxers-and-baggy-T-shirt-clad shape. A thin, worn T-shirt clearly outlined her full breasts and erect nipples in the pale moonlight.

He couldn't stifle a groan.

She startled and jerked to a halt. Her eyes found him in the shadows and widened. "Oh. I'm sorry. I didn't know you were out here."

"Can't sleep?"

"Um, no. You?"

"I'm used to being up nights."

"Are you hungry? I could fix something."

"Thanks, but you don't have to cook for me. I didn't marry you to get a maid or a chef."

"The estate is fully staffed?"

"Yes. And they've been informed that we're moving in."

"Can you trust them not to leak our separate sleeping arrangements?"

The muscles in the back of his neck knotted. Another reason to talk Lauryn into bed. "Good question. Like you, they signed confidentiality agreements, and they've done well with the visiting celebrities thus far. But there are no guarantees."

Her teeth gleamed in the moonlight as she bit her lip, reminding him of her taste and making him hunger for another sample. "Does the house have any suites with adjoining rooms?"

It took a second to pull his brain out of his pants. "The master suite has an attached sitting room."

"There's our solution. I'll tell them I sleep alone because you snore."

He snapped upright. "I don't snore."

She smiled, the first genuine smile she'd offered him since this *thing* began, and her eyes sparkled with mischief. The combo knocked the wind out of him and drained the blood from his brain. "I didn't say you did. I said we'd *tell* them you did."

"Why don't we tell them *you* snore?"

She shook her head. "Be a gentleman, Adam."

He'd never felt less like a gentleman in his life. He wanted to back her into that room, toss her on the bed and spend the rest of the night making her moan, beg and scream his name.

Jeezus, where did that come from?

She took a quick step backward.

Surely his wife wasn't a mind reader? Or had his lust shown on his face? "Lauryn, you don't have to leave. The deck is sturdy enough to hold both of us. We'll think of something to tell the staff—but not that I snore."

A man had his pride.

Her cautious gaze roamed over him and his recently awakened libido reacted as if her hands had done the exploring—a fact his swim trunks wouldn't be able to hide much longer. He shifted his stance. "Want a beer?"

She shook her head. "No, thank you. Were you, um, going for a swim?"

"Thought about it. But I don't know the area and forgot to ask Cassie if it was safe to swim off shore."

"Shark bait wouldn't fill the council seat." The teasing lilt of her voice zapped him with another jolt of arousal. He hadn't known she had a sense of humor.

"No, but it'd make you a rich widow."

Her amusement vanished. "Don't. Don't joke about that."

He shrugged off the concern in her voice. "So why can't you sleep?"

Please say it's because you're horny.

She eased closer to the railing, but kept a couple of yards between them. His tongue nearly fell out of his mouth at the sight of her long legs beneath those short shorts. How had he missed those legs? Had his head been stuck in a hole these past seven months?

"I kept thinking about your family. Are you comfortable deceiving them?"

Not what he wanted to hear. But maybe she was working her way up to the right answer. A man could hope. "It's necessary."

She wanted more, but he wasn't going to tell her about his quest for a larger role in Garrison, Inc. Telling her his family didn't trust him with responsibility wouldn't win her over.

He finished his beer and faced her. "We have a problem."

One golden eyebrow lifted, and so did the lush fullness of her breasts when she reached up to capture her wind-tossed hair in her hands.

"You flinch every time I touch you. My family, particularly my sisters, will pick up on that immediately."

She snatched an audible breath. "I'll work on it."

"We could practice."

A wary, caged light entered her eyes. "Practice?"

"You have a better idea?"

Her low chuckle danced over his skin like dusting fingertips. "You're beginning to sound like a corny character in a bad novel."

"Corny? *Corny?* Me?" No one had ever accused him of that. Loner, risk-taker, ambitious, emotionally unavailable? Sure. His brothers, five and six years older than him, had always dumped Adam in the same category as their younger sisters or ignored him completely. But nobody had ever called him corny.

He didn't like it. Especially not from Lauryn.

"Adam, this isn't junior high or high school where you make out just to see how far you can go before getting caught."

"You made out in junior high?"

She gave him a get-real stare.

Right. She wasn't the type. She was too…what was the word he needed? Prim? Proper? Straightlaced? And that was why she was the perfect bride for him. The council and his family had to believe he'd mended his partying ways.

"I don't do casual sex."

He moved closer, close enough to feel her body heat and catch her scent. "What's casual about sleeping with your husband?"

Her throat moved as she swallowed and awareness tightened her face. Sexual tension crackled in the air around them. "L-let me rephrase that. I don't do meaningless sex. And you agreed. To the no-sex clause."

"Then what do you suggest?" He lifted a hand to smooth her hair, but she flinched out of reach.

"Can't we just be…friends?"

"Friends." The last thing any guy wants to hear from a woman.

He'd never survive four days in paradise with his reluctant bride without losing his mind. And the thought of two years of celibacy made his package shrivel.

He had to come up with a plan. A plan to seduce his wife.

Lauryn wasn't ready for this. Not yet.

Who was she kidding? She'd *never* be ready to try and convince the people who knew Adam best that she was head over heels in love with him. But she'd try. That was their deal.

She clung tightly to Adam's hand as they approached the Garrisons' Bal Harbor estate on Sunday night and hoped she didn't blow it.

She would have preferred staying in the Bahamas and tiptoeing around the growing sexual tension between her and Adam to meeting his family *en masse*, but this morning he'd suddenly insisted on coming home early to organize the move and have Sunday dinner with his family. They'd spent most of the day apart in their respective homes packing boxes for the movers to pick up tomorrow. But that brief reprieve was over and now the spotlight was on her and she had a touch of stage fright.

Knowing she'd be sleeping in Adam's condo tonight didn't help her anxiety level, but the house wasn't ready. Specifically, the sofa bed for the sitting room wouldn't be delivered until tomorrow morning. Since she'd refused to let Adam share her bed and he'd refused to sleep in another room for one night, the condo had been their only option.

Lauryn was so nervous she was almost nauseous. She searched her mind for a distraction. "Mrs. Suarez said something about your brothers getting married recently?"

Adam didn't slow his pace as he crossed the brick driveway. "Parker married Anna, his executive assistant, in August. Stephen married Megan in September, and they have a three-year-old daughter who probably won't be here tonight. My sister Brittany is engaged to Emilio Jefferies, one of Garrison, Inc.'s rivals. If he's here, you can expect Parker to be on his worst behavior. Brooke is still single."

"How will I tell the twins apart?"

"Brooke is a people-pleaser. Count on Mother to be yanking her chain. Brittany is more laid-back."

"And your brothers?"

"Parker's the oldest and he's a control freak. Stephen's okay."

Control freak? Was there tension between Adam and his brother? "Will Cassie and Brandon be here?"

"Not likely."

"That's too bad." Lauryn could have used a friendly face.

"Trust me, it's better to keep Mother and Cassie apart."

Cassie would be a reminder of Mr. Garrison's infidelity. That wouldn't be easy for any woman to take. "I guess so. I wasn't thinking."

The setting sun cast a mellow light over the creamy stucco walls and terracotta tile roof of an imposing Spanish-style house. If Lauryn weren't meeting her in-laws she'd probably find the place attractive in a grandiose we-have-loads-of-money way.

And then it hit her and she almost tripped. She'd married a millionaire. Sure, she'd known Adam came from the same affluent community her mother had, but Lauryn had never made the connection that *she* had married money and soon she'd be living like this. Probably because the money aspect wasn't what mattered. She wanted those diaries. She had no interest in being showered with diamonds and no desire to be a pampered, kept woman. No matter what Adam wanted.

When this was over she'd go back to life as usual, albeit with an extremely nice nest egg.

Adam stopped in front of the mahogany door and hit her with a head-on gaze. "You look beautiful. Remind me to thank Cassie for that dress."

Pleasure rushed through her. "I chose it."

"Very nice. Conservative and tasteful, but with a latent sexuality that any man would enjoy tapping. Remember, don't flinch," he whispered as he cradled her cheek in a warm palm and then he covered her mouth with his. Lauryn didn't have time to react—or not—to the unexpected kiss before the front door opened. Adam slowly lifted his head.

His hand lingered on her jaw line before he released her and then he flashed a disarmingly boyish and guilty grin at the fiftyish-year-old woman inside. "Late again. I know. But I was distracted."

The woman's stern face melted into a smile. "Well, you're here now. Come in. You know what happens when you keep her waiting."

Her? Who?

Adam tugged Lauryn forward. "Lauryn, this is Lisette Wilson. She's the saint who manages my mother. Lisette, meet my beautiful bride, Lauryn."

"So you really did it?" a male voice called from inside.

Lisette quickly shook Lauryn's hand, greeting her warmly and then stepping aside.

A tall, dark-haired, brown-eyed man stood behind her.

Adam ushered Lauryn inside a foyer almost as large as Lauryn's living room. "Ask Brandon and Cassie. They were our witnesses. Lauryn, my brother Stephen."

Stephen appraised Lauryn as he shook her hand, and then turned to an approaching man who looked uncannily like him. Same hair, eyes and a similar build. Definitely a Garrison even though neither man shared Adam's sexy blue eyes. "Pay up."

"The one digging for his wallet is Parker," Adam said dryly. "I can't believe you guys bet on my wedding."

Stephen shrugged. "What can I say? You are the last one anyone thought would settle down. But hey, I bet you would. Eventually."

"This is Lauryn. You might have seen her around Estate. She's the only woman I let play with my…accounts." Adam flashed a teasing smile and wink her way for the benefit of their audience, and Lauryn nearly swallowed her tongue. Adam deserved a standing ovation for his acting ability.

Five more people crowded into the foyer practically forcing Lauryn and Adam against the door and increasing Lauryn's sense of being trapped. She easily identified the two slender brunettes as the twins. Another dark-haired woman, a redhead and an olive-complexioned man made up the group. The names blurred as Lauryn shook hands and accepted what seemed to be genuine welcomes.

This isn't so bad.

"Adam, I never expected you to literally take my advice and settle down," one of the twins said. Brittany, Lauryn decided, because she held hands with the only non-Garrison male. Emilio.

"You mean my advice," Stephen corrected and his sister rolled her eyes. Stephen gravitated toward the redhead. Megan?

Adam's arm slid around Lauryn's waist. For once she was glad to have him to lean on and burrowed tighter against his side. She saw the surprise and the flare of arousal in his eyes as he looked down at her. She hoped he remembered she was acting. "Neither of you get credit. I found Lauryn without your help."

"May I see your ring?" Brooke asked.

With all eyes focused on her Lauryn wanted to squirm. She extended her hand and hoped it didn't tremble too much.

"It's beautiful."

"Your brother has excellent taste." Good. Her voice sounded almost normal.

Brooke looked doubtful. "Adam does? How long have you been dating?"

Panic hit Lauryn hard and fast. She and Adam hadn't discussed that. She looked at him but he'd turned to talk to Stephen. "Um, not long. We met when I interviewed for the job at Estate seven and a half months ago, but we, um, tried to deny our feelings…because of the no-fraternization policy."

She stuck to the truth as much as she could because she hated lying to these people. To anyone, really. She'd spent too much of her youth telling whoppers. And getting caught. She kept waiting for the half-truths of her current life to blow up in her face. One misstep and—

"What is wrong with you people?" a harsh and slightly slurred female voice asked from behind the others. The group parted for the thin woman barging through them like a Coast Guard cutter. Her short dark hair was streaked with gray. Her cold, blue gaze plowed into Lauryn's. Adam's eyes, only

Lauryn had never seen his look as hard. And she hoped she never did.

"Why is it none of my children have the decency to marry in a church?"

"Hello, Mother," Adam said.

The chilly gaze raked Lauryn from head to toe before shifting to Adam. He air-kissed his mother's cheek with about as much warmth as a polar ice cap. "This is Lauryn. My wife."

"So I hear."

Lauryn suppressed a flinch at the caustic tone.

Adam continued as if his mother hadn't rudely interrupted. "Lauryn, Bonita Garrison. My mother."

"It's nice to meet—"

"Are you pregnant?" Bonita Garrison snarled.

Lauryn gasped and lowered the hand she'd extended. "No."

"Good. I need another drink. Lisette!" Adam's mother wheeled around and headed across the vast living room beyond a fat stone column. The housekeeper hustled after her.

"I shouldn't be surprised to find her already working her way through a bottle," Adam muttered.

"That's our mother," Brittany said. "I can't believe you didn't take Lauryn on a decent honeymoon. Three days in the Bahamas? Please. I never took you for a cheapskate."

Adam shrugged. "We have too much to do. We're moving into the Sunset Island estate tomorrow. I'll make it up to Lauryn later."

"You're giving up the bachelor pad?" Stephen said in a surprise-laden voice.

"No. The property's too valuable to sell and it should continue to appreciate. The club will use it the same way I've been using the estate. But Lauryn and I want a home. The kind you'd raise a family in." He quoted her words from the night he'd given her the house tour.

Adam's arm around Lauryn's waist guided her along with the group as it moved toward the French doors on the far side of the room, through which Bonita Garrison had disappeared. Outside, a limestone patio surrounded an Olympic-size pool. A border of tall palms swayed in the evening breeze. Lauryn tried not to gawk, but it was impossible not to be overwhelmed by such opulence.

"Drink?" Adam released her and moved toward a marble-topped wet bar.

Lauryn debated sipping something to calm her nerves versus the possibility of loosening her tongue and tripping over it. And then she noticed Adam's disconcerted expression. She realized he had no clue of her drink preference. "Um, sure. Do you have a dry white wine tonight?"

"Coming up."

"We're late for dinner," Mrs. Garrison groused.

Adam leisurely reached for a goblet and bottle. "Go ahead, Mother. Lauryn and I will join you in a minute. Lisette, would you ask the kitchen to serve champagne with dessert? And join us for a glass."

The housekeeper flushed. "My pleasure, Mr. Adam."

His mother flounced off, leaving her children looking after her with almost identical looks of disgust on their faces.

When Adam handed Lauryn the wineglass, she considered knocking it back in one gulp. Adam obviously shared the sentiment since he downed half his bourbon in one swallow.

"You don't have to wait for us," Adam said and the others filed inside, but Adam caught her elbow and held her back.

"Is something wrong?" she asked.

"Just doing what's expected." He encircled her waist, pulled her close and kissed her. Taking advantage of her surprised "Oh," he skipped the preliminaries and deepened the kiss. She tasted the liquor on his tongue, but it wasn't unpleasant. Neither was the warmth of his body against hers.

She dug the fingers of her free hand into his firm waist and struggled to shut down her knee-weakening, nerve-tingling response to his scent, his heat, the skill of the silken tongue plying hers. But denying the sexual heat he generated wasn't possible. He made all her senses come alive in ways beyond the hot rush of sex she remembered from her wilder days. She yearned to burrow closer, to linger and explore.

What would it be like to be Adam's lover? Would the intimate act live up to the promise in his kisses or would he disappoint her as others had before him?

Don't start liking this.

Too late.

When he finally lifted his head she panted as if she'd run a mile. She licked her sensitized lips and tried to quell her clamoring hormones and catch her breath. "W-why did you do that?"

"We're being watched," he said against her neck. He caught her face when she would have turned and traced the shell of her ear with a featherlight touch. "Don't look."

His five-o'clock shadow rasped deliciously against her skin as he nuzzled from behind her ear to her collarbone, his breath warm and moist. She shivered. Just when she thought she'd dissolve into a wet puddle on the patio tiles he slowly straightened and released her. A dark flush coated his cheekbones.

"If you're ready for battle, let's go."

Lauryn's stomach plunged and she nearly dropped her wineglass. Any lingering remnants of desire vanished. "It gets worse?"

"Usually. Garrison family dinners are not enjoyed. They're endured."

"Then why do you come?"

"Because they're my family." Adam laced his fingers through hers and, palm-to-palm, led her toward what felt increasingly like the lion's den.

And then she remembered her father's favorite quote. "There's a price for every lie you tell. Before you open your mouth, be sure you're prepared to pay it."

The tension throughout dinner was of the clichéd thick-enough-to-cut-with-a-knife variety.

Beneath the superficially polite conversation Lauryn sensed undercurrents between the members of the Garrison clan, but especially between Parker and his soon-to-be brother-in-law, Emilio Jeffries. She'd have to ask Adam to explain the family dynamics later. But for now she was glad the ordeal was almost over. The staff had served the dessert, poured the champagne and left the room.

"Anna's pregnant," Parker announced.

Lauryn lifted her gaze to the brunette sitting directly across from her. "Congratulations."

Anna's eyes shone with happiness. "Thank you. You can see why I for one would have been thrilled if you were pregnant. We could have compared notes."

Lauryn ignored the derisive snort from Bonita and shifted in her chair. "Sorry."

"Perhaps soon," Adam said. He captured Lauryn's hand and carried it to his lips for a tender kiss topped off with one of those charismatic smiles that made her heart flutter irregularly. "I'd like to make a toast to my beautiful bride, the only woman to ever make 'forever' sound like a promise instead of a life sentence."

Lauryn almost knocked over her stemware. She had to remind herself Adam was acting, and that she had no reason whatsoever to turn warm and mushy when he looked at her that way.

"Here, here," and "Congratulations," echoed around the table. Adam leaned forward and whispered a kiss across her lips.

He was good. Very good. And she almost regretted him drawing back. Their gazes remained locked and tendrils of need spiraled through her.

He's your husband. Sex with him would be okay.

No, it wouldn't. You don't love him and he doesn't love you. Wait for someone who matters. Someone who cares about you and not just about getting off.

But she wanted him. More than she could ever remember wanting anyone.

"Well, since we're making announcements…" Brooke's hesitant statement startled Lauryn back into awareness of her surroundings. She blinked and looked away from Adam's mesmerizing blue eyes. Brooke paused, inhaled deeply and then said in a rush, "I'm pregnant, too."

Shocked silence filled the room, and then Bonita barked, "By whom?"

"I'm sorry, Mother, that's none of your business."

"It is my business if you are going to shame this family like your father with another bastard," Bonita bit out.

Lauryn winced, thinking of Cassie. No, her new friend definitely wouldn't be welcome here.

"Who's the father, Brooke?" Adam sounded fierce. Angry. Protective. Lauryn filed that surprising facet to her new husband away.

"I'm a grown woman, Adam. I don't need my brothers to fight my battles for me. Suffice to say, the father is not going to be a part of my baby's life or mine and leave it at that."

Bonita slammed her glass on the table, sloshing half the clear liquid—she'd refused the champagne—onto the damask cloth. The smell of gin filled the air. "Don't expect Garrison money to support your mistake."

She rose unsteadily and left the dining room in a huff with Lisette hot on her heels.

Adam broke the uneasy silence. "Brooke, how are you going to manage the condo complex and take care of the baby alone? The bastard responsible should help—at least financially."

His sister's chin lifted. "I don't want his help, and I'll have day care or a nanny like any other parent."

"What about maternity leave?" Brittany asked quietly.

Brooke looked at the faces around table. "Look, I'm not saying I have all the details worked out. This was a surprise for me, too. But I am having this baby with or without my family's support. Now can we *please* talk about something else?"

Lauryn could feel Adam's tension across the space between them, and she was touched by his need to charge to his sister's aid, but now wasn't the time. Brooke looked too on edge.

Lauryn covered the hand fisted in Adam's lap to draw his attention. When he met her gaze, she silently urged him to change the subject. He inclined his head slightly and turned back to his siblings.

"We have to do something about Mother's drinking. It was bad before, but it's worsened since Dad died."

Lauryn noticed Brooke looked relieved by the diversion.

"What do you suggest?" Parker asked. "Locking the liquor cabinet? It won't work."

"What about rehab?" Megan, Stephen's wife, suggested.

Adam's hand fisted on the table. "It's our best shot. She's not going to quit on her own."

"She's not going to go to rehab voluntarily, either," Brittany added.

"Tough." At that moment Lauryn thought Adam looked hard enough to force his mother into capitulating—as hard as his mother had looked at Lauryn earlier.

A frisson of unease slithered up her spine. Adam wouldn't make a good adversary.

Several tense, silent moments passed, and then Brittany cleared her throat. "On a positive note, Emilio and I plan to get married at Christmas. We'd like you all to be there."

Parker scowled at Emilio and then shifted his attention to his sister. "Is that wise considering we have a spy within Garrison, Inc. feeding information to your fiancé's family?"

"Dammit, Parker," Emilio growled, "Jordan does not have a spy in your company."

"How can you be certain when you've admitted you and Jordan aren't on speaking terms?"

"I could look into it," Adam offered.

"Forget it. I'll handle it," Parker snapped back.

"You're not handling it," Adam insisted. "The information leak has been going on for months. A fresh set of eyes—"

"I said, I'll handle it."

Adam persisted, "I want to help, and I'm more persuasive than you."

"Forget it, *little brother*. We're not talking about charming the panties off women. This is business."

Lauryn's cheeks burned with embarrassment. *She* was one of the women Adam had supposedly charmed out of her clothing.

Adam turned rigid beside her. The men looked ready to come to blows. Lauryn rested a hand on Adam's forearm and then glared at Parker. "You shouldn't dismiss Adam's business acumen. Estate is extremely profitable because of him, and the employee turnover rate is next to nil. He knows what he's doing and he knows how to read and manage people."

All eyes turned on her.

Her stomach sank. Good grief. She'd reacted like one of Pavlov's dogs again with another conditioned response. Why had she opened her mouth? Because Parker's insulting tone hit one of her hot buttons. But this was not her fight and arguing wasn't the way to make a good impression with the in-laws.

Parker drilled her with an unblinking stare—nothing new to Lauryn since her father used to do the same—and when she didn't cower or look away he scanned the rest of the party.

"I don't need Adam's help because I'm looking into brokering a deal with Jordan Jefferies just to keep the peace between our families."

Almost everyone at the table gaped at Parker in surprise...everyone except Brooke, who looked relieved, probably because her pregnancy was no longer the topic of conversation. Lauryn glanced at Adam and found him watching his sister with a frown puckering his brow.

Lauryn only half listened while Parker outlined the potential deal.

Something very important had just happened at this table. And it wasn't Parker's announcement.

And then she remembered the research she'd done for a college psychology paper. She'd been fascinated by the way birth order affected personality and behavior—mainly because she'd needed to understand her own twisted family dynamics and her hackles-raised response to her father's edicts.

If she remembered correctly, the textbooks said middle children often reported feeling invisible and overlooked. It wasn't unusual for them to seek recognition.

She studied her husband.

Gulp. Her *husband*.

Adam seemed far too confident to need anyone's approval—other than the business council's nominating committee, that is. He'd claimed it wasn't the council presidency that mattered, but what it represented.

She fingered her champagne glass. What did that position of responsibility represent?

Recognition of his success from the Miami business community?

Or respect from his family?

Seven

Lauryn had defended him tonight.

Adam couldn't remember the last time someone had stepped up to the plate for him. Not his father, his mother or his brothers. He didn't expect his sisters to because as the older sibling it was his job to look out for Brooke and Britt.

And yet Lauryn had gone to bat for him without hesitation and without him asking her to. That flash of fire in her eyes when she'd stared Parker down had been downright sexy. It made Adam desire her even more.

Would she be as passionate a lover?

With his thoughts fixated on the woman making use of his bathroom, he sat on his bed in his loft bedroom staring blindly at the half wall that overlooked the living room below. Lauryn wasn't the first female to shower here by a long shot, but she was the only one who'd ever made him want to pull up a chair and watch the water stream over her naked curves. Better yet, join her and let his hands and mouth follow the water's path.

That's because by the time a woman uses your shower you've already had her, and you're eager to put her into a cab and send her home.

His women didn't sleep here. Lauryn would be the first.

Moments later the bathroom door opened and Lauryn emerged in a cloud of steam. She'd pinned up her hair, but damp tendrils clung to her freshly scrubbed and flushed cheeks.

How could he have ever believed her mousy? She looked so damned desirable wearing the shapeless baggy shorts and worn T-shirt his teeth ached.

"Why did you defend me tonight?"

She jerked to a halt and hugged the black dress she'd worn to dinner tighter against her chest. The garment had covered her from neck to knees, outlining an hourglass shape that made his mouth water and his hands itch to explore. The sexy little slit in the back hem of the skirt had had him groaning at each glimpse of thigh. He saw more skin on the Estate dance floor every night, but because Lauryn dressed conservatively, that flash of taboo territory had hit him like a bouncer's taser.

She shifted her weight from one long, lean leg to the other. "Something in your brother's condescending tone ticked me off. He reminded me of—"

She mashed her lips together and shook her head as if regretting her words and headed toward the dresser.

He rose, blocking her path and putting them face-to-face with barely a foot between them. "Of who?"

She tipped her head back, met his gaze and then sighed. "Of my father. He was a control freak, too. Very his-way-or-the-highway."

The thought of Lauryn being browbeaten into submission lit a bonfire of anger in Adam's belly. Was that why she was so conservative and quiet now?

"Lauryn, I don't need you to fight my battles for me," he said softly.

"I'm sure you don't." She ducked around him, tossed her dress over the back of his valet chair, and then with her back to him, dug around in her suitcase as if she'd find buried treasure inside.

Adam crossed the loft, stopping behind her. Her scent filled his nostrils and her warmth drew him like a fire does a shipwrecked sailor. He rested one hand on her hip and traced a damp lock clinging to her nape with the other.

She stiffened, but not soon enough to still feel her tremor.

"I don't need your defense, but I appreciate it," he said against her ear.

"It's what a wife would do, isn't it?" she asked without moving.

"No clue. I'm flying blind here."

She slowly turned. He detected a flicker of hunger in her eyes and his lungs jammed.

"Adam… You laid it on a bit thick tonight. I know making your family believe this is real is—"

"You kissed me back. On the beach. By the pool. In the driveway."

Her expression turned wary. "Maybe I'm as good an actor as you."

"You can't fake the arousal darkening your cheeks or widening your pupils." He lowered his eyes to the stiff nipples tenting her shirt. "You can't fake that."

She folded her arms and lifted her chin. "And your point is…?"

"You want me."

"Me and a hundred other women. But part of being an adult is realizing you can't have everything you want."

He spread his arms. "You can have me. Any way you want me."

She hesitated for a moment, catching her bottom lip with her teeth and then her mouth twisted in a wry grimace. "So I've heard."

Not the invitation to share the only bed in the condo he'd been hoping for. "Is that what this is about? You're waiting for the blood test results?"

"No. I'm adhering to our agreement."

At some time during the miserable family dinner he'd forgotten about convincing his siblings he'd settled down, and he'd started looking for excuses to touch Lauryn, to make her breath catch, her skin flush. He'd actively sought opportunities to kiss her because kissing her filled him with an excitement and anticipation he hadn't felt for anyone or anything in a very long time.

How many kisses had he stolen tonight? Four? No, five. After that last one by the car he'd been so hard he could barely fold himself into the Beemer to drive them home.

"Agreements can be amended." He cupped her nape, savoring the warm silkiness of her skin against his palm. "Let me show you how good it could be between us, Lauryn."

Her lids fluttered closed, and then she sucked a quick breath and popped them open again. "No."

It wasn't as if he'd never heard "no" before, but he'd never heard it from a woman who'd almost eaten him alive on three separate occasions. He could accept Lauryn's refusal and walk away if she didn't want him. But she did.

So why the mixed signals? Why make them both suffer? He wanted to kiss her until she begged him to peel off her clothing, toss her onto his king-size bed and bury himself in her wet heat.

He'd bet she'd be as hot as her mouth.

No. Hotter. Wetter. He broke a sweat just thinking about it.

As if she'd read his mind her eyes widened, her lips parted on an unsteady inhalation and color washed her face and neck, warming the skin beneath his hand.

Oh yeah. She wanted him. He pulled her forward.

"Your family's approval," she blurted when he was an inch from her delectable mouth. Her palms spread on his chest and pushed. "That's why you want to win the business council's nomination. Isn't it?"

Talk about a mood-killer. He straightened and released her. "That's personal."

"So you keep saying. But, Adam, the day I became your wife I became part of your personal life. If you don't tell me what's going on I can't help."

He wasn't going to get laid tonight. Unless he changed her mind he'd be sleeping downstairs on the sofa.

Shoving a hand through his hair, he turned and walked toward the half wall and braced his arms on the ledge. He debated how much to reveal. But like she'd said, she was part of this now. "I want a bigger stake in Garrison, Inc."

"Why? Isn't Estate enough?"

"No. It's not. My father kept me out of the Garrison offices when he was alive and now Parker's doing the same. And I'm sick of having to prove myself only to be denied an equal share in the family business."

She joined him by the rail. "But why does that matter? You're successful without Parker's approval."

"I don't want his approval." His frustrated growl sent her eyebrows skyward. "I was groomed to take my place in the family business. I have the education and experience to take a more active role. I can't help wondering if I was denied a place at Garrison, Inc. because I knew about my father's affair with Cassie's mother and had the balls to call him on it."

"You think you're being punished because you didn't keep quiet and take one for the team?"

"Exactly. But I'll never know. Will I?"

"You do realize you're not being kept out because you lack business acumen, don't you? I wasn't lying when I told Parker you run a first-rate organization. I've worked in several places that weren't, so I know what I'm talking about."

Her support expanded something inside his chest.

She tilted her head and considered him in silence for several moments. "You're a typical middle child, you know."

"What does that mean?" And was it an insult?

"Middle children have to find their own niche, their own way to excel, to stand out from the crowd."

"That's…accurate. Parker and Stephen were always tight with each other and with our father. Brooke and Brittany had the girl thing going. I learned early on to entertain myself and go after what I wanted. Alone. If I wanted my parents' attention I had to do something grander, wilder or louder than my siblings. In the process I earned a reckless reputation I can't seem to live down even though I quit that juvenile behavior years ago."

"And you think having a wife will help you shake the bad rep?"

"The right kind of wife, yes."

She wrapped her arms around her middle and turned toward the two-story window wall opposite the loft. He followed her gaze. The lights of a cruise ship leaving the Port of Miami via Government Cut twinkled against the night sky.

The ocean view had been a prime draw in his purchase of the condo. But the view couldn't soothe him tonight.

He looked into her eyes. "You're an only child?"

"Yes."

"And what are typical onlies like?"

Lauryn shifted, glanced away. "Onlies can go one of two ways. Conformist or rebel."

"Which were you?"

Her cautious gaze found his again. "Which do you think?"

He considered her conventional clothing, her restrained hair and body language and her solitary life. "Conformist. Which is a good thing since a woman with a wild reputation is the last thing I need."

And yet the urge to make her wild *in bed* had him aroused to the verge of wanting to say to hell with his no-sex promise. He turned abruptly, crossed the loft and yanked back the comforter. "Let's hit the sack."

She remained by the railing. "I told you I'm not sharing your bed."

"Lauryn, there's only one bed. Since we're moving to the estate tomorrow, I didn't convert the study into a bedroom."

"If I were willing to share then we'd be staying at the Sunset Island estate tonight. I'll take the sofa. Do you have a spare pillow?"

"What's the matter? Don't trust yourself not to jump me?"

Another long stretch of silence filled the air before she averted her gaze. "Maybe."

Her honesty hit him like a sucker punch.

But he wasn't sure he could control himself if she was in bed beside him, either. As badly as he craved her body, he wasn't taking her until she was wet, willing and begging.

Until then, he could survive a few sleepless nights. "Take the bed."

* * *

Lauryn's pulse raced and her palms dampened. Standing at the top of the stairs of the Sunset estate, she weighed her choices.

Three hallways radiated off the balcony encircling the foyer like the points of the mariner's compass inlaid in the foyer floor below. Left? Right? Dead ahead? Which hall led to her birthmother's bedroom?

Downstairs Adam closed the front door behind the departing movers. He'd insisted on emptying her apartment, and the crew had stored most of her furniture and belongings in an empty staff apartment above one of the garages. They'd left her and Adam's suitcases in the foyer.

She heard Adam's tread on the stairs and turned to watch him ascend. Worn jeans and a white T-shirt fit him like a second skin, outlining a body worthy of a pin-up calendar. His biceps bulged under the weight of her overstuffed luggage.

Sexy. Her mouth dried. *But just sex isn't enough anymore. Remember? No more meaningless affairs. You promised.*

But promises couldn't prevent the fine hairs on her body from rising like antennae whenever he was near. She'd never been so aware—so *constantly, completely* aware—of anyone before. And the more she found out about him, the worse her fascination became.

"Found the master suite yet?" he asked as he reached her side.

"Um, no." Her feet had refused to carry her beyond the landing. Now that she was where she'd longed to be for the better part of a year, she was afraid she'd discover this was nothing but a wild-goose chase and the diaries weren't here.

But what if they were? She didn't doubt the outcome—whichever it might be—would change her life. And maybe not for the better.

He tilted his head. "This way."

She followed Adam down the wide center hall toward the back of the house. Her gaze dropped from his broad shoulders to his butt doing a fine job of filling out his jeans.

Control yourself, for pity's sake.

"Our room is over the sunroom downstairs. It's the newest part of the house, added about fifteen years ago."

Before her mother died.

He went through a pair of double doors. A twenty-foot hall led her past a walk-in closet as large as her apartment living room with drawers built into a center island. Adam paused long enough to set her luggage down inside the door and then continued down the hall. Next they passed a bathroom that looked like something out of *Architectural Digest*. White marble floors. A round glass shower stall. A decadent, oversize sunken tub. Enough black marble counter space to fill a kitchen. Opposite the bathroom, an open third door revealed a comfortable-looking sitting room and the new sofa bed. Is that where she'd sleep?

She followed Adam into the sun-filled, semicircular bedroom decorated in beachy colors of sand, pearl, apricot and periwinkle. A massive raised platform bed sat against the interior wall. Its carved scallop-shaped headboard had been painted to resemble the opalescent inside of a shell. The curved exterior walls were all windows like the sunroom downstairs and shared the same view of the pool, dock and tennis courts. A chaise, love seat and small bistro table with a pair of chairs offered perfect places to share coffee or curl up and read a book.

"It's beautiful, and the view is amazing, but there's not much privacy, is there? Anyone looking out the back windows of the house can see what we're doing in here."

"One button closes the curtains." Adam flipped a switch

and a nearly silent motor closed the drapes, darkening the room completely and sealing them in shadowy seclusion. Before her eyes could adjust he hit the switch again and the curtains reopened.

The suite was much smaller than the beach house and much more intimate than his condo. Could she share this space and not give in to the sexual urges rising within her like a tidal surge?

An image flashed in her mind—an image that had haunted her all day. She tried and failed to erase it. This morning she'd awoken before Adam and tiptoed to the loft rail to see him sprawled on the sofa just below his bedroom. The plentiful display of sleek golden skin made it clear he slept nude. She'd wasted way too much time staring down at him and hoping the sheet barely covering his groin would fall to the floor.

Voyeur. A guilty flush warmed her skin.

It's just healthy curiosity. Right?

No. It was more than that. Her early days crush was back, she realized with a sinking sensation in her stomach. And it hadn't returned because of the grand gestures like the expensive car or rings. It was the little things like how Adam had been such a great sport when she'd beat him at Scrabble, or the way he opened doors and held chairs for her and always treated her with respect even though she'd basically sold herself to him.

It was the way he worried about his sister and mother, and how he hadn't ridiculed Lauryn's fear of flying. Instead, during the flight he'd explained how the plane worked, and on the return trip to Miami he'd encouraged her to take the controls for a few minutes. When she'd admitted she liked it he'd offered to arrange flying lessons for her.

She understood his struggle with his father and sympathized with his need to live down a less-than-admirable past. They had that in common.

If she weren't married to him she'd want to date him.

Maybe Adam wasn't the womanizer the tabloids claimed. Maybe he wasn't just another guy out to get laid as often as possible.

He wasn't a guy who shirked hard work, and if he were the playboy the press claimed, he would have stood back and let the paid crew do all the sweating, but he'd worked right alongside the movers today. The scent fresh of male sweat emanated from him.

And maybe you're clutching at straws because you want him.

Adam eliminated the space between them with two long strides. He braced a hand on the window frame beside her head and leaned closer. "The bed's big enough for both of us."

She shouldn't be tempted. But she was. "Adam. We've already had this conversation."

"Lauryn," he replied in the same long-suffering tone she'd used, but laughter and an invitation to sin lurked in his gorgeous blue eyes—an invitation she wanted to accept more with each passing moment.

"You're not making this easy."

"No." He cradled her face. The warmth of his palm felt so good, and the urge to lean into his touch nearly overwhelmed her.

And that was another thing. He was honest—despite their dishonest sham of a marriage. He wanted her and he didn't try to hide that fact. It made her feel a twinge of guilt over being less than one hundred percent forthcoming with him.

He just made wanting him so damned easy.

Sleeping with him wouldn't be a desperate bid for approval or a jab to get back at your father.

But it would still be wrong. In the overall scheme of things giving in to lust would not move her toward her long-term goals, and these days she always thought of the future.

She wanted to back away, to break his hold and put a safe distance between them, but this marriage was all about appearances. Adam had asked the cook to prepare a special meal for their first night in the house. If they were going to make their separate sleeping arrangements believable, public displays of affection and even passion would be necessary. Adam must have spotted some of the staff watching through the windows.

Before she could ask if that were the case he lowered his head and covered her mouth with his. He sipped from her lips and teased with his tongue, stroking and then suckling her bottom lip. Every cell in her body snapped to attention. She loved the way he kissed. Adored the way he tasted.

Last night's kiss in his mother's driveway had been hot, but not nearly as incinerating as this one. This one was a no-holds-barred assault on her senses. Hunger rose within her like mercury in a thermometer, overriding caution, good judgment and restraint and making her crave more than just kisses.

Adam backed her against the window frame. His thigh slid between hers, pressing her tender flesh. He deepened the kiss. One big hand raked upward from her waist to cover her breast. He found the sensitive tip and brushed over it again and again. Her stomach tensed with need. His erection pressed against her belly and the heat of his torso branded hers. She curled her fingers against the urge to cup and caress his hardened flesh, to test his length and breadth.

A niggling part of her brain cried *overkill*. No one watching from outside could see his tongue twining with hers or his hand on her breast. But the rest of her body mutinied. She wanted this. Wanted him. Wanted his touch. Wanted to feel the passion she'd denied herself for so long. She moved against his thigh and bubbles of pleasure floated through her system.

He lowered his hand to cover her mound. Her khaki shorts did nothing to lessen the shocking, arousing contact. She broke the kiss to gasp for air and let her head fall back against the window frame. Adam stroked her through her clothing and a moan sneaked past her lips.

You shouldn't let him do this.

Stop him. You're too vulnerable right now to think straight.

Adam nibbled and kissed her neck while his fingers worked magic. Lauryn lost herself in the heat of his breath against her skin, the nip of his teeth along the cords of her neck, the swirl of his tongue over her pulse point. She clenched her fingers in the silkiness of his hair.

Pull.

Him.

Away.

But she couldn't. Not yet. Pleasure, heady and out of control, rose swiftly until orgasm boiled through her.

Barely able to support her weight, she clung to Adam's shoulders and sagged against the hard window frame. She forced her heavy lids open and stared into Adam's passion-darkened eyes.

"Good?" he rasped between labored breaths.

Shame burned her cheeks. She lowered her arms. "You know it was. But it shouldn't have happened."

She'd slipped up. Big-time. Embarrassed, she turned her head to look out at the empty patio below. A quick scan of the downstairs windows revealed no one watching. "We don't have an audience."

Adam straightened, steadied her and then released her. A

slow smile eased across his lips. "That was for me. I told you. I always go after what I want. And I want you, Lauryn Garrison. Consider yourself warned."

And then he winked and strolled out of the room.

Lauryn's knees gave out. She slid to the floor.

What had she done?

She'd opened Pandora's Box, that's what.

And she wasn't convinced she could put the lid back on.

She'd done it again.

Lauryn's stomach flip-flopped. She'd lost herself in the music and sent signals she hadn't intended to send to her husband—signals that said she was available and sexually interested in more than just faking a relationship.

No wonder Adam had spun her into a tight embrace on the dance floor. The heat of his chest pressed her back and his arms, one around her waist and the other just below her breasts, held her close as he swayed to the music of the Grammy Award winner singing on Estate's main stage.

Adam's lips teased the sensitive skin beneath her left ear and his arousal nudged her hips. It was the urge to push back without the barrier of clothing between them that filled Lauryn with panic.

Her reasons for resisting a physical relationship grew foggier each day. Worse, Adam knew it. She saw the knowledge in his eyes each time he looked at her, felt it in the confidence and increased frequency of his touch and the seduction of his lips. The lovey-dovey gestures were supposed to be for show, for their audience. But she knew better—especially since he was slipping a few in when there was no one around.

He seemed bent on seducing her with flowers, jewelry and a handful of other small gifts, which she found by her plate, on her pillow, on her desk. But it was the easy flow of conversation over brunch each morning that was slowly eroding her defenses.

The man knew how to woo women.

But she didn't want to be just another conquest.

She wriggled herself free and faced Adam on the crowded dance floor. She had to lean close to be heard, close enough to smell the unique scent of his body mingling with his tangy cologne. *Sexy.* Her pulse quickened.

"Would you mind if I headed home early tonight?"

Adam's brows lowered and his eyes filled with concern. He caught her elbow and led her off the floor. "Something wrong?"

Yes, something was wrong. She'd lost sight of her goal and had yet to spend any time searching closets for loose floorboards. Other than the master suite, she'd only taken a cursory walk through the upstairs. Part of that was Adam's fault. He insisted on keeping up the inseparable newlywed image and they were always together. Her only time away from him was afternoons when she worked at Estate. Even then he was only ten steps down the hall in his office.

At six each evening he drove her home to change for dinner at a see-and-be-seen restaurant where he touched her at every opportunity. Afterward they returned to the club and stayed until 3:00 a.m. More touching ensued with occasional dances thrown in. Adam's moves on the dance floor were so sexy she couldn't help but wonder what he'd be like in bed.

And now she was as hot as a downed power line.

Self-disgust welled within her. Four days of living in her birthmother's house—*four days!*—and she had nothing to show for them except a case of overactive hormones and a body clock that no longer knew the difference between night and day.

"I need to catch up on my sleep." The lie caused a pinch of guilt. She needed an empty house to do what she'd come to Florida to do.

If you were honest with Adam about your birthmother you wouldn't have to lie. Soon, she promised herself. She'd tell him soon. She liked and respected him too much to continue lying to him about her reasons for seeking him out.

"I'll walk you out."

And if he did he'd kiss her good-night. Her resistance was already running low. She needed to avoid that talented, persuasive mouth of his before it led her straight to his bed.

"No, Adam, I've already cut into the hours you usually work. Stay until the club closes like you used to."

Adam had never worried about one of his women before, but he hadn't been able to get Lauryn out of his head in the past hour.

Why had she left the club so abruptly? Was she ill?

One minute she'd been dancing so seductively he'd been rock hard and ready to drag her to his office to pick up where they'd left off the other day. The next second she'd frozen and bolted.

He'd leave Estate as soon as he'd personally thanked tonight's performer for coming and turned everything over to his manager.

He let himself into the silent house, reset the alarm and climbed the stairs. Light spilling from a bedroom in the south hallway caught his attention and sent adrenaline pulsing through his veins.

Was there an intruder in the house or was Lauryn still awake and exploring? Had she walked in on a burglary despite the heavy security of the house? Or had one of the housekeeping staff left a light on? The need to see Lauryn, to reassure himself she was okay, suddenly seemed as necessary as breathing. He pulled his cell phone from its clip, ready to dial 911 if necessary, and crept down the hall toward the master suite to check on Lauryn first.

The bed was empty, the spread smooth and undisturbed.

He retraced his steps. The bathroom was dark and deserted. He flipped on the closet light switch. The dress Lauryn had worn tonight lay draped across the center island. She'd made it home and changed. That meant the light in the guest room was probably her. He snapped his phone back into the holder.

In an attempt to get her into bed, he'd turned up the heat since that evening she'd come apart in his arms, and this morning he'd left the lab results declaring them both disease-free on her dresser. He'd also tucked a box of condoms in each bedside table and slipped a jeweled condom compact into her purse. Nothing subtle about that.

Had he pushed too far too fast?

Had he driven Lauryn out of their suite?

He made his way to the guest bedroom. Both the room and bed were unoccupied. Light and a tapping sound came from the walk-in closet. Odd. He silently crossed the room and looked through the door. Lauryn knelt on the floor, rapping her knuckles against the floorboards and then pressing each end.

"What are you doing?"

She screamed, sprang to her feet and spun to face him. One hand covered her chest. "You scared me."

"What are you doing?" he repeated.

Guilt infused her face. She nibbled her bottom lip and hugged her middle. "I'm…I'm looking for a hidden compartment."

That made no sense. He must have misheard. "What?"

She swept a hand through her hair, looked away and then

her gaze returned to his. "This was my mother—my *birth-mother's* house. I'm looking for her diaries."

That made even less sense. "Lauryn, what in the hell are you talking about? Are you drunk?"

But her eyes were clear and she looked steady on her feet. He hadn't seen her drink anything tonight besides her favorite sparkling water with a twist of lime.

"It's a long story. One I should have told you before now and I'm sorry that I didn't. But I didn't know how." The look she gave him made the hair on his nape rise. He wasn't going to like this—whatever *this* was. "Can we— I need to show you something."

She walked toward him and squeezed past him through the door. He followed her to their bedroom closet where she pulled out her suitcase, lifted a liner out of the bottom and extracted two file folders and a pile of letters bound neatly together with a string. She pushed them toward him.

The return address on the letters was the same as this estate. No name. Just the initials *A. L.*

"After my father died I found out I was his child, but not my mother's. Adrianna Laurence was my birthmother. She met my father when he was stationed in Florida. They had an affair and she became pregnant with me. The letters she wrote to him refer to a hidden compartment in the floor of her bedroom closet where she kept her diary hidden. She wrote, 'Only you, me and my diary know the truth.'

"I'm hoping to find the diary and read about their affair. Not the intimate stuff. Just the part about me. And why she gave me away."

He juggled the thoughts bombarding him. There was no way Lauryn could have moved from California to Florida and coincidentally met and married him—the owner of the house her mother had once inhabited. He shifted the folders and saw Adrianna Laurence's name on one of the tabs and his on the other.

"You set me up?"

She winced. "Not exactly."

"How *exactly?*"

She exhaled slowly as if buying time. "I came to Florida briefly after my father's funeral. I wanted to meet Adrianna, but she was already dead and she had no living relatives. I asked around and found out the house had been sold. Almost no one would talk to me. Those who did swore she'd never had a child." She tapped the file folder. "This is all I could find out. It isn't enough."

"You want to claim her estate?" He'd heard crazier schemes to get money. But he hadn't expected such greed from Lauryn. Okay, sure, she'd married him for a million bucks, but he hadn't noticed her going on any wild spending sprees.

"No. I just want the diary or diaries if there's more than one. A slew of research hours later I found out you'd bought the Laurence house, and I knew the only way to get what I wanted was through you."

A sour taste filled his mouth. His stomach churned. "You used me."

"I guess you could say that. You have to understand, Adam, I'd just lost my father. And it felt like I'd lost my identity, too. The woman I'd called 'mother' for twenty-six years wasn't my mother. My parents' supposedly perfect marriage was just a sham. My father married Susan, his best friend's widow, to give me a mother and to give her baby a father. Everything I'd believed in had been a lie. I didn't—and still don't—know what's real and what's fiction. I need to find out the truth—the real truth, not the fairytale they fed me."

It was almost too much to comprehend. "You said you were an only child. Was that a lie, too?"

She flinched. "Except for tonight when I told you I wanted to come home and catch up on sleep, I haven't lied to you except by omission. Susan's baby was stillborn. She and my father never had any other children."

"Why play out this charade? Why not just tell me what you wanted?"

"Oh please, this whole story is preposterous. Would you have believed me?"

Probably not.

She must have read his answer on his face. She continued, "When I was researching you I came across Estate's Web site, and I saw the job posting for an accountant. It seemed like fate. I'm a qualified CPA and I wanted to spend some time in Florida. So I sent you my résumé. Both it and references are real and verifiable.

"I thought once you and I got to know each other, once you had a chance to discover I'm not some crackpot, I could explain the situation and make my request. But it didn't work out that way. We saw each other at most two hours a week and that was always with other employees around."

He remembered her stipulation. She'd said she'd marry him, but only if they lived here. "You married me to get into this house."

"The marriage was your idea. You approached me."

True. "But the house is what cinched the deal."

"Yes. That and the chance to meet Helene Ainsley and anyone else who might have known my mother."

Lauryn had hunted him down and she'd lied to him.

Lies by omission were still lies and potentially damaging. Look at the havoc his father's affair had wreaked on his family. On Cassie.

"What would you have done if I hadn't proposed?"

"I was trying to work up my courage to approach you, but I was afraid that if I did and you said no, I'd be at a dead end with nowhere else to turn. My questions would never be answered."

She lifted a hand as if to touch his arm, but he backed out of reach. He couldn't let the chemistry between them cloud his judgment.

"Adam, I'm sorry I didn't tell you sooner. I just… I didn't know how."

Anger, confusion, disappointment and a sense of foolishness for being duped warred within him. He felt betrayed. Used.

He wanted to walk away from Lauryn, but dissolving the marriage after only a week would ruin all of his plans. For the council seat. For a larger stake in Garrison, Inc.

But could he trust Lauryn enough to carry on the pretensé?

"Did you fake your physical response to me just to string me along?"

He hadn't noticed her pallor until color swept up her neck and flooded her cheeks, but she didn't look away. "You know I didn't."

Her eyes pleaded for understanding, but he didn't know what to think. What to say. What to do.

"When you find the diaries—if they exist—then what?"

"We go on as agreed. I promised you two years. I won't break my word."

Her eyes were clear and earnest. If she was lying she deserved an Oscar.

He picked up the folders and letters. "We'll discuss this in the morning."

She started after him. "Adam—"

He held up a hand. "Back off. I need space right now."

And then he turned and walked away because he wanted to believe her even when everything in him said he shouldn't. Rationally, he knew her story was ludicrous.

And he'd been burned by lies before.

His father's to cover up the affair. His mother's to hide her drinking.

First he'd read the letters and whatever was in the folders and then he'd talk to Brandon to find out where he stood legally in this disaster.

When he had all the facts he'd have to make the decision.

Keep his wife. Or throw her out on her pretty, lying ass.

Eight

"**I**'ll help you look for the diaries."

Adam's voice startled Lauryn so badly she nearly inhaled her orange juice.

He believed her. The balloon of happiness swelling inside her warned her that this was about more than finding the diaries.

She twisted in her chair to face him. Adam looked like he'd slept as poorly as she had. Dark smudges underlined his eyes. He'd already shaved and dressed in charcoal trousers and a black silk shirt even though he didn't have to leave for hours.

Saturdays at Estate were always busy. Lauryn didn't have to go in. She was part of the Monday to Friday staff, but because of the wedding and honeymoon and time spent training her assistant on the new check-writing software they'd recently implemented, Lauryn had fallen behind on a few tasks and wanted to catch up before the Monday deluge of deliveries hit the club.

"Why would you want to help me?"

"Brandon says you haven't broken our contract. Even if I boot you out I'd have to pay you the full million."

She flinched. "I wouldn't take money for a job I didn't finish. But please, let me look for the diaries before we end this."

"We're not ending this yet. I lost my father recently, too. I know how that skews your thinking. And I know what it's like to have unanswered questions."

She fell a little in love with him in that moment. But she squashed those feelings deep inside. Her relationship with Adam was temporary. She couldn't afford to lose her heart to him. Besides, even if she decided she wanted more from their marriage, she wasn't the kind of woman a guy like him ended up with. She'd have to be blind to miss the difference between her and the other guests at the Ainsleys' party or at the posh restaurants where she and Adam dined.

Class vs. brass—of the military brat variety.

Being polite and demure didn't come naturally to her. It was something she'd labored over every day since her annulment.

He poured himself a cup of coffee but leaned against the counter instead of joining her at the table for brunch. "Your story checks out. I found your father's obit online. Sounds like he was a hell of a guy. Shame about the accident."

Adam had checked up on her. She couldn't blame him. "He went out doing what he loved. Flying. Testing new equipment. And still in uniform. The air force defined him. It's better that he died before he had to face retirement."

"My father was the same. He lived for work." A moment of silence passed as if Adam, too, had become lost in his memories and then he shook his head and focused on Lauryn. "I still need you for my original purpose. I want to win that election."

She set her glass on the table, rose and crossed the room, stopping just inches from him. "I won't let you down, Adam."

She'd do whatever it took to help him become the president of the Business Council, and she'd try to make his brother Parker see what a valuable asset he was ignoring.

Rising on tiptoes, she brushed her lips against his cheek. "Thank you."

His arm hooked her around the waist when she would have withdrawn, keeping their lower halves fused. "For what?"

"For helping me. For believing and trusting me."

"You should have been straight with me, Lauryn."

"I know. I'm sorry."

"Are there any other skeletons in your closet I need to know about?"

She considered telling him about her misspent youth. But her rebellious days were long past and wouldn't affect him. Tommy was on the opposite side of the country—very likely in jail somewhere given his yen to make a quick and not always legal buck. Besides, the annulment meant legally her marriage had never happened. Thanks to her father, the ceremony she couldn't remember had been erased from the record books. The whole debacle was too embarrassing for words. She was ashamed of her past, of her obnoxious teenage behavior, her stupid mistakes and her gullibility. And she was afraid Adam would think less of her because of it.

"No."

"Good." He discarded his mug, speared his fingers through her hair and cupped the back of her head. And then he kissed her.

She didn't care if this embrace was window dressing for the housekeeper. All she cared about was the warmth of his mouth and the strength of his body against hers. She hated to admit she'd come to like and even anticipate these public displays of affection a little too much.

He tasted of cinnamon toothpaste and coffee.

His hands slid down her back to grasp her bottom and pull her flush against his tall frame. Hard, hot muscles bunched beneath her hands as she shaped his forearms, biceps and shoulders. His hair was silky and slightly damp from his recent shower, his jaw warm and smooth and freshly shaven.

Adam lifted his head. His labored breaths matched her own and his intense gaze fastened on hers. "Enough. I can't keep driving myself to the brink of control and backing off. I want you, Lauryn, and I'm tired of playing games."

The roughened sound of his voice made her quiver. He was right. They couldn't go on as they'd been. The tension and teasing were getting out of control.

"I want you, too, Adam."

His nostrils flared and his pupils expanded. "Then we can take the day off and start searching the closets. Or we can go back to bed. Together."

Her stomach somersaulted. She wasn't going to fool herself into believing this meant forever. But she liked and respected Adam. And she was halfway in love with him.

"I've waited months to find those diaries. I think I can wait a few more minutes."

His brows shot up as if she'd insulted him, but fire flared in his eyes. "Minutes? You underestimate me, wife."

A smile tugged her lips. "Prove it."

Adam swept Lauryn into his arms and headed out of the kitchen.

Her heart jolted at the sheer romanticism of the gesture. She locked her arms around his neck and held on but squirmed when he reached the foyer and didn't slow down. "Adam, you can't carry me up the stairs."

"Want to bet?"

They met the housekeeper coming down.

"Martina, hold any calls. The wife and I are not to be disturbed."

"*Si,* Señor Garrison." Smiling, Martina hustled away as if eager to give them privacy.

Adam climbed effortlessly. His breathing had barely altered by the time he reached the landing. He strode down the hall, not stopping until he reached their bedroom where he lowered her legs, clamped a hand around her nape and took her mouth. Ravenously.

Lauryn dragged her fingertips from his shoulders down his chest and over the rapidly thudding heart keeping pace with her own. Right or wrong, she'd made the decision to do this, to unleash the passion she'd kept caged for so long, and now she couldn't get him naked fast enough.

Her fingers clutched his shirt and yanked upward, freeing his shirttails and allowing her access to the hair-spattered six-pack she'd admired from his loft Monday morning. She splayed her hands over the hot skin at his waist and soaked up his heat.

Adam snapped his head back and reached for his cuffs while Lauryn started on the buttons of his shirt, working her way from the bottom up. When his cuffs were loose Adam released the top buttons, meeting her in the middle of his chest. As soon as the last disk slipped free, she shoved the silk off his shoulders, revealing dark whorls over his pectorals and the line of hair leading to the waistband of his pants. She raked her nails down the path.

His muscles contracted and air whistled between his clenched teeth. He caught her hands, kissed each palm and then pressed them to her sides. He pushed off her new designer suit jacket. It piled on the floor at her feet. Her blouse became his next target. Making fast work of the buttons, he sent it after her jacket.

Inhaling deeply, he reared back to take in her lavender lace bra. He lifted his hands and with his pointer fingers traced the thin straps from her shoulders down over the swells of her breasts to the tiny bow in the front. He cupped her briefly and then shoved the straps from her shoulders to her elbows, pinning her upper arms by her sides like a lingerie strait-jacket. Then he folded the fabric cups beneath her flesh, exposing her to his devouring gaze.

Her nipples hardened and her internal muscles clenched in anticipation. She held her breath as he bent his head and then his hot, wet mouth engulfed her, laved her, suckled her. She bit her lip on a moan. He rewarded the sound by cradling and caressing her other breast. Need twisted deep inside her. Spiraling. Tightening. She speared her fingers through his hair and held him close until impatience with her restricted movements became too bothersome to bear.

Lauryn reached behind her back, flicked open her bra and shrugged out of the garment. She needed him naked, needed to touch him. Her fingers found and released his leather belt and then the hook of his trousers. She eased the zipper down, reached inside to stroke him and found flesh. Hard. Hot. Smooth. *Bare* flesh.

Gasping, she jerked back. His pants glided past his narrow hips and down his legs. "You're not wearing underwear."

"Never do." Adam kicked his shoes and pants aside. He whipped off his socks and straightened.

His erection rose thick and long from a dense nest of dark, wiry curls. Her fingers curled involuntarily in expectation of touching him, but he captured her hands, laced his fingers through hers and waltzed her backward until the dais on which the raised bed sat bumped her heels.

His arms encircled her, briefly searing his chest to her breasts and his hard length to her belly. Her lungs emptied in a rush. He unbuttoned and unzipped her skirt, letting it drop to the floor to reveal her high-cut lavender lace panties.

"Nice." His growl made the blasé word sound wicked. He knelt, and, hooking his fingers in the elastic, tugged the panties to her ankles. He leaned forward, pressed his cheek to her triangle of curls and inhaled. "Your scent drives me crazy."

Her knees buckled. Adam scooped her up, carried her to the freshly made bed, ripped back the nubby silk spread and lowered her onto to Egyptian cotton sheets. The fabric was cool against her back in contrast to the hot palms skimming her underwear past her ankles, but leaving high-heeled sandals behind.

He sat back on his haunches and looked his fill. "You're beautiful."

She'd heard those words before. But she could see in Adam's eyes that he meant them. He wasn't spewing empty flattery to get what he wanted. He wanted *her*. Not just sex. Not just a female receptacle. *Her*.

And suddenly she realized this wasn't the tawdry, meaningless sex of her teens or the itch to defy her father and test her womanly wings. This was…more. And that worried her a little because "more" wasn't part of their marriage agreement.

Adam feathered the lightest of touches around her ankles, over her calves and shins, moving closer and closer to her apex, but with teasing detours behind her knees, to the outside of her thighs and then finally, finally where she wanted him.

"*Oooh.*" Her hips jolted off the mattress at the electrifying initial contact of his fingers against her center. He stroked, found her wetness and smoothed it over her sensitized flesh with a slightly roughened fingertip.

It was too much. Not enough. Exactly right.

And then his mouth found hers and his tongue plunged deep in tandem with his fingers doing the same much lower. Her cry of ecstasy filled his mouth. He carried her swiftly toward climax, but let her drift back down short of her goal. He repeated his sensual teasing again and again until, tense and desperate, she writhed beside him.

She clutched his hair, his shoulders, his back, begging with actions rather than words. And then she covered his hand with hers, holding him at her center. "Please. Now."

Adam rocked back. His passion-darkened gaze held hers for countless seconds and then he rolled away. Lauryn wanted to scream in frustration, but then she realized what he was doing.

Protection. How could she have forgotten? Even in her crazy, careless, rebellious past she'd never forgotten protection.

He opened the nightstand drawer, withdrew a condom and returned to her.

She should confront him about his cocky assurance that she'd sleep with him. Maybe later.

She snatched the package from his hand, but then made a few torturous detours of her own. He wanted to make her beg? Well, she could return the favor. She lightly scraped her nails over his chest, abdomen, hips and legs, and finally, his sex. His groan, the jerk of his flesh, the dewy drop of arousal at his tip combined to excite her even more. When she couldn't wait another second, she tore open the wrapper and rolled the condom down his rigid length.

Before she could consider her next move he had her flat

on her back, his thighs between hers, and his erection at her entrance. Adam cupped her bottom, lifted and plunged deep.

The air gushed from her lungs on a cry as he filled her. Adam froze with his jaw rigid and his unblinking gaze locked on hers. "Lauryn?"

"Don't stop. Please don't stop."

"You're so damn tight. Were you—"

"No. But it's been a while. This is…good."

The devilish glint returned to his eyes but didn't completely erase the hint of concern. He gently stroked the back of his knuckles across her cheek. "Only good?"

She pressed her heels into the mattress and arched her hips to take him deeper. Pure hunger wiped the smile from his face.

"Really good. *Great*. Adam. I. Can't. Wait. Please."

She didn't have to repeat her request a third time. He withdrew and thrust again and again, suffusing her with a heat that intensified with each powerful surge. With his hands, mouth and body, touching, tasting, thrusting, he rushed her into the fastest and most consuming orgasm of her life. It ripped through her like a tornado, leaving her weak and clinging, winded and shattered. But he wasn't finished. Adam coaxed her into a second and a third before he joined her, his groan echoing through the bedroom.

And then his weight settled over her, his damp skin fusing to hers. Decimated, she held him close, smoothed his tangled hair, stroked his slick back and tried to catch her breath.

Wow. Her teenage affairs had not prepared her for that.

He pulled away and lay beside her, and a hollow feeling opened in her belly, slowing her racing heart.

She wasn't just a little in love.

She'd fallen totally and completely for Adam Garrison.

A man who defined temporary relationships.

She hadn't broken the vow she'd made to save herself for the love of her life. But she'd chosen a man who couldn't love her back.

"How long?" Adam asked Lauryn.

She paused midtap and twisted on her knees in her corner of the empty closet. "How long what?"

"How long since you've had sex?"

Her breath caught and she bit her lip. Pink stained her cheeks. "About two hours."

He shot her a don't-mess-with-me look. She'd been experienced, a sorceress at driving him out of his mind with desire. But tight. Almost virginal tight. The contradiction had nagged Adam in the hours since they'd torched the sheets and steamed the shower stall and then made love again on the bedroom floor. The rug burn on his knees stung like a bitch. But it was worth it. He hoped Lauryn felt the same about the abrasions on her butt.

Damned rug. He'd throw it out and get something softer.

"Nine years," she finally admitted with obvious reluctance.

His mouth dropped open in shock and then he whistled. "No wonder you were convinced you could hold out." A feeling of smugness swelled his chest and a smile tugged his lips. "But that was before you kissed me."

She rolled her eyes. "Don't let your success go to your head."

"My head's not what you're wearing out, sweetheart."

Sweetheart? He didn't know where the endearment had come from. He never called women by pet names.

He resumed tapping on floorboards, shifted to the next quadrant and started his systematic search again. Five minutes later a board gave beneath his hand. He rapped again and heard a distinctive hollow sound. He pressed the end of the board and the opposite end popped up. "Bingo."

"You found it?" Lauryn scrambled over and watched wide-eyed as Adam pried the six-inch-by-two-foot board out of the back corner to reveal the compartment below.

The crazy story was true. He'd only half believed Lauryn when she'd told him.

A dozen leather-bound books the size of paperback novels rested atop a blue lining—a silk scarf, maybe. There were other items in the space. Envelopes, bound together with a yellowed ribbon. A small, carved wooden box and a few trinkets.

He looked at Lauryn. With her hands clasped in front of her chest, she stared at the booty as if hypnotized but made no move to pick up any of the items.

"You okay?"

She blinked. Looked at him. Inhaled raggedly. "I had almost given up on finding them."

After fruitlessly searching three closets with her today so had he.

"I-I'm a little afraid to read them."

And then he got it. "You're worried you might not like what Adrianna has to say."

"Yes. Does that sound stupid?" Her worried expression snagged something in his chest.

"No. I want to know why my father passed me over, but I'm not sure I would have liked his answer. He wasn't known for pulling his punches."

Sympathy softened her eyes.

Adam reached over the compartment and covered Lauryn's linked hands, sharing a connection he'd never felt with his siblings or any one else. He wasn't the touchy-feely type, and while he'd rather run from the emotional upheaval he expected would follow their discovery, he suspected she might need his support over the next few hours.

"Want privacy?"

"No!" she answered quickly. Too quickly. And then she shook her head and squared her shoulders. "I'm sorry. That was silly. If you'll help me carry all this to the bedroom then you can go to work. You could still get there before Estate opens tonight. I'll be fine. Honest."

He couldn't deny the relief surging through him and yet there was also an odd reluctance to leave her. "You bet."

Using the blue fabric as a catchall, he gathered the corners and then lifted and stood. Lauryn's gasp stopped him. She reached into the hole and picked up one remaining object. A piece of paper.

She scanned the page. "It's my birth certificate. My original one."

The turbulent tangle of emotions in her eyes made him want to do something. He wasn't sure what. Hold her? Surely not. "Let's get this to the bedroom."

He waited while she shakily rose to her feet and then followed her out of the room, down the hall and into their suite where he deposited the stash on the small table set in the bow of the window. He studied her pale face, the birth certificate trembling in her hands and decided to get out before he did something sappy like take her into his arms.

Sex was one thing. Getting emotionally embroiled in her affairs was another. "You're sure you don't need me to stay?"

"No. Saturday's Estate's busiest night. And I—I should probably do this alone."

Vulnerable. That's it. Lauryn looked vulnerable—not an adjective he'd ever attached to her before. She was a lot of things—capable, intelligent, composed, beautiful and sexy as hell—but never vulnerable.

He brushed her cheek with his fingertips. "You have my cell number. Call if you need me."

Adam walked away.

But it wasn't nearly as easy as it should have been.

* * *

"You're still awake," Adam said.

Startled, Lauryn looked at him and then checked the clock. Six in the morning already. She'd read through the night. Eight hours. She closed the diary she'd been rereading for the third time—the one detailing her mother's pregnancy and Lauryn's birth.

"She wanted me." Her voice sounded hoarse from the emotion dammed in her throat. She swiped at her dry and scratchy cried-out eyes.

Adam approached slowly. "You doubted that?"

"Of course I doubted that. She gave me away and never tried to contact me even though she knew exactly where I was." And Lauryn had thought so much worse—that she'd been a baby even a mother couldn't love. "But she kept me for two weeks. She tried to be my mother."

Lauryn tapped the stack of diaries. "I don't understand some of the medical terminology in these, but Adrianna had a heart condition. The doctors and her family told her to abort me because it wasn't safe for her to carry a baby to term. She refused and ran away. No one in Miami knows about me because she never told anyone that she'd had a baby and given it up for adoption. Her family thought she'd gone away to have the abortion."

Searching her face, Adam knelt beside her putting his face on level with hers. "This is good?"

She sensed his wariness. Did he expect her to fall apart all over him? Admittedly she'd had a few rocky moments as she read the diaries and her father's letters to Adrianna, but those were private. She wouldn't inflict that on him.

A smile tickled her lips. "Yes. This is good. I have my answers, the ones I craved, and I have you to thank for that."

"No thanks necessary."

She couldn't help touching him. Cradling his face in her hand, Lauryn dragged her fingertips over the beard stubble shadowing his jaw line. His lips were soft against the pad of her thumb, and despite her roller-coaster night desire tightened her middle.

"Adrianna died at thirty-six. I'm ten years from that age. I needed to know if there were health time bombs in my DNA that my regular physicals hadn't picked up. But what she had wasn't hereditary. She contracted an infection in her early teens that weakened her heart muscle. She claims her parents smothered her from then on, never letting her live like a normal woman.

"And then she met my father in Fort Lauderdale while he was on leave. He was the first man who didn't treat her like she was damaged goods because he didn't know. She fell in love with the dashing air force pilot that week even though she knew they had no future. Besides the class differences, my father had already been reassigned to California and was leaving within the month.

"When she discovered she was pregnant eight weeks later she saw having me as her one chance to do what normal women do and she decided not to have the abortion. But the pregnancy weakened her heart, and she was afraid she wouldn't be strong enough to raise a child *if* she survived the delivery. She contacted my father when she was seven months along." Lauryn's throat closed up. Her mother had risked dying to have her.

"I read what he wrote her, Adam. When my father found out about me he proposed, but Adrianna turned him down. There were hints to that in her letters to him when she said she couldn't do as he asked or that he shouldn't try to turn a vacation romance into something it was never meant to be. But I didn't know he'd proposed.

"He wanted me. When Adrianna realized she wasn't strong enough for shared custody they made the arrangements for the adoption. And my father found the perfect solution in Susan, his best friend's pregnant widow.

"After turning me over to my father Adrianna moved back here and had very little life outside these walls. It's kind of sad." Lauryn's voice broke the last word into two syllables.

Adam rose, pulling her into his arms and holding her tight.

She rested her head over his heart, taking strength from the strong, steady beat. Being with him like this felt right. It was as if she'd found her past and her future right here in this house with him. She tipped back her head and met his gaze and realized she had more than DNA in common with her birthmother.

Like Adrianna, Lauryn had fallen for a man with whom she had no future, and like her birthmother, Lauryn intended to make the most of her time with him.

And then she'd let him go. Even if it ripped out her heart.

Nine

Lauryn smelled coffee and her lagging energy revived.

She turned in her office chair and spotted her husband with a to-go cup in one hand and a bag bearing the same familiar logo in the other and a mischievous glint in his eyes. That glint did crazy things to her pulse.

She held up a finger and pointed to her telephone headset.

Adam entered her office and hitched his hip on the corner of her desk.

Almost every day since she'd started working at Estate she'd ducked out around three to get coffee from a nearby shop, but today her assistant had discovered a discrepancy in a delivery that she hadn't been able to unravel. Lauryn had taken over and was still tied to her desk trying to fix it.

"So you'll deliver the missing items first thing in the morning? We must have them the day after tomorrow for the Thanksgiving Day event." She waited for confirmation and then finished the call. Removing the headset, she smiled at Adam, who extended the cup.

"Thanks." She gratefully sipped the chocolate coffee brew. Perfect. Had he known what she always ordered? Or had the barista told him?

He set the bag on her blotter. "Did you know your favorite coffee shop sells five brands of condoms along with the coffee, protein shakes and croissants?"

"I can't say I ever noticed that." But South Beach shops had their idiosyncrasies, so it didn't surprise her.

"You can ask me to bring you coffee anytime, along with anything else the store sells." He added a wink that made her stomach somersault. If this was the way he charmed his women, then it was no wonder "legions" fell at his feet.

He opened the bag to reveal the contents. "Which is your favorite brand?"

Her body caught fire. "Whichever one you're wearing."

"Good answer, wife." He came behind her desk, cradled her face and stroked a thumb over her lips. Her internal muscles clenched and her toes curled. The sex between them had been amazing, and while she should be sated since she'd left his bed mere hours ago, her hormones seemed to be set on simmer whenever Adam was around.

He never missed an opportunity to touch her. To the employees streaming past her open door as the day shift left and the evening crew arrived, he no doubt looked the picture of a devoted, concerned husband. Sometimes he even fooled her.

"You look like you could use a siesta. Want to go home for a couple of hours before returning tonight?" His velvety tone implied resting wasn't the only thing on the agenda. Her skin tingled in anticipation.

She was tired, but happier than she'd ever been. Since

they'd first made love three days ago Adam had abandoned the sofa bed in the sitting room. Loving him and then falling asleep in his arms was far better than any fantasy she could have dreamed up.

Oh sure, she knew there was a good chance there would be a train wreck around the bend with her name on it, but she'd face losing Adam when—*if*—the time came. In the meantime, she'd try to show him why they should renegotiate the two-year clause in their marriage contract.

She covered his hand on her cheek with hers and turned her lips into his palm.

"Get a room," Ricco, Estate's booking agent, called from the open doorway with a wide grin. The staff surprisingly had accepted the marriage without incident. If there'd been any snide comments, Lauryn hadn't heard them. "Lauryn, I have the estimates you wanted."

Adam shifted his hand to Lauryn's nape, clearly marking his territory the way he did each night at Estate, when they went out to eat or at the Garrison Sunday dinners. She knew the gesture was merely for show, but deep in her heart she wished it were more.

Lauryn took the paper Ricco offered with an unsteady hand. When—*if*—her marriage to Adam ended she'd have to leave Estate, and she dreaded that. She liked her coworkers, liked her job and even liked South Beach's quirky atmosphere, but there was no way she could survive hearing the rumors about Adam's latest conquests or seeing the pictures in the gossip columns—pictures that now featured her.

The media blitz Adam had predicted before they'd married had hit. Lauryn braced herself each morning before she opened the paper. She'd found her own face in the society pages several times in the past twelve days since Brandon had issued the press release.

Adam stood. "She'll have to get back to you on those tomorrow, Ricco. We're heading out for a few hours, but we'll be back tonight before the doors open."

His dictatorial tone allowed no room for comment. Funny, but Lauryn's hackles didn't even twitch even though she had a mountain of work waiting on her desk.

"Not a problem." Ricco waved and left them.

Adam extended his hand. "Let's go home, wife."

She grabbed her purse and accompanied Adam outside. He helped her into his car and then scanned the grounds surrounding the club before turning back to her. "The barista said a guy was asking for you at the coffee shop today. Any clue who that might be?"

Her heart jolted, but she dismissed the momentary alarm. "It's probably just another reporter."

Who else could it be?

"You've become a creature of habit, babe."

The voice from her past brought Lauryn to a dead stop as she approached the coffee shop counter. Her stomach pitched. She spun toward the man lowering the newspaper that had been hiding his face.

Tommy.

Ice crackled through her veins.

He sat by a window with a clear view of Estate's employee entrance. Her ex still looked like a biker bad boy from his long brown hair to his Fu Manchu beard and ragged jeans. He tilted back in his chair with a sneer on his face that she'd once found fascinating. Not anymore.

Why had she ever found him attractive?

Because everything about him from his tattoos to his ponytail made your father crazy.

She'd been an idiot to think rebelling would win her

parents' respect, and convincing herself she'd been in love with Tommy had been the height of stupidity.

"Never expected you to turn out so much like your old man. How is the Sergeant?"

"Dead," she replied coldly. "Why are you here?"

"'Cuz we have unfinished business."

"Wrong. What we had was over a long time ago—the day you asked me to be your drug mule," Lauryn whispered and glanced at the curious barista three yards away who stood goggle-eyed with Lauryn's drink already prepared in her hand. She hoped Jan hadn't overheard.

"Thanks, Jan." Lauryn quickly paid for the beverage and then she turned and left the coffee shop without looking back. Whatever Tommy wanted he wouldn't leave until he got it. She heard his boots on the sidewalk behind her as she quickly walked a couple of blocks without stopping until she reached the Ocean Drive beachfront park. She hoped there were no reporters in the vicinity.

"What? You don't want to talk in front of your friends?"

She pitched the drink in a trash can. There was no way she could put anything in her stomach and keep it down. She glared at Tommy. "What do you want?"

His brown eyes raked Lauryn from head to toe. "I see you've married yourself a millionaire. The expensive duds look good on you. A little boring, but not too bad."

She folded her arms and said nothing.

"Too bad that marriage ain't legit."

How could he know about her marriage contract with Adam? "What are you talking about?"

"Our annulment wasn't legal."

Her heart slammed against her ribs and her stomach dropped to her sandals. "Of course it was."

"That means your marriage to moneybags isn't, either."

He tapped the breast pocket of his leather jacket. "Got proof the annulment wasn't signed, sealed and delivered. Your daddy forgot to dot all his i's and cross all his t's."

"He didn't forget." *He wouldn't. He couldn't.* Her father was—had been—anal to the core. He'd never slip up on something as important as separating his daughter from the man he called a thug. Turns out he'd been right about Tommy.

"You sure about that, babe? Because I'm willing to show what I got to the press. They think you're so goddamned perfect. But they don't know you like I do. Bet that new husband of yours doesn't, either."

Panic seized her. She fought to conceal it. Tommy, she'd learned the hard way, fed on out-of-control emotions. In fact, hindsight told her he'd often incited them—the way he had when he'd convinced her she deserved to go to Tijuana for spring break.

"You're bluffing."

"You willing to gamble on that?"

Lauryn's father had handled everything from the moment he'd picked her up in Mexico. She'd been eighteen, scared out of her mind and more than willing to let Rodney Lowes take control. The only part Lauryn had played was to pee in a cup for a drug test and sign where he'd told her on the annulment petition. There'd been a seemingly endless pile of documents.

All she had to do was get her copy of the annulment decree from her father's papers. But his papers were in a safety-deposit box in California, and her mother, the one with the key to that box, was away on a cruise until Tuesday. Susan couldn't retrieve and fax what Lauryn needed.

"Let me see your proof."

He pulled out what looked like an official document, but held it out of reach. "Uh, uh, uh. No touching. I'm not having you run off with it."

"What's wrong with it? It looks fine."

"Besides the missing official raised seal that means the clerk or notary or whoever never sealed the deal? There's this." He shifted his thumb to reveal a faded red "DENIED" stamp.

Her world stopped. Could the officials refuse to grant an annulment? Her father would have told her. He would have helped her get a divorce. Wouldn't he?

"We're still married, babe."

Tommy had to be scamming her. *He had to be.* But she had no way of proving him wrong right here, right now. Even if she could get her mother to call the bank and authorize them to open the safety-deposit box for Lauryn, tomorrow was Thanksgiving Day. Getting a last-minute flight to California would be impossible, and she couldn't exactly request the Garrison's corporate jet service or ask Adam to fly her if she wanted to keep Tommy's threat and her shameful past a secret.

"You know this is bullshit, Tommy. What do you want?" She fought a grimace at her choice of words. *Trashy mouth. Trashy morals.* How many times had her father said those words during her teens? Back then he'd been right and she'd cursed just because she knew how much he hated to hear a woman swear.

Apparently Tommy had resurrected one of her bad habits.

Tommy rocked back on his booted heels and slipped the papers back into his inside jacket pocket. "A little green could make this go away."

"That's extortion."

"I call it insuring your future happiness."

She scanned the park. As usual there were uniformed police officers within shouting distance. "I could call one of those cops over here and report you."

"Go for it. But then the paper would get wind of your bigamist marriage."

Her knees weakened. *Bigamy.* True or untrue, even a hint of this would destroy Adam's credibility and his bid for the council nomination. She cared too much about him to let that happen. And cared too much for him to let him find out what a selfish, irresponsible imbecile she'd once been.

He'd said more than once that he wanted a conservative, proper wife. And she'd been about as far from that as you could get. Telling him the truth meant losing his respect and any chance of convincing him to try to make this marriage permanent.

He'd despise her. Maybe as much as she despised herself.

And then a niggling doubt made Lauryn's back itch. She couldn't remember ever seeing the final annulment decree.

Maybe Tommy wasn't bluffing.

Resignation settled on her shoulders as heavily as Atlas's globe.

She needed time. Time to prove Tommy's accusations were untrue. And she'd have to buy it. "I don't have a lot of cash."

"C'mon, babe, he's a Garrison. One of Miami's most eligible bachelors according to the Internet."

"Former bachelors."

He dipped his head to indicate his pocket. "Is he?"

Despite Adam's plan to pay for Lauryn's makeover, Lauryn had used her own money for the clothes, makeup and hairdresser believing it would give her the freedom to back out of the marriage right up until the last minute if she wanted. All she had liquid was the first monthly marriage payment.

"What'll it take to shut you up? Five thousand?"

"Babe, I wasn't born yesterday. Give me a hundred grand."

"I don't have a hundred thousand dollars!"

"Your husband does."

"Our accounts are separate. I can't touch Adam's money."

"Then I'm talking to the papers." He turned as if to walk away.

Lauryn grabbed his arm. She couldn't let him go, couldn't let him destroy Adam's plans. "Tommy, I'm not lying. I don't have that kind of money and I can't get it."

"Then how much you got?"

If she low-balled him he'd walk. But it galled her to have to reward his evil streak. "Twenty-five thousand."

"Not good enough." He tried to shake her free, but she dug her nails deeper into his biceps.

She couldn't believe this was happening. "I can get my hands on forty thousand dollars. That's it. I swear it."

His eyes narrowed as he appraised her, and he must have seen the truth on her face. "Let's take a walk to your bank. But remember, babe, one peep out of you and I go to the press."

"Lauryn, you okay?" Adam called out as Lauryn passed his open office door.

"Yes," she replied quickly—too quickly—and kept walking. *Tell him.*

But she couldn't. Not yet. Not until she fixed this disaster. She dumped her purse in her desk drawer and pressed cold fingers to her temples.

"You were gone longer than usual," Adam said behind her, startling her into whipping around and lowering her hands.

"I…had a…headache and I took a walk on the beach to get rid of it." She was lying. Sort of. Tommy was a headache and she had taken a walk to get rid of him. But she hated twisting the truth.

"You're pale." With concern in his eyes Adam crossed the room, cupped her shoulders and examined her face. "Need to go home?"

She needed to wash off the stench of Tommy and to come up with a plan. How could she get copies of the documentation she needed? She didn't even know the name of the attorney her father had used back then. Susan would know, but her mother would be gone six more days. Was there a way to call her onboard the ship? But even if she did get a name most offices, public and private, would be closed for the holidays until Monday.

Lauryn's chest tightened. She could lose Adam over this. And she wasn't ready to let him go yet. Who was she kidding? She'd never be ready to end this marriage.

"Lauryn?"

"Hold me. Just hold me." She wound her arms around his waist and pressed her cheek to his shoulder over the steady thump of his heart.

Adam shifted. She heard the click of her office door closing, and then his arms banded around her. His lips brushed her hair.

She lifted her head, chasing his mouth until her lips covered his. His hands tightened on her waist, but he didn't push her away. His mouth opened over hers, his tongue seeking and stroking hers. Lauryn kissed him back with every ounce of love she had in her, and for a moment he almost made her forget the disaster her life had become, the disaster she could make of his.

She shaped him with her hands, memorizing the curve of his skull, the sharp angles of his jaw and the breadth of his shoulders. Her palms flattened over the muscles of his back, his waist, his tight behind. Adam sucked in a sharp breath.

She drew back and looked into his eyes, the eyes of the

man she loved. The man she would lose if she couldn't make this right. "If we don't stop we're going to violate part of the employee handbook."

His nostrils flared and his eyes flashed. Streaks of arousal darkened his cheekbones. "Who are they going to complain to? I'm the boss. Where's your purse?"

"My desk drawer. Why?"

"Because I'm too old to carry condoms in my wallet."

"I don't have any, either."

"Give me your bag."

Alarm shot through her. Her copy of the bank withdrawal slip was in her purse. "Why?"

"I put a condom compact in there last week."

She'd never heard of a condom compact, but it didn't take a genius IQ to figure out what one was. "I'll get it."

While she retrieved her bag and searched inside, Adam locked the office door.

Her fingers closed around a metal square she hadn't noticed before today, but then she rarely had to go into her purse. Adam paid for everything and her keys, lipstick and cell phone went in an outside pocket. The brushed gold lid had her initials engraved on it. *LLG*. Lauryn Lowes Garrison.

Her heart hitched. How long would she bear that name?

She pushed the button and the top opened to reveal a cellophane packet. "What will they think of next?"

"Come here, wife." He took her purse and the compact, dropping the first back into the drawer and the second on the desktop. "Remind me to buy a sofa for your office."

And then he yanked her close and kissed her. Lauryn soaked up his barely leashed desire and reveled in his hurried caresses. His heat, his scent, his taste, she stored them all away in her memory bank. Just in case.

She'd have to tell him about Tommy and when she did

Adam would probably hate her. He'd asked her if she had any more skeletons in her closet and she'd said no. He'd never believe she'd honestly thought her past a nonissue. How naive of her.

But she wanted to get through Thanksgiving dinner at his mother's first and maybe even his mother's birthday party, which Adam was hosting at the club. And then she'd tell Adam the whole sordid truth and pray he understood. Pray he wouldn't hold her youthful indiscretions against her. Pray he wouldn't throw her out.

Adam's mouth traced the cords of her neck while his hands found the zip of her dress. She tore at the buttons of his shirt, his belt, his pants. He had them both naked in seconds. His hot flesh burned her palms, her lips, her tongue. She couldn't get enough of him. She dropped to her knees and took him into her mouth.

"Lauryn," he groaned and speared his fingers her hair. Far too soon he tugged her to her feet and kissed her hard. "I love what you do to me, but right now I need to be inside you."

He backed her toward her wooden two-drawer lateral file cabinet, lifted her onto the cool surface and stepped between her legs. With movements as frantic as hers, his hands shaped her breasts, tweaked her nipples, found her center.

Conscious of employees on the other side of the door, Lauryn shoved a knuckle into her mouth to stifle a cry. She curled the fingers of her other hand around him and stroked his erection. Adam's muffled groan vibrated against her breast, increasing the heavy desire boiling like lava in her center.

He straightened, hooked his hands beneath her knees and pulled her toward him. As soon as she'd rolled on the condom she guided him home and gasped as he filled her. Again and again, he thrust hard and fast.

His hands on her breast and where their bodies joined rushed her toward completion. *Too soon. Too soon. Wait.* She wanted to make it last, to savor the rising heat and the building tension, but climax broke over her like a bursting levy, and she couldn't hold back the waves of ecstasy roaring through her.

His mouth swallowed her cries, and then he fed them back to her as his own orgasm shuddered through him. His head fell to her shoulder. The sound of their labored breathing filled the room and his back heaved beneath her hands.

Her eyes stung. She pulled him closer until not even a piece of paper could slip between their sweat-dampened torsos.

A sense of loss welled within her. She couldn't give this up. Couldn't lose him.

And she'd be damned if she'd let Tommy Saunders ruin this for her without a fight.

Ten

"I want more money."

Tommy.

Lauryn nearly dropped the bedroom phone. She turned and saw Adam just yards away in the bathroom shaving in preparation for Thanksgiving dinner with his family.

"I don't have more," she whispered.

"Don't mess with me, Lauryn. I'm looking at your digs right now. If you don't believe me look out the back window. The place is worth millions."

She walked to the window, looked out at the canal and spotted a small fishing boat with Tommy at the helm. A wave of dizziness reminded her to inhale. "I can't get more."

"Hock something."

"No."

"Then give me that rock on your finger. Tell moneybags

you lost it. He'll buy you another one. Hell, the ring's probably insured. He won't even miss the dough."

She glanced at her engagement and wedding rings and curled her fingers into a fist. She may have come into the rings in an unorthodox manner, but she wasn't giving them up. She checked the bathroom and found Adam scraping away the last of the white foam. "I can't do that."

"Then this canary is gonna sing."

"Don't. Please. Give me a few days. A week." By next Tuesday her mother would be home and Lauryn could fly to California and get the paperwork she needed. She wasn't about to give Tommy more money. Because she realized now he'd just keep coming back.

"You say something, sweetheart?" Adam said from the other side of the bedroom.

"Don't call again," she said into the phone and hung up. "It was someone wanting a donation."

Another twisted version of the truth.

There's a price for every lie you tell. Before you open your mouth, be sure you're prepared to pay it.

She faced Adam. He strolled toward her with his chest bare above his trousers, his face smooth and his eyes searching hers. She couldn't believe how much she loved him. She'd never felt anything even remotely close to this for Tommy.

"Ready for another meal with the Garrisons?"

She didn't think she could eat again until the Tommy issue was resolved. "Can't wait."

"Liar."

The blood drained from Lauryn' head with dizzying swiftness. He had no idea how right he was.

"You've survived two Sunday dinners. You can handle

today." Adam pulled her into his arms and nuzzled a kiss below her ear. "Next year we'll have everybody over here."

She prayed there would be a next year, but at the rate she was going that seemed unlikely.

The ring of his cell phone jarred Adam out of a deep sleep Friday morning.

He forced open a leaded eyelid and looked at the clock. Eight. He'd only been home two hours and the sheets had barely had time to cool after he'd made love to Lauryn. She stirred beside him. He kissed her temple. "Go back to sleep. I got it."

The phone bleated again. Adam slid out of bed and stumbled to the dresser. He snatched up the cell phone and started toward the study so as not to disturb Lauryn as he punched the Receive button. His eyes were too bleary to read the caller ID. "Adam Garrison."

"Have you seen the paper?"

Parker.

"No. I was asleep. We had a big bash at Estate last night. You know I keep vampire hours."

"Your wife made the front page."

Adam's steps stalled in the hall. He turned back to stare at the curvy mound in the bed. "Lauryn? Why?"

"Her husband is claiming she's a bigamist."

"I did no such—"

"Not you. Her *first* husband."

A DEA raid would have been less shocking. "Her first husband? Lauryn's never been married."

The woman in question bolted upright with her eyes wide and something in their depths that soured Adam's stomach.

"That's not what this guy says," Parker continued. "What's more, he's claiming she's a tramp who stayed just this side of the law. You're in deep shit, little brother. I've already put a call in to Brandon for you. You'd better ask your wife who the hell Tommy Saunders is and if she's still married to him."

The dial tone sounded.

Adam lowered the phone and stared at Lauryn. Her face was as pale as the white sheets. "Who is Tommy Saunders?"

She closed her eyes and swallowed. A pained expression crossed her features. "My ex-husband."

"You said you'd never been married."

"I haven't. Technically." She clutched the sheet to her collarbones, reminding Adam of his own nakedness.

The burn of betrayal lit his skin. He yanked on his robe. "Explain *technically*."

"I ran away with Tommy soon after I turned eighteen. To Tijuana. For spring break. He asked me to marry him. I said no, but I woke up married. He'd drugged me. I don't even remember the ceremony. And then he told me he wanted to make us rich by using me as his drug mule to ferry cocaine out of Mexico. I freaked and ran and called my father. Daddy came and got me, and he handled the annulment." The words poured from her in a rush, but the meaning was clear.

"You were married."

"No. An annulment means the marriage is erased. Like it never happened."

"But it did happen."

"Yes, but—"

"You lied. *Again*." Something inside him curled up and died.

"Adam, please—"

"How many other lies are there, Lauryn? How many more ways do you plan to screw me?"

"I didn't think my past mattered."

"According to Parker, it's front-page news. I told you I needed a conservative wife."

"And that's what you got. I'm not the selfish girl I was back then."

"No. Now you're the woman that girl turned into. One who set up, used and lied to her husband. If we're even legally married." He shoved a hand through his hair. "Are we?"

She bit her lip. "I think so."

Damnation. "What the hell does that mean?"

"Tommy claims our annulment never went through. I think he's lying. I paid him to be quiet—"

"You paid him? Paid him how much?"

She curled her knees into her chest. "He asked for money and threatened to go to the press if I didn't pay him. I gave him forty thousand dollars to keep quiet until I could find the paperwork and prove he was lying. But then he wanted more and I couldn't give it to him."

"That's who called yesterday?"

Her hesitation nearly crippled him. "Yes."

Another lie.

She climbed from the bed. The sight of her naked body hit him low and hard before she dragged on the robe she'd left draped across the end of the bed two hours ago. How could he still want her when he knew she was a liar?

"My father was detail-oriented in the extreme and a control freak. I know he wouldn't be sloppy like Tommy claims. If the annulment was denied Daddy would have pushed for a divorce. But I never had a copy of the annulment, so I can't prove Tommy's lying. Not yet. My father's papers are locked in a safety-deposit box in Sacramento, and my mother is away on a cruise. I'll fly to Sacramento and as soon as she gets home and I'll get a copy of all the documentation."

She'd ripped his guts out. Personally. Professionally.

"Adam. Please. Let me explain."

"I think you've said more than enough."

"I love you," she whispered.

Another lie. But this one hurt worse than all the rest combined.

Because he loved her.

He'd fallen in love with his beautiful, lying wife.

And right now he couldn't stand the sight of her. Adam stormed into the closet, yanked down his suitcase and started throwing clothes into it.

"What are you doing?" she whispered.

"Getting away from you. I'm moving back to the condo."

"I'll make it right. I'll fix it. Please just give me a chance. All I need is time."

"You've run out of chances with me, Lauryn. Save it for the next sucker."

She silently watched him dress. A lone tear streaked down her cheek before she dashed it aside.

He returned to the bedroom and thrust a pen and pad of paper at her. "Write down everything you know about your boyfriend. His name. A physical description. Where he's staying. I'm having him arrested for extortion."

She hesitated. And that brief moment combined with the regret and worry in her eyes shattered what was left of his battered heart. She must still have feelings for the jerk.

And then something bitter and ugly coiled inside him.

How blind can you be, Garrison?

"Did you call your lover the minute I proposed and cook up this scheme to get more cash?"

"No. And Tommy isn't my lover. He hasn't been for nine years."

"Forgive me for having a little trouble believing you." He slammed the suitcase closed. "You and the bastard deserve each other."

"Adam, you're wrong."

"Forget your big plans. You won't get another dime out of me, *sweetheart*."

She flinched at his acidic endearment.

He grabbed his suitcase and his keys and headed for the front door. When he reached the bottom of the stairs he couldn't help but look back.

Lauryn stood on the landing, both hands clutching her robe. "Adam, I'm sorry. I never meant for you to get hurt."

"Sorry? You're *sorry?* Lauryn, you have destroyed everything, *everything* that matters to me. Sorry doesn't cut it."

He turned on his heel, went out the front door and slammed it behind him.

Paparazzi milled on the other side of the wrought iron gate, circling like vultures around the corpse of his marriage.

"I don't want any more surprises," Adam said to Brandon. "I want to know every single detail Lauryn neglected to mention."

"Then you need a good private investigator. Ace Martin is the guy for the job. He's discreet and fast." Brandon pulled a business card from his wallet.

Adam knocked back his bourbon. "Hell, for all I know Lauryn could be the Jefferies brothers' spy."

Brandon's head jerked up and his eyes sharpened. "Is that likely?"

As the Garrison, Inc. lawyer Brandon knew about the troubles the company had been having with info being leaked. "I don't know. Maybe. She keeps to herself. She has access to a lot of confidential financial information, but more from Estate than Garrison, Inc. I'll ask your P.I. friend to look into it."

"Do you think she's involved?"

"I hope not." Because if she was Garrison, Inc. would have to prosecute, and while he was furious, and yes, hurt, dammit, he didn't want to send her to jail.

Brandon extended the business card to Adam.

Adam rose from the sofa and crossed the library to take it, but at the last second Brandon snatched it out of reach. "You fell for her."

Adam recoiled. "Wrong."

"You did. You fell for Lauryn Lowes. Even Cassie saw and commented on the sparks between you."

"That was lust." He'd never lied to Brandon before, but Adam refused to admit Lauryn had completely duped him. Hooked him. Duped him. And given him the best sex of his life.

"You've been lied to by women before, and it's never bothered you this much."

Adam crossed to the drinks tray and helped himself. He was as at home in Brandon's place as Brandon was in his. In fact, he was more comfortable at Brandon's than at his brothers'.

"I'm not bothered. I'm pissed off. Everything I've been working toward has been destroyed. Bigamy, for godsakes."

"She would be the one guilty of a crime *if* her ex is telling the truth. Not you."

"I hope to hell he's not. And you're wrong. I haven't been screwed over like this before."

"That's your third drink. One of the things I respect about you, Adam, is that you're around liquor all the time, but you don't abuse it. Are you planning to change that tonight?"

Adam splashed a finger of Booker's into his glass. "I'll take a cab home. You won't be sued for negligence for letting me drink and drive."

"That's not what worries me. And you have been screwed over. What about that redhead who was secretly having an affair with Parker and you at the same time? Or the brunette who faked a pregnancy to try to get a wedding ring out of you. Or—"

Adam winced and held up a hand. "You've made your point. But I wasn't in love with any of them."

Brandon noted Adam's slip by cocking his head.

Damn. Adam emptied his glass. The liquor burned all the way down his throat and hit his stomach like acid. He wanted to drink himself into oblivion. To forget Lauryn Lowes and her lover. His marriage. His decimated plans to win more say in Garrison, Inc.

Parker would never take him seriously now.

But drowning his sorrows ran a little too close to his mother's problem.

"At least Cassie's honest," he muttered under his breath.

"Cassie and I think Lauryn is, too." Brandon refilled his own tumbler. "Lauryn's right. In the eyes of the law once a marriage is annulled no valid marriage ever existed, and the grounds for getting a legal annulment aren't easy to get around. Maybe you'd better focus on that."

Adam looked at Brandon in surprise. His best friend would not mislead him. Intentionally. "You're saying her 'he drugged me and married me' excuse could be the truth?"

"Absence of consent is a valid reason for annulment, but she would have had to prove it. Let Ace find out the details for you. He can also check into her other questionable stories."

"The stuff about her birthmother sounds preposterous, but

it's true. I told you about the letters, diaries and the birth certificate."

"So you did. And you're sure Lauryn doesn't want to petition the Laurence estate? If she wanted money approaching the executers should have been her first move. From what you said she found in that compartment, confirmation of her identity and even a DNA match is a real possibility."

Adam rubbed the back of his neck. Brandon had a point. The Laurence estate was worth far more than the million Lauryn had planned to get out of him. And *he'd* approached *her* about the marriage and the money. Not the other way around.

Could he be wrong about her? Was she telling the truth? Or had she and Saunders concocted a scheme to bleed Adam dry?

And did it matter? Hell yes.

Was she still in love with Saunders? Was she still married to the bastard?

Adam couldn't think about that now when he had enough bourbon in his system to make him want to put his fist through something. Or someone. Saunders.

He caught Brandon subtly checking his watch and realized how late it was. "Why aren't you with Cassie tonight?"

"Because you needed me."

"Yeah. Thanks."

"Are you okay with me marrying your half sister?"

"Brandon, I'm closer to you than I am to my own brothers. As far as I'm concerned, making you an official part of my family is just a formality." He offered his hand and then yanked Brandon close in a bump-shoulders-slap-on-the-back embrace. "I owe Cassie for letting me borrow you tonight."

"She'll join me tomorrow if she can get away from the hotel or I'll join her."

"Sounds like you're doing a lot of commuting."

"I am, and you need to know that because of that I've decided to open an office in Nassau. There's no point in getting married if I'm never going to see my wife."

"You're closing down here?"

"No. Just adding another branch of Washington & Associates."

"Good. Because I'll need you to handle my divorce."

"Why would you come forward when all the rest of the Garrisons are saying is, 'No comment'?"

"Because you've made a terrible mistake," Lauryn said across the reporter's cluttered desk Saturday afternoon. "Adam is completely innocent in this situation."

She'd decided a counterattack was the only way to end the vicious scandal that Tommy's story had launched, and as much as she hated being the center of attention these days, if pouring out her past for public consumption would clear Adam, then Lauryn would willingly humiliate herself by doing so. She also hoped sending the press on the trail of the missing documentation would cut through the Thanksgiving weekend barriers keeping her from getting to California and the truth.

The reporters had been relentless over the past twenty-four hours. The tabloid press in particular had followed her everywhere, and she'd used that to her advantage—she hoped. First thing this morning she'd gone to the police department, trailed by an assortment of paparazzi, and filed an official report on the extortion.

Adam may have already filed a complaint like he'd said he would, but this was her mistake and she would take the steps to rectify it. The money she'd paid Tommy wasn't hers. She hadn't earned it. It belonged to Adam and she wanted to return it. Maybe then he'd believe she wasn't trying to fleece him.

After leaving the police department she'd called the reporter who'd broken the original story, offered her an exclusive and set a time for this meeting. Lauryn had told the woman the whole sordid story. The only detail she'd held back was the marriage of convenience part.

"Do you believe what you've told me exonerates Adam Garrison?" the reporter asked.

"Yes. He hasn't done anything wrong. The mistakes were all mine. Adam didn't know about my past or my annulment. I honestly believed it wasn't relevant, and I was too ashamed of my rebellious teenage behavior to tell him. I'm not that person anymore and I haven't been for a long time.

"But whether Tommy's claim that our annulment is invalid is true or not, I underestimated his desire to make a fast and easy buck. I paid him to keep quiet because I love my husband and I didn't want to see Adam hurt. But now because of *my* mistakes the best candidate for the presidency of the Miami Business Council is being trashed in the news."

The reporter's gaze sharpened. "So you're officially announcing Adam Garrison's interest in the position?"

"Adam would be a great council president. He knows business and he knows the community. But only he can announce his candidacy. My purpose in coming forward is to make sure you understand he is a victim, not a perpetrator." She gathered her purse and stood. "Will this run in tomorrow's paper?"

"As soon as I've verified a few facts."

The woman's condescending attitude throughout the interview had rubbed Lauryn the wrong way. Her last remark raised Lauryn's hackles. *All right. Gloves off.*

"You should have verified the facts before running the first story. Have you considered what will happen if Tommy Saunders is lying about the annulment being denied and you've falsely accused a Garrison of bigamy? That could be considered libel and your job and credibility would be in jeopardy."

The woman paled, her indolent posture turned stiff and her mouth fell open.

Lauryn turned on her heel and left. She didn't believe for one moment that the Garrisons would go to battle to clear *her* name, but they would to clear Adam's.

Despite the tensions within the family, there was a bond in the Garrison clan that she envied. And maybe sacrificing her pride and her reputation would make Parker step forward and show Adam just how important a part of the family he was.

"What is this?"

Lauryn's heart stuttered Monday afternoon at the anger in Adam's voice. She swiveled in her office chair. He stood in her doorway holding up a copy of Sunday's newspaper folded to display her interview with the reporter.

Drinking in every inch of him from his overlong hair to his collarless black shirt and crisply pressed black trousers, she rose, rounded her desk and closed the door. She stopped just inches from him, and tilted her head back to meet his gaze.

She'd missed him over the past three days and hadn't expected to see him today since Estate was closed. He looked stressed and his blue eyes were hard and unforgiving. Her hopes sank. She'd bared her soul for that interview, hoping he'd read it and understand her choices. Would he ever forgive her for keeping her secrets? Apparently not.

What had his family thought of the article? She hadn't been invited to the Garrison Sunday dinner yesterday, so she didn't know.

"It's me trying to make this right. Until I can get to California and find my copy of the original documents it's the best I can do. I need a couple of days off. My flight leaves at five tomorrow morning. I should return Wednesday evening."

His jaw shifted. "I don't want your help. I'll handle it. In fact, you can stay in California. I'll have your belongings shipped to you along with the divorce papers—if they're necessary."

She nearly staggered from the verbal blow, but she held her ground because this was one fight she couldn't afford to lose. "You're sounding a lot like your 'control freak' brother at the moment."

He scowled.

"Adam, you told me you were trying to live down a past you weren't proud of. Why is it different when it's me?"

"I didn't lie about mine."

"I didn't lie about mine, either. I just didn't tell you things that I thought were irrelevant and that you wouldn't want to hear.

He snorted in disgust. "You're saying you were protecting me?"

"I thought I was, but I guess I was only protecting myself. Remember that conversation we had about birth order affecting personalities? I said only children either rebelled or conformed. You're the one who guessed I'd conformed and before I could correct you, you followed up that statement by saying a wife with a rebellious past was the last thing you needed. But that was exactly what you had and it was too late to change that. I didn't say anything then because I didn't want you to think less of me.

"I wasn't a good kid, Adam. For five years I gave my parents hell. I used to dress and act like a tramp because it garnered the kind of attention that drove my control freak father nuts. I didn't value myself or those who loved me. I'm not proud of that, but I can't change who I was. I can only make sure the person I am now makes the right decisions for the right reasons.

"And the person I am now promised to help you win the council nomination. I'm trying by making sure the public knows the responsibility for this disaster with Tommy was my fault and only my fault. You're totally blameless."

His face stayed hard, expressionless. Was she getting through to him at all?

"So tell me, Adam, what would a man who loved someone enough to elope do in this situation? Would he run at the first obstacle? Because when we expose Tommy's lie—and I'm confident we will—the paper's going to want to know why you married me in the first place if you quit loving me after barely two weeks and at the first obstacle. Talk about making you look capricious to your business council peers. And then your pretense of marrying for the sake of the nomination is going to come to light."

He stiffened. "Is that a threat?"

She sighed. "No. I would never intentionally do anything to hurt you."

"You're the one who should be worried about lies coming to light. The 'crush-at-first-sight' bull you fed the reporter is absurd."

Embarrassment warmed her skin, but she'd promised to be one hundred percent honest with him from now on. No more secrets.

"It's the truth. I was attracted to you from our first interview. The attraction only increased after I took the job. You're smart. You have a way with people that makes everyone around you feel at ease and an enthusiasm for your job that's contagious. Your employees fall all over themselves to please you— even me.

"But then I heard the rumors about your legions of women and your meaningless affairs and I told myself to get over you. You were living the life I'd left behind—one I never wanted to return to. Only I didn't get over you. I couldn't."

She'd told him before, but he'd blown her off. She needed to say it again, to watch his face when she said the words.

She took a bracing breath. "I love you, Adam. I fell in love with you the day you offered to spend hours on your hands and knees helping me search those walk-in closets, helping me find out about my family because family is important to you. It is to me, too."

Disbelief flickered in his eyes and then he abruptly turned away, dismissing her. "I'm hosting my mother's birthday party here Wednesday night. I don't want you there."

The stab of pain caught her unawares. "We need to present a united front if you want to come out of this with any credibility at all."

He rounded on her. "Don't you get it? Any chance for the nomination or for Parker to take me seriously is gone. Wiped out by your lies."

"I think you're wrong. And I intend to prove it."

Eleven

"Are you sure you're up for this?" Lauryn asked Susan as the cab pulled away from Miami International Airport and headed toward Estate Wednesday night.

"Of course I want to meet your husband and your in-laws. If Adam's an unforgiving sort, then he doesn't deserve you, and I intend to tell him so." Ever the optimist, her mother smiled and squeezed Lauryn's hand. "But I'm sure that won't be necessary. Besides, I've never crashed a party. It might be fun."

The thought of her very proper mother going anywhere without an invitation made Lauryn smile.

She didn't know how she could have forgotten that Susan Lowes had always been her champion. From the moment Lauryn had greeted her mother's ship through the convoluted confession of the diary search, her marriage, Tommy's reappearance and the scandal that had rocked Miami's elite community, Susan had been nothing but supportive. The only question she'd asked was, "Do you love him?"

When Lauryn had answered in the affirmative, Susan had said then they'd better get back Miami and fix this.

No mother, real or adoptive, could be better.

"Thanks for coming. After the way I acted…" Tears burned Lauryn's eyes and choked off her words. "I don't deserve your support."

Susan's fingers tightened. "You were hurt, Lauryn. I understood. I should have insisted your father tell you the truth on your eighteenth birthday the way we'd planned, but with Adrianna already dead—"

"And my rotten behavior…"

"Well, yes, I admit we did take that into consideration. We didn't want to exacerbate the situation. But still, you had the right to know. And then you were so upset after that business with Tommy, we just didn't want to add to your worries."

"I can't apologize enough for my behavior back then. Every rule seemed to hit a hot button and I overreacted."

"Your dad was bossy because he loved you and feared for your safety. You were running with a dangerous crowd. Although he came across about as subtle as a tank most of the time."

"Amen."

"And he couldn't seem to comprehend that you weren't a new recruit who needed to be broken down and built back up into a team player. The harder he pushed the more you pushed back." She shook her head. "You two were so much alike."

Lauryn gaped. "Daddy and I?"

"Oh yes. Both strong-willed. Both determined to test your limits. The difference is your father found a job that allowed him to channel his wild side and to push himself against the barriers of light, speed and sound—literally."

"I thought my rebelliousness must have come from Adrianna."

"Your father was always a bit untamed."

"But you loved him."

Susan smiled wistfully. "Not at first. Back then we banged heads more often than not. I only married him because I was pregnant and alone and felt I had no other options. But I saw his tender side when he stood by me after I lost my little Daniel and then soon after he brought you home I fell hard. He was a little slower to catch on. But once he did we were good together. I'm gonna miss him for a long time."

Swallowing the sudden lump in her throat, Lauryn covered her mother's hand. Her parents' marriage hadn't begun with love, but it had ended there. Could she hope for the same? Or would Adam never forgive her?

The cab pulled to a stop outside Estate. Lauryn paid the driver, climbed from the car and picked up their luggage. "We'll put these in my office and then find everyone."

The employee entrance was locked at night and she didn't have a key to the exterior doors, so she led Susan past the long line of chicly dressed wannabe guests on the wide sidewalk leading to the front door and stopped in front of the massive guard. "Hi, Deke."

"Lauryn, hey. Been on a trip?"

"Yes, and I brought my mother back with me. Where's Mrs. Garrison's birthday party being held?" She tensed and hoped he didn't refuse to let her in, but he unhooked the rope.

"Upstairs. Red room."

"Thanks."

Inside the music from the downstairs DJ pulsed around them. Lauryn turned away from the milling crowd and used her ID to access a locked door to the offices where she deposited their bags behind her desk. She huffed out a breath and squared her shoulders. Nervousness made her almost queasy.

There was no reason to stall before joining the party. She and her mother had changed into suitable attire at the airport. But she was afraid. Afraid she'd lose Adam tonight. If she hadn't lost him already. But if she didn't go upstairs and try to make this right then she'd definitely need to kiss her heart and her husband goodbye.

"Lauryn?"

"I'm ready, Mom." She retrieved the small gift she'd bought for Bonita from her suitcase. "Let's go crash a party."

His heart wasn't in this.

Adam stood on the sidelines of his mother's birthday bash watching two hundred of Miami's most powerful movers and shakers mingle or dance to the music pulsing through the speakers in the private upstairs room.

He wasn't out there working the crowd, slapping backs, shaking hands and trying to win their confidence for the business council nomination. In fact, he didn't even care whether or not his guests enjoyed themselves. A first for him.

Everyone he'd spoken to had asked for Lauryn. Apparently, her touchy-feely newspaper interview had impressed them.

"Adam," one of his hostess's voice broke into his thoughts, "there's somebody here who insists on speaking to you tonight."

Lauryn? "Who? Where?"

"By the door."

Instead of his wife, Adam spotted Ace Martin, the P.I. Disappointment weighted his shoulders. Disappointment he had no business feeling. He'd told Lauryn not to come. For all he knew she could be in California with Saunders spending forty grand right now.

Was he married or wasn't he? Adam's muscles tensed, but he forced them into action and crossed the room. Had Ace found the answers? Adam wasn't sure what he wanted those answers to be or even if they mattered. His marriage was very likely over either way.

Adam extended his hand. "Ace, thanks for coming."

The P.I. nodded. "Is there someplace private we can talk?"

"My office." He took the freight elevator rather than the stairs. He wasn't in the right frame of mind to charm the guests he'd encounter in the front of the club, and he didn't want to get hung up in a conversation with anyone and delay Ace's revelations even one minute.

The office suite was dark and deserted, but for a second Adam thought he caught a whiff of Lauryn's perfume. *Mind's playing tricks on you, man.* He shook his head. But dammit, he'd missed her. How stupid was that when she'd deceived him and possibly even loved another man?

But when he lay in bed alone at night he kept seeing the honesty in her eyes, and it made him second-guess himself—not a frequent occurrence.

He closed his office door behind Ace.

"Saunders lied," Ace said without preamble. He pulled a file from his briefcase, opened it and spread copies of documents across Adam's desk surface. "Your wife's annulment went through without a hitch. Saunders drugged her just like she said. Medical records backed it up."

Adrenaline shot through Adam. He and Lauryn were still married. Had her claim that she loved him been a lie?

"Every story you asked me to look into checked out. From all accounts, her father was a tough SOB. Rode her hard throughout her teens. She defied him in the typical teenage ways, but other than some underage drinking, never broke the law—or at least there's no record of it. Good student. Popular. Typical kid, if a little on the rowdy side during her high school years.

"Adam, I can't see her being your Garrison, Inc. snitch. Doesn't fit her character. And there's no unexplained money trail."

"What about Saunders?"

"California cops nabbed him yesterday. Dumbnut still had the cash and the forged document on him. He's not the sharpest knife in the drawer. He's offering to return the money in exchange for a lesser charge. Our pretty boy's not too eager to spend more time behind bars. He's been there before for jacking a few cars and dealing drugs."

"Was he alone?"

"Yes. No sign of Lauryn."

Relief coursed through Adam.

Ace closed his briefcase. "Anything else I can do for you?"

Find my wife.

But Adam didn't ask. Even if Ace found Lauryn the P.I. couldn't make her forgive Adam or make her stop caring for her ex.

"Nothing else. Thanks for your help."

"Just doing my job. Nice to find out someone's innocent for a change."

Innocent. But Adam had convicted her. He'd been judge, jury and hangman. She probably hated his guts.

He wrote Martin a check and showed him out. The last thing Adam wanted to do was rejoin the party. He wanted to find Lauryn and apologize.

For doubting her.

For not telling her he loved her.

Too little, too late? Probably. But he had to try.

He returned to the red room and walked right in on Jordon and Emilio Jefferies standing nose-to-nose, fists clenched and looking ready to brawl.

Adam could make out the tone of their angry voices as he approached, but not the words. He had bouncers for this kind of crap, but considering Emilio would soon be family Adam decided to handle it rather than call security and have Jordon turfed.

"Jordon, I don't remember seeing your name on the guest list." And if the man had a spy planted in Garrison, Inc. then he sure as hell wasn't welcome here.

"What? You don't want me to wish your mother a happy sixtieth?"

"If I believed the sentiment was legitimate I might consider it. But I don't. What do you want?"

Jordon's blue eyes scanned the room, alighting on a target Adam couldn't identify in the shifting crowd. "Nothing. Absolutely nothing."

Looking disgusted, he turned on his heel and stormed out.

"Know what that was about?" Adam asked Emilio.

His future brother-in-law hesitated. "No."

Adam would bet his Beemer Emilio Jefferies knew exactly why his brother was here. But pushing for an answer fell right off Adam's priority list when he looked across the room and saw the beautiful blonde standing with his mother and Brooke.

Lauryn had come home.

"You look like her," Bonita Garrison said before Lauryn could escape after delivering the birthday gift and good wishes.

"Who?" Lauryn asked absently. She noted the worried expression on Brooke Garrison's face as Adam's sister stared across the room and looked to see what had caught her attention. Emilio Jefferies and Adam. *Adam.* Lauryn's heart thumped harder, faster and her palms moistened.

"Your mother," Bonita answered, yanking Lauryn's attention back to her. Bonita's eyes, so like Adam's, shifted to Susan Lowes, assessed her and then returned to Lauryn. "Your birthmother. Adrianna Laurence."

Lauryn's throat closed up. She yearned for details, but she didn't want to make Susan uncomfortable by asking for them.

Susan took the initiative. "How so, Mrs. Garrison? I've never seen a picture of Adrianna although my husband did speak of her occasionally."

Bonita looked like she regretted opening the dialogue. Her lips thinned and her gaze drifted to the bar then returned. "The coloring is different. She was as dark as Lauryn is fair. But the bone structure is identical. The profile, the set of your eyes, your chin."

No slurring marred Bonita's clipped words tonight. Lauryn wondered if that was her choice or because Adam controlled the bartenders.

"You knew her?" Lauryn asked with a flutter of excitement in her belly.

"She often accompanied her mother to society functions."

"Really? What was she like?"

"She was quite a trial to her parents, always finding little ways to stir up trouble and draw attention to herself. Reading the interview you did with the paper quite reminded me of her. I trust you've outgrown the need to be the center of attention? Or have you? I'm not sure after this debacle."

"Mother!" Brooke exclaimed.

"I have, Mrs. Garrison. All I want to do now is be a good wife to Adam." *If he'll let me.*

Bonita lifted her chin and looked down her nose at Lauryn.

"Adrianna went out on a limb to save her child. You went out on a limb to save mine. Perhaps you have some redeeming qualities. But that remains to be seen."

"Mother!" Brooke repeated.

"It's okay, Brooke. She's right. I—"

"Lauryn." Adam's voice stalled her racing heart.

She turned and there he was, tall and lean, with his disheveled hair and intensely blue eyes. She flushed hot and then cold. Would he throw her out?

"Tommy lied," she blurted.

"I know." There was something in his eyes, some emotion Lauryn couldn't identify, that made her mouth go dry.

"Adam, get me a gin and tonic. Your bartender refuses to pour."

"Sorry, mother. Everyone has orders to keep you sober tonight." He spoke without looking away from Lauryn.

"Not exactly a happy birthday then, is it?" Bonita sniped and then stalked off. Brooke followed.

Adam shifted his attention to her mother. He extended his hand. "My apologies for my mother's behavior. I'm Adam Garrison."

"Susan Lowes, Lauryn's mother."

Adam's tight smile didn't completely erase the tension in his face. "It's nice to meet you, Mrs. Lowes. You've raised an amazing daughter."

"Yes, I have, haven't I?" Susan squeezed and then released Lauryn's hand. "Lauryn, could you direct me to the powder room?"

Lauryn looked from her mother to Adam and back again. "I'm sorry, I don't know where it is. I don't come upstairs very often."

"That way," Adam pointed toward a set of double doors.

"Thank you." With that Susan turned and left them.

Lauryn wanted to call her back. She wasn't ready for this conversation. Wasn't ready to blow her last chance.

Instead, she squared her shoulders and swallowed to dampen her mouth. "How did you know about Tommy?"

Adam gripped her bicep and led her toward an empty corner where the music and chattering crowd were less intrusive. Once there he didn't release her. She wanted to lean into the warmth of his hand, to grab that hand and never let it go.

"I hired a private investigator."

She couldn't help the flood of disappointment. "I guess it was too much to hope you'd actually believe me."

"Lauryn—"

"It's okay, Adam. I understand. My whole plan to move here, befriend you and search for the diaries was ill-conceived and completely self-centered. I never should have done it. I hurt too many people and I lied too many times."

"You didn't lie, Lauryn. You left things out. Things you didn't consider relevant. And they wouldn't have been if Saunders hadn't decided to twist the facts. Your past, like mine, is part of who you are. We made mistakes, but we learned from them. I changed, and so did you."

He didn't hate her? Her heart swelled with hope. "I didn't expect my past to come back to bite me. But I should have given you the information and let you make the decision. You had the most to lose. The nomination—"

"Forget the nomination. If the council members are too narrow-minded to realize I'm qualified for the job then it's their loss."

"But what about the bigger stake in Garrison, Inc. that you wanted?"

"I'm no longer interested. You were right. I'm doing what I want to do, investing when and how I want to invest, with no one to answer to but myself. And I'm good at it. I've always been a solo player. I shouldn't try to sign up for a team sport now."

"Are you sure?"

"I'm sure." He scanned the crowd and then faced her again. "And I'm not completely blameless in this deal. My reasons for marrying you were…what was it you said? Ill-conceived and completely self-centered."

Did that mean they had a chance or that he was ready to walk away from it all—his plan and her?

"But enough about our mistakes. You know you have every right to contest the settlement of the Laurence estate, don't you? You'd inherit millions."

Her mouth dropped open. She snapped it closed when she realized she was gaping. "I—I didn't know that."

"The estate was supposed to go to the last surviving heir. That's you. After a year's search without finding an heir, the properties were sold, but the monies are currently being managed by a trust."

"Ohmigod. I don't even know what to say to that."

"Think about it. Talk to Brandon. Learn your options."

"Right. Yes. I will." She shook her head. "Why are you telling me this?"

His hand tightened on her arm and then his fingers loosened and massaged tiny circles on the tender underside. Her pulse quickened and tension wound deep inside. "Because you'll be wealthy enough to do whatever you want. To live wherever you want. With whomever you want."

"You know money's not why I wanted to find Adrianna's diaries, don't you? I needed to know I was wanted—that I wasn't a baby even a mother couldn't love."

There. She said it out loud for the first time and found understanding in Adam's eyes.

After several silent seconds he nodded. His hand slid down

the length of her arm until he captured her fingers. He stroked her knuckle above her wedding rings with his thumb.

"The P.I. told me the police arrested Saunders in California yesterday. Saunders has already turned over the money. He'll be shipped back here to face extortion charges." Adam's throat worked as he swallowed. "Unless you want the charges dropped."

Confused, Lauryn frowned. "Why would I want them dropped?"

"Because you still care about him. I know you filed charges to help me, but if you want a future with him, then I don't want you to be an inmate's wife, and I don't want you to waste your inheritance on his legal fees."

Alarm prickled through her. Did Adam still want the divorce? "Adam, I don't care about Tommy, and I don't want to drop the charges. What he did was illegal and he hurt you."

"Then why did you hesitate when I asked you to write down information about him for the police?"

She flashed back to their last morning together in the Sunset Island house—the last morning she'd been happy.

"Because I realized at that moment that everything my father had bellowed at me was right. I was headed down a dangerous path. If I'd stayed with Tommy I'd very likely have been in jail by now. I may not have been born a baby a mother couldn't love, but for five years I did my best to become a teenager a father couldn't. I'm very lucky he and my mother cared enough to stand by me when I was trying so hard to push them away."

Adam's hand tightened around hers. "You didn't hesitate because you loved Saunders?"

The intensity of his gaze tripped her pulse. "How could I when…I love you? But I know I messed up by keeping secrets. And I know you might not be able to forgive me or trust me again. So, Adam…if it's what you want…I'll give you your freedom. But I really want to try to make this marriage work."

He closed his eyes and inhaled deeply. When he lifted his lids again Lauryn's knees nearly buckled at the love she saw shining back at her. Beaming at her. Like a lighthouse beacon.

She mashed her lips together and pressed a fist over her heart. Hope swelled within her like a hot air balloon, making her feel light-headed.

Adam cupped Lauryn's shoulders. "If you can forgive me for being a total ass even when your eyes and my heart told me to trust you, then I want to renegotiate our agreement."

She shifted uneasily. "Renegotiate how exactly?"

"Two years is not enough. Hell, fifty years isn't going to be enough. I want eternity. Not one second less." He lifted her hand to his mouth and kissed her knuckles. "I want these rings to mean the words we said on that beach."

He released her hand only to gently cradle her face and brush his thumbs over her damp cheeks. She hadn't even noticed the tears escaping.

"I love you, Lauryn Garrison. I want to spend the rest of my life showing you that you are wanted. Loved. Needed. And if you're willing, I want to fill your birthmother's house with her grandchildren."

Her lips quivered and happiness blossomed inside her. She took a ragged breath. "On one condition."

"Name it."

"You don't pay me to be your wife. That's one job I'd willingly do for free."

He winked and her heart turned over. "You have yourself a deal, sweetheart, and I'm going to make sure it's one deal you will never regret."

* * * * *

THE EXECUTIVE'S
SURPRISE BABY

BY
CATHERINE MANN

Dear Reader,

What a thrill it has been to work on THE GARRISONS
with so many of my favourite authors! I'm especially
excited to present you with the final book in the series.

Christmas certainly brings to mind family time. And
what better way to commemorate the season than with
the Garrison clan's expanding. Of course, when the
newest family member is Jordan Jefferies, long-time
enemy of the Garrisons, there is bound to be trouble. It
takes a special couple to cement that relationship, and
luckily, Brooke Garrison and Jordan Jefferies are up
to the challenge. With a large family myself, I enjoyed
the privilege of bringing all the Garrisons and Jefferies
together to celebrate the holidays—and, of course,
weddings!

Merry Christmas, Happy Hanukkah and Season's
Greetings to you all!

Holiday hugs,

Catherine Mann

Catherine Mann writes contemporary military romances, a natural fit, since she's married to her very own USAF research source. Catherine graduated with a BA in Fine Arts: Theatre from the College of Charleston, and she received her master's degree in Theatre from UNC Greensboro. Now a RITA® Award winner, Catherine finds following her aviator husband around the world with four children, a beagle and a tabby in tow offers her endless inspiration for new plots. Learn more about her work, as well as her adventures in military life, by visiting her website: www.catherinemann.com. Or contact her at PO Box 41433, Dayton, OH 45441, USA.

To the marvellously talented authors of the first five Garrison stories: Roxanne St Claire, Sara Orwig, Anna DePalo, Brenda Jackson and Emilie Rose. I thoroughly enjoyed working with you all on this project!

And to my critique partner, Joanne Rock. Many, many thanks for your help that made it possible for me to meet my deadline. I couldn't have done it without your fabulous insights—and the sugar jolt from that bag of Jelly Bellies you sent during my final dash to the finish line!

Prologue

July, five months ago

Brooke Garrison ordered her first taste of alcohol at twenty-eight years old.

She reached across the polished teak wood for the glass of wine from the aging bartender at the Garrison Grand Hotel lounge. Her hand shook after the emotional toll of the day, hearing her father's will read, learning of his secret life. At least she didn't have to worry about getting carded even if she had been younger since her family owned the place.

"Thank you," she said, surreptitiously reading the older man's name tag, "Donald."

"You're welcome, Miss Garrison." He slid an extra napkin her way as smoothly as the pianist slipped into his next song. "And please accept my condolences about your father. He will be missed."

By more people than she had realized. "We all appreciate the kind words. Thank you again."

"Of course. Let me know if you need anything else."

Anything else? She would like to erase this whole horrible day and start over. Or at least stop thinking about it, much less talking. She'd already ignored four voice messages from her brother Parker's receptionist.

Tentatively, Brooke sipped the wine, wincing. She watched the candle's flame through the chardonnay's swirl. Somewhere in that glass were the answers to what stole her mother away from her. To what had driven her father to lead a secret second life in the years before he'd died.

Her alcoholic mother's bitter words after the reading of John Garrison's will this morning echoed over and over again through Brooke's head. "The cheating son of a bitch. I'm glad he's dead."

What a hell of a way to learn there weren't five Garrison offspring—but six. In addition to three brothers and an identical twin sister, Brooke had an illegitimate half sister living in the Bahamas, a sister her father had never told them about while he was alive. Instead, he'd chosen to share the news in his will while handing over a sizable chunk of the Garrison empire to Cassie Sinclair—the newly discovered sibling.

Not that Brooke cared about the money. The betrayal, however, burned.

Conversations and clinking glasses of happier people swelled around her while she sipped. She wanted none of the revelry, even made a point of carefully avoiding eye contact with a couple of men attempting to snag her attention.

Brooke raised the long-stemmed crystal to her mouth again. She knew the wine was as top-notch as the fresh flowers and linens around her. Her taste buds, however, registered nothing. She was too numb with grief.

She'd always blamed her mother for her father's frequent business trips. The drinking must have driven her wonderful daddy away. Now she couldn't help but wonder if her father's behavior had some-how contributed to her mother's unhappiness.

And how could she untangle it all in the middle of mourning the loss of such a huge figure in her life? The hotel blared reminders of his presence. She could see her father's imprint on each multi-domed chandelier in the bar, on every towering column.

Brooke circled a finger around the top of her half-full glass, an indulgence she never allowed her-self because of her mother's addiction.

Tonight wasn't normal.

Her eyes hooked on the looming columns in the spacious hall outside the bar—the evening turning further beyond *normal* than she ever could have anticipated.

Through the arched entranceway walked the last man she expected here, but one she recognized well even in the dim lighting. Their families had been business rivals for years, a competition that only seemed to increase once Jordan Jefferies had taken over after his father's death.

So why was Jordan here now?

Brooke forced herself to think more like her siblings and less like her peacemaker self…and the obvious answer came to her. He'd come to her brother Stephen's hotel to scope out the competition.

Brooke took the unobserved moment to study Jordan Jefferies prowling the room with a lion's lazy grace. No, wait. Lazy was the wrong word.

Think like her siblings. Jefferies would only want people to perceive a lazy lope so he could pounce while she was otherwise occupied staring at his blond, muscle-bound good looks.

Yeah, she'd noticed his looks more than once. He might be the enemy, but she wasn't blind. However, she'd considered him off-limits because of the controversy it would cause in her family. Often, she'd heard her oldest brother Parker fume for days over a contentious business meeting with Jordan. The family diplomat, she always tried her best to soothe over arguments and hurt feelings.

For all the good it had done her. The whole Garrison clan had been ripped raw today.

Her mother's voice whispered again… "The cheating son of a bitch. I'm glad he's dead."

The bartender swooped by, breaking her train of thought. "Can I get you anything else, Miss Garrison?"

Garrison. She couldn't escape it anywhere around here, just as futile as thinking she could keep peace in her family.

Why bother trying?

A heat fired through her veins and bloomed into an idea, a desire. And sure, a need for open rebellion after a day of hell. "Yes, Donald, actually you can do something for me. Please tell the gentleman over there—" she pointed to Jordan "—that his drinks for the evening are on the house."

"Of course, Miss Garrison." The bartender smiled discreetly and walked under the rows of hanging glasses to the other side of the wooden bar. He leaned to relay the message and Brooke waited. Her stomach tightened in anticipation.

What would he think of her picking up the tab for his drinks? Likely nothing more than a Garrison acknowledging his presence.

Would Jordan Jefferies even remember her? Of course he would. He was a savvy businessman who would know all the Garrisons. A better question, would he be able to tell her apart from her twin?

He looked from the bartender to her. His gaze met hers, and even in the low lighting she could see the blue of his eyes. Interest sparked in his slow smile.

Jordan picked up his drink and wove his way around the patrons, straight toward her with a deliberate, unhesitating pace. He set his glass beside hers. "I didn't expect such a nice welcome from a Garrison. Are you sure you didn't have the bartender poison my drink, Brooke?"

He recognized her. Or a lucky guess?

"How do you know I'm not Brittany?"

Without ever glancing away from her eyes, he reached, stopping an inch shy of touching a lock of her hair that stubbornly refused to stay pulled back. "Because of this. That wayward strand is signature Brooke."

Wow. He definitely recognized *her* when even her own father had gotten it wrong sometimes.

In that moment, she realized she had more Garrison determination in her than anyone would have ever suspected. Brooke lifted her glass to Jordan in a silent toast.

She'd seen him many times. She'd always wanted him.

Tonight, her family be damned, she would have him.

One

Present Day

"Merry Christmas, I'm having a baby. Your baby," Brooke Garrison corrected the phrasing, wanting to get it just right before the father of her child walked through her office door.

Any second now.

She shifted behind her sleek metal desk from where she managed the family's Sands Condominium Development. She toyed with her hair. Longed for more peppermint ice cream—yes, she'd eaten a scoop with breakfast.

Damn. Time was ticking away faster than the blinking lights on the Christmas tree in the corner of her office, and she still didn't know the perfect way to tell Jordan about his impending fatherhood.

"I'm pregnant, and it's yours." She practiced another tact. "The birth control we used apparently failed. Probably when we were in the hot tub."

Hmm… She shook her head. Bad idea thinking about sharing a bath with Jordan. She swiped back a lock of hair that had slithered free from her French twist. As manager of Sands Condominium Development—a segment of the Garrison family empire—she should be more decisive than this.

Except nothing had ever been more important.

"I'm expecting." Expecting what? That sounded like FedEx should be showing up soon with a package. She kicked off her heels that had long ago started pinching her swollen feet, even without panty hose.

Thanks to her ever-present tan, a by-product of living in Miami's South Beach, she could go without stockings. And why was she thinking about clothing accessories?

Likely to avoid the subject that jangled her nerves.

She should have already prepared the flawless speech. The Garrison family perfectionist, never making waves, she was always organized. Not so much now.

Worst of all, there was no excuse for her lack of prep work. Once she'd dropped the pregnancy news bomb at the weekly family dinner, she'd known it was only a matter of time until word got out. Eventually her future brother-in-law, Emilio, would un-wittingly say something to his own brother—and business partner.

Jordan Jefferies.

When her secretary had buzzed her with the news that her family's biggest business rival would like to see her, Brooke had known that *eventually* had arrived.

Sooooo, what about, "Remember that night five months ago after they read my father's will? When I actually indulged in three sips of wine?" Dumb move having any at all since she never drank for fear of being like her alcoholic mother. "And after that, we had wild monkey sex in a hotel room until—"

The door opened and her mouth closed.

Jordan didn't fling it wide or send it crashing against the wall. He didn't need to. The man in a gray pin-striped suit had the kind of presence that resonated through a room more than any echo of wood pounding wall. The diamond cuff links and tailored perfection of him contrasted with her memories of their raw, heated night together.

Six feet three inches tall, he nearly skimmed the mistletoe dangling from her door frame. As quietly as he entered, he closed the door behind him.

The lock snicked. She flinched. His baby kicked.

Jordan turned to face her and strode toward her desk, his handsome face an unreadable mask. As she took in his perfect blond hair, she resented her stubborn strand that wouldn't stay in place. He knelt briefly and straightened, coming back up with her shoes. A whiff of his aftershave drifted across the steel desk, sending her back to the morning she'd hugged a hotel pillow to inhale the scent of him. Before she'd left him sleeping.

"Hello, Brooke." He placed one shoe on her desk, but kept the other black leather pump cupped in his hand. "Don't bother getting up on my account."

"Since you have my shoes, I believe I'll keep my seat." And camouflage her burgeoning stomach behind the office furniture for a few more minutes. A technicality, sure, but it offered a semblance of control.

At least he wasn't shouting, but then he'd had time to absorb the news about her pregnancy. She just needed to be sure he knew—believed—the child was his.

An odd thought struck her. Could she have used telling the family—in front of his adopted brother—as a passive-aggressive way of getting the news to Jordan? While she considered herself a savvy businesswoman who earned her place in the family corporation, she had a reputation for avoiding all-out confrontations in her personal life.

Had she dodged a bullet? Or merely made matters worse? She tried to get a read off Jordan's expression, but he kept her shuttered out with his best executive poker face.

His thumb caressed the leather shoe—and, my, how she hated the way that simple gesture had her curling her toes against a shiver of longing for his hands on her again. It must be hormones. She'd read in one of the pregnancy books that the middle trimester brought an extra surge of sensuality, something she hadn't believed until this moment.

"I'm pregnant," she blurted. So much for a dignified speech. Definitely not a time to add Merry Christmas.

"So I hear." His blue eyes heated over her, unblinking.

"And it's yours."

"Of course."

Arrogant, *sexy* ass. All wishes to avoid confrontation slipped away as something unusually contrary snapped inside her. But then she never acted as expected around this man. "Why are you so sure?"

"Because you told me." He walked around the edge of the desk and set her shoe on the mouse pad. "I've doubled my father's fortune by knowing who to trust and who's a liar."

"You're awfully sure of yourself."

"I've never been wrong before, Brooke. I'm assuming it was during the hot tub. We got a little carried away then." His silky blue eyes oozed sensuality at just the mere mention of that steamy encounter.

She gulped. "Uh-huh. That would be my guess."

He tucked her wayward hair behind her ear. "Besides, your soulful brown eyes aren't a liar's eyes."

She forced her gaze to stay firmly locked with his—while vice-gripping the edge of the desk so her chair wouldn't roll back. She wasn't ready to reveal her stomach, to be that vulnerable. Not yet. "You're saying I'm a sap?"

"I'm saying you're a good person. Far more so than I am, actually." His hand fell to the leather blotter she'd cleared of paperwork for this meeting. "Besides, what would you gain by telling me this? Nothing."

"Ah, so your belief in me has more to do with logic than any mystical eye-reading abilities."

"Brooke. Quit stalling."

Babbling Brooke. Her father used to call her that whenever she got nervous. Yet she'd worked so hard to cultivate a cool facade after years of her mother's hurtful, drunken jibes.

Jordan was right. She was stalling, and all because she suffered from a silly, ridiculous—shallow—moment of self-consciousness. She definitely didn't look like the same woman who'd crawled into bed with Jordan five months ago. Why couldn't he have stayed on the other side of the desk for this conversation?

So much for vanity.

She rolled her chair back across the rose-colored Persian carpet and presented him with an unfettered view of her green dress clinging to her pregnant belly.

Holy hell. Jordan's mouth dried up.

He'd heard about the *pregnancy glow* from friends and workmates, and quite frankly had thought it to be pure bunk. Until now.

Brooke's creamy skin had a touch-me luster. Her

silky brown hair glistened with an extra sheen he could swear had multiplied since he'd last seen her.

And the new swell of her breasts… His hands itched to explore them all over again.

Finally, he let his gaze land on the curve of her stomach where the baby grew. Now *that* stirred something else altogether inside him. Something primal.

His child.

He'd known from the moment he heard the due date that the child was his. However, seeing the proof here in front him, seeing Brooke so amazingly full of his baby… He felt an all-new connection to her and to the life they'd created together. He wasn't going to be shuffled aside, especially not by any stubborn Garrison with her fortress of family support.

Jordan corralled his thoughts and narrowed his focus to her chin with that signature Garrison cleft. People might call him the hard-ass in the boardroom when it came to dealings for Jefferies Brothers, Incorporated, but he decided it wouldn't hurt to let her see how this moment had rocked him.

He sat on the edge of her desk and exhaled long, hard. "Damn, Brooke, that's amazing."

Her gorgeous smile told him he'd struck gold.

Her hand fell to rest over the slight curve. "I'm still getting used to it myself. That's why I haven't gotten around to telling you, yet."

He figured it wouldn't be prudent to mention she'd found time to tell her whole freaking family.

Alienating her gained him nothing and risked everything. "What matters is we're here, now, together."

Together. The word stirred memories of their shared night. Those recollections linked up with the heat surging through him now simply by looking at her, by watching her pupils dilate in response.

Why not let his attraction to Brooke—an attraction that had full well been reciprocated by her—be turned to his advantage?

He reached again to stroke a stray lock back from her face. He took a slow moment to test the feel of it between his fingers, then graze her cheek with his knuckles, her skin as soft as her hair.

"Jordan," she began, her brow furrowing in a surefire precursor to a discussion he hoped to forestall. "I know this could get complicated, but I'll have my lawyers contact yours about making sure you have—"

He dipped his head to capture her next word with his mouth. She tasted like peppermint and temptation.

The peppermint was new. The latter part, he remembered from that fateful night five months ago when they'd crossed paths in the Garrison Grand. He'd been scoping out the competition as he worked on building his Hotel Victoria.

Sure he'd seen her before, but there had been something about her that night, something vulnerable that had called to him. Before he could say bad decision, they'd been making out in an elevator on their way up to a room.

Lips and tongues meeting pretty much the way they were now. Yes, he definitely remembered that, as well as the graceful line of her back under his hands. The feel of her fingers gripping his shoulders. All of it stirred him again with a surprising jolt.

He couldn't afford to lose control. He needed to corral his thoughts with so much at stake with their child, not to mention the business implications of a family merger with a Garrison.

Jordan eased his mouth from hers and tucked her head against his chest as he worked to slow his heart rate. The gusts of her breaths along his neck told him she was every bit as affected by him— which didn't help calm him.

Still, his hands smoothed along her back. The timing to woo her over would be tough for him with the preparations for opening his Hotel Victoria next month, a smaller hotel than her family's Garrison Grand. But he was certain it would rival the Garrison property in luxury—and attract the same clientele. Hell, yes, he'd earned his ruthless business reputation honestly.

He would need that same drive now to win her over. Not only because of the baby, but also because he knew the chemistry he and Brooke shared didn't come around all that often. In fact, he couldn't think of any other woman who turned him inside out with the stroke of her hand the way she could, not even the ex-Playboy bunny he'd dated—and broken up with shortly before that steamy night with Brooke.

Jordan nuzzled her ear. "No lawyers." He nipped the lobe, tugging on her diamond earring gently. "A judge. Two rings." His hand slid around to cup the sweet fullness of her. "And a bouquet by the end of the week, because this child will be born to married parents."

Two

Marry him?

Was he out of his flipping mind?

Or maybe she'd lost hers. Brooke pulled out of his arms so she could regain her balance in the rolling chair. Certainly Jordan's kisses had a powerful effect over her, a large part of why she'd run from his bed so hard and fast five months ago.

The utter loss of control she'd felt with him scared the spit out of her, then and now. "Marry you?"

"Of course." He stroked two fingers down the length of her ever-errant stray lock of hair until she thought maybe she would leave her hair that way from now on. "It makes perfect sense. You're carrying my kid. Our families have been feuding long enough, don't you think? That sort of contentious environment can't be good for a child. Now that Emilio is engaged to Brittany, the rift has started to mend. We can solidify that by marrying each other and fully merging the two family corporations."

Wow, he'd almost had her thinking he possessed a heart, right up to the last word…*corporations.* She pushed out of her chair and stalked away from him, toward the Christmas tree, pivoting back with a huff. "Shall I give you a club to go with your caveman orders?"

"You want romance?" His blue eyes narrowed, then turned heavy lidded, sexy. "I can give you romance. I simply thought a practical woman like you would appreciate the no-nonsense approach to business dealings."

"Whoa. Back up there, Mr. Romeo Incorporated. You romanced me more than enough five months ago, thanks all the same."

Jordan's heat seared her now, as well. "Then answer my question."

She couldn't regret that night because she refused to let her baby ever feel like a mistake. And the sex had been beyond amazing, but good heavens, she wouldn't enter a marriage based on attraction and business mergers. She also refused to risk a sham of a marriage like her parents lived.

"No." She crossed her arms under her breasts. "I will not marry you."

His jaw flexed.

"Be reasonable, Jordan. We barely know each other."

"We've known each other for years."

"As business acquaintances who've sat in a large meeting maybe three times or passed each other in the same restaurant on occasion." Strange how memorable each of those encounters seemed. She'd always noticed him, but placed him in the off-limits category.

Until that night.

That night when Brooke had been mourning the loss of her father. The loss of an image. She'd always been Daddy's girl, running to him when her drunken mother's barbs were too much to bear. To find that her father had lied to them all, as well…

She couldn't think of that now. She had her own child to consider. Providing a stable home for her baby had to come before some illogical desire to lose herself in another kiss from Jordan.

He scooped up one of her shoes and tapped the heel against her mouse pad. "Yet suddenly you've decided to avoid me."

"Because I wasn't ready to tell you about the baby." She decided he didn't need the extra ammo of knowing why she'd run scared from his naked side.

"Or because the fireworks between us were too much for you to handle."

Apparently he was more intuitive than she'd given him credit for.

"The same could be said for you." Okay, so perhaps her pride stung at the fact he hadn't gone out of his way to pursue her.

"I called you."

"A week later." There went her pride again.

He set her shoe down, his eyes narrowing with a predatory gleam. "You tell me to stay away, and I'm supposed to ignore what you say? Does that mean when you say you won't marry me, I'm supposed to ignore that, too?"

He was a wily one. No wonder her oldest brother said Jordan made such a fearsome adversary in the boardroom. Which brought up yet another complication since the baby's father just happened to want a toehold in her family's company. Marrying her would give him that connection to the Garrison business he'd always craved.

God, she hated the path her mind was taking. But damn it, he was the one who'd said they could merge corporations. If that didn't give a woman the right to be leery, she didn't know what would.

"Don't be obtuse, Jordan. I won't marry you. We don't know anything important about each other as people, anything outside the bedroom." Don't go there with the thoughts. "To base a marriage on a brittle foundation of sex and mutual business interests would be catastrophic and horribly unfair to our child."

"All right then." He smiled—wow, how he smiled. He shoved away from the desk and strode toward her. "Let's get to know each other better.

For our child. We're going to be linked by this kid for the rest of our lives. It's the Christmas season. Let's celebrate and use this time to build a stronger foundation."

"That sounds logical." If she knew him better, then she could better judge his motivations for wanting to be a part of her life as well as the baby's.

"Good, good." He nodded as he walked by her, past the Christmas tree.

No kiss? No more trying to persuade her to marry him? That was it?

"Jordan?"

She eyed him warily as he strode toward the door, paused and glanced back over his shoulder.

"I'll pick you up at eight tonight for our date." The door clicked closed behind him.

Date?

She'd thought they were going to get to know each other, as in meet at the lawyer's office to draw up visitation agreements, perhaps have coffee afterwards. But dating?

She'd just been royally maneuvered, and she wouldn't give over complete control that easily. Yes, she could see how *dating* would be a good idea, however, she resented the way he assumed she would fall in line with his plans. She didn't want the world to know about them yet, damn it.

Time to show Jordan Jefferies that while she might be the quiet Garrison, she had every bit as much determination as the rest.

When it came to how they would get to know each other, she could make plans of her own.

At six-thirty that evening, Brooke pulled her BMW convertible past a row of palm trees and a hibiscus hedge into the side parking lot of the Hotel Victoria—eight impressive floors of brass and glass set on the South Beach shore.

The construction workers should be gone for the evening. She knew from casual conversations with Emilio that Jordan had opened an office in a completed suite where he could oversee the last stages of finishing the hotel, and he always stayed late. The place was his well-known pet project of Jefferies Brothers, Incorporated's many holdings. So he would undoubtedly want to spend every free moment overseeing the construction.

She'd worn sunglasses in hopes of keeping a low profile. It helped that no one would expect to find a Garrison here. The world could know about her relationship with Jordan when she was good and ready.

Now she just had to get past security.

Brooke flipped open her cell phone and punched in Jordan's private number he'd given her five months ago, a number she'd almost used at least a hundred times. The ringing stopped.

"Jordan?"

"Brooke, you're not backing out."

"Who says I'm breaking the date?" she retorted.

He thought he knew her. She would enjoy surprising him. "I'm downstairs."

"Down where?"

"Outside your place. At the Hotel Victoria. Could you please tell your security guy to let me up?"

His two-beat hesitation offered the only sign she'd shocked him. "I'll be down in less than a minute."

Sure enough, before she could step out of her car, Jordan pushed through the back entrance toward her. She tugged the picnic basket with her and slammed the car door.

His steps faltered briefly, his gaze hooking on her Little Red Riding Hood basket. "I made dinner reservations for eight-thirty."

"I can't wait that long to eat. I'll be starving way before then." She stopped in front of him, the basket between them. "Would you be responsible for depriving your baby of food?"

He brushed his thumb over the dimple in her chin. "What game are you playing here?"

She didn't want to be tempted by his touch, especially when they would be alone for the evening. But going out in public together? She wasn't ready for that yet. "I don't want to go out. I'm tired and my feet hurt. I want to enjoy my dinner and relax without a bunch of curious people watching us, or worse yet, asking questions."

"Fair enough," he conceded. "Let's go inside." He took the basket from her and guided her toward the hotel entrance.

Letting him steer her with the heat of his hand on her waist, she couldn't deny the curiosity itching over her to check out the rival hotel of the Garrison Grand. Inside, she inhaled the scent of fresh paint, undoubtedly soon to be replaced with a more exotic aroma.

No question, this place targeted the same clientele as her family's South Beach property, yet she couldn't help but be struck by the décor contrast. The Garrison Grand stayed with a theme of mostly pristine white, with the richest of wood, marble and steel accents.

The Victoria fired through her in a blast of bold reds and yellow, with brass accents. Cherrywood, marble and decadence were the only decorative themes in common.

Best not to think about marble, though, which could too easily lead her to memories of the marble spa tub they'd once enjoyed.

The brass doors to the elevator swooshed open, and she stepped inside with Jordan—and more memories. Had she made the right decision today? She tried to avoid looking at him, but the mirrored walls made that impossible. "Your hotel is beautiful."

"*You* are beautiful."

"And *you* are not going to get me against the elevator wall that easily again, Romeo."

His low laugh followed her as she walked out of the elevator, then she realized she didn't know where to turn. Jordan touched her elbow and guided her left toward the double doors at the end of the corridor. He swiped his key and she found—not what she'd expected.

Wait. "I was thinking we would eat in your office."

Not in a sitting room that obviously connected to a bedroom.

Control slipped elusively away. She longed to call for a time-out and simply plop to rest on one of the comfy buttercream-yellow and burgundy sofas or seats stationed throughout the lobby. Or better yet, kick off her shoes and take to the beach beyond the glass wall, wade through the aquamarine waters.

"I'm living and working from here now, just until they finish up the last touches to the hotel. Saves time leaving my house for every call." He tugged at the knot in his striped tie and slowly slid the length free from his collar.

At the deliberate, sensuous glide of the silk against his cotton shirt, her stomach flipped and it had nothing to do with an acrobatic baby. "Okay, can I get you something to drink? I brought water, and uh, water. Oh, and milk."

Let him see what life with her would be like. No wild nights at a bar. Of course he could always go to his own minibar and mix himself something to drink. She waited…

He extended a hand. "I'll have the water."

She reached into the basket and pulled free a bottle of sparkling water. She poured it into two crystal glasses with ice from the minibar, topped it off with a twist of lemon before flipping the lid closed on the basket again... To find him in the doorway with his cell phone in hand.

He covered the mouthpiece. "I'm canceling our reservations at Emilio's restaurant. It seems you have dinner well in hand."

Emilio's? Her mouth watered for the amazing Cuban cuisine offered at El Diablo. Being a captive to her hormonal cravings really sucked sometimes. She chewed her bottom lip and stared at the basket of... She couldn't even remember what was inside anymore.

Jordan covered the phone's mouthpiece. "I had this assistant once who was pregnant. She ate cheeseburgers for lunch every day for a month. She vowed nothing else sounded good. You know, we can pitch the stuff in your basket and I can place a delivery order at El Diablo's—for the baby."

She released her lip from between her teeth, slowly. "For the baby?"

"Absolutely."

"Okay." She rattled off her order before her pride could get the better of her, each delicacy filling her taste buds with anticipation.

"Got it." His smile and wink took away some of the sting to her pride at losing a bit of control in her plan.

He relayed her order, doubled to include himself. Finally he closed his phone and ditched his suit coat over the back of a wooden chair, the wide bed visible through the part in the slightly open connecting door.

She took in the framed prints on the walls, each

photo portraying a stage of construction of the hotel. All but one small family photo resting by his computer… She started toward it, curious, but Jordan waylaid her.

He took his glass in one hand and her elbow in his other. "The balcony?"

Since she could swear he'd phrased it as a question rather than an order, she decided to go along. "The balcony, yes."

Lord love him, after she sat, he even thought to swing another wrought-iron chair around to prop her tired feet while they enjoyed the final fading rays of the day. He really was pulling out all the stops.

Sinking back into her seat, she sighed at the amazing view of the waves rolling against the private beach. "You've got a great piece of prime property here."

"Thanks."

She enjoyed the beauty of the sculptured landscaping, empty now, but soon undoubtedly to be flooded with people. "Who needs blood pressure medicine with a mood stabilizer like this?"

His eyebrows drew together. "A lot going on to stress you out lately?"

She rested her hand on her stomach. "I'm excited about the baby, don't get me wrong. But the news certainly frightened me at first." She didn't have much in the way of positive role-modeling for motherhood.

"I wish you would have told me."

"The thought of doing that really sent my heart pounding." She pulled out the pins from her French twist and shook her hair loose in the ocean breeze.

"I'm that scary?"

"I wouldn't say scary, exactly." Intimidating. "Pushy." That sounded nicer.

"You're as diplomatic as the rest of your family," he answered wryly.

Actually, she was usually the family diplomat. "I don't believe you mean that as a compliment."

He stayed silent, his executive face in place as he studied her for a lengthy moment while seagulls scavenged along the talcum-white shore for a late-day snack. "So clue me in to what I have done to warrant such great fear. You don't tell me about our baby for months. After being left out of the loop about my own child, I come to you directly—calmly, I might add."

He had a point. She stared at her feet, guilt pinching as much as her shoes. She kicked off the heels and wiggled her toes. "Uh, I'm sor—"

"Wait, hold that thought. I'm not finished." He held up a hand. "Then I do the heinous, awful thing of proposing marriage. And when you crush my spirit by turning me down, I ask you out on a date." He thumped himself on the forehead. "Damn. I sure am one helluva jackass."

Laughter bubbled inside her. "Okay, okay, you've made your point. You've been more than fair, and I was wrong not to tell you sooner. I apologize, and I really mean it. This is simply something I've needed time to become accustomed to myself, but I'm here with you now. No matter what happens with these dates of ours, you will be a part of our child's life if that's what you want."

"Don't doubt that for a second."

His steely determination sent a shiver up her spine and her arms around her swelling waistline protectively.

"When Emilio told you about my pregnancy, did you let him know about us?"

He shook his head, leaning back in his chair, water glass tapping against his knee. "I wanted to speak with you first." His eyes widened. "So your whole family doesn't know I'm the father yet. Not even your twin. Damn. You're a good secret keeper. I could use someone like you in my company."

"That's why I didn't want to go out tonight. I've kept the baby news under wraps by wearing bulky clothes and staying away from the social scene for the most part, but my stomach has really popped these past couple of weeks. Once you and I are seen out in public together, people will make the logical connection. I need to tell the family about us first."

"Let's do it then. Call a family meeting."

He had to be kidding. He actually wanted to be there when all the Garrisons heard she'd hooked up with Jordan Jefferies? Of course, she would have to inform her family sometime.

"Actually, we all gather every Sunday for dinner so that would be the easiest, most logical time."

"All right, if you think this is the best way. They're your family."

The problem was, there would be no best way to tell them about Jordan Jefferies—the head of her family's rival company. A rivalry that still existed even though somewhat softened since Emilio entered the fold.

She stared up at the stars just beginning to wink at her and willed her heart rate to slow. After all, she needed to keep a level head. She still had a whole weekend of date nights to get through with Jordan before the big family confrontation.

And for now, just making it back out Jordan's door without glancing in the direction of his bed seemed like a Herculean feat.

Three

Guess who's coming to dinner?

The phrase kept clicking through Brooke's head during the drive to her family's estate late Sunday afternoon.

The words only drummed louder as Jordan pulled past the security gates up the brick drive toward the ambling stucco mansion with a red tile roof—her childhood home. She suffered no delusions that this would go smoothly. The boardroom hatred between her family and Jordan was longstanding and deep.

She still could hardly believe they'd accepted Emilio into their family, in spite of his partnership in Jefferies Brothers, Incorporated. It said a lot for how much Brittany loved Emilio. However, there wasn't love present this time, and she feared her family would sense that.

Jordan slid the Jaguar into Park behind the line of other luxury cars. Apparently her siblings had already arrived.

She was lucky to have been born into her family's wealth, and she worked her tail off managing the Sands Condominium Development to prove she deserved it. Still, that hadn't stopped some from labeling her a silver-spoon, trust-fund baby. It also hadn't stopped many two-faced people from wanting something from her. Brooke rubbed the goose bumps along her arms in spite of the temperate Miami December afternoon.

Jordan rounded the hood to open Brooke's door and lead her up the stairs to the massive mahogany and glass double doors. Garland and bows draping the entrance reminded her of a holiday she hadn't found time to begin preparing for.

Before they even made it to the top step, the doors swept open to reveal an older lady in a starched blue dress and white apron. "Good evening, Miss Brooke."

"Hello, Lissette. Could you please let them know in the kitchen that there will be one more for dinner?"

"Of course, Miss Brooke, we'll have yours out directly."

Noise rattled from the dining room, clinking silverware against china. Requests for passing this and that, a normal sounding family dinner.

Little did they know…

Jordan glanced down at Brooke. "Your face is pale. Are you all right? Do you need to sit down? We don't have to do this today. We can keep right on with our apartment dates—"

She squeezed his arm. "I'm fine." Although she had enjoyed their simple dinners at his place and hers. How she wished they could keep it simple, and yes, hidden, for a while longer. "But thank you for worrying."

He winked.

Her heels clicked along the tile floors as she made her way across the foyer past the winding staircase, the click, click echoing up to the cavernous ceiling. A Christmas tree—at least twelve feet tall—twinkled. Perfectly wrapped gifts lay beneath. The decorations were beyond lavish this year since Brittany and Emilio would be celebrating a Christmas wedding in three weeks with the reception held here.

Brooke forced even breaths past her lips. All the more reason to reveal the news now and give the dust time to settle so she wouldn't ruin Brittany's big day.

They stopped in the dining room entry, waiting. She took the unobserved moment to study her family at the table.

Her brother Parker would blow a gasket. Even with the softening influence of his new wife, Anna, her oldest brother was still unrelenting when it came to his business dealings. His dislike—wow, what a way to soft-soap that—for Jordan was common knowledge.

Her brother Adam had always been emotionally distant from all of them, only just beginning to open up since his surprise marriage to the straight-laced Lauryn.

At least Stephen wasn't here. One less angry brother to worry about.

Her gaze skipped over her mother—downing a glass of wine—and settled on those most likely to be her allies. Her outgoing twin, Brittany, sat with fiancé Emilio Jefferies.

Even with Emilio's new standing in the Garrison family, Brooke suffered no delusions. Jordan was the power force behind Jefferies' attempts to one-up Garrison Inc. by any means possible.

A shattering glass silenced the room.

Brooke jolted as all eyes shifted to Bonita, the matriarch. Her wineglass in shards at her feet, Bonita clapped her hand over her mouth and pointed a wavering finger toward the entryway.

Perhaps Brooke should have made this announcement alone after all.

"Mother, everybody, I've brought someone along for dinner. He obviously needs no introduction."

Brittany snorted.

Brooke shot her twin a *you're-not-helping* glare.

Her impish twin crinkled her nose with an unspoken *sorry*.

Brooke nodded briefly before stepping deeper into the room, forcing her tense facial muscles to smile, damn it. Just pretend things were normal. She paused in front of her chair at the table set for seven, ever aware of the looming man at her back. "I realize this is likely a bit of a shock, but for the sake of family unity, I would appreciate it if we could be civil adults and welcome a guest."

She gauged the noiseless diners around the table. Stunned silent? Or quietly accepting? For a woman who didn't do confrontation, she figured she was making a heck of a good show. "We'll all be seeing a lot of each other in the future since..." She swallowed down the lump in her throat and avoided looking at her mother. "Since..."

So much for her bold approach.

Jordan's hand fell to rest on her shoulder. "I'm the father of Brooke's baby."

She glanced back at him in a quick moment of gratitude that he was there to speak the words she found so hard to say.

Bonita moaned and reached for her Bloody Mary resting by her full water glass while a maid still hovered around the broken glass at her feet. Where was she finding all these drinks? Her brothers usually did a better job at keeping them out of her hands. Things were definitely spiraling out of control.

Parker's chair scraped back as he stood. "Brooke, move."

She shook her head. "Not a chance, Parker."

Her brother kept his eyes pinned on his rival. "Damn it, Brooke, I said *move*."

Jordan's fingers twitched on her shoulder. "Don't speak to her that way."

A vein throbbed in Parker's temple. "Who the hell are you to tell me how to speak to my sister?"

"I'm the man who's going to marry your sister."

Before she could remind Jordan she'd only agreed to date him, he'd gently moved her aside as Parker shouted, "Like hell."

In a blink both men launched across the table.

The candelabra toppled into a crystal serving dish of asparagus. Gasps echoed. Someone yelped. China and silverware clinked and scattered.

She'd seen her brothers scuffle in their younger years, but that had been simple roughhousing. She'd never seen an all-out fight before. An honest-to-God, muscles bulging, men-out-for-blood pounding on each other.

It wasn't pretty. And it wasn't sexy. All the polish of their everyday ways negotiating deals in boardrooms peeled away to reveal the true cutthroat nature that had propelled them to the top. Their rawness scared her as they rolled off the edge of the table onto the floor in a crash of shattering glassware and honed bodies meeting tile.

The women shot to their feet, advanced a step, then backed away. The other two men at the table simply lounged back. What the hell was wrong with them?

Brooke stamped her heel. "Adam, Emilio, step in before one of them breaks something vital."

Her brother and Jordan's lumbered to their feet as if in no big hurry to end the show.

Adam strode past, leaning toward her. "This has been a long time coming between them. Sure you don't want to let them just work it out of their systems for a while longer?"

"Adam!" she warned a second before Parker landed a punch to Jordan's jaw, not that Jordan even flinched. Instead, the father of Brooke's child flipped his rival on his back in a move that slammed them both into the serving cart.

There went dessert.

Emotions swirled through her—guilt over bringing Jordan into this lair without more forewarning. Annoyance at him and Parker for not staying civilized.

And ohmigod, divided loyalties.

Adam sighed. "Okay, okay…"

Her brother, the middle of the Garrison brood, nodded to Emilio for assistance. The two men made their way toward the pair still duking it out.

Bonita whimpered between gulps of her Bloody Mary. "Another Garrison bastard."

Brooke grabbed the edge of the table to steady herself. The last thing she needed right now was condemnation from her mother, even as much as Brooke wanted to defend her child and her illegitimate sister Cassie. Focus on getting the men quieted down first so she could sit and rest her throbbing feet. Her aching heart.

Emilio and Adam dodged flying fists to grab an elbow and haul the two apart, no easy task given the thrashing men were hyped on adrenaline.

Brooke kicked her way through the shattered remains of the meal on the floor. "Stop it, Jordan. *Now.*"

Somehow her calmly spoken words in conjunction with the reverberation of her stamped high heel must have penetrated his rage. He turned to look at her.

Thank God Adam quickly grabbed and pinned both of Parker's wrists behind his back before her oldest brother could make a furtive move to take advantage of Jordan's distraction.

Anna rushed past a toppled chair to stand beside Brooke, sliding an arm around her shoulders. "Parker, put a lid on it. You're upsetting your sister and that can't be good for her in her condition." She rested a hand on her own slight baby bump. "Or my condition, either, for that matter. Can't you see Brooke's swaying on her feet?"

Brooke winced. She hated sounding like a wimp, but it did seem to take the wind out of the sails for both men. Parker eyed Jordan warily while Jordan strode back to her side.

"Do you feel all right?"

Not really, but the last thing she wanted was to launch another argument of people blaming each other for upsetting the pregnant women.

Brooke chose her words carefully. "I'm upset. Who wouldn't be? I didn't expect that everyone would do a happy dance, but I expected civility."

Anna stared down her husband.

Parker grimaced. "Damn. Sorry, Brooke. The last thing I want is to do anything that would harm you or your baby. You're my sister, kid, I just…" He shook his head as if to clear away the fog of rage. "I just didn't think."

She noticed he hadn't apologized to Jordan, but she figured it was best to leave that one alone for now. At least they weren't hitting each other anymore.

"Lissette," Anna, the ever-efficient, called, taking charge, "the dinner table is out of commission for tonight. So I believe we'll all have a light supper out on the veranda. It's a lovely temperate evening. Have the cook bring us something simple, whatever she can put together quickly."

Brooke could hear the implied part of quick, meaning they wouldn't have to endure this horrible gathering much longer.

Anna hooked her arm through Brooke's and ushered her toward the door. "Let's find a lounger where you can put those feet up."

"That obvious they're swollen, huh?"

Bonita joined alongside them with an unsteady gait. "You should quit trying to squeeze your feet into those heels. When I was carrying you and Brittany, my ankles swelled up like balloons. You girls caused me trouble from the first trimester and haven't stopped since." She tossed back the last of her drink, extending it for someone to refill.

Brooke wondered if she could borrow some armor to wear around her mother. Or earplugs. How come everyone else seemed able to ignore the comments except her?

Luckily, Lissette was otherwise occupied which sent a frowning Bonita off hunting for her own damn refill. Hopefully, the decanters would be empty.

Brooke swung wide the double doors to the veranda. A gust of fresh night air caressed over her with a much-needed cleansing freshness. She turned to speak to Jordan—only to find he'd stayed behind with Parker.

They weren't throwing punches, but their intense expressions showed their words were equally as powerful. Just her luck, the high ceilings bounced echoes around like racquetballs. Every word of their exchange pummeled her.

Parker stuffed his hands in his pockets. "I always knew you were ruthless, but I never suspected you would sink so low as to deliberately knock up my sister to secure a piece of the Garrison pie."

She heard Jordan deny it. Heard him tell Parker what an ass he was and how Emilio already owned a piece of Garrison Incorporated. Besides, Jefferies Enterprises could take on Garrison just fine on its own.

Brooke heard it all. Yet still, after a lifetime

of growing up in a family that didn't know the meaning of enough power, she couldn't help but wonder if Parker was right.

of growing up in a family that didn't know the
meaning of money, power or the results it helped
wouldn't Parker the rich

Four

Standing behind Brooke outside her condo door
after the family dinner from hell, Jordan worked
his jaw side to side. Parker Garrison packed a
mean right hook. Not that Jordan planned on admitting it.

At least he'd given as good as he'd taken. And
he had to confess, after so many years of conten-
tion between them, it had felt damn great to let
loose on the guy.

Except then he'd looked up and seen Brooke's
pale face.

Jordan hadn't realized until then how emotional
the cool beauty could be. The family's disapproval
really had her worried. He would have taken them

all on if he hadn't seen how fast they backed off once they, too, noticed how the confrontation upset her.

Well, everyone except their sloshed mother.

He hadn't been predicting a red carpet reception, but he'd expected basic courtesy, more like what they'd settled into afterward during the cool—brief—dinner on the veranda.

Jordan reached to touch Brooke's shoulder just as she opened the door and stepped into her condo. Closing the door behind him, he sealed them both in the sleek silver and pink luxury of her home. What a strange time to realize that while he'd viewed every inch of her luscious naked body, he'd never seen where she lived. Now he realized she had been keeping a part of herself from him by insisting they always meet at his place.

He took in the luxury living space sprawling in front of him in a study of silver, white and pinks. Definitely a woman's domain. No question, it was stylish and high-end, but not a place where he could see himself relaxing. He had a quick mental flash of his own childhood home, as swank as the Garrison complex…

But a hell of a lot warmer.

Jordan brushed aside thoughts that didn't change a thing about his path with this woman. If he let Brooke see the slightest chink in his resolve, they would be toast. Even now, he could tell from the brace of her shoulders and the way she chucked her purse onto the sofa, tension still lingered.

He closed the distance between them and rested his hands on her shoulders. He responded to the feel of her beneath his hands. His body aroused in mere seconds any time he got near her these days. But, yeah, she was definitely tense.

Jordan rubbed his thumbs along the kinked muscles in her neck, considering all the ways a man could help a woman relieve this kind of stress. The possibilities tantalized. "Are you going to tell me what's going on with the silent treatment, or do I have to start playing twenty questions?"

He leaned to kiss the nape of her neck, taking his time to absorb the scent of her. She swayed toward him with a whisper of a moan. Then he could almost feel the return of her resolve starch up her straightening spine.

She shrugged off his hands and turned on her heel, her Garrison chin firmly set for battle. "Is it true what my brother said back at the house, right after your fight? Did you sleep with me just to gain a deeper toehold in the Garrison empire? Did you try to get me pregnant on purpose?"

Crap. She'd overheard? Jordan clenched his jaw, then winced at the stab of pain. He hoped Parker was enjoying at least a couple of bruised ribs.

"Ah, the whole Garrison-Jefferies rivalry." He considered the best way to reassure her. She likely wouldn't believe an outright denial anyway. And to be truthful, in the past, he'd done anything possible to get the inside track on Garrison, Incorporated.

Anything to get ahead. "It's a reality we both have to deal with. Isn't that why *you* slept with *me?* To piss off your family? What better way to strike back at big brother Parker and your mother."

"How can you think that?" Her brown eyes went wide, then definitely glinted with guilt.

He reminded himself of her pale face and kept his own stirring anger in check. "For the very same reason you believe the only reason I'm with you is to gain access to your family's stock."

Sure, a union between them made good business sense. But he also couldn't miss that the more time he spent with Brooke, the less he thought about corporations. The apartment dates, with just the two of them, had given him far more insight about her than twice as many outings in a distracting public crowd could have.

Pointedly, he held her gaze until finally she looked down and away, striding toward the kitchen in an obvious move to avoid him. "We don't have much reason to trust each other, do we?"

He watched her walk, the gentle sway of her hips beneath the dark clingy fabric, the hint of bare calf at the slit of her hem. His mind mentally traveled up that patch of skin to silky thigh.

"I guess not." Following her, he lounged in the archway linking the kitchen to the dining area, trying to hang on to the conversation long enough to address her fears about him. "How do we get past that?"

"More dating?" She pulled out a large bottled water from the refrigerator and filled two crystal glasses. "Time."

"Exactly." He'd solidified his point about dating. Apparently he'd done well enough in hiding his own restlessness. And since he didn't want to let on that his thoughts kept straying to her possible choice of lingerie tonight, he distracted himself with figuring out what it was about this place and her mother's home that bugged him.

He took the glasses from her, returned to the living room and set their drinks on the coffee table. "How about we start small tonight?"

"What do you mean?" She eyed him suspiciously.

"Let's sit." He would make her more comfortable by connecting with her the best way he knew how. Their words might do battle, but the heat between them had always been in perfect harmony.

Warily, she perched on the edge of the over-stuffed white sofa. "Okay? What now?"

"Do you trust me with your feet?"

"That's a strange question."

Kneeling in front of her, he pulled off her shoes and tossed the high heels under the coffee table. He sat on the sofa and swung her legs onto his lap, gripping her feet in his hands. He kept his eyes off the way her hem hitched higher, knowing he'd never survive this if he continued torturing himself with thoughts of undressing her. Instead, his thumbs worked a gentle massage along the arch of her instep.

"Ahhh…" Her head slumped sideways to rest against the couch. "Uhmmm, okay…"

The sweet hum of approval in her throat would have encouraged any man, and he looked forward to hearing her make that same sound when he touched her in many, many more places. "I take that as consent to continue."

"A definite yes." She reached behind her and cleared away half of the pink throw pillows so she could settle into the crook of the sofa.

Her shoulder shifted, sending her full breasts in a tantalizing shimmy of movement while she made herself more comfortable. His mouth went dry, and he reached for his water. He'd been with too many women to count, and none had this powerful effect on him.

After he replaced his half-empty water glass on the coffee table, he pressed his thumbs back into the graceful arch of her right foot and decided to see if he could tease a smile back to her face. "Since you're in a yes mood, how about you marry me?"

She didn't so much as flinch, much less open her eyes. "Don't push your luck."

"Can't blame a guy for trying."

Sure enough, the corners of her mouth twitched with a grin as she relaxed deeper into the cushions, hugging one of those froufrou pink pillows.

The business world hadn't labeled him persistent without cause. He would win her over. He was patient as well as persistent, a combination for success.

Never had the stakes been so high, and not just on the business front. He refused to let his child be born without his name. From a young age, he'd known too well how vulnerable a young kid could be without a father.

He'd been told how Emilio's biological father had abandoned his responsibilities. When Emilio's mother had died, Emilio would have become a ward of the state if Jordan's parents hadn't adopted their nanny's orphaned son.

Jordan refused to be like the man who'd left an innocent kid alone and helpless. Sure Brooke had plenty of family, but never would he let his child wonder why his own father hadn't cared enough to be there.

His hands gripped tighter around Brooke's feet as if he could somehow will her to stay with him. "You're just as sexy in sandals as you are in heels."

She opened one eye to peek at him. "Are you jumping on my mother's bandwagon and telling me I have fat feet?"

He would rather guide conversations away from that drunken bat. "You have beautiful feet, with pretty red toenails. I just want to know why you won't pamper yourself. Take it easy during your pregnancy."

"I'm letting you pamper me right now. Don't ruin it by grouching at me." The hint of a pout on her lips gave him an almost irresistible urge to mold her mouth against his for a taste.

"Fair enough." He let his hands glide up to her ankles, his touch growing lighter.

When she didn't object, he inched his way higher to her calves, more of a stroke now than a massage against her bare flesh. Her honey-toned skin still carried a light tan left over from the summer.

Her chest rose and fell evenly. Had she fallen asleep? He skimmed his fingers to the back of her knees, a place he remembered well as being an erogenous zone. Her breathing hitched, then increased.

Oh, yeah. Her eyes might be closed but she was totally awake and not stopping him.

He could continue farther up her dress, likely without protest from her. But he'd better not take the risk now. He'd won time with her. He needed to use it wisely.

Jordan inched his hands from beneath the hem of her dress.

Her lashes fluttered open, and her arms lifted.

Hell, yeah. He couldn't stop the smile from sneaking over his face, and she grinned back. So he waited for her to make the next move.

Her arms hooked around his neck as her mouth parted to greet his with a sigh of acceptance. He wanted to touch all of her, but restraint seemed to be working more in his favor. He planted his hands on either side of her on the couch, careful to keep his full weight off her. As much as he ached for closer contact, he needed to be careful of the growing swell of her stomach. Why couldn't she see that he simply wanted to take care of her and the baby?

He let the kiss play out, glad to connect with her on a level where they communicated so well. Angling to rest his weight on one elbow, he allowed his other hand free rein to roam along her side, upward to cup the fullness that had been tempting him all evening long. The near-immediate beading of her nipple through the fabric followed by that sweet hum of pleasure he'd been hoping to hear encouraged him.

Her slight wriggle against his thigh urged him to keep right on pursuing this path. But the more logical strategist in him knew better.

Damn.

Reason insisted if he took the easy way out for the sex he wanted so badly, he might never understand her reasons for resisting an engagement. Without that information, he would ultimately lose. He had one window of time to finalize this deal, and no amount of killer kisses or soft sighs of approval could sway him from closing the most important transaction of his life.

Jordan eased back with a final sweep of his tongue, a last nip on her bottom lip. "Not that I'm complaining, but what's going on here? I was expecting to work my ass off for a simple quick kiss."

She traced a fingernail along the back of his neck. "You said my swollen feet are pretty."

Women were more complicated than any boardroom negotiation he'd ever undergone. "Your feet are perfect, and if they're swollen, it's half my fault since it takes two to make a baby."

She'd mentioned the comment her mother made. Could a drunk mother's ridiculous throwaway comment bother such a successful, confident woman?

Of course it could. And what a strange time to notice there were no photos of her parents in the condo that he could see. In fact, the walls and mantle bore just watercolor artwork. The only photo he could find…a small photo in a silver frame on the end table. He scooped it up to find five young Garrisons on the beach, Brooke and Brittany not more than five or six. His thumb gravitated to the image of Brooke, no questioning which was her with that sneaky strand of hair sliding from her ponytail.

Brooke raked her fingernail from the back of his neck around to trail along his sore jaw. "I'm sorry my brother hit you."

"I'm not." He smiled in spite of himself and replaced the photo on the end table. "That was the most fun I've had in a long time."

"You're crazy."

"It's a man thing. I expected it." He shrugged off the fight and stifled a wince at his wrenched shoulder as he sat up again. He tugged Brooke to sit in the crook of his arm. "Since we've told the family, what do you say tomorrow we go out to dinner on our own? I'll pick you up after work."

"Why don't we meet here at my place instead?"

She plucked at the hem of her loose-fitting black dress. "Or we can meet at yours and dine on the balcony again."

He frowned. "You don't want to go out with me."

"It's not that." She kept picking at the fabric, her fingers pinching a loose thread with unwavering attention. "I'm just not ready for things to be so...public."

Jordan walled off his impatience. He was starting to learn that while this Garrison had a reputation for being less confrontational than the rest, she was still every bit as stubborn in her own way. "What sort of timetable do you have for telling the rest of the world this is my baby?"

"I'll know when it's right." She finally snapped the stray thread on her dress and pulled a tight smile.

He could already see how much the thought of making this decision was torturing her. Informing her family had taken her months. Taking him to dinner had left her pale, her hands clammy and her feet puffy.

How much more stress would it bring her figuring out how to tell her workmates and the rest of South Beach about their relationship? Without a doubt, gossip would flow. Things had only begun to die down from Emilio and Brittany hooking up. And while Emilio as a partner in Jefferies Brothers had his own issues with Garrison, Incorporated, the animosity between Jordan and Parker went off the charts.

Brooke had to know the baby's paternity would be grist for a hungry rumor mill.

He studied the dark circles under her eyes and made an executive decision. The sooner everyone knew about their romance, the better. And by everyone, he meant all of South Beach in one fell swoop.

Jordan tipped a knuckle under Brooke's chin and brushed a final kiss across her lips. "All right, then, as you said, when the time is right, the world will know."

The next morning, Brooke raced past her personal assistant at the condominium development with a smile and a wave, late, thanks to her restless dreams about Jordan. The massage had tweaked her every last hot button, convincing her that having Jordan in her bed again would be a very delicious idea. But he'd pulled back when she'd been wanting, forcing her to think about their future and not just her keen hunger for him.

Her waking thoughts were equally as agitating as she recalled his kiss…and the way his thumb had gone straight to her image in the photo. He'd known the difference between her and her twin even as children. God, that rocked her.

She only half registered her assistant's call of, "You have a visitor," before Brooke threw wide the door to her office to find—

Her mirror image.

Well, her mirror image without a baby bulge since her twin wasn't five months pregnant. "Good morning, Britt. If you wanted the scoop about Jordan, we could have done lunch today and talked about your wedding plans at the same time."

In spite of being twins, they hadn't always been as close as Brooke would have wished. Brittany had often complained that everyone treated her like a child. However, since Brittany's engagement to Emilio, she'd become closer to her family.

Brittany leaned forward, gripping the portfolio briefcase on her lap tightly. "Are you all right?"

Brooke sank into a chair across from her sister rather than sitting behind the desk. "Yesterday's showdown with the family wasn't fun by any means, but at least that hurdle is passed. Mother reacted pretty much as expected, and both men walked away without broken bones."

"And?"

"And what?"

Brittany eased back in her chair, her eyes sympathetic. "You didn't read local newspapers over breakfast this morning."

The papers? A bad feeling shivered up her spine. "I overslept. I grabbed a bagel on my way out the door." A bagel the baby suddenly seemed determined to kick repeatedly. "Why?"

Her twin opened the monogrammed portfolio bag and pulled out a newspaper—the *South Beach Journal.*

Brittany flipped the paper open. "You're the lead

feature in the social section. Or rather, I should say, that you and Jordan are big news."

Brooke's stomach settled with a dull thud, followed by a roaring denial in her head. Blinking fast, she wiggled her fingers for the paper and sure enough, the lead story plastered a photo of her beside a photo of Jordan.

The paper shook in her hand. "How many more?"

"Three that I've seen, and, of course, it's on the Internet." Brittany twisted her princess-cut yellow diamond engagement ring around and around her finger. "I hear big cash offers are already starting to roll in for the first photo of the two of you together."

"Great." Brooke slammed the paper closed. "That makes me feel much better."

"You could pose and donate the proceeds to charity."

"Don't make light of this, please. This is my life. My baby's life." She blinked back tears of frustration. "This explains why Parker has been trying to reach me all morning. I thought he wanted to badger me about Jordan, so I ignored the messages from his receptionist, Sheila, uh…" Brooke pressed her fingers to her aching temple, the woman's full name escaping her.

"McKay." Brittany finished her twin's sentence. "Sheila McKay."

"Yeah, right. Although learning the reason for the calls from his receptionist doesn't make me any more inclined to answer." She glanced down at the paper again. "I wonder if Jordan knows yet. Damn. What am I saying? Of course he knows. Mr. Perfect would never oversleep and miss checking the news."

"Emilio has already gone to see Jordan and make sure his head doesn't explode over this."

Brooke swiped away a lone tear. She hated feeling so out of control of her life, a by-product of growing up with an alcoholic mother, no doubt. She could only imagine how someone as strong-willed as Jordan would react to having his life scooped this way. "I wonder which of Mother's staff sold the story."

"It could be anyone. We have so many people in and out of there making deliveries with my wedding less than three weeks away."

"I'm sorry to add stress during what should be a happy time."

"Shush. It doesn't have to be all about me. As a matter of fact, it feels good to be able to offer support for a change instead of always being the one needing it."

"Thank you for being here. It's going to be tough winning over the brothers. And I don't even want to think about Mother." Brooke shuddered.

"Of course, I'm here. I owe you, anyway. Remember when the news rag got the pictures of me making out with the chauffeur and you told Mother and Dad it was you? Since you never got in trouble, they let you off with a slap on the wrist. Me, I would have lost my car."

Brooke welcomed the laughter to replace well-ing tears. "The shock on the chauffeur's face was priceless."

"No kidding. If he couldn't tell us apart, then he didn't deserve to have me."

"Damn straight." Brooke's mind skipped back five months to the night she and Jordan made the baby, when he'd most definitely known one twin from the other. Still… "Everything is just changing too fast for me."

Brittany squeezed Brooke's hand. "Once Emilio and I are married, they'll be that much closer to realizing they have to accept all the Jefferies into the Garrison family. Maybe there will even come a time when Garrison, Incorporated can merge with Jefferies Brothers."

"Perhaps." Brooke forced a tight smile although she really wanted to scream. Even her own sister saw this relationship in terms of a business negotiation.

Still, Brooke wasn't so certain things would be settled with her family that easily.

By the end of the week, Jordan wondered why he hadn't managed to settle this wedding issue yet. He tried to take comfort in the relationship being public now. A Friday night dinner at a back table in his brother's restaurant counted as progress.

She hadn't been happy about the newspaper articles, but as he'd hoped when he'd had his secretary leak the story, Brooke had quit worrying about secrecy. They'd begun dating openly in earnest.

He had to admit, he'd enjoyed the hell out of the past week although he should be focusing on the upcoming opening of his Hotel Victoria. He had a stack of work and telephone messages sitting by his computer right now—although at least he could ignore the five messages from his ex. Damn, she was persistent. When she'd called out of the blue yesterday, he'd told her he was seeing someone else now. If she wouldn't listen to words, distance seemed the best option. His secretary would have to tell her he wasn't available.

Jordan put his ex-lover out of his mind, into his past, and realized he didn't feel the least regret. He had his mind and intentions firmly set elsewhere, something others began noticing, as well. Emilio had even caught him watching the clock during a late-day board meeting.

Of course, he didn't bother masking his attraction to her. While romancing Brooke every night this week, he'd also worked to win her over by easing tension with her family.

An unhappy family made for an unhappy Brooke.

So he'd taken Brooke to Brittany's restaurant/lounge for supper one night. To her brother Adam's club another. He'd made a point of being where her family congregated, and sure enough, the press hadn't gotten over their fascination with snapping photos yet. He couldn't blame them. Candlelight played well across her beautiful face—and wreaked havoc with his self-control.

Still, in spite of his best efforts, aside from Brittany, the reception from the Garrison clan stayed at subarctic temperatures. The disapproval was starting to chafe.

He wanted to enjoy this Friday night away from her family, *without* thinking about another Sunday dinner with the Garrisons. His jaw still hurt from the last gathering. Not that he would ever let that arrogant ass Parker know.

Maybe he and Brooke could skip the family dinner if he came up with a better plan for the weekend, a different tactic for winning Brooke over. He'd been thinking how important it was for his child to know he or she had a father who cared, a father who was there. How he wouldn't be like Emilio's old man and run out on responsibilities.

Perhaps Brooke needed a reminder of the scars an absentee father could leave on a child.

Jordan waited for the waitress to finish serving their after-dinner lattes before he reached across to take her hand. "Would you like to fly down to the Bahamas and get away from the paparazzi?"

Her eyes lit as bright as the oversized flickering candle between them. "Yes."

His hand over hers, he thumbed along the soft inside of her palm. "Visit your half sister."

"Definitely, yes." She sagged back in her seat, the relaxed atmosphere of the nightclub and music appearing to calm her more than anything else this week.

Might as well go for broke. He explored the smooth skin and perfect manicure. "And tie the knot."

She snatched her hand away. "No, thank you."

He kept his smile in place and chased her hand back down, soothing her with a kiss over her knuckles. He lingered to nip the gold band on her thumb. "Can't blame a guy for trying."

She narrowed her eyes. "I can stop dating a guy who won't listen."

That caught him off guard. He never overplayed his hand. Although it had been a while since he'd dated, after all. In fact, he'd broken things off with his last relationship shortly before that first night with Brooke.

And there hadn't been anyone since then. A fact he wasn't ready to consider for too long. "You would really cut us off from being together, after the great week we've had, just because I want to marry you?"

"I don't like being manipulated."

A smart man listened, and he'd never been accused of being stupid. "I asked you a simple question, which you answered. I'll back off."

"As long as you understand. I watched my parents live in a loveless marriage. It destroyed them and hurt all of us. Maybe that's something you can't grasp."

Apparently he hadn't overplayed at all. She'd just shared a vital piece of information with him. But Jordan also understood that he had pushed as far as he could for one night. He'd won on the dating issue, and that was going well. So he would continue with the dates. Have her sister Cassie add persuasive insights for Brooke. Let the romantic Bahamas work some magic.

And keep the engagement ring/wedding band set in his pocket ever-ready for use.

Five

The Bahamas midday sun baking overhead, Brooke stared out the limousine window and stretched her legs in front of her. The hem of her skirt teased her calves, her whole body hyperaware of the smallest caress ever since Jordan had reawakened every last hungry hormone inside her. Who would have thought a pregnant women could be so sensually focused on a nonstop basis?

Brooke plucked at her loose peasant blouse, the limo suddenly stuffy. Their morning flight had been early and a bit tiring, but already she could feel the tension seeping from her muscles with each mile closer to seeing her half sister. And how awesome to be away from all the media scrutiny.

If only her need for Jordan didn't make her so physically edgy.

She couldn't deny that Jordan had come up with the perfect way to spend their weekend. She only wished she could gauge *his* feelings. The man never gave anything away. He just kept that sexy smile and sleepy-eyed look focused on her, always lightly, teasingly touching her in some way.

Like now.

Jordan's thumb caressed the inside of her wrist. "How do you feel?"

Oh, if only he knew. She'd entertained the most vivid dreams about him just the night before, her imagination cut loose in sleep to imagine all the things he could do to her body with just his talented touch.

"I'm fine, just a little tired. But mellow, totally." She swept a hand to encompass the seaside road leading up to her sister's estate in an exclusive gated community of stucco homes. "Who wouldn't be relaxed at a place like this?"

"You should take it easy," he said for about the fiftieth time this week, making her wonder if he was avoiding her bed out of concern for her health.

"It's not as if I worked this morning. I only flew in an airplane, for goodness' sake. I even called my doctor before we left to get an official okay to travel. Remember?"

"I want to meet this guy." A twitch flicked in the corner of his eye. "Check his credentials."

She resisted the urge to go on the defensive. Of

course he wanted to interview the physician who would deliver their child. She would feel the same way in his position.

"*Her* credentials, and you can come to the next appointment."

"That's it?" His tic stopped. "No arguing?"

"My family always says I'm the peacemaker type."

"Peacemaker." He frowned. "I would rather you be honest with me than hide your feelings."

That sounded too much like the start of a conversation that could steal her deliciously pleasant imaginings of running her hands down his bare, sun-warmed chest. Thank goodness the limo pulled to a stop outside her sister Cassie's rambling home. She'd seen Cassie often enough since their father's will was read, but this was the first time Brooke had visited the Bahamas mansion.

The driver opened her car door, and she swung her legs out. Conversation would have to wait anyway as her sister already waited for her on the front porch, a towering man just behind her—Brandon Washington, Cassie's fiancé and the Garrison family lawyer.

Gold-and-green garland framed the entranceway and the couple, reminding Brooke that holidays should be spent with relatives. Cassie had lost not only her father this year, but her mother, as well. Brooke was glad to see that Cassie appeared to be moving past the grief and on with her life.

If only they could have consoled each other.

However, forging a relationship with Cassie had taken all the Garrison siblings time. Brooke resolved to lure Brittany here with her once things settled down after the wedding.

Jordan's shadow stretched over her. Was the man able to sense when she even *thought* the word wedding?

The realization reminded her how dangerous it might be to indulge her fantasies about Jordan this weekend. She needed to be careful not to wade in over her head with this man, something she feared would be all too easy to do given the magnetic spell he held over her.

Brooke angled her head back to whisper, "Jordan, do you want to know what would honestly relax me the most right now?"

"Absolutely."

"Could you and Brandon make yourselves scarce so I can have some low-key alone time with my sister?"

Jordan squeezed her shoulder, tormenting her with all the things they shouldn't do this weekend. "Consider it done."

Brooke advanced the rest of the way up the stone stairs, a smile firmly in place, and blessedly she saw nothing but welcome in Cassie's outstretched arms. She stepped into the hug she had needed so desperately since telling her family about the baby.

Beside her, she could see the men shaking hands

and thumping each other on the back as Brandon extended his congratulations.

Brooke's eyes filled with tears, and Cassie pulled back, tut-tutting. "No, no, this is a happy time. Dry up those tears."

"Hormones. I can't help it." She swiped the back of her hand along her cheeks. "I'm sad, I cry. I'm happy, I cry."

"Fair enough, then. Let me look at you while you finish sopping up those tears." Her sister stepped back, smiling. "Pregnancy most definitely suits you. You're gorgeous."

Brandon whistled low. "Amen to that."

Cassie swatted him lightly on the stomach. "You could be a little less enthusiastic in saying that, my dear."

The high-powered attorney slung an arm around Cassie's shoulders and dropped an unabashedly adoring kiss on his fiancée's cheek. "I'm a one-woman man, and you know it."

Cassie softened against him, her marquise-cut diamond engagement ring glinting in the early-afternoon sun. "Just so you don't forget it."

Rings, rings everywhere. Brooke resisted the urge to stomp her foot in frustration.

It was as if Jordan had special ordered all these engaged couples and their happiness just to tempt her. Instead she felt tormented by the ease in the relationships of her siblings with their loved ones. This was how things should be.

She was right to stick to her guns about dating rather than jumping into some marriage of convenience.

Jordan clapped Brandon on the shoulder. "How about you give me a tour of the place while our ladies here talk baby stuff?"

"Sounds like a plan to me, Jefferies. Let's start out by the pool house bar." Their voices drifted on the sea breeze, leaving the sisters alone.

Brooke reached to hook arms with Cassie, relaxing when her sister seemed to have no problems with the continued affection. "Thank you for welcoming us on such short notice."

"It's no trouble at all."

"Are you sure? Our visit is so last minute. We can stay at the hotel."

Since the reading of their father's will, her sister controlled the Garrison Grand-Bahamas nearby.

"Don't be silly. I have plenty of room and kept Mother's staff after she passed. We're fine."

"Okay, then." Brooke walked alongside her over the threshold into the splendor of Cassie's home, a busy, wonderful mix of contemporary, colonial and Queen Anne. "I must admit I welcome the extra time with you. We have a lot of lost years to make up for."

"I always thought my life was full here, and my mother truly was okay without the trappings of a wedding ring or marriage certificate." Cassie's eyes lingered on a portrait of John Garrison with Cassie's mother, the bronzed beauty who had held his heart if not his name. "But now that the tension has passed since the reading of our father's will, I *am* enjoying having siblings. Of course the big family is nothing new to you."

Brooke tore her gaze away from the image of her father and continued with her sister toward glass doors leading outside to a dense garden. "Just because I grew up with brothers and a sister doesn't mean I value you any less. It just took me a while to see past..."

"My getting such a large portion of your family's estate?" Cassie sat on a stone bench near a huge fountain.

Brooke sagged to sit beside her, the verdant scents from the tropical flowers not strong enough to override the acrid air of betrayal. "Dad lying. You had the truth all those years. We had a lie. That was—still is—hard for me to see past." She slid her hands protectively over her stomach. "I want my child to have a life filled with the truth."

"So you came here for more than a place to prop your feet and sun your face."

Her mind crowded with images—that portrait of her father with his other family, so many engagement rings, and largest of all, Jordan's face coming toward hers for a mind-numbing kiss. "I think perhaps I came here for answers."

"Ah, sister dear, the problem is, just because I found a way or your other siblings did for whatever reason, doesn't mean that's right for you. Everyone has to find their own path."

Which left her with nothing more than a host of questions and two swollen feet. If only life were as simple as tossing a penny into that sparkling fountain so she could wish her world right again. She stared into the bubbling waters, her mind mixing around the images of the portrait, rings—Jordan's handsome face. Simply the thought of his kiss made her skin tingle all over as if she'd plunged herself into the fountain.

At this rate, how would she ever manage to resist falling into bed with him?

Moonlight glistening on the surf, Jordan looped his arm around Brooke's side and enjoyed the gentle kick of his child against his fingertips. The little one seemed restless tonight.

And something was up with the baby's mother, as well. He wasn't sure what churned around in that beautiful head of hers, but she'd been jittery since they'd arrived. Not the reaction he'd planned for.

He'd hoped bringing her here would advance his cause. With luck, this midnight walk by the water would calm her and romance her. But he wanted more than romance from her. He wanted commitment. He wanted to plant his ring on her finger the way Cassie Sinclair's hand sported Brandon's rock.

No question, Brandon was one astute dude on a lot of points. Brooke Garrison was a hot pregnant woman.

Her pink dress with the gauzy wrap draped around her shoulders complimented her new curves. The simple elegance seemed all the more perfect with her bare feet furrowing in the sand. He couldn't help but notice how her dress tied at the shoulders, simple little strings he could so easily tug and undo…

Stop. Many more thoughts like that and he would have her ducking behind a dune.

"How was your time with Cassie?" He thought of all those photos packed in every corner of the house. The outward structure of the place might resemble the South Beach Garrison mansion, but no question, John Garrison had found a home here. It was that element that had been missing from Bonita's house, even Brooke's condo. He just hadn't been able to pinpoint it until now. Could Brooke distinguish the difference?

"Good. Very good, actually. It's a journey forming a sister bond once we're already grown-ups, but we're definitely well on our way to the friends part." She kicked her way through the surf. "Cassie's an amazing person."

"All the Garrisons are definitely overachievers." He leaned in to sniff her neck, catch a hint of her perfume.

"Is that a compliment?" She tipped her head toward him, then pulled back as if reminding herself she shouldn't give in.

What might things be like between them once they got past all the stop-and-start negotiations of this marriage deal? A no-holds-barred Brooke was something he wanted to see.

"In my book it is." Their child would probably be a supercharged handful, and yeah, he looked forward to the challenge.

"Do you ever take vacations? Just pick up and leave all the work behind?"

"I'm here, aren't I?"

"You're here because you want to win me over. That's different."

She'd figured that out? He should have realized she would. Still, that didn't make the effort wasted, especially if it worked. "I'm lucky my job takes me to amazing places. I tag on an extra day to sightsee when I can."

"What about after the baby comes?"

Ah, now he saw where she was going with this, and he liked that her thoughts were finally on the future. "Obviously a child means we'll both make changes in our lifestyles. I expect that. I look forward to it."

Did she trust his answer? He couldn't tell, and she'd stopped talking so he searched for something to fill the silence that would reassure her. "I did just pick up and leave once, six months after I graduated from college. Emilio and I backpacked across Europe."

He hadn't thought about that awesome month in… Hell, he couldn't remember when he'd dredged up memories of that time.

She snuggled closer against his side as they strolled. "You're really close to your brother."

"We are. Always have been since we were kids. And now he's the only family I have left." Jordan paused. "Or rather, he was. Now I've got this baby—and you."

"Sounds like the perfect sort of vacation."

"It was great, until..." Crap. He'd meant to dig up pleasant words to soothe her.

"Until what?" She glanced up at him.

He settled for, "We went home."

"Come on, Jordan." She squeezed his side. "You've heard about me and my father and how painful the past months have been. This sharing thing needs to be a two-way street."

The pain of that time kicked over him. The power, even after so many years, surprised him more than a rogue wave. "We came home early because our parents died."

She stopped in her tracks, her hands falling to rest on his chest. "Oh, God, Jordan, I'm sorry. I knew they were dead, but I didn't realize you'd lost them both at the same time. That must have been so difficult for you. How did you lose them?"

"In a boating accident. Emilio and I came home from Europe and assumed control of the business in Dad's place."

"And you never took a vacation again." Her eyes glinted with a sympathetic air that made him uncomfortable.

He wanted to win her over, but not this way. "Like I said, I'm seeing the world on my terms.

When the baby comes, I get to make my own schedule because I'm the boss. I promise, the kid will get trips to Disney. Don't worry."

She stared into his eyes and he wondered if she would press him on the issue of his parents. He braced himself.

Finally, she looked away and started walking again. "So when this baby asks about how Mom and Dad met and decided to start a family, what do we say?"

Relieved to be off the hook from more emotional topics, he answered with the first thought that popped to mind. "We tell him or her the truth."

"The truth?" She snorted on a giggle. "Isn't that a bit much for a child?"

"Not the way I see it." His emotions still too damn raw, he needed—welcomed—the distraction of splaying his hands over her shoulders, sliding them up into her hair. A whiff of her perfume caught on the breeze to tempt him again.

"How do you see it?" Her words hitched with a betraying breathiness.

He stepped closer, skimming against her, each brush a hot temptation. "I would say that I saw a one-of-a-kind woman who knocked me off my feet."

Her chest swelled with a gasp, her fuller breasts pressing against him as she leaned. "That's nice."

"Not nice so much as smart. I know special when I see it." When he felt it. Like now. He soaked in the silkiness of her hair against his fingers.

Her lashes fluttered closed, then half-open again. "You're using those stellar corporate boardroom skills on me."

"Why is it so difficult for you to trust what I say?" He shoved aside a punch of guilt over the newspaper leak. He had been thinking of her peace of mind.

"It's been a tough few months, learning about my father." She waved a hand in the general direction of Cassie's house. "Finding out about this other life of his. It can shake a person's trust, especially when I already had doubts about the whole happily-ever-after gig in the first place."

"I can understand that." That wasn't what he'd intended in bringing her here, damn it. He worked to steer the conversation back on path. "My parents had a great marriage. I've seen how it should work."

"They loved each other?"

"Yes." The loss squeezed his gut again.

She stared at him. Waiting. For?

Hell. She was talking about that *L* word, or the lack thereof between them.

He'd promised to be honest with her. He'd been able to go to the press to make things easier for her, but this would be different. He knew that.

He hooked his hands behind her waist, wishing this could be simpler, wishing they were free to take their time and let the simmering passions and feelings build.

Then again, would they have ever made time for that to happen if not for the pregnancy? The sand shifted under him as he thought of all he would have missed if he'd stayed away from Brooke Garrison. "Feelings grow over time. We have a lot to build on."

"Thank you for being honest."

At least he'd answered right. An exhale of relief gushed out of him in time with the receding wave. The next curl of the ocean around their feet sent desire pumping through him, an urge to forge ahead. "Then let's be honest about what feelings we already have."

Feelings?

She was awash in them at the moment. Sensual longing more than tingled over her now. It burned until she ached to sink deeper in the waves for relief.

Or submerge herself in the sweet release she knew she could find in Jordan's arms.

Maybe that was her answer after all. Quit worrying so much about the rings and happily-ever-after family portraits. The baby wouldn't be born for a few more months. Why deny herself the pleasure of exploring what she and Jordan did have figured out? How to bring each other unsurpassed pleasure.

Before she could change her mind, Brooke tucked her hand behind his neck and arched up on her toes to press her mouth to his. His low growl of appreciation rumbled against her already sensitive breasts a second before his arms secured her to him.

Water soothed around her feet, languished warm liquid touches up her ankles as Jordan toyed with the knots holding her whole dress together. Silk swayed along her calves, teasing between her legs while his mouth covered hers, his kiss growing deeper, more insistent. Her fingers gripped his hair, holding him to her while she let the desire for him wash over her as relentlessly as the waves stole the sand from beneath her bare feet.

He palmed her bottom and nestled her closer, closer still, as near as she could get in her condition—and likely as far as they should take this out on an open beach.

She'd been wanting this, thinking of this. Why was she hesitating? She wouldn't. "Let's go to my room."

Six

At the bold scoop of Jordan's arm behind her knees, Brooke gasped with surprise. He gathered her up into his embrace and charged across the beach toward the private entrance to their suite. She laced her fingers behind his neck and held on, savoring the strength of his body and the fluid movement of muscle.

Her heart raced as fast as his feet. "I can walk, you know."

His hold merely tightened, tucking her hip close to the hard heat of him. "I'm not wasting any time for you to change your mind."

She threw back her head and laughed, the stars overhead not even close to competing with the sparks of sensation showering through her. She rested her head against his shoulder. "Not a chance of that. I want this. I want you."

"I'm not going to argue with you." He thundered up the lanai steps, across the small patio and angled to open the outside door to her room. His jaw slanted closer and on impulse, she arched up to brush a kiss along the bit of bruise that remained from his fight with her brother.

She would always associate the sweet scent of the greenery on the porch, the crash of the island waves with this moment, her senses all on high alert. He carried her over the threshold and lowered her to her feet. She sank her sandy toes in the thick rug and stretched upward.

Her hungry mouth locked to his, her fingers yanking at his shirt. The cotton fabric bunched in her fists still held the heat of his body which made her yearn all the more for the real thing. She flung away his shirt and flattened her palms to the pulsating warmth of his chest. She ached to feel that strength over her, under her, all over her.

Jordan swept away her shawl, the crocheted lace slithering down her body to pool around her ankles. The heat of his hands on her uncovered shoulders sent a shiver of anticipation through her.

He tugged the tie on one shoulder, then the other, the satiny top easing down until the fabric hitched on her breasts. Leaving her covered. For now. But thanks to the dress's built-in bra, once the top fell free she would be fully exposed.

Her hands gripped and twitched along the back of his neck, his bristly hair teasing along the sensitive pads of her fingertips. He murmured words of encouragement in her ear.

Not that she needed any. But the whisper of his breath against her skin incited a fresh wave of want.

Jordan slid his fingers under the gauzy fabric, teasing inside to test the creamy texture of one breast. The dress inched lower. Her breathing snagged in her throat.

She couldn't think of a time she'd ached for anything as much as she longed for the feel of his palms on her breasts, heavy with need.

"Jordan…" Was that husky plea hers?

His steamy gaze darn near seared through satin. The ties from one shoulder still in his hands, he teased the tip along her collarbone, over the top of her breasts. He nudged the dress lower bit by bit, layering kisses beneath each new patch of skin he unveiled. Finally, her satiny dress fell free from her chest, skimming down her body, leaving her wearing only panties, just a thin scrap of Lycra separating her from him. She pressed into his cupping palms with a needy groan as her dress joined her shawl around her ankles.

A moment's unease snaked through her as she wondered what he would think of the unmistakable differences in her body. She waited, her hands stilled on his chest by anticipation mixed with anxiety.

The night breeze through the open veranda doors did little to cool her overheated flesh. Jordan's hungry and oh so appreciative gaze upped her temperature even more. Her heart kicked into a speed that almost made her dizzy.

"And I thought you were beautiful before." His hands skimmed from her breasts to shape over her stomach.

He seemed to mean it and she exhaled her relief.

The baby booted him. He jerked a hand back, his eyes wide. "Wow, that was so…incredible."

She laughed, enjoying sharing this moment with him, having him touch their growing child. "Pretty intense, isn't it? It doesn't hurt, although this soccer star wakes me up sometimes."

He stared at her stomach, stunned as he placed his hand back again in a broad span of warmth. "Amazing." Eventually he looked back at her face again. "Are you sure we're clear to take this further?"

Unease—and she hated to admit it, even a touch of insecurity—crept back up her spine. "Are you going to be one of those men who's afraid to touch a pregnant woman?"

"Hell, no," he answered without hesitation. "But I also think I should be man enough to check about restrictions."

"No restrictions. Well, except we can't pull out a trapeze."

"You would have used a trapeze before?"

She rolled her eyes, but welcomed how his charm eased some of the starch from her spine. "In your dreams."

Brooke relaxed against him, the brush of her legs against his dragging her back under his spell.

His hands roved over her with unmistakable impatience. "I'm not much for circus tights, anyhow. So other than the trapeze?"

"Pretty much anything goes as long as it's comfortable." Although she did remember one chapter in her *What to Expect* book that had interesting possibilities. "As the baby grows, I will need to use inventive positions."

"Inventive positions with me, you mean."

"Possessive, aren't you?"

He stayed silent, his face solemn for three slow blinking seconds before he smiled deep creases into his face. "Let's get back to those inventive positions."

"I'm not that large yet."

"We could always practice now."

Practice for later? Assuming they would still be together and having sex when her pregnancy advanced to that stage months from now. The intimate, vulnerable image sent a shiver through her.

"You're sexy now," he whispered against her ear and nipped her diamond stud between his teeth. "You'll be even more so then because it's my baby you're carrying."

"You're a smooth talker." She backed him toward the bed, brushing against the unmistakable reaction to her nakedness.

"I mean what I say." He closed his eyes briefly as she continued to skim against him, his throat moving in a long, slow swallow. "It doesn't pay to be caught in a lie."

"But you leave out parts of the truth."

"Then, I guess you will have to ask the right questions."

Just what she wanted to hear. She flattened her hand to his chest. "Do you want me to touch you here?"

"What do you think?" He stared down at her with eyes blue-flame hot.

"Answer, please." Yes, she wanted, needed the words.

"I've wanted your hands on me every damn second of every day since you left me in that hotel bed over five months ago."

He couldn't be much clearer than that. She wondered if there had been other women since then, but given his propensity for honesty, she wasn't sure she could handle the answer.

"Nobody but you since that night." His hands slid into her hair and tipped her face to his where she could see the honesty of his words.

She tried not to show how much that meant to her, tried not to *let* it mean so much to her. "Are you a mind reader, too?"

"Not a mind reader, but fairly good at judging expressions." His fingers traced down her spine. "A boardroom necessity."

"Remind me not to play cards with you." But back to the more pressing questions for the moment, something that seemed all the more urgent with his hands curved to her bottom. "Do you want my hand higher while I kiss you…or lower?"

"See if you can read my expression."

It seemed she had fairly astute expression-reading skills herself. Brooke arched up on her toes to press her lips to his while skimming her fingers down, down, down until they skimmed the heavy hard length of his arousal.

No question, he wanted her.

Her senses seemed more finely tuned than ever before, her awareness sharply honed. Any apprehensions she may have had about baring her pregnant body to his gaze evaporated under the obvious heat and passion of his attention.

His tongue dipped and swooped through her mouth while he made swift work of his shirt buttons and flung the garment away, quickly bringing them flush against each other. Flesh meeting flesh.

She sighed. The sweet abrasion of his bristly hair brought her breasts to tight peaks of near unbearable pleasure until she couldn't stop herself from wriggling against him. Wanting more. Already craving release.

"Patience, Brooke. Patience."

Damn it all. She was the most patient, calm person on the planet. If she wanted something now she deserved to have it.

Jordan trailed a finger down her spine until he

reached the top on her bikini panties resting just below the slight bulge of her stomach.

She stopped her caress and reached around to clamp his wrist. "I'm not getting fully naked until you lose more clothes."

He grinned. "What a hardship." Jordan spread his arms wide. "Have your way with me, woman."

Brooke unbuckled his belt and slid the leather free slowly, deliberately, then giving the length a shake and snap that echoed through the room.

Jordan's eyes widened. "My quiet one has even more fire than I knew."

Laughing, she tossed away his belt and grabbed hold of his pants. She tugged him forward and nipped his collarbone, while opening his zipper fly. "Still interested in talking?"

"Uh, not so much."

"Thought so." She slipped her hands into his pants and shoved them down and off in a deft sweep that left him gloriously naked. "Now don't move until I tell you."

Finally, finally she could touch him again and she let herself. Let her fingers, just the tips, glide over him along his chest, arms, wrists and hands.

His muscles rippled from the restraint of standing still when she could see clearly in his eyes that he wanted to leap forward. Tanned, defined abs begged for her attention and she obeyed, then surveying lower, lingering.

She remembered well the feel of wrapping her

legs around his solid thighs, then inching higher to dig in her heels. She adored the feel of those strong and powerful legs and worked her way back up again until her palms cupped his hips, and she stood face-to-face with him.

What new things would they try tonight?

She saw his biceps contract for action a split second before he scooped her up into his arms again. Brooke squeaked. "Stop! You really should stop carting me around this way. I'm too heavy."

"Not even close." He carried her past the settee over to the sprawling bed and gently settled her into the middle of the puffy comforter.

"My turn," he growled, and before she could answer—not that she could find words at the moment—his mouth closed over her breast.

Slowly, torturously so, he began his journey over her body, a trek that mirrored her exploration of his, except he kissed, licked, sipped his way over her heated skin and sensitive crooks until her fists twisted in the sheets. Until muttered pleas whispered on panting sighs.

Jordan grabbed a pillow and tucked it beneath her hips, offering the perfect angle to compensate for the gentle swell of her stomach. He slid over her, bracing his weight on his elbows and stared into her eyes, his heat pressing, waiting.

She flung her arms around his neck to urge him toward her for another of his mind-drugging kisses, but he wouldn't be budged. With slow deliberation, never looking away, refusing to let her so much as blink, he pressed inside her again, deeper. Fully. And waited.

If not for the stark strain of tendons budging on his neck, she wouldn't have known how dearly this restraint cost him. A fresh wave of pleasure scorched through her at his tenderness in the midst of such passion.

She arched up to kiss him, bit his lip and demanded, "More, now."

In case he might be left with any further doubts, she rolled her hips against his and, oh my, he got the message. Then she forgot about who was in control of the moment because it was all she could do to keep from screaming out her pleasure, which would only bring the whole house running. Instead, she buried her face in Jordan's shoulder and moaned a litany of encouragement to continue more of this, and yes, a little bit of that.

The rocking pressure of him moving in and out of her body brought back memories of their first time. The familiarity mixed with a sense of newness, risk, because they no longer had the option of walking away from each other forever.

A scary thought she shoved away before it could steal the blissful sensations tightening inside her. She grappled at his shoulders, scratched down his back then flattened her hands to absorb the warm feel of his sweat-slicked skin. Her fingers contracted again as the sweet need inside her rose higher, higher still until…

She dug her nails into his flesh, her head flinging back as she gasped once, again and again with the rippling waves of release. Dimly, she heard him join her as the tide seeped back out, leaving her limp and panting as he slumped over to lay beside her.

Their hitching breaths mingled in the light breeze swirling through the room. She rested her head on his chest and knew there was some reason she should gather her scrambled thoughts. Except that would require, well, the ability to think.

For some reason, her brain never worked as advertised when it came to dealing with Jordan.

Languid from loving and being loved, Brooke kept her arm over her eyes and felt the cool drift as Jordan slid the sheet from her, wafted it in the air and covered her body.

And left.

Watching from the veil of her eyelashes, she saw him tug on his boxer shorts before padding across the room to open the French doors. Her muscles pretty much mush after round two, she couldn't bring herself to slide from the bed, but that certainly wouldn't stop her from enjoying the view. Moonlight streamed over his golden nakedness, the broad planks of his steely shoulders.

He seemed so solid *and* exciting. Could she trust her judgment? Jordan had such sound arguments for why they should be together, and without a doubt what they'd shared in the bed had been beyond compare.

She'd thought she could be happy simply enjoying the sexual side of their relationship, but with the cool splash of air bringing a dose of reality, she couldn't ignore more rational thoughts nudging her as firmly as the tiny foot under her ribs.

Was she greedy to want more from Jordan? What she saw in Cassie and Brandon's eyes for each other?

Not that she begrudged her half sister her happiness. Heaven knew, Cassie deserved every bit of her hard-won peace after the tumultuous childhood she'd suffered as John Garrison's illegitimate child.

Brooke wrapped her arms around her own baby protectively and rolled from her side to her back.

Her parents' mixed-up union had caused so much pain for so many. John Garrison had hurt Cassie by never committing to her mother in much the same way Bonita and John had torn each other to shreds—yet never letting each other go.

Relationships were complicated enough in and of themselves. Add children and the issues multiplied exponentially.

Brooke turned back to stare at Jordan's toned body clad only in his boxers. He could take over her life as fully as his long-limbed body had sprawled over the bed after he finished loving her.

She needed to be more careful than ever to keep a close guard on her emotions.

Seven

Jordan usually hated those first few moments of waking when he had no guard over his thoughts.

This morning, however, he could find plenty to be happy about. Starting with the woman whose bottom snuggled against him, her warm bare skin and the rustle of sheets stirring memories of the night before.

Being with Brooke had been even more amazing than he'd remembered—and his recollections were mighty amazing. His plan for her to grow closer to him was working.

He hadn't, however, expected how much he would be drawn to *her.*

For about five seconds he tried to convince

himself it had to be because he'd been without since the night they'd shared in the Garrison Grand. Even when his ex-girlfriend had tried to lure him back into her bed, he hadn't been tempted. They'd been connected through business dealings, but that's all it could be. Memories of Brooke had tormented him then and now, ensuring his ex-lover held no more appeal.

Fresh flowers by the bed wafted sweet scents and an idea his way. He reached past her to snag an orchid from the vase. She'd told him once that she no longer suffered from morning sickness, so he figured it was safe to approach her.

Jordan sketched the flower along her jaw. "Are you awake?"

"Little bit." She inhaled with a low hum of appreciation.

Nuzzling her ear, he grazed the flower along her arm, teasing the inside of her elbow. "Wanna be more so?"

She mumbled something half-intelligible. He grazed the flower around her breasts until she peered over her shoulder at him with sultry sleepy eyes. He recalled well that same expression as he stared back at her on top of him when they'd explored more of the positions that best accommodated her pregnancy.

He grinned back at her. "I was thinking we could start working on another of those inventive positions."

She tried to roll to face him, but he kept her trapped in place with his legs.

"Don't I get to touch you?"

"We can touch very soon, beautiful, very soon." His throbbing body echoed the sentiment.

Jordan skimmed the flower lower, along her stomach, over her hip to the very top of her thigh. She wriggled with eagerness. At the glide of her hair against his chest, he almost dropped the orchid.

She snatched the flower from him. "Enough. More."

He couldn't help but smile at her contradictory words. Her intent, though, he understood. He slid his fingers between the juncture of her thighs, teasing the core of her and finding her ready for him. She arched against his fingers with that sweet whimper of hers that made him want more—more of her, more time to explore all of those positions. Even the less inventive ones as long as she was the woman under him.

She grabbed his wrist to halt his play, her fingernails stabbing into his skin and not distracting him in the least from what he wanted. "Jordan, either you finish or let me take over."

No misunderstanding that.

Jordan hooked a hand under her knee for just the right angle to slide inside her. Her damp heat clamped around him in time with his own groan. He buried his face in her silky hair, making the most of the advantageous position to stroke her breasts, so full and apparently sensitive if her writhing response offered any indication.

Their gentle rocking set the sheet slithering to the floor, the brush of chilly morning air doing little to cool the sweat beading on his body. The sunrise slanted through the blinds to play along the creamy expanse of her skin. He set his teeth to hold back the driving need to finish. He would wait for her, watch for signals of her nearing satisfaction.

And *yes,* his focused attention paid off. Her skin began to flush, her head arching back as she panted faster, faster still…

She gasped out a litany of need as she came apart, taking him along with her in a mind-blowing explosion of sensation. His forehead fell to her shoulder, his eyes closed while he simply *felt.* Her. All around him, against him. Aftershocks rocked through her so hard she shook in his arms, finally settling with a sated sigh.

As he stroked a hand through her hair, he thought again of how much he enjoyed how she made her needs heard in bed. If he could just get her to be as communicative about her thoughts. Because while she'd been physically responsive, he couldn't miss that this time she'd held something back. She'd shuttered her eyes from him at the last minute as if closing herself off from him.

He was losing ground at a time when he should be gaining. What the hell had gone wrong?

More importantly, he needed a plan to get back on track with planting his engagement ring on her finger.

* * *

Sunday night, Brooke forced her feet to climb the steps toward her mother's front door, Jordan only an inch from her side. She couldn't decide which was worse—facing her mother or going back through the gate past the snap-happy reporters intent on snagging photos.

She gripped Jordan's elbow tighter for support. As much as she'd been shaken by making love with him again and even feared how easily he could steal her willpower, she couldn't help wishing they'd been able to stay in the Bahamas a while longer. But she'd promised Brittany they would go over last-minute wedding plans tonight.

The decorated door loomed, bracketed by ornate porch lamps and twinkling garland.

"Hey, beautiful?" Pausing on the top step, he stroked her cheek, thumb grazing her lips with the tempting familiarity of lovers. "You look like you're heading to the gallows. We can always turn around and leave right now."

Mother or the media? Tough choice. But there were others to consider.

"We skipped the dinner part of the evening." She repressed a shudder at the thought of sitting for a meal with all that dissension stirring as tangibly as her roiling stomach. "The least we can do is show up for dessert since I promised Brittany. It's not like I can exactly hide from my family forever."

"You're not alone facing them anymore."

A sad smile tugged at her lips and heart. "A blessing and a curse."

He cocked an eyebrow. "Thanks."

Contrition nipped. She shouldn't take out her bad mood on him. "Sorry, I didn't mean that the way it—"

His thumb tapped her mouth closed. "You don't have to be the peacemaker with me. I'm a big boy. I realize it won't be easy winning your relatives over. Thing is, I'm persistent and determined."

His words along with the unrelenting glint in his eyes sent a mix of reassurance and apprehension down her spine. "They're my family. I can handle it. Let's just concentrate on keeping things as quick and low-key as possible."

"As you said, they're your family. You call the shots."

As long as she didn't try to send him packing. Then he always stepped in with more pressure for time. Well, she'd wanted to use this time to get to know each other. This driven part of him, however, she'd known from the start. What was she looking to learn by agreeing to these dates?

She wanted to know the man and Jordan kept his inner self well cloaked behind charm and smiles.

A raised voice from inside pierced through the door. Her mother was on a roll about something, not that it took much to set Bonita off anymore.

Brooke braced a palm against the stucco wall to steady herself. She should have expected this.

Were her mother's drinking and outbursts worse? Or were her own nerves simply edgier because of the pregnancy?

Jordan's hand fell from her face to grab her elbow. "Forget it. Let's blow this pop stand."

Brooke actually considered taking his suggestion until the door swung open. Brittany stood framed in the open portal. Eyes wide and frantic, she grabbed her sister by the wrist and hauled. Seemed like everyone was looking for a lifeline.

"See, Mother?" Brittany tugged her over the threshold, delicate diamond bangles jingling on her arm. "Brooke is here after all."

Her mother swayed in the archway between the living room and the hall with a crystal tumbler that could have been iced tea. Not that it ever turned out to be something so innocuous.

Her normally perfectly coiffed black hair fluffed in disarray around her face, the streaks of gray more visible than usual. For years, Lissette had helped Bonita keep up at least an air of togetherness. Apparently even their housekeeper couldn't withstand Bonita's binges that seemed to grow longer each month since her husband's death.

"Well, daughter dear, better late than never. Where were you and your... What are we supposed to call him? You're not engaged, and boyfriend doesn't sound right." She stumbled forward to lean on Brittany, her fingers clenching the glass and showing off a chipped manicure. "Isn't the current phrase baby daddy? Or do I have that backward, Brooke? You're the baby mama."

Jordan slid an arm around Brooke's waist, his jaw tight as he ushered her into the hallway. "Mrs. Garrison, Brooke and I are the parents of your grandchild."

"Of course I know that." She waved her drink in the air, sloshing some over the side to spill on the marble floor. "All of South Beach knows, thanks to that horrible media sensationalizing having children out of wedlock."

Bonita was in full form tonight. Even Jordan winced over the last comment.

Her siblings trickled from the living room into the hall with wary steps, all but Parker who plowed forward. "Mother, I think perhaps it's time for us to call it a night—"

Bonita passed her glass to her son. "Fine, here. Take it. This one's tepid anyway." She stumbled toward the stairs.

Brooke heaved a sigh of relief she heard echoed by everyone else.

Then Bonita turned, her eyes surprisingly lucid—and venomous. "It's not that I blame you, Brooke. You simply followed the pattern set by your father. Your siblings already proved that. Brittany has always run wild. And Stephen didn't even know he had a child until she was three."

Stephen parted through the press of siblings and joined Parker. "Mother, you're going too far tonight." He advanced toward his brother's side, both men grasping one of Bonita's arms to escort her with a practiced synchronicity that stung Brooke clean through. "Parker and I will help you up the stairs, and Lissette can settle you into bed."

Bonita slapped his arm away and took a step toward Brooke. "Watch yourself, young lady, or the genes will win out."

Brooke tried to force words free to stop the poison spewing from her mother's mouth, but it was all she could do to stay steady on her feet. It was mortifying enough to have Jordan view her family's awful secret, much less live it. She wouldn't disgrace herself by calling for a chair and footstool right now.

Brooke inhaled slowly, exhaled through her lips. She'd read in those pregnancy books about relaxation techniques. She found a focal point—the custom-made jeweled star topping the Christmas tree. She stared and breathed, and slowly her mother's diatribe faded to a dull blob of sounds.

Distantly she heard Jordan's voice, low, steady, with a steely edge of anger. Brooke wanted to tell her mother she would be wise to heed that steel. But the focal point wasn't staying still anymore. The darn thing was rising, and the room was growing dark.

In a brief moment of clarity, Brooke realized she was passing out just as she heard Jordan shout and felt the solid comfort of his arms catching her before she hit the floor.

* * *

So this was what fear felt like.

Jordan Jefferies had never experienced it before now, but sitting in the hospital waiting area, not knowing what was wrong with Brooke and their child, scared the hell out of him. Brooke had regained consciousness quickly enough in the car, but stayed groggy during the interminable drive to the E.R. to meet up with her obstetrician.

At least the Garrison crowd had gone stone silent since they'd all arrived at the hospital. Smart move.

Her siblings and their significant others sat along the sofas. Bonita occupied a chair by a coffeepot. The alcohol would have to work its way out of her system. For now, they had a wide-awake drunk on their hands, who at least had enough sense to shut her foul mouth.

He restrained his anger for the upset she'd caused Brooke. One look at her sent his blood simmering. How dare she talk to Brooke the way she had?

Brooke was a strong, confident force in the work world. He'd seen that in action when the Garrisons had rolled out their Sands Condominium Development project. She'd turned it into the most successful South Beach property that year, selling every last unit for record-breaking prices. He found it hard to reconcile the strength of her obvious business acumen with the softer side she gave her family.

The buzz of a pager yanked his attention back to the present. All three Garrison men reached to check their devices.

Parker winced. "Mine. Sorry. From my receptionist. Business will just have to wait."

Parker Garrison actually putting off business? A shocker, but one Jordan was too preoccupied to wonder at right now.

The double doors swished open and the doctor emerged, a woman around fifty who, thank God, had sharp eyes he would trust in a boardroom. They'd only briefly exchanged greetings before Brooke had been swept away into an E.R. examining room.

The doctor nodded to Parker Garrison's pregnant wife, Anna, before turning to the whole group. "Brooke is stable. The baby appears to be fine."

Appears? He stepped closer to the obstetrician, wanting, needing more details, damn it. "I'm Jordan Jefferies. We didn't have a chance to speak when Brooke came in, but I'm her fiancé and the baby's father."

The woman nodded. "You're still not technically a relative, but Brooke has given me the go-ahead to speak with you. She knew you would be worried, that her whole family would be concerned."

Worried? Understatement of the year. It was all he could do not to blast through those double doors to be with her.

Brittany drew up alongside him, her brothers standing behind her in a wall of support, for once united against something beside him. "And what's the diagnosis?"

The physician stuffed her hands into her lab coat.

"Brooke's blood pressure is elevated, enough so that I'm ordering an overnight stay in the hospital."

His mind raced with options. None of them good. "Are you saying she has preeclampsia?"

Brittany reached out a hand to both him and Emilio at the same moment. Jordan wasn't sure if she was steadying herself or offering comfort, but he damn well couldn't bring himself to pull away.

His mind raced down daunting paths, thanks to the pregnancy and delivery books he'd read over the past week. Women who developed preeclampsia could have seizures or die. Babies could be deprived of air and nutrients to the placenta and be born with low birth weight and other complications.

The doctor relaxed her official stance and gave Jordan a sympathetic look. "Dad, stop thinking ahead and imagining those worst-case scenarios. Her problem hasn't progressed to preeclampsia as of now. We've caught this early, which is a hopeful sign. But this is definitely a warning that her body is under stress."

Stress had caused this? Of course. He'd seen firsthand the toll taken on her from family confrontation. No wonder the evening had sent her blood pressure skyrocketing.

Jordan's jaw clamped tight. This wasn't the time or place to confront Bonita Garrison, but he planned to put himself between Brooke and her family in the future. If Brooke wouldn't protect herself from them, he damn well would. "What do I need to do for her?"

"For now, I want Brooke on bed rest for a couple of weeks, low-key living and a special diet." She gave his arm another pat. "Hang in there, Dad, you can come back to her room and see her in about five minutes. She's been asking for you."

Brooke wanted to see him? Thank God he wouldn't have to figure out how to angle his way into the place where he needed to be most right now. Relief rattled through him so intensely, he barely noticed the doctor leaving and Bonita sobbing her way toward the ladies' bathroom.

Five minutes and he could see Brooke. Jordan swallowed hard and wondered how one willowy woman and a barely formed baby could knock the ground out from under him in a way nothing else had before.

He didn't like this feeling one damn bit.

When he looked up from the ugly tile floor, he realized that he wasn't alone. Emilio stood silently on one side. And what the hell? Parker waited on the other, his black eye from their fight still not fully faded.

Jordan stared at the line of Garrison offspring and while they unquestionably loved Brooke, he didn't trust they could keep her safe from Bonita's talons. There was only one way he could make sure Brooke had total peace and her every need met. "I'm taking Brooke home with me."

Her brother Adam quirked a brow. "Isn't that for her to decide?"

Jordan planted his feet and his resolve. "Like any of you would handle the situation differently if you were in my shoes."

He watched her three brothers wince with chagrin, then resolution as they glanced at the women beside them. Her brothers might be his adversaries in the Jefferies-Garrison war for power, but they certainly shared the same drive.

Emilio grinned. "Good luck convincing her without upsetting her, bro."

And thank God for brothers who could wrench a much-needed laugh out at just the right time. Emilio gave him a quick, hard hug and stepped away to comfort his fiancée, leaving Parker still standing beside him.

"You care about my sister," Parker said, the words sounding more like a statement than a question.

Jordan gave a simple nod. More and more every day. More than he'd expected or knew how to take in.

Parker sighed long, hard. "Okay, then. We'll gather up Mother and head out. Let Brooke know how worried we are for her and the baby."

Jordan glanced toward the ladies' restroom with no sign of Bonita yet. Still he kept his voice low, but level. "About Bonita. Normally I make it a point to stay out of other people's family affairs, but Brooke and our child are my family now."

Parker frowned. "Your point?"

This wouldn't be easy to say or hear, but after a night like this, he couldn't keep quiet. Especially when Brooke needed his help. "It seems to me that hiding the liquor bottles isn't working anymore."

Jordan waited for the explosion, a fist or at the very least a bark to mind his own business. Yet none came.

Only a heavy resolution in the air as the eldest Garrison nodded. "I'll look into inpatient rehab clinics first thing in the morning."

No victory here. Just a hard truth. Jordan kept his silence.

Parker sagged back against the wall. "I'm certain the brothers will be on board to join me in an intervention for Mother. Brittany's probably going to want to stay with Brooke." He looked back at his siblings and all nodded in agreement, Brittany swiping at a tear streaking down her face. Parker turned back to Jordan. "We'll let you know how it goes."

A few short words exchanged, but enough. They'd been adversaries for a long time. Working together didn't—and wouldn't—come easy. But given Emilio's marriage and this baby, their families would have to get along.

Bonita was a destructive force to those around her, and he wanted better for Brooke and their child.

Speaking of which, now he just had to figure out a diplomatic way to persuade her to move in with him, without raising anyone's blood pressure. That would most definitely take a Christmas miracle.

Eight

Brooke let the soft leather of the limo seat envelop her, her feet propped up and a water bottle clasped in her hand. Jordan sprawled beside her, working away on his BlackBerry.

Hot.

Silent.

And always present during her every waking moment in the hospital.

She kept her other hand pressed to her stomach to reassure herself the baby still rested safely inside her. The smell of the hospital and fear clung to her senses even miles away. Everything had happened so quickly, from passing out to waking in Jordan's car as they raced to the E.R.

Now the world had slowed, in every sense. She couldn't work. Couldn't go anywhere. The helplessness pinched, but she didn't have a choice. Already maternal instincts to protect this precious life burned so strongly. She would do whatever it took to keep her child safe.

Although so far, she hadn't needed to do much beyond dress herself. Jordan had taken care of everything, checking her out of the hospital and whisking her away in the limo. However, when she got to her place, she would regain some control. Her assistant could bring any pressing work over, and Lissette's niece had been looking for part-time employment. With someone who could help during the day, she should be fine.

She could do some paperwork at home to keep from going stir-crazy. Parker had even offered to send over his receptionist, Sheila, to take care of business errands, but Brooke reassured him her staff at the Sands could handle things.

One morning off work, and already she was going stir-crazy. She needed to calm herself, for the baby's sake.

Brooke stared out the limo window, counting palm trees whipping by to steady her thoughts...as they passed the exit to her condo. "Hey, we missed the turnoff to my place."

Jordan glanced up, tucked his BlackBerry in his briefcase on the seat beside him and focused the full attention of those yummy blue eyes on her. "I know.

I didn't want to give you time to stress about this. Stressing isn't good for you or the baby."

"Stress about what?" Was the doctor keeping something from her? Her fingers curved around her stomach.

Jordan stretched his arm along the back of her seat. "I'm going to take care of you."

Ah, now she saw the way this was going. "You're using this as an excuse for us to move in together. I don't want to stay in a hotel room for weeks on end."

"Not at the Victoria." He toyed with her hair, loose around her shoulders. "At my house, with a full staff to wait on you while you stay on bed rest."

"Your house?"

"Yes, or actually my parents' old home, but mine now. I bought out Emilio's half a long while back."

He lived in his parents' old house? The notion teased at her heart, thinking of him wanting to stay close to memories of his mother and father. If only he would show this softer side of himself to her more often.

It was his charge-ahead side she had to worry about. She forced her attention back to what he was saying.

"You can't take care of yourself alone at your place, Brooke, you have to know that. Do you want me to move into your pink palace? Or would you rather go home with someone in your family taking care of you?"

The thought of staying at the Garrison estate

with her mother… "That's dirty pool for a guy who swears he doesn't want to piss me off."

"I'm simply showing you the options." His fingers tunneled through her hair to massage her neck, tease her senses. "Do you have a better idea?"

Brittany was getting ready for her wedding, even more so now that she wouldn't have Brooke's help. And she didn't really know her sisters-in-law well enough to be comfortable living with them, even as nice as they were. All of her female friends worked full-time, living alone in a condo like she did. "I thought I could hire someone."

"I've already got a full staff taking care of the house." His thumb worked along her spine in muscle-melting strokes. "Think of it this way. Since our dates out on the town have been curbed for now, we can have the same sort of getting-to-know-each-other time at my home. More efficiently."

She stared out the limo window as they drove deeper into South Beach with each palm tree that whipped past. Rollerbladers zipped along the sidewalks despite the cooler temperatures. Tourists filled crosswalks, the older contingent moving in for the winter months.

His argument had merit. Still, she wondered if he harbored further ulterior motives. "I can't have sex until the doctor clears me."

"She warned me again in the hall." He winced. "Stringently."

She grinned at just the thought of that conversation. "Not much privacy in this baby-birthing process, is there?"

"Apparently not." He rested his head against the side of her forehead, nuzzling her hair. "I'll miss being with you more than I can say. But if you can go without sex, so can I."

No sex. Already she mourned the loss. With Jordan touching her, she couldn't deny how uncomfortable holding back might get. "You're really serious about us moving in together, temporarily anyway."

She let the implications rain down around her, this new facet of Jordan's commitment to her. She had been watching him for any false moves, any sign that he was in this relationship with ulterior motives or to somehow bring down the Garrison empire. But his tenderness and thoughtful generosity now... She couldn't deny that she was moved.

"Totally. And if you can't consider your own health, think about the baby."

Of course, Jordan being Jordan, now he was really playing dirty pool. Except he'd hit on the one argument guaranteed to sway her. "For the baby, but I need to set some ground rules."

"Fair enough." He stared at her with those boardroom blue eyes, his make-the-best-deal-possible eyes.

"And you have to *promise* to follow them."

"You're good at catching nuances." He winked, humor easing his intensity. "I've heard you're as tough as the rest of your family across the bargaining table."

"Another dubious compliment." Although she had to admit, while a peacemaker in personal relationships, she enjoyed releasing her suppressed aggressions in the workplace. "But on to those rules. Just because I gave in on this doesn't mean I'm relenting on my reservations about marriage."

The notion still scared her to pieces, and she didn't plan on thinking about anything that would stress her out.

"Understood."

"And I think it's best if we don't share a bed." She figured she should cover all the nuances he may have tried to sneak past her.

His eyes crinkled at the corners as his smile increased. "Because you're afraid you can't resist me?"

"That's quite an ego you're sporting."

"Or sense of humor." He grazed her lips with his thumb. "I'm trying to make you smile back."

His gentle touch stroked her scattered emotions. "Sorry. I'm just…scared."

All levity faded from his gaze, and he slid his hand to cup her face. "Ah, damn, of course you are."

"I could handle it if this was just about my health, but worrying about the baby, that's too much." The concerns bubbling inside her were so much bigger than anything she'd ever faced.

"Worry is against doctor's orders." He smoothed his other hand over her stomach in a gesture of intimacy she couldn't bring herself to stop. "Set your mind on something else."

She blinked through the fears, accepting he was right, knowing she needed to try harder for their baby's sake. "Such as?"

"Have you thought about names?"

The limo stopped at a light while hordes of pedestrian traffic crossed the street. She let herself settle into the warmth of his touch and the buttersoft leather seats as they shared the moment, planning together for their child. "It would have helped if the little one had been more cooperative during all those ultrasounds. Then we could have known whether to choose girl or boy names."

"We?"

He'd doubted she would include him? Further proof he didn't know her well if he thought she could be so small-minded as to cut him out of such a huge decision about their baby. "Of course, you should get a say in this, unless you come up with something horrid. What's your mother's name?"

"Victoria."

"Your hotel's name," she murmured in surprise. How could she not have known that? Yet another reminder of how far they needed to come before she could even consider tying her life—and the knot—with this man.

He shrugged.

"That's really touching." She wanted the same sort of closeness with her own child, something better than her relationship with Bonita. "I'm sorry about how my mother behaved earlier."

His eyes took on that sharp look again. Predatory, unrelenting. "You have nothing to apologize for."

She still felt guilty for not thinking through her actions more that night five months ago. "The first time I took you to dinner, my brother beat you up—"

"Uh, you mean *tried* to beat me up."

Male egos. She stifled a laugh. "Right," she said, then sobered. "Anyway, and the next time we showed up at my house, my *mother* goes on the attack, verbally rather than physically."

"You were the one who was hurt. I should have stepped in sooner."

As if that would have made a difference. Her hands shaking, she set aside her water bottle. "No one can stop her when she's on a roll like that."

However, she needed to stop her mother in the future since there was no way she could allow Bonita to jeopardize this baby's health. Anger stirred at what her mother's tirade had nearly cost them.

He rested a hand on top of her clenched fist. "I don't think this is a wise discussion for you to be having."

"Think happy thoughts and all." She forced even breaths in, out, in again.

"Exactly." He raised her hand to his mouth and grazed a kiss across her knuckles, once, twice and again until her fist unfurled and the gold band on her thumb appeared again. "Tell me a *happy* child-hood memory."

She offered up the first thing that popped to mind. "My mother used to paint. She would take her art supplies to the beach. Brittany and I could build sand castles and splash in the waves."

"That's a great memory." He thumbed along the inside of her wrist as the limo pulled up to the iron gates outside his family home on the north end of the strip.

"I hadn't thought about it in such a long time. The bad memories tend to overtake the good ones." She eyed the opening gates, envisioning them closing behind her. Closing her in with the manicured bushes and trees. "I guess you and I need to make sure those bad feelings between our families don't overcome the good stuff we're working on."

He studied her as the limo rolled along the brick paved driveway, past a fountain with an angel in the center. "I agree, as long as thinking about that doesn't stress you."

"Hmm… If I was a Machiavellian type of person, I could really milk this to my advantage and pick the name I want."

"As long as we don't have to name the kid Parker, I think I can handle just about anything."

Much-needed laughter rolled up and past her lips. She clapped a hand over her mouth. "I'll think about names and get back to you."

"Fair enough." He winked on his way out of the limo.

Before she even reached the walkway, he swept her into his arms. She started to argue, but they'd already been down this route and he seemed insistent on carrying her. Today, at least, she had a valid reason to accept the ride without worry of losing control of the situation.

She looped her arms around his neck as he took the stone steps and wound his way through a columned courtyard to the front door. She barely had time to take in the warm honey-and-blue hues of his home since he introduced her to the staff in a quick flurry before heading toward the lengthy staircase with a deep mahogany railing curling around the foyer.

The long hall seemed narrower because of the framed artwork. Landscapes mingled with portraits of a heart-tuggingly young Jordan, as well as Emilio. Already, she could feel her eyes drifting closed as much as she wanted to stay awake and look around at this slice of family-centered heaven that was his home. Doggone it, these pregnancy near-narcoleptic moments seemed to hit her harder every day.

The world shifted, and she blinked awake again as he settled her in the middle of a towering four-poster bed. Jordan wafted the fluffy duvet over her with cocooning comfort—and then the first hints of claustrophobia. It only took her one sweep of the room to realize…

She wasn't in his bed, but she was most definitely in his suite.

A week later, Jordan took the stairs in his house up to the second floor with anticipation. He had food and a present for Brooke, both of which he thought would lift her spirits.

No question, he enjoyed having her under his roof more than even he'd anticipated. He'd brought her here because it was the right thing to do for her and the child.

He hadn't expected it to be so right for him, too.

Especially after living alone for such a long time, sometimes at the hotel, sometimes here. The bachelor life had suited his career aspirations well. He'd envisioned there being more of a pinch in adding her to his routine. Instead, the past days had been entertaining, spent sharing meals, talking, learning the fundamentals about each other. Her favorite color, food, music.

Pink—no surprise.

Chili—for now. Subject to hormonal change.

Oldies and soft rock—he had a concert in mind for when she was on her feet again.

He hoped that would be soon, for the baby's safety as well as her sanity. He couldn't miss the restlessness growing in Brooke with each passing day. He'd done his best to keep her occupied, sending in contractors to renovate a bedroom into a nursery when she wasn't tackling some work from her office. He hadn't met a woman yet who wasn't thrilled at the prospect of a bottomless budget for decorating.

Except Brooke didn't seem the least bit thrilled tonight, lying on the sofa in the sitting area between their rooms. She appeared downright irritable staring at her feet propped on a pillow at the other end of the sofa. Her fax machine hummed quietly on the far side of the room even though she didn't so much as glance at the papers spewing out in her work area.

He stepped into the room, rested the wrapped package against the couch and placed the carryout container on the coffee table—none of which elicited any reaction from her. "Brooke? Don't you want supper from Emilio's? There's a container of chili in here with your name on it." Even the mention of one of her favorite foods didn't change the weariness on her face. "We can order something else, if you're having a different craving."

She shook her head. "No. That's fine. Thanks."

He swept aside the pillow and rested her feet in his lap. He savored the chance to touch her, look at her. Her simple red cotton dress clung to the luscious curves of her breasts and to her stomach, the increasing swell a reminder of how little time he had left to cement things between them. He'd always hoped for a marriage like his parents', and this pregnancy had prevented him from finding that with Brooke. Yet. He could still hope they would find that magic, but only if they both tried.

As much as he wanted to tunnel his hands under her dress for unfettered access to her, he limited himself to stroking no higher than her knees. Two minutes into the massage, she still hadn't relaxed.

What the hell? "All right, I'm stumped. What gives?"

"It's all this." She swept her hand to encompass the stacks of wallpaper books and paint samples.

"Baby preparations? I told the contractor and interior designer to let you pick whatever you want."

She swung her feet off his lap. "But you're picking decorators and knocking out walls and trying to take over my life."

Okay. At least she'd been honest, not that he understood her in the least. What was he supposed to do? Back away?

However, he couldn't fight with her, even if the doctor had reassured them she was rapidly improving. Her blood pressure was already down to normal. A few more days with her feet up, just to be safe, and she would be cleared in time for Brittany's wedding.

Still, he wasn't taking any chances by arguing with her. "Regardless of whether or not you live here, I need to set up a place for the baby. I would like your input. If you end up living here, great. Regardless, it will give you something to do while you sit around. I know you've decreased your workload, and I thought this would fill the gap with something lighter."

"I figured I could still help with my sister's wedding through phone calls."

"I'm cool with whatever doesn't stress you out."

Her brown eyes snapped with irritation. "You're not the one with the final say in that."

Damn. He wanted her to quit veiling her thoughts from him, and he'd sure gotten his wish today. No doubt about where she stood on that issue.

Unfortunately, he'd been having the final say on most everything in his life for a long time. He took a deep breath and tried to be patient.

"I worry you don't know when to stop pushing yourself. I know you're bored."

"Bored is too mild a word. If my family didn't visit, I would go nuts." Her head fell back with a heavy sigh. "Although I'm starting to wonder if you've locked Mother out of the front gate. I really expected she would show up by now, not that I'm complaining about her absence after our last encounter."

He started to lead the conversation in another, less stressful direction, then changed his mind. Bottled-up stress was worse, according to her doctor. "How long has she been an alcoholic?"

"For as long as I can remember. Even when she painted on the beach, the jug of sangria went along with her." She looked down from the ceiling to meet his eyes. "It's not like we were neglected. We always had round-the-clock nannies—and each other."

"That doesn't negate what your mother put you through."

"I know."

He stared in her eyes and saw the milky-brown darken with frustration, pain, then helplessness. Her siblings had wanted to keep the news of Bonita entering rehab from Brooke. Jordan realized now that she should know. He would face the wrath of the Garrisons, if need be.

Jordan thought about reaching for her hand, but she still had those stand-back vibes going. "Your brothers met with your mother to discuss her problem."

"They did what?" Her eyebrows rose in surprise, before slamming down again. "Wait… You knew and you didn't tell me?"

"Do you really think you could have participated in an intervention in your condition right now?"

"Okay, fair enough." Her stiff spine eased. "What happened?"

"They checked your mother into a rehab center the day you were released from the hospital." How would Brooke feel about that? He couldn't get a read off her. "Are you okay with this?"

"Of course. It's a good thing. I just can't help but feel I should have been there." She took his hand, the distance between them fading for the moment. "Thank you for telling me, though. I understand you're trying to pamper me, but I can't take your keeping things from me. There have been too many secrets in my family. If I found out you were lying to me…"

He felt her slender fingers curl around his, understood the gesture she'd made in reaching out to him. Now he faced another dilemma. Tell her the truth about what he'd done with the newspaper leak and risk everything. Or roll the dice that she would never find out.

Damn it. He knew what he had to do. "I need to tell you something."

"Hey, why the scowl? It can't be worse than having to think about my mother in rehab."

"This honesty stuff, I want to be straight up with you."

Her delicately arched eyebrows pinched together. "You're starting to scare me, and that's not good."

"Then I'll just spill it. The newspaper leak about our relationship wasn't an accident."

Her hand went ice-cold in his.

She eased her fingers free. "You started the media frenzy?"

He hadn't meant to stir all the gossip about her family, but that was beside the point. It was his fault, and he took full responsibility for the strain he could now see it had placed on Brooke. "I'm not going to make excuses for my behavior. All I can say is that I would do things differently now, and I'm sorry."

Brooke hugged her stomach protectively for another long stretch of time before nodding. "You wanted to get the announcement over with all at once."

"What makes you think that?" He'd expected anger, tears even, but not an understanding of his motives. He'd always prided himself on playing things close to the vest. What people didn't know they couldn't use against him.

Having someone see through him so thoroughly was uncomfortable.

She shrugged. "That's what Parker would do, and you two are a lot alike."

Well that bit. Hard. "You're that mad at me, are you?"

"I'm disappointed, but I understand. But you have to realize that when you make unilateral decisions that affect both of us—without telling me—you're not easing stress for me. You're increasing it, especially after the passive way I've handled family relationships for too long. Whether I sense something's off or find out later, it tears at me."

Guilt hammered at him, made all the worse by how easily she'd let him off the hook, even going so far as to take some responsibility by mentioning how she'd dealt with her family in the past. *I'm sorry* seemed too little to offer.

"I won't excuse what you did, Jordan, but I can see where you came to your decision and forgive what happened." Her spine straightened with unmistakable steel. "As long as you promise never to lie to me again."

"That, I can do." And he meant it. He was ambitious, even had a reputation for being ruthless—which he wouldn't deny—but he prided himself on honesty. No question, the newspaper thing hadn't been one of his wiser moves, hindsight. "Are you ready for supper?"

She inched away from him and stood in an unmistakable back-off message. "As long as we're being open with each other, I need some space tonight."

She hesitated and he thought—hoped—she might relent. She reached toward him…

And snagged the carryout bag of food before turning back to her bedroom.

Not bothering to stifle his grin at her accepting at least one of his gifts, he watched Brooke walk away and disappear behind her door. He wanted to follow her, but would leave her alone and let her sleep. Rest was the best thing for her and the baby. For tonight, he figured he'd wrangled more forgiveness than expected.

However, he hadn't figured on being so damn disappointed at the missed opportunity to share chili and a movie with Brooke.

Brooke wrestled with sleep and the covers, the confrontation with Jordan leaving her frustrated and restless.

She stared at the clock—2:00 a.m. She'd seen midnight, as well, but must have drifted off.

God, she hated this helpless feeling of losing control of her life. Her family had staged an intervention with her mother, a huge, life-changing moment.

While Brooke sat around with her feet propped up, unable to handle stress. No wonder Brittany had been so edgy when she'd come to visit after Brooke left the hospital. The whole family must have gone through hell, and yet they'd all continued to tiptoe around her. Doing the right thing wasn't necessarily easy.

Why couldn't Jordan have told her sooner? Her

mother seeking help was a good thing, the right thing. Hope warred with skepticism.

And therein lay her main problem, trusting that her mother would make it through the program successfully. Trusting, after a lifetime of mixed signals from her parents.

Trusting Jordan.

Even with their dates and living together this past week, it still seemed like too little time to know each other before committing to marriage. Her parents had dated for two years before marrying and look how that had turned out.

If only she could recapture—and trust—that intense sense of rightness she'd felt the night she'd decided to sleep with him for the first time.

The night they'd made this baby…

She'd seen him many times. She'd always wanted him.

Tonight, her family be damned, she would have him.

The decision echoed in her mind all the way up the elevator to the room she'd secured for herself and Jordan Jefferies.

Her head spun more from the touch of his hands on her body than from any effects of alcohol. She'd felt the attraction between them for years, but never imagined the sparks would combust through her with such intensity.

His palms, sweeping down her back during their frantic kiss down the hall.

His palms, cupping her bottom to pull her closer as they stumbled through the door.

His fingers, making fast work of her clothes in order to torment her.

And even when she demanded her place on top, still those talented hands teased her senses to the edge of fulfillment. Stopping short. Taking her to the brink and back again until they both tumbled over in a tangle of arms and legs and uncontained cries...

Brooke woke with the sheet twisted around her ankles, her body achy with want for what she'd experienced with him, an intense completion remembered in her dream.

Yet she hadn't found the same relief tonight.

She reached to click on her bedside lamp. As always, there waited a pitcher of water along with fresh fruit for a late-night snack. She snagged a pear and crunched. If she couldn't satisfy her sexual hunger, she would settle for feeding another appetite.

What was it about that time with Jordan that haunted her so? A sense of control in that moment, of equality. Except by the morning after she'd felt so *out* of control, she'd run from him, was running still.

Her eyes gravitated to the open door. Jordan must have checked on her after she went to sleep and then left the door open. She stared through at the books of fabric samples resting by the small sofa in the sitting room. He'd given her choices, but that didn't stop her from feeling smothered.

She glanced away only to see a blue wrapped

package propped along the edge of the couch. Vaguely, she recalled Jordan had been carrying something—that—when he'd entered the room. So he'd bought her a present to win her over.

She munched on the pear and studied the gift with trepidation. With the dream having left her pensive and vulnerable, she wasn't sure she could take more of Jordan tonight.

But curiosity nipped and nibbled.

Tossing the rest of the pear into the trash can, she kicked free of the sheet and swung her feet to the floor. Her satiny nightshirt slithered over her skin in a sensual caress that reminded her all too well of her dream, of the real-life night that had been anything but a dream, yet most definitely fantasy material.

She padded across the room and sat on the edge of the sofa. Her fingers fell to rest on the top of the gift and tapped restlessly. If only she had her impulsive twin here to help her decide what to do next.

Memories of childhood Christmases shuffled through, of Brittany picking up each wrapped present, touching it, shaking it, then confidently proclaiming what she suspected it contained. Fifty percent of the time, Brittany was right. The other half, her guesses were so deliberately outrageous, no one bothered to tease her over being wrong.

Brooke stared at the package. Not jewelry. Not clothes. Too big to be a photo album. Too small to be furniture, even unassembled.

Finally, curiosity won out over caution. She tugged

the present around and began tearing the blue-striped paper away to find—bubble wrap. Lots and lots of bubble wrap protecting something underneath. No wonder she'd been unable to hazard a guess.

She ripped at the tape securing the covering. She slowly realized some kind of framed artwork was inside. He'd bought her a picture? Or a painting?

Without question, he was showering her with attention. He *was* trying. But she didn't want to start off their relationship with the notion that she could be purchased. A last swipe cleared away the plastic...

And stole her breath.

He hadn't bought her some exotic piece of art. Instead he'd chosen a watercolor—obviously meant for a nursery—of two little girls playing on the beach, making sand castles.

Jordan remembered her telling him about the happy memory from her childhood.

The thoughtfulness of his gift touched her as firmly as his hands ever had. *This* side of Jordan she simply couldn't resist. Not tonight with the dream still teasing at the corners of her mind, not with an ache of loneliness and yearning for more stirring inside her.

Resting the painting carefully along the sofa, Brooke stood, her eyes and intentions firmly planted on the connecting door leading to Jordan's bedroom.

Nine

Jordan woke the moment he heard his door hinges creak.

He held still, watching through narrowly open eyes as Brooke made her way across the room toward him. Even in the near pitch-dark he could see she was not in any distress, so he kept his silence, biding his time to discover what she had in mind. He never knew anymore around her, and that bothered him.

She stopped by his bed, seemingly unaware that he continued to study her through the veil of his eyelashes. She plucked at the edge of the covers.

Holy crap. She couldn't be about to…

Brooke slid in beside him. He couldn't stop the

rush of air gusting from his lungs any more than he could contain himself from reaching to wrap an arm around her. The flowery scent of her hair teased his nose as she snuggled against him.

"Trouble sleeping?" he asked. His hand slid to her stomach and began rubbing soothing circles. "Is the future soccer star kicking you awake?"

Bad idea, touching her. Especially when this could lead nowhere.

She settled alongside him, her head resting on his shoulder. "Something woke me up. Not the baby though."

"Can I get you anything?" He smoothed his hand from her belly to her back. He'd noticed she'd begun pressing a hand to her lower spine over the past week.

"I needed to be with you." She flattened her palm to his chest.

His body tightened in response to her cool fingers on his overheated flesh. The rasp from the ring on her thumb seared along his skin, and what a time to think of how he could envision the vine pattern etched on the ring. He'd come to know her that well.

He clenched his jaw and started counting backward from one hundred. By seventy-eight, he gave up and accepted that he would simply have to live with the pain. "Okay, if you want to sleep in here, no way am I going to object."

He continued the back massage, a mix of heaven and hell to have her in his arms, feel her soft curves against him, under his hands. He reminded himself that if he kept himself in check and won her over, he could be with her again. The opportunity to have his child raised by the two of them together was worth any wait.

And the idea of a life with Brooke grew more appealing the longer they spent together.

She stroked along his ear. "I don't feel much like sleeping."

Neither did he, but for a different reason. He focused on the click of the ceiling fan overhead, the white noise helping keep him grounded. "Then we'll talk." She'd said something earlier about resenting feeling controlled, so he opted for a more neutral question. "What would you like to do tomorrow after I get home from work?"

"I wish we could go to all the parties for Brittany and Emilio this week."

No wonder she was restless. "I'm so damn sorry. Being stuck in the house must be boring. What do you say we check with the doctor about going for a drive along the shore? As long as we don't travel far and you're not walking around, I'll bet it's all right. We can take a limo so you can prop your feet."

"That would be nice," she answered with zilch in the way of enthusiasm.

Ah, damn. He remembered she wanted to make decisions, too… "Any other ideas?"

She sighed. "I don't mean to sound cranky. That really is thoughtful, like the beautiful present you bought."

So she'd finally opened it. He had to admit he'd been disappointed when their argument had forestalled him giving it to her. At least he had the satisfaction of knowing she appreciated the gift. After purchasing it, he'd wondered if perhaps she might prefer a chunky diamond bracelet instead—as the other women he'd dated would have. Without question, his last ex would have preferred diamonds over any painting.

He needed to remember Brooke wasn't even similar to any other woman.

"I'm glad you liked it. When I saw it in the gallery window, I had a feeling you might." And how strange that he found himself seeing Brooke in any number of things he came across in the course of a day.

"I unwrapped it after I woke up." She cuddled nearer, her knee nestling too damn close between his legs. "I was dreaming of you."

"I'm glad." He dreamed about her every night, a notion that sent him throbbing against the gentle pressure of her thigh.

Hey, wait. She couldn't mean her dream in the same way as his…?

Her hand skimmed over his hip.

Damn.

He grasped her wrist. "Brooke, honey, as much as I enjoy touching you and you touching me, we can't have sex. Not until your doctor clears you."

"I know. I just needed…" She shrugged, her body grazing against his and sending the satiny fabric of her nightshirt slithering over his chest in a tempting whisper. "I wanted to thank you for the painting you bought for the nursery."

Jordan allowed himself the satisfaction of toying with her hair. "You're welcome."

"And I'm sorry I was crabby earlier. It really is tough for me, sitting around all the time."

She settled her head against his shoulder with a sigh that pressed her breasts against his hot flesh. He welcomed her ease with their closeness, even as her sweet curves tempted him.

He would definitely have to call the doctor about a limo ride for Brooke. The doctor had said Brooke was doing well. She might soon be moving back to her condo…away from him.

Jordan brushed aside thoughts of time ticking down for them and focused on her current frustration. "I'll talk to your family about visiting more."

"They're visiting plenty." She scrunched her nose. "I've talked to people until I'm blue in the face. I'm restless. I need…you. This."

So did he. He stroked her back again, tried to calm her to sleep before they both lost their freaking minds. "Shh. Relax."

He could feel all the tensed muscles knotting along her shoulders. She truly did need to relax. Being this edgy couldn't be good for her. If only he could take care of her sensual needs without having sex—

Inspiration lit. He smiled, the thrill of what he *could* do for her sending a rush through him.

He cut the restraints and let his hands roam freely to her breasts, lush from carrying his child. Her response was immediate and gratifying as she moaned, arching into his palms.

Her eyes drifted closed, her panting breaths pushing her against his hands again and again. "Jordan, the no-sex problem. Remember?"

"I remember." He would never do anything to risk her health or that of their child. Sure he wanted her, but he was man enough to wait for his own gratification. "We're not going to have sex. I'm just going to help you feel less…restless."

His hand slid to her hip to caress high and higher still on her thigh. "If that's what you want."

She edged closer, guiding his fingers. "I definitely want, but what about you?"

"We can worry about me another time." He tucked a finger inside the band of her low-cut panties and rubbed along the smooth skin of her stomach. "Tonight's about you."

He covered her mouth with his while sweeping away her underwear. Sighing into his kiss, she kicked free the scrap of satin. He sought, found, the tight bud between her legs. His thumb teased back and forth, eliciting another happy hum from her. As much as he wanted to watch her face, he enjoyed kissing her too damn much to stop, took pleasure in the feel of her frantic hands grasping at his shoulders, her fingernails digging into his skin.

Soon, sooner than he'd expected, her chest rose

and fell rapidly. She moaned repeated don't-stop urgings as she pressed more firmly against him. The speed of her response to his touch surged through him. He opened his eyes to take in the beauty of her face as she found her release, her grip digging deeper into him.

Three gasps later, she sagged onto her back, her head burrowing into her pillow. Puffy breaths slid between her lips. And yeah, he took plenty of satisfaction in knowing how much he affected her. He might have transferred a boatload of her restlessness to himself, but it pleased him no end to see the way she relaxed into his arms now, her cheeks still flushed and her mouth swollen from his kiss.

"Better?" he asked, unable to take his eyes off her.

She smiled slowly. "Much."

He gathered her close until she settled with a final sigh. He stroked her hair away from her face while she relaxed against him, her breathing evening out with sleep.

"Good night, beautiful," he whispered against her hair.

He knew how right it was for her to be in his bed. Why couldn't she understand it, as well? As much as he wanted to take reassurance from her presence here, from her joy over the painting, he couldn't forget their argument earlier. He'd never met anyone as stubborn as Brooke in a quiet, determined way that crept up on a person.

Jordan glanced at the clock—4:00 a.m.

He knew without question sleep wouldn't be coming to him as easily as it had for Brooke.

It would be a long three days until her next visit to the doctor.

Brooke settled in the back of the limo after her OB appointment and allowed herself the huge sigh of relief she'd kept restrained at the clinic.

Thank goodness she could do away with being chauffeured around now that the doctor had cleared her. All looked good with the baby and her blood pressure. She wished Jordan could have been there with her—knew he wanted to be—but he'd been stuck in traffic blocked off by an accident. He'd called once the wreck was cleared, but she'd already been on her way back to the exam room. There simply wasn't time for Jordan to make it across town to meet her.

At least she could surprise him with all the good news—and an ultrasound photo of their son.

A baby boy.

She let images of playing on the beach with her little one stir in her head. She allowed those dreams to shift with Jordan stepping into the scenario. For the first time she could imagine a future with him, a happily-ever-after where they let love grow between them.

Love.

The word still gave her heart an uncomfortable squeeze, but she waited through it rather than shying away as she'd done in the past.

She concentrated on all the good news she would share with him soon. Not only was she okay to attend her sister's wedding and return to work, but she'd been cleared by her doctor to resume *all* normal activities.

Including sex.

After their steamy encounter the night of her dream, they'd begun sharing a bed, a tormenting pleasure. She'd wanted more during those nights, yet took comfort in the strength of his arms. Without question, she slept better with him at her side.

Tonight, they wouldn't sleep, not for a long while, anyway.

And tomorrow? She would worry about that in the morning. Because right now, she couldn't think of anything other than making tracks to locate Jordan and find the nearest bed. Lucky for them both, the Hotel Victoria offered plenty of options.

Jordan glanced at the time on his computer screen, wishing he was with Brooke rather than at the Hotel Victoria. He would have been if not for the traffic jam on the causeway that had eventually sent him back to his desk.

He wanted to find Brooke and hear about her visit to the doctor. He'd tried to call her, but she wasn't picking up her phone.

He glanced at his clock again. What was keeping her? Memories of that terrible night in the E.R. tormented him. He shoved up from his chair, ready to start checking the roads if she didn't show up soon. Maybe he'd misunderstood her earlier, and she'd simply gone to his house.

Jordan reached for the phone to call his house-keeper just as the door began to open.

Relief socked him. Dead center. "Brooke—"

Except the woman in the doorway wasn't the mother of his child. Instead, he found the last person he expected—or wanted—to see right now.

His ex-lover, Sheila McKay.

He put up his guard as fast as he rose to his feet. She'd been persistent the past few weeks, trying to get in touch with him. Apparently she didn't accept rejection easily. "Sheila, my assistant shouldn't have let you up here."

He'd tried to be calm and civil when he'd stopped dating Sheila over six months ago, but she'd con-tinually attempted to jump-start their relationship. Shortly after he had broken up with her, she'd taken a job as a receptionist at Garrison Inc.—and promptly worked to lure him back with valuable insider information.

Sheila sashayed into his work area on spiky high heels. "Your assistant must be taking a coffee break, because I didn't see anyone except a few whistling construction workers."

How in the world had he ever found this con-ceited woman attractive? Her blond hair, blue eyes and Playboy bunny history didn't matter. She paled in comparison to Brooke.

He glanced at his watch pointedly. "This isn't a good time. I'm on my way out. I'll escort you to your car."

Sheila perched a hip on his desk, unmistakably encroaching on his personal space. "It'll be worth your while to wait. I have some pretty interesting inside scoop from the Garrison camp on some stock purchasing plans."

There had been a time he and Emilio accepted any tidbits on the Garrisons she offered. That time had passed. He'd promised Brooke honesty and he meant to follow through on that vow.

He thought he'd been clear with Sheila in their last phone conversation that they were done. And when she'd persisted by leaving messages, he'd made his point again with silence. Apparently subtlety didn't work with her. "Sheila, I'm not in the market for any information you have about the Garrisons. If you've even glanced at the newspapers, you know I'm committed to Brooke now. Besides, any relationship you and I had ended months ago."

"Oh, that's right." She shrugged her long hair over her shoulder. "You have your own in with that family now."

His jaw tightened over the notion of gossip like that upsetting Brooke. "Watch yourself, Sheila. You're overstepping."

He rounded the desk, set on ushering Sheila out— and away from *his* files—on his way down to the car.

"I need to get home to Brooke. She had a visit to the doctor today, and I want to hear how it went."

Sheila stepped in front of him, blocking the pathway to the door. "It must be tough for you, having her on bed rest."

Why hadn't he seen through this woman from the start? An image of them as a couple flashed through his mind. He winced inwardly at the memory of himself then, the kind of man who didn't always take the time to see beyond the surface when it came to bed partners.

Then nearly six months ago, Brooke had blazed into his life with so much more than surface attraction. The heat had transformed him into something different, someone he liked a whole lot more. That knowledge made it ridiculously easy to push this superficially beautiful woman away from him. "It's tougher for her with the cabin fever, which is why I'm leaving now."

"I imagine a strong man like you is experiencing a different fever altogether." Her painted lips curved in a knowing smile.

Enough wasting time. He cut straight to the chase. "Sheila, I'm committed to making a future with Brooke and our child."

"So? I'm not looking for a serious relationship. That doesn't mean we can't have fun." She reached to cup his neck. "You look like you need to let go and relax."

Her touch left him cold. No surprise. He gripped

her arms, ready to move her gently, but firmly, away. "Sheila, it's time for you to go—"

A gasp stopped him midsentence.

Damn it. He knew before he looked. Brooke had made it back from her appointment.

Tears clouding her vision, Brooke jabbed the elevator's down button again and again. Sure, it didn't make the thing arrive any faster, but the action provided an outlet for her anger—and disillusionment.

A traffic jam?

She'd been an idiot to believe his lame excuse. She couldn't help but think of how often she'd seen a similar scenario play out with her parents. Her father would always offer an excuse as to why he couldn't spend more time at home. Her mother would cry—then drink.

Now Brooke knew all too well what her father had been doing during the time away. Seeing his other family. She wouldn't be so naive as to think Jordan wouldn't do the same to her. And to do so with some painted-up Sheila person...

Sheila?

Wait. Now she realized where she'd seen this woman before. She'd worked at Garrison Inc. as a receptionist. Her brother had even offered to send her over to help with paperwork while Brooke was on bed rest. How damn coincidental to find her brother's receptionist here.

Or was it?

A woman intimate with Jordan, yet she worked for Parker? At the least, it whispered of conflict of interest. At the worst, it screamed setup. Could this Sheila person be a corporate spy sent to scoop secrets from her family's business? Parker had said often enough that Jordan would do anything to win one over on the Garrisons.

Fury mingled with the disillusionment. She dashed her wrist across her cheek, swiping away foolish tears. She would be stronger than her mother.

However, for the first time, she sensed how deeply the years of betrayal must have cut Bonita.

"Brooke, hold on." Jordan's voice stroked over her a second before she felt the heat of him stopping behind her. "Nothing happened between me and Sheila McKay."

"Of course it didn't." She jabbed the button again. "I walked in."

Although who was to say she hadn't arrived at the tail end of a heated goodbye. She choked on the thought and the ball of tears at the back of her throat.

He sidestepped between her and the glowing down button. "Nothing was going to happen."

Right. "Has she or has she not been spying on my family's business while she worked for Parker? You promised always to be honest."

She hated the way he hesitated. But she wouldn't start crying again, not in front of him.

He pinched the bridge of his nose, eyes closing. From frustration? Or simply to gather his excuses?

Jordan looked at her again, his blue eyes appearing genuine—damn him. "In the *past*, Sheila and I saw each other. And yes, over the last few months she has brought information in an attempt to patch things up." He held up a finger to stop her from speaking. "But I have not slept with her since the first time you and I were together. Something changed for me that night. I didn't fully understand it then. I just knew no one interested me once I'd been with you."

His words rang true. Except…

"How do I know if I can trust you?"

He'd lied to her about the newspaper leak. He'd easily hid the truth about her mother's intervention. Although he'd made an eloquent case for why he'd tried.

Bottom line, she didn't want to be in a relationship full of secrets. Even if it cost her the family she'd just begun to dream about.

"Brooke…" He cupped the nape of her neck and rested his forehead against hers. "It's not good for you to upset yourself."

"No need to worry about me or the baby. The doctor gave me a clean bill of health today." She thanked God and all the saints for that. How could any woman have handled that scene in Jordan's office without some serious stress?

The sight of that viper's hands on him punched a hole clean through her.

"I'm so happy for you. Both of you. That's great news." A smile creased his handsome face. "Come on. Let's go home and talk about this."

Lord, she was tempted. His words sounded logical, his smile heartfelt. She wanted to believe him, which scared her most of all. But she couldn't cave to temptation. Besides, she had to tell Parker about the leak so he could make sure Sheila never set foot inside Garrison, Incorporated ever again.

Admitting that Parker had been right about Jordan all along hurt her pride almost as much as her heart. If only she could rest her head on Jordan's shoulder and give him a chance to persuade her.

The swoosh of the elevator doors opening cut through the silence, breaking her free of the momentary weakness that could lead her to lean into him. She shook off the allure of his looks, his charm, and whatever it was about him that seemed to hold her captive.

Despite what he thought about her seeming weakness around her family, she had always protected herself with space and distance, quietly insulating her heart from the jabs of those closest to her rather than fighting with angry words. She might not argue with him, but she would damn well think about this before sharing another ounce of herself with him.

Brooke inched away from him, pivoting back into the elevator. "I need time alone to mull this over."

"Fine." He held the doors open with flattened palms. "I'll stay out of your way at home tonight."

She knew if she walked into his house again she would end up in his bed. "I'm going to my condo. I can take care of myself now, remember? I've given you what you wanted these past few weeks with dates and getting to know each other. Now give me what I need. Space."

Brooke jabbed the close button. Thank goodness he took the hint and released the doors.

The elevator music swaddled her in claustrophobic memories of another time, another elevator, she and Jordan so hungry for each other.

As the chimes dinged with each passing floor, she realized her triumph would be short-lived. With her sister and Emilio's wedding only two days away, Brooke would see Jordan tomorrow night at the rehearsal dinner.

And the next day, she would face him as she came down the aisle in a church. Even though she wouldn't be the bride, the symbolism of the moment would be damn near unbearable with her heart already breaking.

Ten

Jordan popped a caviar canapé in his mouth at the reception, his mind still full of images of Brooke at the church service. She had never looked so beautiful to him as she did walking down the aisle this afternoon at the wedding.

Too bad the service had been for her sister and his brother. But as the maid of honor, Brooke had still been making her way toward him. Her Christmas red dress skimming her body. Hair swept up. A small bouquet shielding her stomach.

He'd barely noticed the bride in her beaded gown and veil—well, other than her train so long it could have clothed a couple of people. No. His attention had focused soundly on Brooke as she stole his breath then, and at the reception now.

He and Emilio had spent most of the evening before having a brother-to-brother chat after the bachelor party. They'd discussed the Sheila McKay debacle and the need to sit down with Parker soon to clear the air on that subject.

His sibling had also offered some words of wisdom about pursuing Brooke. Namely patience and honesty. Brooke was without a doubt the most sensitive of the Garrison clan.

Even at the reception on the Garrison estate, he couldn't take his eyes off her as she stood on the veranda talking to her sisters-in-law. They all wore the holiday crimson dresses, Brooke's higher waistband for her expanding stomach the only difference in the gowns. Their smaller rose bouquets lay discarded along the patio wall now that staged photos were complete. The Christmas themed wedding reminded him of the holiday he longed to spend with her. The gifts for her and the baby he'd wanted to share.

Reaching to snag another hors d'oeuvre from a passing waiter, Jordan nodded to Brandon as he strode by to claim his fiancée from the group of women. Jordan got good vibes from Brandon and Cassie after the way they'd played host and hostess to him. His memories of Brooke in the Bahamas kept him hopeful he could salvage some of the relationship they'd been working toward.

Except she was still keeping him on the deep freeze. No talking beyond polite exchanges in front of others. Blatant avoidance of any alone time.

She looked gorgeous, but tired. Moonbeams and the tiny white Christmas lights strung throughout the shrubbery accented the shadows under her eyes that no one would see except for somebody who knew her well.

Footsteps behind him shook him free. He turned to find Parker approaching, thrusting a drink his way. Given the dry ceremony, he knew the glass wouldn't contain more than sparkling water. Good, since he needed to keep his mind clear. A seemingly subdued Bonita Garrison had behaved so far during her day out of the rehab clinic. She'd even been polite in a brief—very brief—exchange with Cassie and Brandon.

But he wasn't taking anything for granted.

Jordan took the drink. "Thanks. I appreciate it."

Parker leaned back against the stone wall littered with poinsettia and rose arrangements. "I hear from Brooke that you and my receptionist Sheila McKay had a meeting this week."

Jordan tensed, unwilling to go another ten rounds with Parker at a family shindig. "Believe it or not, Emilio and I were just discussing the need to sit down and have a talk with you about Sheila." Aka the witch. He tried not to harbor such extreme ill will against a woman, but in Sheila's case, he would make an exception. "I thought Brooke would wait until after the wedding to tell you—to reduce chances of an uproar at the big event."

Parker tipped back his glass before answering, the sound of the tide tugging at the shore mingling with tunes from the band inside. "Brooke was pretty fired up when she talked to me. She wanted to make sure I knew so I could fire Sheila—pronto."

He tried to read Parker, but failed. The guy looked relaxed enough. Jordan stared into his drink. "Should I be wary of some kind of poison?"

A calculating grin split his adversary's face. "Maybe three weeks ago, but you're safe now. Unless, of course, you hurt Brooke."

"Your sister is tougher than you give her credit for. I'm pretty sure it's me who's the injured party this go-round." Jordan winced as he remembered Brooke's scowl when she'd caught the bride's bouquet just before Brittany and Emilio left to start their honeymoon in Greece. "All the same, I owe you an apology for the McKay incident."

Parker stuck out his hand. "Apology accepted."

Jordan stared at the hand suspiciously before shaking it slowly. "You're okay with things that easily?"

"Oh, I'm pissed." Parker grinned in contradiction to his words. "But I don't blame you. I'd have done the same in your shoes. It's business." His grin faded. "However, when it comes to family matters, I'm not nearly as forgiving. If you mess around on my sister, the next fist fight won't end well for you."

"Brooke is the only woman in my life, now and forever, if she'll have me." He stared through the crowd, searching for Brooke on the veranda, just to reassure himself she was still okay, but no sign of her. Just a few minglers, and Adam slow dancing on the beach with his wife Lauryn.

Jordan looked away from the happy couple wrapped up in a world of their own. He needed to clear the air with Brooke's brother, and to do that, he needed to be totally up-front. "Sheila McKay did come to me this week and offer more insider secrets in hopes of resuming our relationship."

"Since you're here telling me this, I guess that means you turned her down on the sex." Parker powered on, "So why haven't you talked to Brooke? You can convince her. Hell, I've witnessed your persuasive powers in the boardroom."

"Maybe… Except I can't help but think either she trusts me or she doesn't."

"She has a lot of reason *not* to trust people. Mother has wreaked hell on her over the years. For that matter, finding out Dad hadn't been honest with us about much of anything didn't help, either."

Jordan remembered the first night he'd spent with Brooke had been partly instigated by a swell of emotion she'd experienced after hearing her father's will. No doubt her ability to trust had been raked over serious coals that day.

He stared through the open French doors to where Bonita sat on a small settee looking suitably subdued as she spoke with a guest. Maybe there was still hope for some healing between Brooke and her mom at least. "I'm glad the intervention seems to have taken for your mom."

"Time will tell." Parker scooped his glass back for a long swig. "Okay, so I'm not saying you're the first man I would have chosen for my sister, but on second look, you're not all bad. You can hold your own in a fight."

Jordan certainly hadn't expected that. "Thank you."

"And I've been ticked off at you often enough to say with authority that you're a helluva businessman."

"Thanks, again." The guy was making a genuine effort and deserved something in return, for Brooke, for the baby and because he sensed that Parker could make an astute ally if they committed to working the same side of the fence. "Same to you on both accounts."

And damn, he meant it.

Glass in hand, Parker rattled the ice from side to side. "Seems as if this family linkup is a foregone conclusion, given Brittany's marriage and your baby."

"Apparently so." A year ago, he couldn't have imagined sharing such a civil conversation with Garrison. But a year ago, he'd also been too caught up in the thrill of the rat race to see the deceit in Sheila McKay.

"I've been doing some life review stuff lately, thanks to all those family support meetings we're having to go to with Mom's treatment." The ice clinking stopped. "I think it's time you and I laid down the arms and joined forces."

Holy crap. Garrison was actually suggesting… "A merger between Jefferies Brothers and Garrison, Incorporated."

Could it ever work? Hell, maybe there could be some benefits. Benefits cagey Parker was already seeing.

"It would take negotiating, but yes, basically."

Jordan let his brain wrap around the notion of blending the two corporations, abandoning the competition that had consumed them both for so many years.

A competition that had led him to keep his distance from Brooke in spite of his attraction to her the first time she'd glided through his radar.

The notion had serious merits and incredible possibilities. For that matter, it might create a lot more peace on the home front. Of course, he couldn't make that kind of business move without having Emilio on board. Not that he could see his brother arguing, not since his marriage to Brittany. "I'll have to confer with Emilio since we're partners in the holding, but I'm more than intrigued by your offer."

Parker relaxed his stance, his eyes glinting with a business acumen and excitement. "Staking a monopoly on the hotel and entertainment segment for this area would make you and me happy."

Jordan could feel himself warming to the notion,

the possibility of what they could accomplish with their combined drives. "For just South Beach? You think small, Garrison."

Parker's laughter rumbled free and they clinked their glasses together with the promise of a greater business celebration yet to come.

If only his problems with Brooke could be so easily negotiated and resolved. To hell with waiting for her to figure this out on her own. He could at least talk to her.

Jordan searched the crowd again to find her, tell her. Convince her. Except the bridesmaids had all scattered, their gathering spot now occupied by Brandon and Cassie sitting on the stone railing sharing a single plate of food.

He scanned the beach where Adam and Lauryn still danced. Then glanced over at the open French doors to the foyer where the band played, Stephen and his wife, Megan, making the most of the music, as well.

He looked through the window to the dining area with all the food. Bonita was helping her granddaughter, Jade, tuck a napkin in her shirt to protect her flower girl dress from her snack.

Still no sign of Brooke.

"You're right, Garrison. I need to make things right with Brooke. I don't want more time to pass with her so upset, especially without reason." He couldn't see her anyplace. "I have to speak with her."

"She just left." Anna spoke, having somehow snuck up behind the men undetected. She slipped an arm around her husband's waist. "Don't bother asking where she's gone. I swore not to tell."

She'd left? Hidden was more like it. "So you do know."

Anna gauged him through narrowed eyes. "As much as I would like to watch you squirm a little—I do still owe you for that sucker punch to my husband's gut—I've also seen how miserable my sister-in-law is without you."

And he couldn't even take pleasure from that because he hated to think of Brooke unhappy. "Then where the hell is she?"

Anna bit her lip, but hesitated only a moment.

"Think—" she tapped her forehead with a manicured nail "—and you can figure it out. If she wants to run from you, where would she go to get her head together?"

His mind churned with what he knew about her, what he'd learned during their intensely compacted time together. The answer took shape. "She would go to family. But everyone is here except the bride and groom." He scanned the family decked out in gowns and tuxedos. His gaze hooked on Cassie. Her sister. A confidante—who would be flying home in the morning. "She's going to Cassie's place?"

Anna stayed silent, but smiled slightly.

Parker's grin, however, was full-out. "I know that look on my wife's face, Jefferies, and you're on the right track."

Okay, thank God. He just had to find her before

she made it to the airport. "So there's time to stop her before she joins up with Cassie and Brandon to fly out."

Anna frowned a definite no, apparently still bent on not speaking on the subject.

"Why would she leave ahead of them—"

"God," Anna blurted, "for a smart guy, you're really not thinking like your corporate shark self today. You must actually be in love. It wreaks havoc with a guy's brain if he doesn't get things straightened out. She's taking the family yacht to the Bahamas so she'll get there after Cassie returns. And don't start hollering about her health. She hired a nurse to accompany her, just to be safe."

He exhaled his relief at having found her and, thank God, that she had the foresight to watch over herself and the baby, even during a short trip to the Bahamas.

Then the rest of Anna's words penetrated his thoughts.

In love?

In love.

Damn straight. He loved Brooke Garrison. Not just because she carried his child, but because all other women faded around her. She was it for him. His chance to have what his parents shared, and he didn't want to waste another second apart from her.

Now he just needed to convince Brooke he wasn't a scumbag so he could tell her how damn much he loved her.

* * *

Brooke lounged on one of the yacht's deck chairs, searching the starlit night for answers to the confusion swirling inside her. A gust of wind rolling in off the ocean sent her clutching her lightweight sweater closed over the bridesmaid gown she still wore.

She probably should have just gone back to her place, but all the love and sentimentality of the wedding had left her so weepy, she needed to get away. Far away, before she puddled into a serious crying jag. Thank goodness she'd been able to hire a nurse to come along on such short notice, the only way her sisters and sisters-in-law would help her leave.

In the middle of the swirl of aching feelings, a memory of spending time with her father on their yacht brought her an unexpected comfort. Right now, she appreciated the total quiet here and she needed that utter peace for her baby after the emotional hubbub of most of her pregnancy. Here in the quiet, she could sense her father's presence, could almost hear his apology. He hadn't been perfect, but he had been there for her as best he knew how. She could see that now as she viewed the world in a way that involved less extremes and more middle ground.

The past couple of days since seeing Jordan with Sheila McKay had been hell. She missed him more than she could have imagined. How could he have worked his way so completely into her life in such a short time?

Or had this been a long time coming?

She wanted to trust his explanation about the incident with Sheila. Her instincts shouted that he'd told her the truth. But her heart wanted a clear sign that her love was reciprocated.

Yes, she loved Jordan Jefferies. She couldn't deny it any longer. Maybe in some corner of her heart she'd always known but had been too afraid of the family fallout to pursue the possibility. She wasn't afraid of her family's disapproval anymore.

She was, however, afraid of making a mistake, for her own sake and that of her baby. How would she ever know for certain?

Her gaze shifted from the stars—Orion wasn't offering up any answers anyhow—down to the opaque ocean. A dim light chopped through the darkness, another late-night boater. The gently lapping waves might not have solutions either, but at least the rhythmic sound lulled her at a time she desperately needed ease from the agitation.

The drone of the other boat grew louder, the beam closer. The sleek craft took shape, smaller than she'd expected. Who used a ski boat this late at night? A hint of anxiousness stirred in her gut. She started to rise and alert the captain, when one of the crew came out onto her deck.

"The captain said to let you know we have company. But no worries, ma'am. The boat's one of ours. There's a family member on board."

"Thank you for the update." Family?

Brooke rose from the chair and walked toward

the metal railing, curious. Concerned. Her relatives should all be at the wedding. Jordan didn't know where she was. She'd only told the girls because she'd thought someone should be aware...

The ski boat drew nearer, two towering males becoming visible, a pair of tall figures in tuxedos standing. The craft drew up alongside. She backed a step.

Parker *and* Jordan.

Her heart did a quick flip-flop much like the fish plopping in the ocean. She should have known Jordan would find out and follow her. Especially after she'd turned him away. And somehow he'd won her brother over to his side. Which led him here.

Someone had ratted her out. Now she faced not only Jordan but her meddling control-freak brother, as well. Still, her pulse picked up speed at the sight of Jordan, who'd come all this way for her.

She gripped the rail and shouted, "Parker Garrison, you traitor. You're officially out of my will."

Her brother slowed back the engine as the boat neared the yacht. "You've been saying that since you were six and I kicked over your sand castle."

Yet another instance when her family had tried to dictate her life to her.

She'd put a lot of time and dreams into that sand castle. All she'd ever wanted was a happily-ever-after of her own and damned if she would let her brother mess that up, even if he meant well. She'd had enough of putting her own needs on the back burner just to keep the peace. Making the right decision about Jordan was too important for her and her child. "I meant it then, Parker, and I really mean it now. Don't interfere in my life."

"I think you should hear Jefferies out."

"*You* think?" Her fingers clenched around the railing, and it was all she could do not to stamp her foot in frustration. "What gives you the right to decide?"

Jordan stopped Parker with a hand to his arm. "She's correct. She makes the decision as to whether I go or stay." With an agile leap, he stepped up and out onto the bow of the ski boat, his balance steady as the craft rocked beneath him. "You know that we have to talk sometime. But I won't come on board unless you want me to."

"I don't want you to." Her lips lied even as her heart cried out for her to give him a chance. "I need time to think."

"Fair enough. I'll go back."

Her next argument stalled in her mouth. He was giving up that easily? Disappointment melted through her veins...until she realized he hadn't moved. She knew. He was waiting for her to tell him flat out to go. Somehow she couldn't force those words past her lips.

She blinked against the whipping ocean wind plastering her bridesmaid dress to her body. Those weren't tears of hope stinging her eyes, damn it.

Okay, maybe they were. She could at least listen to what he had to say as long as he stayed off the yacht and on the bow.

Sea spray splashed up across Jordan's shoes, but his feet stayed planted, his attention focused solely on her. "While you're thinking, I want you to consider the fact that I love you."

Drat, there went her heart with the flip-flopping again. But she still needed her sign that she could believe those beautiful words she'd been longing to here.

"I love you, Brooke Garrison, and no matter what happens between us, I want you to have this." He held out his hand with a small jewelry box in his palm. The sort of little velvet box that held a ring.

He lowered his hand as if to toss the box up to her.

"Wait!" she shouted. "Don't you dare throw that at me. What if you miss?"

"I won't," he said with such assurance she almost smiled at his predictable arrogance.

"How about you hold on to it while you keep talking." She fisted both hands to resist the temptation to motion him up onto the yacht and say to hell with signs. He'd said he loved her, and she wanted his diamond on her finger like the ones all the other women in her family now possessed. Even though she always could have afforded whatever gems she pleased, she found herself craving the emotional commitment that came with this particular stone.

Caution and pride overrode impulse to take what she wanted without weighing the cost.

"I can't make you believe me." Moonbeams glinted on his blond hair, casting shadows along the serious lines of his face, her hunky charmer completely somber. "That trust has to come from you. I'm willing to wait as long as it takes for you to believe me."

Jordan opened the box. Starlight sparked off the ohmigod-huge diamond inside.

"So you're proposing—again." Did he really think she could be bought with a big rock? A beautiful big rock held by the man she loved.

If this were real, what a memory it would make, her handsome man in a tuxedo proposing from the bow of a boat. All the practical, cautious parts of her cried out for the beautiful romanticism of it to be real.

He shook his head. "No, I'm not going to ask you to marry me again, unless that's what you want." Jordan extended his hand, his feet so sure against the jostling waves that could too easily send the priceless gem to the bottom of the bay. "I am, however, asking you to wear my mom's ring."

His mother's? Was this a trick? "That's an engagement ring."

"Wear it on your right hand if you want." His voice carried strong and clear on the night breeze whipping over the water. "I've been saving this to give the one woman for me. No matter what you decide, this ring could only belong to you."

Wow. Her sign.

How funny that she'd been searching for a big symbol for why she could trust him, and the answer came to her in a way she'd never expected.

The sentimentality of his ring touched her heart so much more than anything he could have bought. He could *purchase* anything. But this was like the time he'd chosen the painting for her. He understood her, the essence of her and what she would want. He knew her heart.

And as an added bonus, he'd even said all those humbling words in front of her brother.

She saw the two men, side by side, both so self-assured, successful and yes, more than a little arrogant. But men a woman could count on. Men who were willing to lay it on the line for a woman—one woman.

Jordan was a man to trust. She knew it now without question.

He'd won his chance to stay, a chance to tell her more about why he loved her.

She stepped back from the rail and crooked her finger at him. "Okay, then. Come aboard and we'll talk."

A deep smile creased his face, but she could swear she also saw relief in his starlit blue eyes.

Jordan climbed the ladder to board and she got a close-up look at the ring—an emerald-cut diamond with tapered baguettes. Beautiful for its sentimentality even more than the magnificence of the cut and size. Victoria's ring had been worn with a love that lasted all her days.

A whistle sounded from the ski boat, from Parker. "Hello? So, Brooke? Do I go or stick around?"

She stared at the diamond, his mother's ring. She'd known about Jordan for a long time, thanks to gossip and common business dealings. He was the last man to show a softer side to anyone. Yet, he'd done so here, tonight. And now she knew she was woman enough to stand up to him during those times his stubbornness got the best of him.

"Parker?"

"Yeah, kid?"

"You're back in the will." He winked. "Be happy."

The engine on the ski boat gurgled to life again as her brother backed the craft, then roared away into the night.

Leaving her alone on the deck with Jordan.

Jordan tipped her face up to his. "Is this a yes or a no?"

The yes already sang inside her, begging to be set free, but goodness, she deserved to revel in this moment. "Could you repeat what you said out there?"

She expected him to grin that arrogant smile of self-assurance. She'd all but told him he'd won, after all.

Instead, his face stayed sober. Intense. "I love you, Brooke. Not because you're carrying my child, although Lord knows that stirs something inside me I never could have imagined. I love you because you're you. And when I'm around you, I'm a better me. Together, I believe we can build one helluva lifetime."

He'd made his case well.

Joy rushed through her as strong as any tide tugging the yacht. "I guess we're a very lucky couple, because I happen to love you, too."

She rested her hands on his chest. A gust of breath rocked through him at just her touch. She understood the feeling well. Brooke arched up to meet his kiss, his mouth warm and wonderful and blessedly familiar against hers. A yearning, equally as familiar and growing stronger every day, began to build inside her. A longing they would be able to fulfill, thanks to her doctor's okay.

She looped her arms around his neck to deepen their kiss—

A tiny foot booted inside her. Hard. Hard enough so that Jordan jerked back in surprise.

He shook his head as if to clear his thoughts. "Wow, I guess I should be used to that now, but it's still so damn amazing."

She grasped his hand to flatten along their child. "I totally agree."

They stood together for—well, she lost track of the time until he lifted her hand, the ring magically appearing in his other hand.

"Brooke, will you marry me?"

He'd asked. Not demanded. She hadn't expected two signs in one night. But then she'd never expected to fall so utterly in love with Jordan Jefferies.

She extended her fingers. "Yes, I will marry you, and love you and share my life with you. Together."

His eyes closed briefly and she understood the feeling. She knew him now as well as he knew her.

His eyes blinked back open and he slid the ring onto her finger, sealing its placement with a kiss to her hand. Then he let out a shout that sent her laughing just as he scooped her into his arms again. He took her place in the lounger, cradling her in his lap.

She'd expected he would take her below deck, but at the moment he seemed to be more interested in holding her, kissing her, stroking her and drawing out the moment in a way she would cherish all her life.

Especially since she knew they *would* eventually end up below deck.

Finally, he pulled back, his thumb fiddling with the ring on her finger. "If you prefer something of your own choosing for an engagement, we can pick it out together. I won't be offended if you wear this on your right hand."

She shook her head, lifting her hand so the moonlight could catch the facets of the cut. "It's perfect."

"You're sure? You really don't want to go jewelry shopping?"

"You silly man." She clasped his face in both hands, his five o'clock shadow rasping tantalizingly along her skin. "We both have enough money to buy anything we want. This ring is about things so much more important than money. Sentiment. Family. Love."

He stroked his knuckles down her cheek, his eyes shining with a hint of awe and a lot of love. "You really do trust me, then."

"This ring and the fact that you knew to choose it for me tells me everything I need to know."

His killer, gorgeous smile returned. "And to think I almost screwed up by spending a mint."

"You can still do that if you really want."

His laugh rumbled against her chest and she enjoyed the chance to laugh along with him with ease, secure in their love.

"How did you manage to get this ring and still find me so quickly? I haven't been gone long so you must have set out in the ski boat right away."

He stayed silent and the answer slowly dawned on her. "You've been carrying this set around? For how long?"

"Since the day I left your office, right after you turned me down the first time I asked."

And to think the sentiment, his understanding of family, and yes, even the seeds of love had been there right from the start if only she'd been able to see through her own fears. "I guess I'm the one who's been silly."

"Not at all. You're a wise one, Brooke Garrison. It's good we're getting this right."

"It's going to stick. This marriage idea. The way we love each other."

"Damn straight. And it's only going to get better." He eased up from the lounger, keeping her in his arms as he turned toward the stairway leading below deck. "Merry Christmas, beautiful."

She nipped his bristly jaw with a kiss. "Merry Christmas, to both of us."

Epilogue

He'd seen her many times. He'd always wanted her.

Tonight, once her family finished their meal, he would have her.

Jordan covered Brooke's cool, slim fingers tucked in the corner of his arm as they sat together at the reception dinner after their wedding. Eager to make things official, they'd scheduled the nuptials for the first weekend after Emilio and Brittany's return from their European honeymoon.

The January ceremony had been a small family affair at a chapel on the beach in the Bahamas. They'd had enough with media frenzies and gratefully accepted Cassie's generous offer to host the private reception. A lavish event, the house full of candles, flowers, food—and family.

He'd never seen Brooke look more beautiful than at their ceremony, with the Bahamas sunset streaming across her creamy skin and her golden yellow dress. The glow had glinted highlights on her dark hair, swept back in a twist—with a lone strand slithering free, of course.

He stared around the table of smiling faces and couldn't help but contrast this happy gathering with the tense confrontation the first time he'd eaten with her relatives last month.

Tonight, her two sisters wore their green bridesmaid gowns, his groomsmen in tuxedos. He'd chosen his brother and his new business partner, Parker, surprising himself with the decision as well as the oldest Garrison offspring.

Brooke squeezed Jordan's arm, smiling and nodding in the direction of her brother as steel drum music wafted softly in the distance. "I can't believe you two are speaking, much less that Jefferies Brothers and Garrison, Incorporated are officially merging. And to have Parker in the wedding, too, I'm thrilled—and still a little stunned."

Jordan set aside his fork with a clink against china. "It was worth it to see the shock on his face. It's not often anyone can render that guy speechless."

Parked arched a brow as he silently finished the last of his Bahamian rock lobster.

Anna stroked her husband's shoulder. "No brawls today, dear."

"Don't worry." Parker captured his wife's wrist to kiss her palm. "I wouldn't risk upsetting you or my sister in your delicate conditions."

Anna rolled her eyes, eyes that held a definite twinkle of excitement as she smoothed both hands over her expanding waistline. "There's nothing delicate about me right now."

"You're all the more gorgeous." Parker placed his hand over hers on her stomach and directed his words to her pregnant swell. "Right, John?"

Jordan took in the spontaneous family moment with an inward grin. Well, hell, the guy had a softer side after all. And what a sign of how far they'd all come in a month for Parker to name his child after the deceased patriarch who'd stirred so much turmoil for his children.

For that matter, having a serenely sober Bonita sit at the same table with Cassie was an event even Jordan had doubted could happen. Bonita had completed her four-week program at the rehab clinic and now attended A.A. meetings at least every other day. Brooke's mother had even approached them with her hopes to stay sober and be a healthy grandmother to her grandchildren. She radiated a quiet determination that boded well for her *and* her family.

Anna broke the long, affectionate look with her husband and shifted her attention to Brooke. "Have you two chosen a name for your little guy?"

Jordan slid an arm around his wife's shoulders. *Wife.* Damn, that had an amazing ring to it. "I think I have the perfect name picked out, but I'll need to run it past Brooke first."

No more unilateral decisions when it came to their future. He'd found a real partner in this quietly determined woman who'd been smart enough to make them explore their feelings for each other before committing.

She elbowed him gently in the side. "About the name thing, I'm not going to agree with Uncle Fester no matter how nicely you ask."

"I think you'll like this one better. We can talk later." He reached to the sprawling centerpiece and pulled an orchid free. Gently, he tucked the flower behind her ear, wondering if she recalled their time here together when he'd teased her naked flesh with a similar blossom.

From the warming of her brown eyes, she most definitely remembered.

Brooke tipped her face to kiss him while the family applauded. The cheers and clapping faded and Brooke eased back.

Their kiss may have been short but it was powerful. His body heated in response to her unspoken promise of the pleasure they would enjoy once they reached the yacht, anchored in the harbor. He stared into her eyes, tempted to leave now, until chuckles from around the table pulled him back to the moment.

Blushing, Brooke turned to Cassie next to her. "Thank you so much for arranging such a lovely dinner—" She stopped abruptly and clasped her half sister's wrist. "Hey, is that a wedding band I see along with the engagement ring?"

Cassie exchanged an intimate grin with her fiancé—or rather apparently her former fiancé. "Brandon and I eloped. We had a secret wedding two weeks ago. We just got back from our honeymoon."

Squealing, Brooke threw her arms around her sister as Brittany rushed from her chair to join in the hug. The genuine emotion between all three women couldn't be missed. In spite of the havoc John Garrison had brought to them, they'd managed to forge a bond and find peace.

Brooke finally pulled back to reclaim her chair. "Why didn't you tell us?"

Brandon clasped Cassie's hand in his. "We didn't want to take away from your special day."

"Take away?" Brooke waved aside the notion. "This only adds to the joy. I'm so happy for both of you. This should be a double reception. Right, Jordan?"

"Absolutely. Congratulations!" Jordan lifted his glass of sparkling water to toast the new couple. "To Brandon and Cassie."

Brandon lifted his crystal glass, as well. "And to Jordan and Brooke."

Little Jade jumped up to stand on her chair. "And to my new baby brother or sister on the way!"

Laughing, Stephen wrapped an arm around his blushing wife, Megan, while patting Jade on the shoulder.

After everyone replaced their drinks and the catering staff began clearing away the china, Cassie led the way to the three-tiered wedding cake being served outside. The warm night and scent of the ocean beckoned. Beyond the sets of French doors, torches on the beach led down to the water.

"Jordan, wait just a moment." Brooke stopped him just shy of the open door and tugged him behind a decorative potted palm.

He braced a hand on her back. "Is everything all right?"

"Totally." She leaned forward, her body brushing his. "I couldn't have asked for a more wonderful wedding—and husband."

He cupped her face for a kiss, this one far longer than the one at the table as he made the most of even this brief private time together. A prelude to more they would enjoy soon. Not soon enough.

The sweet sweep of her tongue teased his senses along with the scent of the flower in her hair.

She nipped his bottom lip as her hand slid inside his tuxedo jacket. "So tell me more about your idea for a baby name. I'm too curious to wait."

"I like it when you're impatient." He skimmed his knuckles along the side of her breast before addressing her question. "What about naming our son Garrison?"

Jordan waited for her verdict while Brooke's eyes took on that soft brown mulling expression. God, he loved how he understood her.

"Garrison Jefferies." Brooke tested the combination, a smile slowly spreading over her face. "I like it, I love it. I love *you*."

He gathered her close again, a pleasure he looked forward to pursuing further throughout their honeymoon. Thanks to Brooke, he'd learned the importance of enjoying life along the way. Already, he could imagine making a lifetime of memories, filling their house with photographs, turning his place into their home. "I love you, too, beautiful." He curved a hand over their growing child. "And you, as well, Garrison Jefferies."

Garrison Jefferies—now that it was official, their child's name settled inside him with a rightness as special as the woman in his arms waiting to share wedding cake with all their relatives.

And wasn't that the biggest surprise of all? Especially to a man used to being ahead of the curve on everything. He'd known the name choice offered a nice symbol of their combined empires.

He'd just hadn't realized how damn amazing it would be to join the Garrisons and Jefferies into one family.

* * * * *

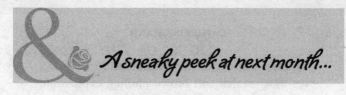

A sneaky peek at next month...

By Request

RELIVE THE ROMANCE WITH THE BEST OF THE BEST

My wish list for next month's titles...

3 stories in each book - only £5.99!

In stores from 16th November 2012:

☐ *His Chosen Wife – Anne McAllister, Christina Hollis & Susanne James*

☐ *Christmas with Him – Jackie Braun, Christine Rimmer & Shirley Jump*

In stores from 7th December 2012:

☐ *Billionaires & Babies – Maureen Child, Katherine Garbera & Emily McKay*

Available at WHSmith, Tesco, Asda, Eason, Amazon and Apple

Just can't wait?

1112/05

The World of Mills & Boon®

There's a Mills & Boon® series that's perfect for you. We publish ten series and, with new titles every month, you never have to wait long for your favourite to come along.

Blaze.
Scorching hot, sexy reads
4 new stories every month

By Request
Relive the romance with the best of the best
9 new stories every month

Cherish™
Romance to melt the heart every time
12 new stories every month

Desire™
Passionate and dramatic love stories
8 new stories every month

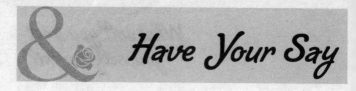
Have Your Say

You've just finished your book.
So what did you think?

We'd love to hear your thoughts on our
'Have your say' online panel
www.millsandboon.co.uk/haveyoursay

- Easy to use
- Short questionnaire
- Chance to win Mills & Boon® goodies

Visit us Online

Tell us what you thought of this book now at
www.millsandboon.co.uk/haveyoursay

YOUR_SAY